"I WILL FIGHT YOU, I SWEAR IT, UNTIL HELL ITSELF SHOULD FREEZE!"

"Fight me then," he said.

She bolted, leaping from the bed, and raced wildly for the door. He caught her inches before she reached it, sweeping her up hard into his arms.

"Lady, lady," he whispered softly. "You know I cannot let you go."

He laid her down upon the bed, stripping away the cloak as he did so. She inhaled on a shaky sigh, her eyes tightly closed. "Do it then," she whispered fiercely. "Be quick, dear God, be merciful!"

Startled, he looked down at her, a smile curving his lips. "Quick? Never! But, aye lady, merciful! That I *do* intend to be!"

Shannon Drake

Knight of Fire

AVON BOOKS ◆ NEW YORK

KNIGHT OF FIRE is an original publication of Avon Books. This work
has never before appeared in book form. This work is a novel. Any
similarity to actual persons or events is purely coincidental.

AVON BOOKS
A division of
The Hearst Corporation
1350 Avenue of the Americas
New York, New York 10019

Copyright © 1993 by Heather Graham Pozzessere
Cover art by Paul Stinson
Inside cover art by Steve Assel
Back cover author photograph by Lewis Feldman
Published by arrangement with the author
Library of Congress Catalog Card Number: 93-90409
ISBN: 0-380-77169-1

First Avon Books Printing: December 1993

AVON TRADEMARK REG. U.S. PAT. OFF. AND IN OTHER COUNTRIES, MARCA
REGISTRADA, HECHO EN U.S.A.

Printed in the U.S.A.

RA   10 9 8 7 6 5 4 3 2 1

For "Maw," Mrs. Gwen Cumbess,
and Barry,
with lots of love

Prologue

1088

    *I*t was, oddly enough for this rugged, stormy part of the country, a beautiful day. When so very often the wind blew with a keening ferocity, when so many mornings were tinged with gray mist, when so frequently the greens and golds and deep purples of the cliffs and rises were blanketed with clouds and the skies were split with sudden, startling streaks of lightning. This was not such a morning. It was cold, the air was clean and crisp, and a soft blanket of snow covered the earth, yet the violets showed through in occasional patches where the snow had melted, and a variety of colors could be seen to enhance the whiteness of the snow. The day was dawning gloriously; the sky was cobalt-blue, the sun shone overhead in an orb of golden glory.

It was a beautiful, beautiful day.

Perhaps that was the most incongruous part of being tied to the stake, of smelling the acrid scent of smoke on the air that came from the burning torches, set into the ground now, so very near the stake with its piles of deadly-dry straw and hay and sticks and larger branches. Death, so very, very close to her. Time itself fading, and memories rushing in.

"When does it begin?"

She heard the whisper, harsh on the air. Her uncle's men-at-arms were all around her, solemn, with downcast eyes trying not to meet hers. None of them was anxious for this task—she had known half of them all of her life— yet by their laws, she had been condemned.

"When?" came that pained, hushed whisper again.

"Soon, soon!" An older, harder voice. "Robert said she must be executed within an hour of the dawn, and so he must order the torches lit soon!"

"Ah, but do ye think he can?"

"I think he must, lest he surrender all in the end, laddie! There will be no turning back now!"

"They say, of course, that it cannot happen, that *he* surely will not allow her to die by the flame, that he would rather scorch the earth itself—"

"*He* cannot come!" came the older, weary voice once again, surely that of a warrior who had fought with her uncle, Laird Robert, for quite some time. There was a deep sadness in his voice that seemed to touch her from the nape to the base of her spine, chill her, terrify her as she had not been afraid before.

There was anguish in that voice. The task ahead of them—this execution, *her execution*—was a horror to him, yet one that he believed would take place.

For there could be no help for it.

Even if *he* were to come, he would be so sorely outnumbered, riding in with the fifty men with whom he had ridden out. His own life would certainly be the sacrifice. And just as certainly, Robert would not let him die easily, he would certainly be drawn and quartered, beheaded, that grisly trophy then taken to prove that the Scottish lords would not bow down to the son of the bastard king of England. Though Malcolm, the Scottish king, had been forced to bow down to William I before, and might soon be doing the same with the son, the Scottish lairds would be kings unto themselves, and were very hard to best, for they would flee into their rough and rugged lands when necessary, and return to fight again. Seizing a man such as Bret d'Anlou, slaying him, displaying his proud dark head, would surely be an incredible boon to the fierce warriors here . . .

And what man, what noble lord, would risk such a fate, even for . . .

His wife.

Ah, but one he had obtained through misfortune alone.

One who had fought him, tooth and nail. One who had promised from the start to be his enemy. One who had battled and betrayed him.

One he might be well rid of, and yet . . .

" 'Twould be death, sure in itself!" came the younger man's whisper once again. "The man is no fool, and that's a fact. Robert's plan must be to catch the bigger fish with the smaller, and then, the smaller fish may yet swim free!"

"Nay, laddie," came the answer, sadly. "For what escape is there here? No matter what strength has that wretched bastard's son William in London, we are far from London town, and here, Robert's men, embattled and bruised as we might be this morn, do stretch forever. Stare about ye, lad. See the men at arms, fierce, wild warriors out of the highlands not even the Romans would trouble themselves with, boy. See the line! Who would come here, who would brave this? And if *he* were to come, the torches already burn near the kindling, once that fire is lit, 'twill burn like all hell itself! He would see that, lad. The lady is doomed. We can only pray that Robert intends to have her strangled first, ere the flames can kiss the sweetness of her flesh. She is his kin, and one of us. He can not truly wish her the horror of the inferno!"

"Who will set these flames?" the younger man asked, his voice heavy, strangled itself. "What man can walk to yon stake, meet those eyes of hers, and set a blaze against such proud and tender beauty?"

"Who would defy Robert?" the older man asked in turn, sad and weary again.

Who indeed?

"She betrayed him, lad. And all of us. Betrayed her kin!"

"Kin what turned her over to *him* when it was expedient that it be done!" the young man reminded him.

She wished that she could see him, this young champion of hers. She would like to thank him for his care.

Yet she could not see him, could not twist, could not turn. Ah, but that young lad had seen the very crux of it indeed. The very uncle who condemned her now had coerced her into marriage with the man, her support for whom now branded her a traitor in the eyes of the men here today, who held her very life in their hands.

The one they thought must save her now. Who had once, in his turn, called her traitor for clinging to her father's people here.

Nay, that was not fair! He had understood her. Whatever his own determinations, he had always understood her. No matter what his dictates or commands, he had given her his compassion, even when she had hated him for his very empathy.

How strange that she could see all this so clearly now. How horrible that she could remember all the beauty she had touched so fleetingly, that she could long to see his face, touch him, just one more time. Speak to him, tell him . . .

That she loved him as deeply, as passionately, as she had ever despised him; wanted him, would sell her very soul for just two minutes to whisper those words.

She would not have those two minutes.

These men. She could not see the lad who had spoken so gently behind her. But she could see the lines of deadly men that stretched out across the rugged white-cloaked hill to her left and right.

So many of them! What a sight they all were against the day! The lovely hillside, beautiful in its glittering white winter color, rising to the rocky craigs above. The endlessly blue sky rising atop the craigs. The men stretched to either side of her upon . . .

Upon her stake. Hewn of rough oak, and planted solidly in the ground. She, elevated perhaps a foot on raw planking . . .

The better for the fire to burn.

The kindling set in great piles about her, strewn with dry straw and grasses, so that the flames might rise with a merciful swiftness. Flames she could not escape, for thick rope bound her from the shoulders to the knee. Those ropes were all that kept her standing now, for she had no strength left. She refused to betray to these men the fear that lurked behind her deep-green eyes, and she prayed that she stood there with dignity, silent, furious, proud to the end.

Held there, bound to the knee . . .

Yet, below the knee, the breeze pulled upon the white linen fabric of her tunic, hinting, teasing, of freedom. Likewise, her hair was free, for she had lost her veil in her scuffling with her uncle's men, and the soft wind plucked and played at the long golden strands, winding them around her like so much additional rope. She was nobly dressed, as befitted her station . . .

Her tunic was of the softest white linen, hemmed with fur, the round neck richly, beautifully embroidered with tiny seed pearls. A girdle of delicate gold links lay smoothly about her hip, ornamented with tiny gemstones—rubies, sapphires, emeralds as deep, as shimmering, as green as her eyes must be now as she fought the burning of tears beneath her lids. Nothing of hers would be touched; nothing taken or salvaged from the flame. Robert's men were no thieves.

Nay, they were warriors. Proud, fierce, independent Scotsmen.

They were a wild group. No close-cropped Norman hair here, and few faces clean-shaven, as was the Norman manner. Here, the men's hair was long, thick, wild, and, often enough, unkempt. Faces were grizzled with shadow and beard. There was little chain-mail armor to be seen, and few men wore helmets to protect their pates against the Norman swords and battle-axes. Many were clad in furs, or simple tunics. Some wore armor of leather and their shields were most often made of wood. They were reckless fighters, and fiercely independent. They were a people who had long clung to their rugged terrain, who fought so many battles among themselves that they were well-prepared to take on any foe . . .

Had they been at Hastings those many years ago, Allora thought fleetingly, the Bastard might not have taken the day at all . . .

Not that the men who followed her husband were any less fierce or hardened. Many of them claimed to be descendants of the Viking Rollo who had long ago laid claim to much of Normandy. They were ruthless in battle, fearless, disciplined, and yet capable of taking on a foe as if they were indeed the berserkers who had cast themselves upon the coastline.

Perhaps in that they were all alike, for the Vikings had sailed their ships against these coasts as well, wreaking havoc upon the rugged harbors of the Scottish and Irish. Blue eyes and blond hair were scattered here and there among the ranks, evidence of a Nordic heritage. A bright-red mane of wild hair could be seen occasionally down the endless line as they waited, the morning now coming on full.

Some of the warriors were on foot, some mounted, their steeds thrusting great clouds of mist into the air with each impatient breath.

They waited . . .

Why, she thought in sudden agony, why was Robert waiting?

Did Robert himself wait . . .

Wait to see if Bret would come?

She was not afraid to die, she told herself. She was not afraid to die . . .

Oh, be damned with such lies to herself! She was terrified to die here today. Frightened of the agony, not of the world to come. She believed in God; believed that death would surely bring her back to many she loved deeply.

Yet it would also rip her away. She would never see Brianna again, never hold her again. She would never know if the child she carried now was a daughter or son, so cruelly taken from life, before life could begin.

She would never see Bret again . . .

She was shaking. Only the strong cords of rope that tied her to the stake upon the beautiful white hill kept her standing that glorious gold-and-mauve morning.

Tears burned her eyes, and she fought them back furiously, determinedly. They had all called her traitor, so it seemed.

The uncle who would slay her.

The husband . . .

Who could not come for her, who might well, after everything, be glad of the freedom that this very act would give him.

Ah! But he must, by honor, fight back for the wrong done him here! His wife—*wife!*—burned upon the very border land they so disputed! For Bret bowed to yet another William. Damn them all, another William! Damn William! Since Hastings, that detestable Norman and his family had reigned, yet in all these years, they had been compelled to fight in order to hold what had been conquered. She hadn't even been alive when the Bastard had first set foot upon English soil, seeking to be king, and yet, in the end, it was he, dead now himself, who was bringing about her demise . . .

The Bastard! It was he who had first demanded her father betrothe her to his own man, he who had later demanded that her land be taken and then held.

He who had forced her upon *Bret*, and Bret upon her.

He who had caused the tempest and the travesty . . .

And the love.

She nearly shrieked out loud with the onslaught of anguish and terror that suddenly settled over her. Maybe that was the worst of it. Not the flame, nay, never the fire. Not the sudden expunction of the beauty of the day, the snuffing out of all that was sweet scents and glorious sights. Nay, nay, there was the pain. *Bret*. With his broad shoulders and towering height, steel-blue stare and ink-dark hair. Fierce, deep, commanding voice. Seeming so indomitable! Demanding, hard, relentless, ruthless . . .

And yet, upon occasion, so very, very tender.

After all the times she had fought him, hated him, longed to best him in any way . . . sweet Lord, longed only for him . . .

Indeed, she loved him. Loved him so desperately. And at the very least, through it all he had wanted her, claimed her, sworn that she was his, and that he would have her.

She could not lose life now. Not life and love . . .

Precious Brianna. And Bret. And the seed of life she carried now.

Maybe, from the very beginning, her loyalties had been divided. Perhaps, from the very first time she had seen his raven-dark head, felt the touch of his steel-blue eyes, she had known that she could not stand against him, no matter what the fight.

From the first time he had touched her, she had known the anger.

And the longing.

She had felt his incredible strength.

And her own weakness against it . . .

"*He* must come!" her young champion whispered hopefully once again.

He must, he must . . .

Some feared him more than they might the king himself, for he was the son of a great Norman noble and also the grandson of a long-gone king, a *Saxon* king. He was known for his strength and for his mercy, for standing against both the Conqueror and William Rufus when he so determined, for granting what few boons fell the way of the defeated. He judged swiftly and with great prudence; his mercy was swift, his vengeance even more so . . .

She knew them both—his fury and his tenderness.

She started suddenly, clenching her teeth tightly together as she heard the thunder of hooves approaching from behind her. She twisted her head in time to see that Robert had come before her. Her uncle with his ruddy complexion, thick red hair, and wild red beard. And at his side, his closest companions: David of Edinburgh, lean and handsome and tawny-haired, his features contorted, his hazel-green eyes glazed, and Duncan, David's half-brother, his hair a shade darker, his watery eyes a shade paler.

David rode with his hands tied behind his back, led by Duncan. He would have fought for her, she knew. He had sworn an oath of peace with Bret, and his own judgment would be swiftly forthcoming. He had fought Robert when Robert had condemned her, and her uncle would not let him interfere now, she was certain.

Once, she had nearly wed David. And once, she had spurned Duncan, and perhaps that very act too had brought her here now.

Her nemesis, indeed. His eyes were bright, unlike David's agony-clouded gaze. Nay, it was excitement that tinged Duncan's eyes, and pleasure. He could not wait to light the fire, she thought. He had been her enemy forever, and he longed for her death.

"Niece, it is with the greatest sorrow that I come to this day!" Robert told her solemnly from the back of his heavy stallion, then whispered, "Jesu! But that I could undo this!"

Perhaps, in his own mind, he spoke the truth, for Allora and Robert had once been very close. Indeed, it was quite ironic, for she would have refused to wed a Norman lord until she'd had no breath left in her body if she hadn't been forced to wed Bret to obtain her uncle's freedom and perhaps save him from execution. What strange memories! Yet it did seem that there was, this morning, the greatest sorrow in his eyes, no matter how bitterly he had spoken against her last night, no matter how determined he had been on this action.

Ah, so it seemed! She had loved him as a child, loved him deeply. She had been willing to do anything for him. Even to wed the Conqueror's choice, a Norman lord who would come here and hold the isle.

She had learned that her uncle could be absolutely ruthless and determined. She had been stunned by some of the things he had tried to do.

This should not shock her now, yet at this moment, she believed that he was sorry. Ah, and surely he was! He had wanted to rule the Far Isle through her. She was his brother's daughter. But she had defied him, and thus he certainly felt he had no choice. And since she knew what other acts he had been more than willing to perform in his pursuit of freedom for the border lands, she knew that he would not hesitate to kill her now.

She met his eyes, fighting to keep her lip from trembling, determined to keep her voice steady. "My lord uncle, you have determined on this course. Be done with it then."

"If you could still swear before God that you would join with us and by your life vow to trap your Norman, give him over to us, and then open the gates of the castle of the Far Isle . . . ?"

She smiled, suddenly finding the strength to stand by herself against the hardness of the stake. "I am condemned by

my peers, so you tell me, Uncle. As a traitor. Yet again you
would send me back, only to betray my duly-wed husband
again? We have covered this ground before, Uncle. I have
sworn before God that I never intended any ill to my own
people. I have played Bret falsely enough in the past, with
your fine assistance. I'll not do it again."

David edged his horse closer and spoke to her in a
hushed, pleading whisper.

"Swear it! Be free from this threat of fire, Allora, give
life a chance! Tell them anything to save your life. Bret
would understand! Sweet Jesu, lady, he would want you
alive!"

"Nay, David!" she said softly in return, sorrier for this
man who cared so deeply for her than she was for herself. "I
cannot buy my own life with the price of another's! That's
what it would be; they would kill him so quickly!"

Duncan followed his half-brother, his voice no whisper,
rather a cackle upon the air. "Watch your tongue, brother,
for your life lies in a precarious balance now as well. Ah,
don't you see it?" Duncan bit out, his eyes hard upon
Allora. "The once-proud beauty of the Far Isle is nothing
more than *his* creature now, bowed down before him. If
she is so determined to burn for him, then *let her burn!*"

"Duncan!" Robert said sharply. His eyes remained steady
upon Allora's, with their same depth of sorrow. "Allora,
give me *something!* Anything to give to my men, a reason
why you should be freed! You know that I can betray no
weakness, as you are my kin, so give me something that I
can give to them!"

"Give you Bret?" she said softly.

"Aye, give me the damned Norman!"

"Saxon-Norman," she reminded him.

"Allora!" Robert snapped harshly.

"Think of it, Uncle! You and my father wed me to this
man for your own gain—and now, you demand that I entrap
him for your own gain!"

"You were with us when you wed the man! You've
turned against us since!"

"I never turned against anyone, Uncle. You were mistaken, and misinformed, and you condemned me falsely.

Be that as it may, I will not help you murder him now!"

"Allora, you are beaten, you are about to die!"

She smiled again. "Never beaten!" she said softly, using her uncle's own words. *Never beaten.* The Scottish king had been forced to pay homage to the English one; yet it was true, the Scottish lords were never beaten. They retreated into their highlands, into their cliffs, their mountains—into their pride.

"If you think that he can save you—"

"I don't think that anyone can save me, Uncle. He was called far off when I so foolishly fell prey to you! But I will not be used against him. I am condemned; my hour of execution is here. Have done with it then."

Robert came still closer, his great horse's hooves crunching upon the kindling set around her. His voice was raspy, pained, his whisper was only for her.

"I shall see that you are strangled, sweet niece. That the agony of the flame never touches your flesh in life." He hesitated a moment. "I loved you, Allora."

"I, too, Uncle. Once," she said softly. "And then I watched with growing horror the things that you did, and I am not surprised to die by your hand. Love and kinship meant more to me, Uncle, than it did to you. I can say clearly now, even as I am about to meet my maker, that I despise you, and your greed, and your treachery!" And then she bowed her head. She would not say more.

She clenched her teeth tightly together, closing her eyes, leaning hard against the stake. She was starting to shake again. Flashes of the past were suddenly streaking before her eyes. She had heard tales of drowning men, that all that had happened through the years swept through their minds in the last few precious seconds of life.

That was what she saw. The past. The tempest, the beauty.

All that had brought her here.

She could see it, for surely she was drowning now!

"So be it!" came a sudden cry, and Robert whirled his horse about and raced away, followed by Duncan leading David on his horse.

Allora heard the roll of a drum begin.

Now, now, any second now . . .

Keep your eyes closed! she warned herself. *Let it be swift, let it be merciful.* She trembled from head to foot, then felt that she was beginning to pass out. Good! A much better way to die.

Dear God, forgive me my sins. Dear God, if I could but see him one more time . . .

The drumroll stopped. It seemed that a hush had fallen over the crowd of men upon the white hillside. She opened her eyes.

Dear God! Did she dream? Was this some sweet illusion?

Far, far across the field, she could see them. A line of mounted men, stretching out upon a ridge. They seemed to glitter like a host of gods in the golden sunlight, steel swords and decorated shields catching the rays, reflecting them, chain-mail armor glinting where it was bared.

Her gaze was suddenly riveted to the center of the line, and her heart seemed to leap and shudder.

A single horseman dominated the line—mail and sword, shield and helmet all catching the light of the sun. He sat upon his horse like Thor, the ancient god of thunder, furious, resolute . . .

He came forward just a few feet in front of the others, his massive war-horse, great Ajax, shimmering white beneath the sun, pawing the ground in a great show of impatience.

Again, her heart slammed within the wall of her chest.

Bret!

Nothing of his face could be seen. He wore a rectangular helmet ornamented by stag horns on either side. If she were closer, his eyes might be visible, burning cobalt-blue. The hard set of his chin might be visible beneath the face plates of the helmet. His coat of mail was covered by a white-and-gold tunic and a great crimson cloak.

He was here! Dear God, he was here!

His horse reared suddenly, pawing the air. Taller upon his mount than any man behind him, with his uniquely devised helmet, with his broad-shouldered form, with his very grace, he was unmistakable. The grandson of one king, champion of another, so fiercely proud and determined, and willing to dare any challenge to have his way.

"Light the fire!" someone roared.

Robert. It was Robert's voice she heard.

She smelled the acrid scent of smoke. They meant to light the kindling at her uncle's command.

Because he was here. In truth, because he was here!

Bret . . .

Nay, he could not be here! He could not have come so quickly. She saw only what she had seen before, when she first met him—a man, a warrior, indomitable, defying death itself.

A drowning man saw his life pass before his eyes.

Surely, she was drowning now!

For her life—indeed, her life had just begun with him!— began to pass swiftly through her mind's eye.

What had brought her to this had begun in very much the same way.

When this man, this warrior, this great, fierce lord had first come into her life . . .

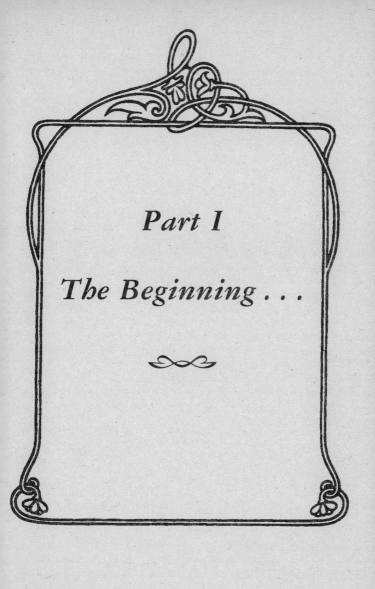

Part I

The Beginning . . .

Chapter 1

1086

"*H*e is up to something devious, I daresay. The man is ever thinking, plotting—grasping!" Ioin Canadys, lord of the Far Isle, exclaimed in agitation.

"Aye, Father!" Allora said swiftly, but giving him scant attention at the moment. She agreed entirely with his words, and felt a great deal of empathy, yet despite their reasons for being here she was entirely enchanted by the city. She hadn't traveled very much in her near-seventeen years of life, and nothing had quite prepared her for the wild, hectic day-to-day bustle of London. Below her—and very close to her window!—fishermen hawked their catch, peddlers sold their wares, and even little children—ragged, but aggressive creatures with soot-smudged faces—roamed the streets, trying to sell their posies—much-needed against the stench within some of the city walls. The streets were deeply grooved and muddy, but there was so much activity upon them. And the languages! Old Saxon English combined here and there with a spattering of Norman French; some people were apparently determined to join the Norman regime with all speed, some were equally determined to have nothing to do with it. Cries rose to her ears, dogs barked, and occasionally, harsh Norman words were bellowed out in dark orders as the king's own men hurried about. The buildings were terribly close together and there was so much life within so very little space.

Her father had not been happy to bring her here, but she had been desperately determined to come. Allora had spent her entire life hearing about the Norman monsters, and now

17

she was set down dangerously close—right in their very midst! She was deeply worried, of course, but she was still absolutely fascinated.

His hands clasped behind his back, Ioin paced the room in this London manor that stood not far from one of the king's own residences, the fortress he had ordered built to keep the Londoners under control soon after he had taken the city. They called it the White Tower, and it was an impressive stone structure, housing great stores of supplies, endless numbers of the Conqueror's men, and, when in residence, the king himself and his family.

The *loathed* king, although Ioin was careful that he neither stated nor inferred such an opinion to the king himself. They had come here on a mission, and he would see that his mission was fulfilled. If that meant supping with the Bastard Conqueror and maintaining a civil conversation throughout the meal in the Conqueror's despised Norman French, then that was what they would do.

It was only when safely in their own realm—the border right before Scotland, where King Malcolm III had long given safe harbor to any member of the old order in England—that they dared speak bluntly—and freely—about the bastard king.

Allora, watching her father, sighed softly, her gaze then turning again to the window that looked out over the city below. She shared her father's feelings, certainly. She hadn't even been alive when the Norman had first seized the English crown, but she had heard horrifying stories about him all of her life. She had ridden through Yorkshire, which had been decimated by the king in one of his reprisals, and she had seen that it would take decades for the land to bloom again. No matter what the Conqueror's claims, Allora's heart went out to the old order, to the people slain, left landless, homeless.

She distanced herself from it, of course. Though William claimed that the Far Isle and much of the border region ruled by her family to be English territory, they knew better themselves. For hundreds of years, the Far Isle had been a minor kingdom itself. Through the years, the isle had been more closely associated with Scotland to the north than with England below. It was now to Malcolm of Scotland that the neighboring lords paid homage. Though William disagreed, he had thus far been very busy quelling one rebellion after another. He hadn't been able to do much to stake his claim as absolute overlord of the Far Isle and its nearby lands.

And they might well have lived in peace, never to have felt the too often brutal hand of William the Conqueror— until Robert had joined with other rash lords and come farther south to aid another brief, and very short-lived, rebellion in Northumberland. Robert had been seized; Ioin Canadys, head of the family, and not one to allow his younger brother to spend endless years of imprisonment or face the possibility of execution for treason, had swiftly sent messengers down to London, seeking terms of negotiation for his brother's release.

William, Allora was convinced, was a cunning and sly man, one who could be ruthless. She could not forget what she had seen in some of the northern country where he had wreaked his revenge. She had met him, briefly, in her father's company, having been in his hall with a number of others awaiting an audience, and despite herself, she had been impressed by the man. He was not so very tall, but he was built with heavy muscles; a broad-shouldered man who had hacked and thrashed his way through countless battles. The years—and the battles—showed upon his face; it had a leathered look, yet remained strong and striking. His eyes seemed to see everything, so piercing, so swift to study and judge, then hold secret his judgment. She had felt those eyes on her in the brief moments when he had spoken with her father, courteously thanking him for coming to London and assuring him that they would come to some agreement. He had touched her hand, brushed it with his lips, and murmured a soft *"Damoiselle,"* and she had felt a curious streak of tremors at his touch, something that seemed to hint of the man's great power.

Many of her father's people had feared his journey here, to London, certain that William would instantly take him hostage as well. But they had ridden south with only twenty men, for Ioin had been determined not to be cast into a position where he must do battle; he was not afraid of being taken himself.

William would be a fool to seize him, and the Conqueror was anything but a fool.

Of all the border lords, her father was the most reasonable, and by long-standing consensus, the others were swift to look to his lead. He was trusted and loved by Malcolm, and had served as a negotiator between the kings oft enough. By seizing her father, William would invite insurrection for years to come. And besides, negotiating with Ioin for Robert's release might well bring the Conqueror great concessions.

So they were safe. As safe as any man or woman might be within William's realm.

Except that her father was right to fear what concessions this ruthless king would demand. William did little without careful thought, and he had most certainly given the idea of her uncle's release very careful thought. He knew what he would ask of her father, Allora had seen it in his eyes in those few moments in which they had so briefly spoken.

"I fear," Ioin murmured, "that he will seek some heavy toll for this last of Robert's rebellions!"

Allora left the window seat to go to her father's side, setting a hand upon his shoulder and encouraging him to sit before the warmth of the fire. They had been given the upstairs section of a very comfortable manor in which to live. The property belonged to one of the king's nobles, and was at the king's disposal. They each had been given a handsomely appointed bedroom, and between them, this room where they spoke now with its broad oak dining table and tapestried chairs.

"Father, you mustn't worry," she told him, though it was like suggesting he not breathe. "The king needs you and your support. He has offered us this place with his own servants to care for our well-being, and Robert will join us at the evening meal in the king's own hall, for though he is a prisoner here he is a noble one, treated much more like a hostage than the traitor the king claims him to be. Things will work out well enough, Father, I am certain of it. But you must take care not to worry so much."

He patted her hand absently.

"Pour me wine, daughter," he said. "That, at least, is fine in this London town we've come to. The Bastard does order that the very best of wines be brought from France!"

Allora swiftly left him, striding to the round table by the windows that overlooked the street below. She started to pour the wine her father had requested, but she found that she paused in the very act, staring down as a cacophony of noises suddenly drew her attention.

A triumphant horn was blown, announcing the arrival of the troops streaming through the streets in a near-deafening march. It seemed that hundreds of horses pawed the earth, that a thousand footsteps touched down upon it.

All of her life she had seen men-at-arms, fighting men. Her father had within his employ a hundred housecarls, trained fighting men. Then there were the neighboring thanes, his allies, and other border lords.

But she had never seen anything quite like this.

There came a rider at the head of them, followed by a man who carried a streaming gold-and-blue banner. She couldn't quite make out the design upon it, but the colors were striking. And the man who rode before that banner . . .

She shivered suddenly, watching him. She couldn't see his face, for he wore a helmet that shielded not just the top of his head, but his cheeks and nose and forehead as well. Silver stag horns rose at either side of the helmet, and she imagined that just the sight of the rider might give some men pause in battle. He rode a large horse, a silver-white horse with a wild-flowing white mane and tail. He was clad in mail, a long shirt of it beneath a tunic that blazed in the blue and gold of his shield. The horse itself was tall and the man seemed taller atop it, dominating even the size of the host that followed behind him. His thighs were covered in dark leather leggings and a great sword hung from his saddle as did his shield. As he rode, making his way through the narrow street, the people cheered wildly, barely making way; it seemed they longed to touch him, to have some brief encounter with him. In turn, he raised a gauntleted hand and greeted those around him.

As the man and his army rode nearer, Allora began to see that though they were incredibly disciplined, the warriors in these ranks were not entirely pristine—this group had come from battle. Men supported other men as they walked, tunics in differing shades were darkened by stains of blood. Below her, as the leader approached, she saw that his gold-and-blue tunic was torn and muddied, and though he rode straight in his saddle, he also rode with the posture of a weary man.

For a startling moment, it seemed that he paused beneath her window. The shimmering silver helmet lifted, and the man stared up at her.

She stared back, wondering at the dark eyes that glared at her from within the helm. It seemed that he stared a long time, yet it couldn't have been more than seconds. Surely, the horse hadn't really ceased to move. Yet suddenly, she found herself blushing hotly and moving in from the window as swiftly as she could.

But no, the horses had not stopped moving. She could hear their hooves upon the earth, hear the tromping of all those feet. How many of the Conqueror's men returned that day under the leadership of the strange man in the horned silver helmet? Two hundred? More? Or did their vast movement within the confines of the narrow street make it seem there were so many when in truth, their numbers were not nearly so great?

Allora didn't know. She looked at her father, who had come to her side, as he stared down at the multitude moving beneath them now.

"So there *he* comes," Ioin muttered, "the great Earl of Wakefield . . ."

She glanced at her father quickly, startled by the tone of his voice. It held a certain note of bitterness, but none of mockery. He might have hated the man, yet it was obvious he admired him as well.

"Who is he?" she asked.

As though he hadn't heard her, her father continued softly, "Back from Normandy."

"There's rebellion in Normandy?"

"There's always rebellion when a man tries to hold as much as William would hold. And when he has decided to split up his holdings as he has! England will go to one son, Normandy to another, and the one in Normandy is already giving his father a rugged time of it!" He shook his head sadly, then stroked her gleaming hair.

"In this, daughter, I am blessed!" Ioin said softly, smiling at her with gentle tenderness. "Your mother always thought I missed a son, but I could not imagine not having my daughter; could not imagine not having my people stand behind me—my brother, my family, my kin. And I cannot imagine battling over what is mine to give!"

"The truth of it, Father," she told him lightly, "is that I intend to pray that you live forever."

"Ah, but no man lives forever. William knows that, you see. So I am grateful that the Far Isle will be yours, and that Robert and the family will always honor my wishes. We are different, we are."

Allora arched a brow, but held back her words. She had seen the rough border lairds with their mountain- and seafaring heritage battle like wild creatures, yet they seemed to recognize their own laws and respect each other's right to property.

Perhaps that respect was what the Normans lacked?

Nevertheless, watching this triumphant procession through the city toward the court where the king was in residence was a good thing—it had stopped her father worrying about Robert and William for a brief time as he stared pensively after the young Norman nobleman.

"So who is he?" she inquired. "A truly despicable wretch, the worst of the Normans' henchmen?" Her tone was teasing.

But her father shook his head slowly, then poured and sipped some wine. "Nay, he's young, and wild. But at ten the lad had a fair head upon his shoulders." He turned to her suddenly. "He is not to be taken lightly, daughter. Take care if you find yourself near him!"

Startled, Allora said, "Father, I hardly think that I shall be anywhere near him!"

Her father sniffed warily, staring at the street below, where at last only the dust and dirt rustled up by the returning army remained. "William has said that we will dine in his hall tonight, Robert as well, that we may see as how my brother has endured no ill treatment—despite the charge of treason against him. I promise you, Allora, this man of his will be there tonight. Keep your distance—and mind your tongue."

She sighed reproachfully. "Father, I do not intend to jeopardize your position here. I shall use the diplomacy the Normans are so very fond of themselves in all that I say and do."

"Nevertheless, take care."

Even as he said the words, there was a sudden pounding on the door below. Laird Ioin leaned out the window, staring at the young messenger boy who had come below.

"What is it, lad? Ye're about to wake the dead!" Laird Ioin called down to him.

The boy was about twelve, with large, slightly protruding ears, bright eyes, and a quick smile. He placed his hands together solemnly and bowed low to Ioin.

"The king summons you to his hall to dine, my lord!" he called back. He bowed again, his cheeks pinkening. "And your lady daughter as well. Come quickly, milord, for the king has asked that you sit at his table, and he is most anxious that you grant him this small favor!"

"Small favor, humph!" Ioin said, so softly that only Allora could hear him.

"I pray that you are ready, milord?"

"Indeed, lad, if you are to be our escort to the king's table, you will not wait long."

Allora stared at her father, then swiftly ran from the window and to the small but pleasant room that had been hers since her arrival. She dug quickly into a trunk for the veil that matched the gown she wore, a gold-and-amber linen tunic with long slit sleeves that displayed the elegant beading on the sleeves of the shift she wore beneath it. The veil was gossamer, barely covering the brilliance of her hair. Her father had bought it during one of his trading excursions into the far north country where the Viking jarls

still ruled on cold and distant islands; islands where their
kinsmen brought all manner of riches from all about the
world. She had a beautiful circlet of twined gold and silver
that held the veil atop her head, and when she had duly
attached the piece, she smoothed down her skirt, determined
that she would prove to this Norman court that the border
lairds and those of highland descent were not the barbarians
they were so oft reputed to be.

She returned to the center chamber, seeking Ioin's eyes.
"Am I presentable, Father?"

He didn't answer her for a long moment. "I should have
left you home, Allora!"

Distressed, she frowned, touching her skirt, then the
elegant veil. "What is amiss?"

"Nothing, and there the dread of it!" he said softly. He
stretched out a hand to her. "Come, daughter, we enter the
den of lions now, eh?"

She smiled and took his arm, her fingers warm around
it. She squeezed slightly. "We shall have what we will!"
she told him determinedly. "Remember, Father, you are a
powerful man. William needs you!"

He answered with some small sound in his throat. It was
not as reassuring as she might have wished, and despite
herself, she felt a shaft of unease sweep up her spine as
she hurried along at his side.

In the street below she discovered that the king had sent
a conveyance for them, a canopied wagon with handsomely
covered chairs within and a drapery that kept the passen-
gers' privacy. The driver sat on a seat that was lifted up
outside of the canopy.

The king's great tower, the White Tower, was not so far
from them that they could not have walked the distance
easily enough. Still, Allora found herself fascinated once
again by everything that she was seeing. She had always
been very aware of a wonderful world just beyond her
reach. Her father's own fortress had long been a place of
culture where the learned and skilled of countless countries
loved to come. Monks often filled the solars, dutifully
crafting exquisite editions of the Gospels. Lute players
came, dancers, magicians, even Greek scholars who taught

her the lessons of their ancient playwrights. She'd even been moved to tears once, when she had learned that the noble and brilliant Socrates had been executed by poison.

For treason against the state. So they claimed.

Just as they who held Robert claimed that he had committed treason.

She gave herself a mental shake, assuring herself that no ill would come to her uncle, her father, or her. William had been holding Robert for quite some time now, and no ill had come to him as yet. Had the Bastard wanted to kill Robert, he would have done so.

No, her father was right. William was treacherous. He did not want them dead.

But then . . .

They entered the gates and came to the massive structure Londoners called the White Tower. It was built of stones of the color that gave it its name, so she had heard. It was a fantastic place, as busy as the streets, with men-at-arms moving about rapidly, and animals of all sorts. There were a number of women there as well, and she heard laughter rising here and there and flushed as she felt her father's eyes upon her.

She was not so innocent as he might imagine. She was not a fool, and though Ioin might well be shocked, she had heard a great deal from a number of her married kinswomen. She was well aware that the laughing women— the sound of their voices so very husky in the nearing darkness—were prostitutes. "Where there's an army," a cousin had once warned her, "ye can of this be sure— there'll be women!" And her cousin had gone on to say that she wasn't sure she should describe just what kind of women . . .

But her cousin's sniff said it all.

Allora's cousin Elizabeth had nobly told her that marriage, of course, was to be endured. Yet her cousin Bridget had winked and promised her that there was *enduring*, and then again, there was *enduring*. And Bridget and her young swain, Keenan, did indeed seem to laugh together as an occasional couple here seemed to do.

But the differing opinions of her kinswomen didn't seem to matter much at the moment. Allora was still fascinated by everything going on around her. She had seen camp followers before, of course, but these seemed to be of a cut above the ragtag women who so often followed behind the highlanders. These women were well-dressed. Their perfumes met high on the air and mingled.

They were as intriguing as were the rest of the people in this great city of London. They didn't look so very different from many of the great ladies she had met so briefly thus far in the city—they just sounded different. And certainly, she thought, they behaved quite differently.

"There!" exclaimed her father, pulling the drapery further back. The conveyance came to a sudden stop and their driver was swiftly around the wagon, placing a footstool at its rear for them to descend. They swiftly became part of the throng of people that had passed among William's guards to come sup with their king.

They needn't have felt as if they had been specially selected for the evening—at least fifty men and women entered the gleaming tower, and swept along the stairs to the upper level where the king had his court this night.

Even here, it was still wickedly busy, with great hounds mingling with the multitude of people. Servants in the king's colors rushed about with massive trays of fruit and meat, trickles of sweat beading upon their faces, their shoulders burdened down with their loads. Strong-armed men carried the heaviest loads; pretty lasses hurried about with pitchers of wine and mead to wet the dry throats of the cacophonous crowd.

"Ioin!" came a cry. "Ioin! Brother!"

It was Robert! Younger than her father, a bit shorter and bigger in the shoulders, it was clear that he was far more a man of action, while Ioin weighed his thoughts before his pride or anger could make him act too quickly—or carelessly.

The two men clasped one another fiercely. Robert, with his rich, thick beard and ready smile, drew quickly away, pulling Allora into his great bear's hug next. He kissed the top of her head, then moved back. "'Tis not that long since

I've seen you, lass. And still . . . ah, lady! 'Tis fair certain the young fool David frets behind!"

She blushed slightly, aware that her uncle knew the depths of her feeling for the young man who awaited them all back home, David of Edinburgh, tall, lean, fair, so very much like her father, careful in his thought, passionate and sure in his actions once he had set forth upon them.

He had long intended to ask for her hand in marriage. Her father would, she was certain, bless the union. They were wonderfully companionable. But the matter of Robert's arrest and very possible execution had sent them all into action, putting all else behind them for the moment. "He need not fret for me, Uncle," she chided him quickly, placing a hand gently upon his arm. "For my heart is true!" she promised him with sparkling eyes. "It is for you—you old fool!—that we all fret!"

Robert roared out his laughter, then his voice lowered and he spoke very softly to both Ioin and his daughter. "We'll pull the wool over the eyes of that scruffy bastard king yet, eh? He mastered England, never the land of the free Scots!"

Allora refrained from mentioning the fact that the king considered their border lands to be a part of England rather than Scotland. Her uncle could still hang.

Prudence, rather than argument, was in order.

"Aye, Robert, but this is grave serious!" Ioin warned, his brows furrowed.

Many men—including his own—might call William bastard behind his back.

None did it to his face.

"I'm not guarded here," Robert said swiftly. "Not in this great hall where Norman henchmen mill about. He's a fair enough warder, is the king. I eat as well as his own men, and have a certain run of the place. So you need not fret unduly, Ioin. The Bastard wants something—thankfully not my life!—and we've just yet to discover what it will be."

The fire suddenly snapped and rose, a dog yelped and leaped away from a burning ember. The hall seemed to fall silent for a moment as all eyes turned toward the man now entering.

Allora found her gaze pulled his way as he walked straight to the head table, his strides long and very certain.

Arrogant strides, but then, Norman strides were . . .

Still, no matter what his ancestry, this was an arresting man; he was very tall, and startlingly dark, his hair nearly blue-black. It was not cut so short as many of his people liked to style their hair, and neither was it tonsured. It was a head of rich, thick, wavy blue-black hair, burnished in the fire and candlelight that now blazed so hotly.

He was dressed simply enough in earth-colored breeches and boots, a long-sleeved shirt beneath his knee-length tunic, the shirt an amazing, clean shade of white, the tunic a blazing blue embroidered with gold. It moved with him when he walked, adding to the grandeur of that sweeping, hard movement.

To the arrogance . . .

She caught sight of his face as he came forward, and was startled as her heart seemed to shudder, stopping for a moment, and then began beating anew at a frantic pace. She didn't know what emotion it was he caused to rise within her. Surely, it could not be fear, for she was surrounded by others here.

Lions, Norman lions, the lot of them!

It wasn't fear, she told herself angrily, and yet she still felt the same curious sensations as she watched him. Something leaped along her spine, and chilled her heart. He was both startlingly handsome and forbiddingly austere. His features were hard as granite, and yet near-perfect—a straight nose, a rugged, determined chin, high, bronzed cheekbones, and deep, rich, dark eyes that blazed fiercely, brilliantly in the firelight. His brows were ebony, etched in high, defined arches. It was one of the most arresting faces she had ever seen, one of the most compelling, and one of the fiercest—all in one.

And equally fascinating to the company around her, Allora thought, for the people who had milled about so loudly in the king's hall were silent, watching this man as she did herself. He was very tall, yet his grace as he swiftly approached the king was mesmerizing.

And amazingly enough, the Norman king, who had been seated in his specially carved chair, rose to greet this man who so arrogantly advanced upon him. The table was between them, with roasted eels curved upon a large silver tray. Yet the Conqueror reached across the table to embrace the man and call out a warm welcome. "Drink, my friends, in salute! Welcome my great warrior home. Where I cannot ride, he rides in my stead. Heartily I welcome you, friend!"

When the king had spoken, the others seemed to come to life, swiftly gathering around the man. Allora turned to ask her father or her uncle who he might be, then it occurred to her that it had to be the mighty Earl of Wakefield, the man who had ridden beneath her window that afternoon with the same swift arrogance. The man with the striking helmet.

She whirled back to stare at him through the crowd. With or without that helmet, he was . . . imposing. She felt a strange shivering sneak down her spine once again. Her father had warned her . . .

What exactly had he warned her? He didn't seem to hate the man, and yet . . .

He had been wary of him. Aye, but this Earl of Wakefield was the king's man, and that in itself bore warning! Ioin hadn't really needed to say a word to her. She knew exactly where her loyalties lay, and she knew exactly what she thought of William the Conqueror, William the Bastard . . .

And that, she thought swiftly, *was* her father's warning. She needed to heed her tongue, which, of course, none of them did when they were near the warmth of the fire upon the Far Isle.

She turned again, anxious to find her father and uncle, yet it seemed she had been parted from them. She started forward, then discovered that suddenly a Norman lord stood before her, clean-shaven, his hair cropped close, his face lean and cunning.

Then she found herself suddenly lifted off the ground as the Norman grasped her by the arms. In seconds she was backed against a wall and held within the shadows of an alcove that stood just off the great hall. She decided swift-ly—and with only a trace of alarm—that many a romantic tryst had been doubtless held in such a place.

"Sir, if you will let me go—" she began mildly enough.

But the man with his licentious eyes was quick to break in upon her. "Ah, *damoiselle!* A wondrous creature to behold after a long and perilous journey. Did some magic fairy bring you here? Perhaps the gods do live in Valhalla, and have loaned you to us for the evening. In God's name, fair lady, who are you?"

The words were polite enough, flattering, but the look in the man's eyes was frighteningly hungry, his tone taunting. She gritted her teeth, not with fear, but with impatience. She disliked him on sight, that look in his eyes, the dark hollows in his cheeks. He was surely of the nobility, for his tunic was richly tufted with fur at the neckline and the hem which hung about his booted feet.

She could not escape him without some answer.

"Nay, sir," she told him, "I am not brought from any Valhalla for your liking, I am most certain. Trust me, sir, that I am no goddess, but rather a demon from the most barbaric north. Now, sir, if you would let me by—"

He eased her to her feet again but clutched her arm, dragging her swiftly back when she would have passed, his strength startling her, as did his boldness. Even as a Norman lord, he must realize that she was a guest especially invited by the king.

"Ah, but I am in love, I think, smitten this very sec-ond!" he cried. And to her distress, she discovered that he had swung her around, and that he actually had the awful audacity to try to kiss her lips.

Jesu! There would be war in this very hall if her father or uncle were to see . . .

She would not scream and bring attention to this scene.

There was so much conversation going on in so many high, nasal Norman voices that she doubted that all but the most bloodcurdling screams might be heard anyway.

She had far more of her uncle's blood than her father's at times, she thought as she swiftly drew back her knee and brought it up mercilessly hard against the man's groin.

The sound that escaped him was deep and pained, and then he spoke through clenched teeth, his lips gone white and thin.

"Lady, you will rue the day you dared injure me—" he began in a raw fury, his fingers tightening like a vise around her arms.

Yet he broke off suddenly, his voice catching on a high note, his fingers falling from her arms as he was plucked out of the dark alcove and set some feet from her. "D'Anlou!" Allora heard him gasp with a sharp intake of breath.

"And you, de Fries, the biggest fool in Christendom! What in God's name do you think you're doing?"

A hand, none too gentle, landed on her own arm now, wrenching her back out before the fire. Any word of thanks she might have had died on her lips. The man did not want her thanks—he had barely bothered to glance her way. He did not know her, she was certain.

She knew him.

The wretched Earl of Wakefield.

"William will have your neck if you are not wary, milord!" Wakefield continued, obviously deeply irritated. "Apologize to the lady!"

"She is no lady," de Fries replied sullenly. "She told me she was a demon from the north, and aye, that she is!"

She suddenly felt Wakefield's eyes upon her, sharp and interested now.

"From the north—old Ioin's daughter, the princess of the Far Isle!" Wakefield said. He seemed somewhat amused now. He disliked de Fries, she thought, yet had no greater wish for bloodshed in this hall than she did.

And as for her . . .

Aye. To him she was someone to be swiftly dismissed. Still the situation must be . . . managed.

"Apologize," he told de Fries again. His eyes remained upon Allora, though he did not touch her now. They weren't black, as she had thought. Not brown, not black. They were blue. Deep, dark blue. Cobalt in this shadowy place.

Sharp as the steel of his sword, she thought fleetingly.

"There is no need for this heathen to voice an apology,"

she said, her voice surprisingly low and even, her fury yet apparent in that controlled tone.

"Bret, I swear, she hurt me most sorely—" de Fries began anew.

"Hurt you sorely! De Fries! 'Tis a lady standing here, a lass, the fair princess of the Far Isle. Man, have some pride, some sense! She is but a little thing!" Wakefield mocked him, irritating Allora still further. She was, perhaps, slim and petite, but he might be quite startled by the strength within her.

Then again, perhaps not. De Fries was a strong enough man, and Wakefield had plucked him up as easily as he might a broken branch.

"Wait till she hurts *you*, my grand Lord Wakefield!" de Fries retorted angrily.

"Nay, she'll not hurt me," Wakefield said, cobalt gaze slipping disconcertingly from her head to her feet. "For I should not be the fool to put myself in a position for her to do so! I repeat, she is a slender little woman! And there will not be bloodshed over her in this hall."

"No bloodshed," she agreed swiftly. "But neither, milord, am I so *little!* And I do so solemnly swear, I can be a demon to fear indeed—and will become one if you *both* do not choose to let me pass!"

Her eyes were upon Wakefield.

And he responded quickly, seeming startled by her audacity. "I fear no demons, lady—especially those I can see. And," he added with a trace of amusement, "those barely out of the nursery."

Ah! He had known the barb would stick!

She was not *so* very young. Most women her age were wed already. But in this court, against the many who had played these games so very long . . . perhaps she was just a babe.

He must have heard the sound of her teeth grating fiercely together, and remained amused, so it seemed. But before she could snap out a reply, he was speaking again to de Fries, angry now, the amusement gone from his voice. "The lady of the Far Isle is a guest within this court, de Fries. You will apologize to her."

De Fries locked his thin lips tightly together and bowed in a curt manner. "Lady, my apologies!" he snapped. He turned on his heel and was swiftly gone.

Allora watched him for a moment, then realized that Wakefield was still with her. She returned her sizzling gaze to his.

"Now, milord, if you will excuse me as well . . . ?"

"Ah, but lady, I cannot! Your father was quite distressed that you had disappeared within this goodly crowd. I was sent by him—and the king—to escort you to the table. I am glad I came when I did."

"How so?" she said lightly, inclining her head with minor interest.

" 'Tis a pleasure to serve any young *damoiselle* in a matter of such distress," he said smoothly.

"Ah, but my dear Wakefield," she retorted, "when you arrived, I was no longer in distress, but had quite competently taken care of the matter myself."

An ebony brow arched high. "You were in darkness, lady. Pressed from the crowd. You think that Jan de Fries would have given up so easily?"

"He was near crippled."

"He was but gasping for breath."

"He was sorely injured. He assured you so himself!" she insisted.

"Was he?" From his great height, he looked down upon her, crossing his arms over the considerable breadth of his chest.

"Indeed!"

"Well then. It seems the moments for both danger and gratitude are gone. The king summons you to the table."

"The king must wait."

"Kings do not wait, milady."

"Even those who have seized their crowns?"

"Especially those who have seized their crowns," he promised her swiftly.

She was startled by the answer, certain he would have stoutly defended William's right to the throne of England.

"Especially the Conqueror," he continued softly.

"The Bastard," she heard herself saying. She instantly regretted the words. Her father had warned her to guard her temper and her tongue.

He still watched her. She could not read his thoughts. But he shrugged.

"The Bastard—the *Conqueror* nonetheless," he told her.

"He has not conquered me."

"Take care then that he does not."

"I am not English."

"That is debatable."

"Not if I refuse to debate."

Those steel-blue eyes flickered over her. "*Damoiselle*, you should learn to bend. In the midst of a heavy wind, it is often the best course of action." He offered her his arm.

She lowered her lashes, stalwartly refusing to take it.

"Will you take my arm, *damoiselle?*" he asked her again, very softly.

Take it! She longed to break it. Yet she thought of the way he had plucked up de Fries. As if the man were made of nothing more substantial than air.

He dared offer *her* no harm! Not here, not in this court! Yet . . .

She wasn't afraid that he would suddenly harm her, pounce upon her. She was afraid because she could . . . *feel* something about him. Tremendous heat and energy. A force like lightning. He was a man who made her long to bolt away . . .

And yet she would long to then come back, and watch him. Feel him, see what he would do.

"Lady?" An ebony brow arched again.

And then she knew the meaning of bending. Her chin high, her eyes blazing—fingers shaking!—she accepted that which was offered to her.

She set her hand upon his arm.

And she trembled inwardly, for it did indeed seem that she had set her touch to fire and steel.

Almost as if fate itself gave her fair warning . . .

Chapter 2

❦

"**T**ell me, milord," Allora murmured as they moved carefully through the company crowded into the hall, the men eager to call out greetings to Wakefield, the women anxious to touch his arm or sleeve, "do you offer a threat to my uncle?" Even as she spoke the question, she was aware she was being studied. Just as they had been swift and eager to greet Wakefield, the crowd within the king's hall was eager to examine her, staring at her boldly. One woman in an elegant purple tunic and elaborate head-dress gazed straight at her in a most speculative fashion, then whispered to the man in the mustard hose and brown leggings standing beside her.

"I offer no one a threat, milady," he assured her, "until he—or she—threatens me."

"And then they die?" she inquired, pausing. "Is that why you are the incredibly great and indomitable Earl of Wakefield?"

He arched a brow again, and she found herself breathless, staring at him. He was indeed a striking man, his gaze so searing, his features rugged and handsome. He seemed somewhat amused by her again, yet despite his assurance that he posed no threat, there was a warning in his tone. As if she were an annoyance to him, like a child might be. And he would tolerate an annoyance for only so long, but then . . .

But then what? She was disturbed to realize that she both dreaded coming to such a point . . . and yet would be fascinated to challenge him to it. But really, how foolish. She was in her father's company, and her uncle's. The king was anxious that they would come to some bargain

36

tonight. She could really do or say as she wished as far as this man went. She had the safety of not only her father's broad back, but the king's as well.

The look Wakefield gave her now was one of impatience. "Milady, I do not call myself either great or indomitable, and I do assure you, I am aware—as is William—that though a man may be great, he can never be indomitable."

"How amazing," she said. "He might certainly have fooled most of England."

"But not all of it."

She arched a brow, then realized that there were numerous people still watching her—or them. The lady in the purple; another very beautiful young woman in a golden-yellow tunic with a delicate embroidered white shift beneath. She had ink-dark hair and almond-brown eyes, and skin as pure as cream.

"You are not fooled by the Conqueror, milady? You do not find him great—or indomitable?"

She stared at him again. "I pay fealty where fealty is due," she said. "Why are they staring at me so?" she demanded then.

He laughed softly, and it seemed that he replied to all her words. "You are the princess of the Far Isle. Many wondered if you would be barbaric, or perhaps hugely tall and well-muscled, like a warrior-queen descended upon them. You are new to the court, milady. They did not expect one so young, nor so intriguing. Everyone will wonder just what the king will want of you."

"Of me?"

"You're his subject, milady."

"I told you—"

He was growing truly impatient now. "You claim your land to be part of Scotland, which in itself means nothing, since Malcolm and William ever barter over the border—and Malcolm does concede, lady, let me warn you that! William sees that the isle is his—"

"Another place he would *seize!*" she whispered.

"Hear me, lady. And trust me, I can argue this more fairly than any other man! Edward the Confessor did swear to William to leave him England. The English were not so fond of a foreign prince as their sovereign, and Harold Godwinson had long served as the highest noble in Edward's kingdom. On his deathbed, Edward then gave England to Harold—but William could not forget an inheritance this size, sworn to him first by Edward, and then—under difficult circumstances, I admit—by Harold himself. To William, this was not a conquest or seizure. He came and took, legally, and beneath a papal banner, what was his."

"I know my history—"

"Then bear it all in mind!" he warned. "Your king will have your obedience."

"Does he have yours?" she demanded. "Or are you so swift to speak your mind with him?"

His eyes swept over her, and she felt that strange sensation of dancing heat once again. "I serve the king, as my father serves him. I serve him well, and so, milady, my opinion is a valuable one."

"I see. You are so very valuable that the king dares not command you."

"Milady, you are from the far north—"

"A barbaric land?"

"Perhaps a foolish land, or a land filled with fools! While here, milady, you should curb your tongue, for wars have begun—and men have died—over less than the words you so rashly speak."

"It is not William I insult—" she began to say, worried anew about her uncle, but she broke off quickly, realizing that she was telling the man in exact terms that she *was* insulting *him*.

She flushed, swiftly asking another question. "Why does that woman continue to watch me so?"

"Which woman?"

"The dark-haired lady, behind us."

"You've eyes in the back of your head?" he demanded.

"I can feel her watching me."

"Ah. Lady Lucinda."

"Almond eyes, fair skin—"

"Indeed, she's quite beautiful."

"And rude."

His lip curled. "And you are the very heart of gentle and courteous diplomacy!"

She gritted her teeth. "I am not one of these people."

"Scottish rather than English."

"Anything—other than Norman!"

He arched a brow again, amused and annoyed. "That rather remains to be seen, doesn't it?" he suggested softly, his gaze sweeping her once again. It made her feel desperate for a moment. Hot, flushed, longing to lash out—at him.

And very anxious to be away from him, his warmth, his power, his strange influence.

But he continued then, answering her question. "Lady Lucinda is anxious to wed. She is no doubt a bit worried about the king's plans for you."

"But he should have no plans—"

"Nevertheless, milady, you asked a question; I gave you an answer. Lucinda does assume, I imagine, that you will do as you are commanded by God, king, and father."

"They are not one and the same!"

"Perhaps she isn't staring at you, but at me."

"Why?"

"Perhaps she is worried about my affections."

"How insufferable!" Allora gasped, then realized—despite the fact that this man seemed to force such responses—just how rude she was being. She bit her lower lip, but too late. He was, once again, certainly annoyed, but more than that, amused.

He lifted his hands in a shrug. "I am worth a great deal," he told her.

It was no boast, just a simple statement of fact. Most probably, he was. And she was suddenly certain that he was right, that the woman was watching him more so than her.

And that the almond-eyed beauty didn't care at all what Wakefield was worth. She cared that he was the man he was, so darkly, ruggedly striking, so tall, young . . .

Stop! She commanded herself, and spoke quickly, mockingly.

"Ah, but why should she watch? Surely she assumes

that you also would follow the commands of God, king, and father?" Allora taunted softly.

"Milady, you fail to realize that I have proven myself to God, king, and father. And in my service and loyalty, milady, I am left to govern myself. Shall we sit? The king—and your father—will be growing anxious."

He didn't let her reply, but turned swiftly, now practically dragging her the last few feet to their table. Definitely, his patience was at an end.

Allora had been afraid that she would be seated next to the Norman knight, but that was not to be the case. When she reached the table, he swiftly handed her over to her father, and she found herself between Ioin and her uncle. It was still not a comfortable position—Bret d'Anlou was to her uncle's left, and the king himself was to her father's right.

She was the only woman at the head table that evening. Mathilda, William's queen had passed away. For all his faults, the king had been a loving husband, and no woman was at his side now.

Allora found herself studying the king. He was neatly, handsomely attired, his face clean-shaven, his hair clipped short. His eyes were grave, his voice very deep, his manner pleasant. It seemed nearly impossible to believe that he was the man who had bested and conquered an entire race of people; he could behave in so very civil a manner.

She took her eyes from the king for a moment, and stared from her position at the king's table down the length of the planks that sided from it in a U fashion. There seemed to be so very many people present. Close to where she was seated, Allora saw the nobility; handsome men, beautiful women, all dressed in brilliant colors, laughing, talking, sharing wine. The lesser folk came next down the long planking, their clothing not quite so rich, their laughter not quite so loud. Beyond them, down at the end of the table lengths, were most of the clergy. Around them all, servants bustled swiftly, carrying an inexhaustible supply of food and drink from the kitchens.

"We are missing one of the realm's most beautiful

matrons this evening," she heard suddenly, and her eyes were drawn back to William, who was still speaking pleasantly in his native Norman French—the language which was spoken at court. His eyes were focused down the table from her, upon Bret d'Anlou. He lifted his wine chalice. "I had sent notice to Fallon that she should join us this evening. Where is your lady mother this eve, Bret, on the night of your most triumphant return?"

The question seemed to have the slightest edge of steel to it. Curious, Allora studied Bret d'Anlou, certain he would swiftly be on the defensive, stuttering out a reply, perhaps.

But the man seemed not at all unnerved. He sipped wine from the chalice before him and slowly set it down, shrugging his broad shoulders lightly. His eyes, their blue so startling against the rugged bronze of his face, fell without hesitation on the king. "I cannot believe that my mother did not send her regrets, Your Grace! I can only imagine that she pines, for my father remains in Normandy along with Robin and Philip. Surely, she awaits Father's return. And then again, sire, you know Mother."

Allora straightened, amazed by the man's words, then pleased—certain the Conqueror would explode at such a cryptic statement. For some reason, she would have dearly loved to see the towering, arrogant knight fall victim to the king's famed temper.

A small smile curved her lips as she waited for the axe to fall. Then a flush crept over her cheeks, for Bret d'Anlou's steel-blue gaze touched upon her own. He arched a brow, then gave his attention back to the king. "In truth, sire, you have known Fallon far longer than I!"

Now Bret's blue gaze remained fixed upon the king, and William suddenly grinned. Allora had the feeling that the king had been goading his young champion, and was actually quite pleased with his answer.

There would be no explosion.

She shivered, feeling the touch of d'Anlou's gaze once again.

"It is a pity she is not here tonight," William said.

"A pity indeed," Bret agreed.

The king's eyes left his and fell upon Allora. He smiled.

"So, *damoiselle*, are you enjoying yourself?" he inquired.

"London is fascinating," she assured him.

"I refer to this evening, milady. I hoped you would be comfortable. Therefore I ordered that you be seated between your father and uncle; yet I hope, too, that you are making friends at this court."

She forced a smile. "I seek no enemies."

"Few of us seek enemies. They seem to find us on their own," he murmured dryly, then continued. "You have, I see, met the Earl of Wakefield?"

She felt Bret's eyes on hers. She nodded, her forced smile still in place. "Indeed, yes, we've met. He so very courteously brought me to this table at your request."

"Without his father, I might not have taken England. Without Bret, I might not have kept it some of these past years."

"The man," she murmured, eyes downcast as she fought to keep the sarcasm from her voice, "is assuredly a treasure!"

"Indeed! Yet he is a younger son," the king said with a note of regret. "His father's titles fall to his brother."

"Your Grace," d'Anlou said firmly, "you have given me a worthy title—"

"Aye. A title, and land. Decimated land," William said with a sigh. "It becomes difficult to parcel out a kingdom that has already had so very many parcels taken."

"What a pity you owed so very many men!" Allora said lightly.

Her father cleared his throat, his fingers winding around hers beneath the table. But William laughed. And Bret d'Anlou was quick to speak, with a certain amount of irritation edging his voice, as if he was wearying of the entire conversation. "Your Grace, I've ample freedom of movement, and, therefore, opportunity always lies ahead. I am satisfied with the lofty title you have given me. I will improve upon my land and fortune by my own hand."

"Bravo!" William exclaimed.

"A treasure indeed!" Allora couldn't help but add. Yet she looked up, compelled to do so, and shivered at the fire in the cobalt eyes that accosted hers.

He had ceased to find her amusing. Indeed, he seemed very aggravated and anxious for the evening to end.

No more than she!

William chuckled softly, staring at her. "Ah, milady! Treasures come in many varieties. Young d'Anlou is worthy of much!" he assured her.

Then William turned to gaze at Allora's father, and she was startled anew by the dazzle of cunning in the man's eyes. "Ioin, you have eaten little! Come, man, I swear there is no poison in this food!"

Ioin folded his hands together on the table before him. "I've little appetite, Your Grace. Worry has cost me the hunger I might have summoned for this fabulous feast."

"Worry?" the king said. "But your brother sits there at your daughter's side, safe and well. He has enjoyed his time within the tower, I daresay. It's my understanding you led many a guard a merry chase with your ability at chess, eh, Robert?"

Robert shrugged, grinning. Her uncle certainly *wasn't* the worse for wear, Allora noted.

"And still," William continued, "Robert Canadys took part in a serious rebellion against me." He speared a piece of fowl with a small dinner knife and nibbled from it. "I have given it all very careful consideration. The border land is incredibly important to any sovereign. Isn't that right, Bret?" he demanded, turning back to d'Anlou.

Like Allora, Bret d'Anlou seemed to realize that the king's conversation was heading somewhere. He answered without fear, but with a certain knowing wariness. "Indeed, sire. All borders do bear their own importance. Malcolm, however, continues to pay you homage—"

"And to harbor Saxon fugitives, and plot rebellions right along with them," William said flatly.

"It is not rebellion for a man to hold what is his! And perhaps, for some, all did not end at the battle of Hastings!" Allora exclaimed. Surely, this man had to realize that a conquered people were not going to be happy! Then she realized that everyone at the table had gone silent, and that to a man, they were staring at her; her father with a look of horror on his face, the king with anger, Robert with amusement, and Bret d'Anlou . . .

With strange, shimmering eyes. As if he'd love to silence her, if he only had the right to do so.

Well, he did not. But her father did, and she was alarmed at the worry that now tinged his gaze. She shouldn't have spoken, she had to hold on to her temper. They were bargaining for her uncle's life, and no matter how civilized William might pretend to be, he had proven that he could be entirely ruthless.

The king's eyes remained upon her, but once again, when she awaited an explosion, there was none to come.

"For some . . ." William murmured. "Ah, like those who reside upon the Far Isle?" he asked softly.

"King William—" her father began with dignity.

"Nay, Ioin! I'm speaking to your daughter."

Allora's breath caught as she returned the gaze of the king staring so intently upon her. "Malcolm is the king of Scotland," she reminded him.

William smiled, biting off another piece of meat. "It is part of a territory that gave homage to Edward the Confessor; therefore, milady, I see it as an English possession."

She felt her lower lip trembling slightly. No deception here. He meant to seize them all!

"If you have tricked us—" she began.

"I don't believe the king is suggesting such a thing!" Bret d'Anlou interrupted her sharply. There was a clear warning in his tone.

The king laughed, raising his chalice to Bret. "Nay, lady, there is no treachery here. I promised your father safe journey here and safe journey home. However, I promised nothing to your uncle!"

Allora gasped. "Then you are demanding that my father sacrifice his home for his brother's life—"

"Allora!" her father cried out.

"No demands as yet, milady, only a suggestion for a solution to a most difficult problem." William stared at Bret again. "It is imperative that I strengthen my defenses on the north border! Don't you agree? With my own son fomenting difficulties in Normandy, I need to hold very strong against Malcolm—and my own subjects in the north of England."

With the king staring so intently at him, Bret was plainly obliged to make a careful reply. "Aye!" he said very softly. "It is imperative to strengthen the border."

"Ah!" William exclaimed distractedly, for the entertainment had suddenly arrived. Hounds howled as they were kicked out of the way. A trained bear came bounding in, its keeper close behind him. The animal rolled on the floor, rose on its hind paws. A smattering of applause greeted its antics.

Allora couldn't watch the creature. Her eyes remained on the king. He felt her gaze, and turned to her, smiling. She quickly averted her eyes to stare at her hands, folded before her on the table.

Applause rang out again. The bear was balancing on a long pole suspended across two chairs. The animal stood up and waved its paws in the air. Then it jumped down. A woman screamed, a number of men laughed.

The bear and the trainer, both seeming to gleam in the firelight, stood before the company. The bear fell to its feet and the man bowed. And both turned and left the hall to the sounds of more applause.

"I need the Far Isle!" the king said softly.

Ioin half-rose to his feet; Allora knew that both she and Robert were ready to stand with him.

But the king lifted a hand to stop them, then lowered it swiftly. "Sit down! I do not intend to seize it from you, Laird Ioin!" he assured her father. "Rather, it should be yours for your lifetime; then it will rightfully fall into your daughter's holding."

Allora exhaled a great draught of air and realized she had been holding her breath as the king spoke.

"Which leads us to the matter of your daughter," William continued.

Allora tried to swallow down a gasp of dismay. Once again, her father grasped her fingers beneath the table.

"I'd not have the girl harmed, not even for my life—" Robert began angrily.

"Robert, by the grace of God, please! I've no wish to harm the girl," William said impatiently. "She is quite useful in all that I propose."

"And that is?" Allora whispered.

William lifted his wine chalice, his eyes sizzling in the firelight when they touched upon her now. "The Far Isle is your land!" he said softly to Ioin. "Yet I am overlord, and that will be doubly assured by the man who will wed your daughter. No loss to you, yet a great gain to me. And Robert Canadys walks free."

Allora choked in astonishment, then sat frozen, unable to speak. Her gaze flew to Bret d'Anlou as she thought with a simmering anger that yes, the fool, arrogant Norman had known what he was talking about.

The king, indeed, had plans for her.

Oh, aye! He was treacherous, the king. But no! This could not be put upon her like this!

Her father would refuse.

Her uncle would refuse.

But then . . . what would become of Robert Canadys?

"Who is the man?" she heard her father ask raggedly. "I'll not have her wed to some fool—"

"Nay, nay, Laird Ioin!" William said, his voice jovial and with just a small bite to his laughter. "I offer up my very best!" he said softly.

His very best. His Norman best! It couldn't be.

There was a silence.

"No—" she started to whisper.

"Who?" her father demanded again.

"Bret d'Anlou, Earl of Wakefield," the king said.

This time, amazingly, it was Bret who gasped in astonishment. The great Norman knight was so stunned, in fact, that he rose swiftly to his feet, staring at the king with such a fury he couldn't quite seem to hide it.

"Your Grace! I am amazed that you could have such thoughts and not think to consult with me upon them!"

Perhaps this was good. Even in her shocked condition, Allora realized that d'Anlou protesting the marriage would help to quell the idea far more effectively than her own words could do.

But to her dismay, her father was suddenly on his feet as well, staring at the towering Wakefield. "Bret d'Anlou," he said indignantly, "this is the insult you offer to myself and to my daughter?"

In that moment, Bret d'Anlou grasped control of both his temper and the situation. He inclined his head deeply to her father. "Laird Ioin, I swear before God, I would never seek to insult either you or—any member of your family. You must forgive me, as the king has managed to take me quite by surprise. For I had assumed that my family would be present in such a situation; and because, frankly, my affairs tend to circle around some startling distances from your homeland. I do not begin to imagine that I could offer the Far Isle the full-time support so worthy a property deserves."

It seemed William had put them all in quite a position.

"Perhaps this bears deeper thought by all parties; there should be time to look within our hearts," William said magnanimously. His smile was bountiful.

His tone warned that they had best indulge in some introspection—until they managed to see it his way.

Allora stood, fighting the trembling that had seized hold of her. She was ready to explode; words threatened to tumble from her lips, words in which she told the king just what she thought of his treachery and cunning—and his Norman knights.

She couldn't; her uncle's life remained on the line.

"If you'll excuse me—" she choked out.

The king himself rose, reaching for her hand. "You would leave us all so early?"

She grated her teeth very hard together, then managed to speak courteously. "Alas, Your Grace, but I believe that I shall go and attend to my—thoughts!"

"Ah!" the king murmured.

"I shall see my daughter to our rooms—" Ioin began, but the king set his hand upon Ioin's shoulder and interrupted quickly.

"I would have further, private conversation with you and your brother, Laird Ioin, away from this crowded hall. Whatever the future may hold, I am quite certain that the

Earl of Wakefield will be delighted to see Allora safely to your quarters."

D'Anlou bowed stiffly to the king. "Milady?" he said to Allora, offering her an arm once again. His furious cobalt eyes silently warned her not to refuse.

And once again that evening, she found herself taking his arm.

Were she a cat, she thought, the hairs upon her nape would have risen.

And as she touched his arm, she nearly jumped from the heat within it. She might have touched new-molded steel, still burning from the smith's fire.

"Milady?" he repeated.

She lifted her chin; held her ground.

"Laird Ioin, your daughter will be most safely delivered to your quarters!" he vowed, and turned swiftly, near dragging her along with him.

And as they left the king's hall, she was now painfully aware that all eyes followed her exit, more so than they had her entrance.

With even greater speculation.

Chapter 3

*I*t wasn't until they were out of the hall, down the stairs, and into the night that Allora was able to wrench free from his hold. And in the bailey before the wall of the tower, she shivered from the sudden chill in the night air and stared at him, her heart pounding fiercely.

There was so much she could say. She felt that a stream of fury could come spewing from her any second, and so she braced herself with all possible dignity and managed a curt "Goodnight, milord d'Anlou!" Then she spun around and started walking across the bailey.

A hand fell upon her shoulder; she was stopped dead in her tracks and then swung around. Those blue eyes were upon hers with nearly as great a power as that of his hand upon her shoulder.

"I didn't realize that you were staying in a roadside ditch while in London, milady."

"I am not!"

"Then why do you expect me to leave you so, when I have assured your father I will see you to your quarters?"

"Because, milord, I am quite anxious to be rid of your company—"

"Nay!" he interrupted, his deep voice laced with sarcasm and controlled anger. "Ah, lady! *You* are anxious to be rid of me—while *I* am pining to hear more of your insults!"

"All the better reason to leave me be, milord!" she warned him.

"I told your father that I would see you safely to your quarters."

"I assure you, I shall arrive there safely, and my father shall never know that anything was amiss."

"I gave my word," he said softly, then continued, "Lady, I will see you safely back one way or another, I do promise you."

"But—"

"You are a fool!" he snapped suddenly, harshly. "London is teeming with those who would take any advantage."

"You mean that I might be abducted? Forced into something against my will?"

"Indeed."

"But that is what the king plans himself, so what danger can I be in here?"

"Milady . . ." He bowed deeply, gently took her hand. Then he swiftly jerked her against him and she was made aware of his size and strength, and of the extent of the anger within that he had managed to hide so very well. "I must admit, I believe I would by far rather wed a hedgehog than find myself chained in name to such a *sweet* and *delectable* creature as yourself, who possesses such a golden richness of hair—and such a wealth of daggers within your tongue! Indeed, lady, the night has not been much to my liking."

"Ah, but you, my great lord d'Anlou, can change this!" she cried, suddenly frightened by the force with which he held her, by the taunting mockery of his words. "Do remember, you have served so very nobly, you have proven yourself to God, king, and father! Why, milord d'Anlou, do recall! *You can stop this monstrosity before it begins!*"

The sudden great tick in his bronzed, long-corded throat gave her swift and frightening assurance that she had aimed well—and hit her mark. His fingers tightened upon her arm.

"If you will just be so good as to let me go—?" she said, no mockery in her words now, a plea having swept into the tone of her voice.

"I will see you safely back."

"But *you* are the worst thing to have happened to me!"

"Nay, lady, I have no intention—and surely no interest!—in taking any advantage of your ever-so-lovely person. Neither do I intend to slit your wondrous throat. I will see you safely to your quarters."

"But—"

He swore violently in French, an oath she surely shouldn't have heard, and then he suddenly swung her up into his arms, and, holding her so, walked with hard, long strides toward the tower entrance, where guards stood attentive, watching the tower, yet watching them now as well. "Jean-Luc!" d'Anlou roared impatiently, and even as Allora struggled against his hold, a boy in neat brown leggings and a forest-green tunic came hurrying around one of the tall stone walls, d'Anlou's huge white horse being led by the reins in his grasp.

"I'm not riding that beast—" Allora began.

"Indeed you are." And of course, she was, because he had thrown her atop the animal as if she weighed no more than a bag of flour. And in seconds he was behind her, nudging the animal into a trot that carried them swiftly from the tower and down the muddied street.

"Afraid of Ajax, milady?" he taunted softly in her ear.

"I am not afraid of any beasts—including Norman ones!" she hissed in return.

It was a short ride as the manor house where Allora and her father were staying was very near to the tower. D'Anlou was apparently quite aware of where they were staying. Perhaps he had seen her and noted the place that afternoon after all.

And perhaps anyone close to the king had known where William was housing Laird Ioin of the Far Isle.

The great white horse came to a halt right at the manor door. D'Anlou leaped down and reached for her; she had to admit, as good a rider as she was, that she was startled by the distance from the horse's haunches to the ground. Yet she came to it gently enough, by the strength of his arms, and when she was down, she was quick to back away, knocking against the horse's flanks and managing to lose her headdress. D'Anlou caught the circlet and wisp of material and she snatched it from him. "I am safely returned!" she told him. "Have mercy upon the both of us and leave me be, I beg you!"

"You are still standing in the street, milady," he said simply.

And so she turned, her mind and spirit well-battered for the day, and hurried toward the door to the house.

So he would rather wed a hedgehog!

"Ajax, *attendez-moi!*" d'Anlou commanded the horse. And even as the door was opened by Joseph, the stooped, white-haired servant, Bret d'Anlou was behind her.

"Good evening, Joseph," d'Anlou said swiftly, before she could speak. Oh, aye, of course he knew Joseph, the king frequently housed visitors of import here, and surely, the great and magnificent d'Anlou would know them all!

"I—" Allora began.

"Milord Bret!" Joseph said with pleasure. " 'Tis good that you are back, and good that you serve the king, so we all say! How fares your family, milord?"

"All well, by the grace of God, Joseph; all well."

"If you'll both excuse me—" Allora began anew.

"There's an exceptional cask of Bordeaux in the kitchen, milord," Joseph offered cheerfully. "I'll bring it to the hall above promptly. The fire burns there now against the damp chill of the night. Please, milord, milady, I shall be delighted to serve you immediately."

"But I wish to—" Allora began more determinedly.

"Come!" d'Anlou said, and she bit back a furious reply for old Joseph was still watching them closely. D'Anlou's hand was on her arm again, indeed, his fingers were tight around her arm once again, and she was being ushered up the stairs. When they reached the solar from which she had first seen him earlier that day, she wrenched away; they were far enough from the servants to vent her rage.

"I wish to be alone! I am exhausted, I am furious! Do you understand? I believe that I am speaking your language, and that, surely, you must understand!"

"There are just a few more things I would say to you."

"Milord, most certainly there must be a hedgehog out there more anxious for your company!"

Alas, what a mistake her words were! It seemed they were barely out of her mouth when, lifted by her upper arms, she found herself flying toward one of the tapestried chairs by the fireplace, and then abruptly seated with him upon one knee before her. "I swear if you do not learn to curb your tongue, I will agree to this marriage for the simple pleasure of tying a gag about your lips."

"You wouldn't!" she gasped, and then, to her own horror, she heard herself continuing, "Not when there are so very many willing and able hedgehogs out there! And you needn't fear, I will never agree to marry you; my father will not have it, my uncle will not have it, my *people* will not have it."

"Milady—"

He broke off when there came a loud, crashing sound. Instantly on the alert, d'Anlou was on his feet, drawing his sword from the scabbard at his hip as he strode toward the door.

"Damn him!" came a hoarse curse. "Damn the man to a rude and bloody hell, by God! May the devil come take him!"

Allora leaped up herself, her heart thundering in desperate alarm as she recognized the deep voice of her father.

Ioin burst into the room. Allora noticed immediately that he had been drinking, and drinking heavily.

The bastard king had apparently been pouring rich French wine into him since she had left the table. His eyes were red-rimmed and glassy; his handsome, grizzled face was heavily flushed.

"Father!" Allora gasped. He had to cease his commentary on the king now! D'Anlou stood here with them; Joseph listened just below.

"You!" Ioin saw d'Anlou, and the sword held by his side. "You!" he repeated. Then he laughed. "Ah, but William is a wily bastard! He would seize all the land; one way or the other, he would seize it all. Well, he can't have it!"

"Ioin, you need to go to bed," d'Anlou said quietly.

"I'll not have it!" Ioin roared. Then Allora gasped again in horror as her father drew his sword and came rushing wildly at Bret d'Anlou, mighty Earl of Wakefield.

"Nay!" she shrieked, for d'Anlou was sober, his gleaming weapon held at his side. He was ready. All he need do was lift it in self-defense.

And her father would be dead.

"Nay!" she cried again, ready to rush forward and throw herself against the hard-muscled Norman.

But there was no need. D'Anlou stepped to the side, swinging his blade only to stop the fall of Ioin's steel. Her father's weapon flipped upward and clattered to the slatted wood floor.

Ioin himself flew back against the wall, and then he, too, crashed downward to the floor. Rolling over, he leaned against the wall, rubbing his head and moaning softly.

"Father!" Allora cried, sweeping down to his side. But d'Anlou was already on a knee across from Ioin, reaching up to right him against the wall as he slumped to one side. Ioin's eyes were closed for a moment.

"Father!" Allora cried softly once again.

Ioin's eyes opened and lit upon d'Anlou. "That was foolish of me, eh?"

"I think you erred in balance due to the wine, Laird Ioin," d'Anlou said with a small curve to his lip.

"But it might have been some battle, eh?"

"Every man is aware of your strength in battle and in peace, sir."

Ioin closed his eyes again, leaning back, shaking his head. Then he opened his eyes and stared at d'Anlou. "It isn't *you* that angers me, d'Anlou. You know that."

"Aye, I know."

Allora stared from one to the other of them with amazement.

"Thank you for not skewering me through," Ioin said very softly.

D'Anlou inclined his head, now offering Ioin a hand to stand. Allora frowned, ready to help her father herself. He was a tall, broad, well-muscled man, and yet did not hesitate to accept d'Anlou's help.

Ioin groaned and made his way to the table to sit. He propped his elbows up and then held his head within his hands. He groaned again.

At that precise moment, Joseph arrived at the entrance to the hall with a tray loaded down with goblets and wine.

"Bordeaux, my lords," Joseph announced, coming into the room.

Ioin groaned a third time.

"Perhaps not tonight," d'Anlou told Joseph quickly, steering him back toward the door.

Joseph was obviously startled, but departed.

"There's no way to trust the king, no way at all," Ioin said glumly.

"He has his point, my lord," d'Anlou said. "Malcolm pays homage, then harbors more rebels." He sat across the table from Ioin, shaking his head. "Trust me, sir, in this: William believes with his whole heart that England is rightfully his. Not by conquest, but by inheritance. He considers the Far Isle a part and parcel of England—"

Ioin swore softly. "How quickly he forgets history!" he said impatiently. "Not two hundred years ago, there was no such England! Alfred was king in Wessex. Elsewhere, others ruled—as kings themselves. Athelstan conquered Northumbria in 927. Eric Bloodaxe, the Dane, was king of York. Sweyn Forkbeard was recognized king in 1013, and just years later, Canute ruled in the north, and Athelstan ruled the southern Saxon nobles." He shook his head sadly. "The kingdoms were ended, the great earldoms begun: Northumbria, Wessex, Mercia, and East Anglia. Four then—and the Conqueror comes and titles are created from thin air . . ." He paused, looking at d'Anlou.

"Indeed, Laird Ioin, *my* title is newly created. The land it grants me lies in a devastated region in the north. Titles are rewards, Laird Ioin, as we all know. As William said, no king can pay thousands of men with great riches."

"I have no quarrel with any just reward you have received d'Anlou—rather with the king's concept of his domain. The Far Isle was long a kingdom in itself."

"As you said—Wessex was a kingdom. Mercia was a kingdom. They came together for the better good."

"Scotland remains a kingdom."

D'Anlou smiled, and Allora was startled to realize that he liked her father very much—and her father him.

"Laird Ioin, my very point! William will have *your* loyalty."

"You knew nothing of this marriage the king speaks of, did you," Ioin said, more statement than question.

"Nothing."

"But there's nothing to worry about," Allora interjected quickly.

They both looked up at her, startled.

As if they had forgotten that she was even in the room.

"Wakefield won't do it," she assured her father. "He has promised me that he governs himself, and so we will all be set free of this foolishness."

Neither of them answered her. They looked at one another.

Bret d'Anlou rose then, looking down at Ioin. "I bid you rest well this evening, Laird Ioin." He bowed deeply to her father and turned to leave, only to find Allora blocking the way.

He inclined his head to her. "Milady." And putting his hands upon her shoulders, he set her aside and strode swiftly from the room, his booted footsteps ringing against the floorboards.

Allora watched him go, then spun around, hurrying to take the seat across from her father where he had been sitting. "Father, this will work out. He wants none of it, that is clearly evident. You mustn't—"

"Allora," Ioin interrupted her wearily then, groaned, pressing his hands upon his skull. "I wouldn't mind the treachery so much if it weren't for the bloody French wine. Native ale is the best for a native man."

"Father, why didn't you say something? Why didn't *he?* Why didn't we just agree here and now that it wasn't to be, and the whole lot of us could have merely told the king so!"

Her father studied her sadly. He reached out a hand, curling a strand of her hair around a finger, very tenderly stroking her cheek. "I never should have brought you. He might have forgotten I had a daughter."

"Father, the point—"

"Nay, lass!" he said softly. "Bret d'Anlou held his silence then for my sake—and for your own."

"What?"

Her father shrugged. "Perhaps d'Anlou might have the power to gainsay the king. His father and brothers remain in Normandy now, but if they return . . . William is in their debt, and they are a highly popular family among the Normans as well as the Saxons."

"Then," she murmured, "if he really does have the power to govern himself—"

"Then the king would find some other man. Perhaps an older one, perhaps one who even rode on his conquest with him. He is determined that you will wed one of his nobles. Perhaps he will not fully twist d'Anlou's arm. He *will* twist mine—else execute Robert."

Allora sat back, feeling as if buckets of icy water were being tossed over her. Perhaps she hadn't realized until that very moment just how deadly determined the king could be. The word *no* was not in his vocabulary—in any language. She felt ill. Indeed, d'Anlou could walk free. The king would find another man, and another. And it wouldn't matter if he was young or old, if he had teeth or not, if he had ten grown children of his own: the king was determined that the heiress to the Far Isle would be safely wed—and thus governed—by one of his own.

A strangled sob escaped her, then she quickly grasped control of her emotions, knowing that Ioin watched her with the greatest heartache.

His daughter's heart and happiness—for his brother's life.

Ioin shook his head. "He is a fine man."

"What?" Allora said carefully.

"A fine man. A bit wild, perhaps, but a good one."

"D'Anlou?" she whispered.

Ioin nodded absently. "If he were one of our own, perhaps one of Malcolm's—"

"He is not. He is a Norman," Allora said icily. "We have lost all if we give way to such a thing!"

"Aye, daughter! There's the rub!"

"What do we do?" Allora asked.

"We find a way."

She shook her head. "He holds Robert. And he will kill him."

Ioin lowered his great head. "I don't know. I don't know," he murmured. "Perhaps we sleep on it. Perhaps I will think more clearly when my head is freed from this blasted Norman wine!"

Allora heard desolation and despair in her father's voice. She leaped quickly to her feet, running around the table to set her arms around his great shoulders. "You're right, Father. We'll sleep on this. And the morning will bring us an answer. Come, *please*, let me get you to bed."

She got him up. He leaned upon her and for a brief moment, she wished that d'Anlou were back—just long enough to get her father into his bed. But she made her way down the narrow hall to the bedroom where he slept, managing to get him just to the bed before her shoulders gave and the big muscled man fell flatly down upon it. She tugged off the leather boots that rose as high as his knees, then drew the fur covering over him as the night was chill.

"Allora!"

She had thought him sleeping or passed out. He caught her hand. "Daughter . . ." he said haltingly. "In all things, you have been my greatest, most precious jewel. I—I will find a way—"

"Sleep, Father!" she said softly, and kissed his brow. His eyes closed. She left his room and hurried to her own.

Once in her room, and drawn by the shimmering moonlight streaming in through the opening, Allora walked to the window and looked down upon the street. The king's Norman guard could still be seen. Far across from her in a two-storied wooden house with a warm thatched roof, she could see that a friar remained awake, working by candlelight on some manuscript he carefully crafted. Below her, dogs suddenly began to growl and then yap, fighting over some bit of discarded meat they found upon the street.

She looked up. The moon was glowing full over London town. Leaning out, she could just see it rippling its golden spell over the Thames.

She had been so delighted to come here to London, so fascinated by the city itself.

She inhaled suddenly, closing her eyes, seeing his face again. *A fine man, a good man.* So her father had said. An arrogant one, so sure of himself, never bested in battle, born to the right people, at the right time.

The Conqueror's own man. With his ebony-dark hair and steel-blue eyes, mocking her ignorance, mocking her youth, determinedly striving for patience . . . touching her.

She started to shiver, and swiftly closed the shutters. She shed her finery, still shivering, and quickly donned her bleached linen nightdress. She threw herself upon her bed, huddling under the covering. She was exhausted, but sleep seemed very far away as she lay there, staring up at the ceiling. D'Anlou would refuse; he did have the power to do so, her own father had assured her.

There was nothing to fear from him.

And still, she felt a strange heat seeping through her body, felt the warmth dancing down the length of her spine. With unnerving ease, she saw his face as clearly as if he was in the room with her. Eyes, penetrating. Jaw, clean-shaven, so firmly set. His mouth, lips, generous, full, sensual . . .

She pulled the covers even tighter about her and, twisting and turning, tried to settle into sleep, without success. Memories of the night seemed to flash before her: arriving at the king's hall, feeling the eyes of so very many strangers, all upon her. The women, the women all watching . . .

Her.

And him.

Then there was the very lovely dark-haired Lady Lucinda with her exotic almond-colored eyes. She and d'Anlou probably knew one another well . . .

Once again, Allora found herself tossing and turning. Growing warm. She rose and hurried to the window again, casting open the shutters, welcoming the chill, damp evening air.

She stood there until she began to shiver fiercely again. She had so wanted to come to London. Now, she just wanted to go home.

To get Uncle Robert, and run. To go home just as swiftly as they could, to a place where things were familiar, where people were all that they seemed. David would be there, his words gentle, his arms strong around her, his heart one with hers. They would wed as quickly as possible, and then she could be no man's pawn. The Conqueror would not conquer *them*.

She loved David. If only he were with her now. David with his . . .

His what? she mocked herself.

Fury drove her back from the window again. For the life of her, she could not—for just a moment!—remember his face. All that she could conjure was the image of steel-blue eyes . . .

With a groan she turned and threw herself onto the bed again.

She had to escape London. Escape. It was her only hope.

But how? How to leave here with her uncle alive?

Then she turned, and at last began to drift off to sleep, one thought finally giving her peace at last.

She would ask Robert himself. For though her father was strong and judicious and ruled so wisely, his great strength lay in his mercy.

Her uncle's strength lay in his recklessness—and his cunning.

Surely, Robert would think of something.

Yet even as she drifted to sleep, her dreams were plagued by thoughts of *him*. Mist rose all around her, smoke, fog. Great billowing clouds of gray. And he was there. Upon his great white Ajax, wearing his stag-horned helmet, riding hard, coming, coming through the mist . . .

And oddly enough, she was calling out his name . . .

Chapter 4

*H*e burst into his father's town manor, his head near splitting, his temper very sorely frayed. To his astonishment, Eleanor had waited up for him, or tried to wait up, at least. She was seated in one of the high-backed chairs at the long, polished table in the handsomely appointed hall. Her head was upon the table, resting on folded arms, and she had apparently slept—awaiting his return.

His entry might have awakened the dead.

"Bret!" she cried, lifting her head, smiling. She pushed back the chair and stood, running to meet him. She gave him a warm embrace, her blue eyes dazzling, her hair, every bit as dark as his own, streaming down her back.

"Little one!" he murmured, hugging her in return. She drew away from him quickly, hurrying down to the end of the table where wine and goblets waited. She looked back at him, even as she poured the wine.

Suddenly, she set the goblet back upon the table and ran back to him on light feet, throwing her arms around him again. "Oh, I've missed you sorely. It seems so very long! I suppose it hasn't been *that* terribly long, but six weeks can seem so long! How is Father, how are my brothers? Mother frets so every time you all go to battle, but then, she has lost so many people in her life, we can only begin to imagine the depths of her suffering! How is Robin? Did Philip's wound heal without mishap? We were dreadfully worried, but Father's note assured Mother that he was well—"

Despite his headache, Bret laughed softly, catching his sister's hands. He had been away a long time, and this evening, listening to her chatter, it seemed he had really come home. "Father is well, strong as an oak, and Robbie,

61

of course, is just like him. Aye, Philip's wound has healed very nicely, with the help of a young and very lovely countess, and we just might find ourselves visiting him in Normandy, *if* we wish to see him. They all send their love, and I'm sure will head home soon enough. It may be difficult, now that William has given Normandy to his eldest son Robert; he plans on England being for William Rufus. He cannot give Robert independence; the Conqueror cannot quite let go of anything that is his. So Father stays, since Robert does not resent him as he does so many other men; but truly, I don't think that it will be much longer. I was summoned because the king fears new rebellion to the north, and I am familiar with the territory—" He paused, winking. "And since it's there I have acquired my magnificent earldom upon the scorched earth!"

Eleanor laughed softly. "Whatever brings you home tonight, we're all delighted." She frowned suddenly, sensing that something bothered him. "What is it?" she asked him soberly, walking down the length of the table to pluck up a goblet and hand it to him. "We heard as soon as you came into town, of course. The entire city of London knows of your return. What took you so long to come here?"

He took a sip of the wine, suddenly pensive as he thought of Ioin Canadys. It was amazing what properties wine could hold.

His father had told him that William nearly lost the Conquest by not having enough wine on hand. English ale and English water had given his great conquering army tremendous difficulty and illnesses. Bowel discomfort had nearly given the Saxons back their country!

But tonight, fine French wine had nearly made Ioin Canadys lose his senses.

Bret was well familiar with French and Norman wines himself.

And just as comfortable with good English ale.

He took another sip of the wine and strode down the length of the room to the hearth, then strode back again. He pushed out a chair and sat upon it heavily, throwing his feet up upon the table and leaning back.

"Bret?" Eleanor said worriedly.

" 'Tis the king, Eleanor. The wretched, wretched king!"
he said softly, and sipped his wine.

She stared at him, her concern clear in her beautiful
dark eyes, and he was sorry to be the cause of it. He
drew his feet from the table and stood again, coming to
her, smoothing back her hair. "I'm sorry; you musn't be
upset. I was delayed, of course, because I had to meet with
William and give him all Father's dispatches and advise him
of the situation in Normandy. Then, of course, I had to stay
to dine. And then—" He paused and looked around the hall,
empty except for the two of them. "Where is Mother?" he
asked. "The king asked for her at dinner, yet I do not
know how he could have imagined I might have seen her,
since he tends to be demanding of a man's time! She was
apparently invited to dine at the tower tonight. I believe I
excused her absence easily enough, although God knows
it is amazing that he expected her. Ah, but then again, the
king *is* amazing in his demands!"

Eleanor frowned again. "Mother is with Elysia and Gwyn,
spending the night in vigil at the abbey. Since she was thus
engaged, the king could make no comment on her not
appearing at his table tonight. It was a difficult decision
for her. She is so very anxious to see you. And she misses
Father terribly."

"Ah! Indeed, she must!" Bret said softly, and a smile
curled his lips. Now there was a match for the king—
his mother, Fallon! All these years she and his father had
found happiness—despite the fact that Fallon had been King
Harold's daughter by his Danelaw, or unofficial, marriage.

William liked to refer to Harold's children by that marriage as bastards—as much bastards as he was himself.
Fallon knew better, as did her husband, Alaric d'Anlou.
When William chose not to understand the ways of the
people he had come to govern, he did not.

Fallon had never managed to endure the king, and though
she had learned to abide his company when Alaric was with
her, she avoided it at all cost when her husband was not
in residence. Bret could well understand. Her mother, her
brothers, cousins, friends—all had rebelled at various times,
and each time a member of the house of Godwinson gave the

king the least bit of trouble, he looked to Fallon to blame. She had never betrayed her own family—though Harold's own sister had chosen to offer her fealty to William when he had approached London.

Yet once Fallon had come to peace with her marriage, she had never betrayed his father, either.

Bret loved them both. Deeply. And admired them with all his heart.

Until this moment, though, he hadn't quite thought of what would happen when Fallon learned that William was trying to dictate a marriage for her second son. Her temper would fly; no doubt she would be determined to defy the king.

"Sweet Jesu!" Bret whispered suddenly.

"Bret! You've been gone six weeks and now you sit there and say things that make no sense!" Eleanor scolded him. "You're frightening me."

He shook his head, biting his lower lip. "I'm sorry, little one."

"I'm not quite so little!" she said with a sigh.

He grinned suddenly. She *wasn't* quite so little anymore. She was fifteen—and growing very beautiful. She was the youngest of their brood—except for Gwyn, who had arrived as quite a surprise to them all, and was two years old now.

"Eleanor, I am sorry!" he told her. He shook his head again. "Let me begin from the beginning."

"Please."

"I arrived today to the warm greetings and applause of the city. It really is quite amazing what one generation can do, isn't it? Not so long ago, William came and conquered. Now the people he conquered cheer him against his own son in Normandy." He shrugged. "Nevertheless, it was with a certain feeling of well-being and triumph that I rode through the streets. I bathed and changed at the tower, Ajax was scrubbed and brushed and well-tended, and I sat in council with the king. And then it came time for the evening meal . . ."

He studied his goblet, then drained it of wine.

"I heard that the king had several of the most infamous Scottish rebels in to dine tonight," Eleanor said as he paused. "In fact, Mother was so curious about them that she nearly swallowed enough of her hatred for the king to accept his invitation to dine." She hesitated offering him a small smile. Then she pulled out the chair beside him and sat, her blue eyes alight. "Are they as wild as they say? Grizzled with hair, barbaric? They've said that if William does hang Robert Canadys, Canadys will laugh at his executioner, all the way to hell and beyond. Oh, and the girl! There's rumor aplenty about the laird's daughter, too. She is tall and wild, and some say she has even sliced off one breast like the women did in the legends of the ancient warrior goddesses. But they also say that she is golden, and beautiful, and easily the death of any man."

Was she? Bret wondered. Beautiful? Aye, like a golden angel. Wild? Aye? That too.

"She has both breasts," he said dryly.

Eleanor stared. "Then you did see her—and the Scottish lairds."

"English lords—so says William," he commented, his tone dry once again. "Aye, sister, I saw them all," he said softly. He stood, pouring more wine into his goblet, remembering at the same time that it was an excess of wine that had been the downfall of Ioin Canadys this evening.

"And?"

He sipped his wine, thinking over the question. "Ioin Canadys is not at all wild or barbaric, Eleanor. I first saw him years ago, when I rode north with Father beneath William's banner and our own. I have seldom seen a man negotiate such reasonable terms with such courage. In truth, William admires Canadys greatly himself; thus his fear, I believe. If Ioin dies, his property goes to his daughter. But control of their family clan will fall to Robert, and he is ever ready to lead hundreds of men to their deaths. No, Ioin Canadys is no monster."

"Then the one who is to hang—"

"Is not so great a monster, though he is not a man of peace. He is simply convinced that his fealty belongs to Malcolm and to none other."

"Then—"

"Malcolm has forever been a thorn in William's side, swearing fealty to William himself but never meaning it."

Eleanor was silent for a moment. "Then it was the daughter with both breasts who has upset you so?" she inquired, a small curve to her lip.

His gaze shot swiftly to her.

"Ah!" Eleanor said softly. "So she is a beautiful, golden, towering thing with a barbed sword—"

"No barbed sword, not in William's hall tonight. But a mercilessly barbed tongue. Aye, sister, *there's* the Canadys who's the dangerous one." Recklessly wild—there seemed so much of her uncle within her! She didn't know her father's strength, she didn't share his manner of thinking deeply, of seeking all answers, of looking to all men—and women—involved in a situation.

It would serve her right if William did find a toothless old wretch to wed her.

Nay! An old man might die too quickly. She deserved to suffer with some young, rotten-toothed, bandy-legged bastard—for years and years.

Yet even as that caustic thought swept through his mind, he felt a faint revulsion at the idea. Indeed, she was wild. Razor-tongued; foolishly, fiercely independent. But she was a golden beauty, not so tall—nor, thankfully, mutilated as Eleanor might have imagined. Her face was stunningly exquisite, finely, delicately fashioned, her nose small and exceedingly straight with just the slightest tip at the end—exaggerated, of course, by the way she managed to keep it in the air. Her lips were full, red, tempting. Her brows were the color of honey, cleanly arched over the arresting emerald of her eyes. Her skin was as pure, as silken, as ivory, inviting the hand to reach out and stroke it.

Indeed, Ioin Canadys had a very beautiful daughter. But one with a deep and abiding hatred for all things Norman, and if she was aware that his blood was somewhat salvaged—to the view of many, other than William, of course—by his mother's royal Saxon line, it wouldn't mean anything anyway. He served William, and there was no denying that he did. His father served the king, and for his mother's sake, he knew, his father had always done his very best to see that in serving William, he also spared the conquered peoples as best he could. Alaric's men never raped, pillaged, or destroyed. Bret, the son of a Saxon princess and one of the Conqueror's greatest champions, had never led an easy life despite his exalted birth. To survive and prosper with any sanity, he had come upon his own code of honor. And in time, Bret had learned to live with that code, at peace with himself.

He was a good subject, a loyal subject, one who dared to speak the truth to the king and yet remain a strong champion.

And now this!

"What?" Eleanor demanded.

Startled, he stared at her. "William wants control of the Far Isle. So he wants Ioin Canadys to give his daughter to a loyal Norman knight."

"Who?"

"Me."

Eleanor gasped, rising swiftly to her feet. "Sweet Mary!" she said softly. "I had thought that you had all but come to terms with Lord dePont to marry Lucinda. It would bring you the stone castle outside Windsor, all that land, the manor house in Dover, and—"

"And instead," Bret murmured, "the king would have me gain a wild fortress where the villeins would assuredly despise my very presence, where it is wet and the wind blows wildly day after day and the cold is one that can seep into the very bones!"

"What of Lucinda?"

He lifted his wine goblet and drank deeply once again. At long last, the fruit of the vine was beginning to warm his blood. Lucinda. Warm, sweet, exotically beautiful, and very much in love with him.

"Knowing the king," he said, his teeth grating, his tone acidic, "he has already determined on a new mate for her as well. He's just informed Canadys and me of his desires; I imagine poor Lucinda knows nothing of them as yet."

Eleanor came to him, touching his arm. She gently took the goblet from his hands. "The king will listen to you. He needs you! He grows older, his family is ever more rebellious, and besides, he likes you. Admires you. Where would he be without Father? He must listen to you."

"Indeed?" he asked his sister, smiling, amused by her wonderfully passionate cry of support.

"Indeed!"

His smile faded.

"What is it?" she demanded softly.

He shook his head. He suddenly felt sober, painfully sober. "Father is in Normandy," he said huskily.

"Oh!" Eleanor gasped, following his train of thought exactly. "And *Mother* is here."

"And by the saints, if she hears of this . . ." Bret said, then rose and went to stand before the fire, watching the blaze, listening to it snap and crackle. Fallon was always so careful, but only because of Alaric's relationship with the king. She had curbed her tongue, she had kept many thoughts to herself on many occasions . . .

But she was a vibrant, passionate woman—and one who still lived with a bitter hatred for the man who had battled her father, for the Conqueror who had caused his death. If that same man now threatened the happiness of her son, there might be trouble indeed.

And Alaric remained in Normandy with Bret's brothers Robin and Philip. Who would stand between Fallon and the king now, when she thought one of her brood threatened?

"Bret?" Eleanor said.

He turned, came to her, grasped her shoulders, his eyes burning into hers. "Sister, swear to me that our conversation will never, ever go beyond this room!"

"Oh, Bret! I swear! But what will you do?"

He felt the tension in him; winced that he might have hurt her. He released her shoulders, and turned back to the fire again.

What, indeed?

"Is she—so horrible?"

He shook his head, studying the flames. "She seems so very young—not so many years older than you."

"Not too young for a bride!" Eleanor quickly assured him. She seemed to search for something promising to say to him. "And she is very blonde—"

"Hair like the richest gold," he agreed wryly.

"Then will it be so terrible?" Eleanor asked.

"Aye!" he said very softly. "For she despises me."

He drummed his fingers against the wooden mantel. One of the hounds the family kept came suddenly to him from beneath the table, pressing its great head against him. He idly scratched the hound's ears, then closed his eyes. The news would be out by morning, he was certain. Fallon would hear, she would come to him to see if it was true . . .

And then she would accost William, no matter how hard Bret tried to convince her he could wage his battles on his own.

If the king even thought to harm a single hair on his mother's head . . .

Then he could accost the king himself, grow rash and let fury ride, and . . .

And he and Fallon could find themselves hanged for treason, right along with Robert Canadys. Then his father and his brothers could come home and fight and find themselves hanged and . . .

"Damn that little Scottish witch!" he swore with a sudden violence.

Eleanor jumped back slightly, staring at him. He forced a cold smile to his lips.

"My future bride!" he added lightly.

"Then you do intend—"

"To marry her? Oh, aye! And God help us both, for I swear, if she causes me one more wretched moment, there shall be hell to pay!"

He strode back to the table and again filled his goblet with wine. He drained the rich red liquid swiftly, praying for the warmth to come again. It failed him. He drank more, feeling Eleanor's frightened eyes upon him. "Drink with me, sister. Congratulate me on my coming marriage!"

"Bret," Eleanor said softly, "you are going to awaken with a dreadful headache!"

"I will bear with it!" he said grimly. "Just so long as I may sleep tonight!" He snatched up the handsome earthern wine carafe and clasped it to his chest. He went to his sister and kissed her forehead. "Remember, Eleanor, not a word to anyone. I am intrigued by this marriage, and am anxious to take over something rich and so fantastic as the Far Isle!"

"Oh, Bret!" She sighed unhappily.

"Swear that you are with me!" he said warningly.

"Brother, what else could I do?"

He smiled, but despite the wine, his smile was cold. He left her in the empty hall and climbed the stairs to the chambers above the hall, still holding tight to the carafe. He came to his own room. It was a large, comfortable chamber, heated by a huge fireplace where a blaze burned warmly in anticipation of his use this night.

He strode to the window and looked out at the full moon lighting up the night. He lifted the wine. "To you, my wretched little Scottish princess!" he said softly. Perhaps he shouldn't feel so bitter. She was young and stunningly beautiful. Marriage was a thing of gain and convenience.

He had simply thought that he would wed elsewhere. He closed his eyes tightly. Did he love Lucinda? She cared so very deeply for him. Aye, he had cared for her, and deeply, too. But had he loved her? He didn't know if he had ever really questioned himself about it before. She had been beautiful, too, and the right age for marriage. She was richly endowed with land, and he had the strength and power to govern it well and wisely for her. The marriage would have simply been . . . right.

And now this.

He thought of Allora once again. The searing, fire-lit flash in her eyes when she taunted him. *Ah, milord! So you will govern your own affairs!*

So passionate, so furious. Beautiful indeed, rich as well. Young. Exquisite with her soft ivory flesh.

Definitely equipped with two breasts, he mocked himself. He knew that full well because he had touched her. He hadn't really meant to do so; he hadn't wanted to touch her, but when his temper flared he couldn't have stopped himself from seizing her when he did.

So he knew. That she was no towering maid, but was rather small, possessed of a wild energy, a wild heart, a hauntingly curved form, a beautiful face.

All the virtues one might ask of a wife . . .

Except that this wife would be his enemy until the very day he died.

Quick to inform him of it.

Quicker still to fight him . . .

"May we both be damned!" he cried aloud to the night.

He turned to his bed, set down the wine, and stripped off his tunic and boots.

Then he crashed down upon the bed.

Finally, it had been enough wine, enough riding, enough hours awake. Enough.

He closed his eyes, and slept soon after his body touched the softness of the bed.

Chapter 5

*I*t was not a difficult feat for Allora to reach her uncle in the morning.

Ioin Canadys did not awaken early. Allora came to his room when the first cock crowed, finding him curled in a tight ball and sleeping so deeply that he snored with a vengeance. The effect of too much wine, she knew. She smiled tenderly, covered him anew, and hurried downstairs, telling Joseph that she was just going out to walk in the early-morning air, to see a few sights, perhaps purchase a few trinkets.

"Look out for my father," she charged him with a smile.

"Aye, milady, that I will do, and gladly. But you shouldn't be out alone, you should never go about this town unescorted—"

"Joseph, I will not wander far, I promise," she told him firmly, and before he could protest, she slipped out the door and hurried down the street.

She didn't ride, though her small black mare, Briar, was housed in a stable behind the manor. She hadn't that far to go, and she didn't want to hand her horse over to a tower groom, or wait for Briar's return when she had finished with her mission. As it happened, no one did disturb her. There were hawkers on the street. Fresh fish seemed in abundance this morning, along with fresh-baked bread. She ignored the tantalizing scents and hurried to the tower.

Once there, she was stopped by a guard. She identified herself as Lady Allora, niece to Robert Canadys, and assured the guard that the king would have no quarrel with her visiting her uncle. But the guard, though seemingly entranced after she had given him her sweetest smile, insisted on asking his superiors. An older man appeared next, one who must have endured many a battle, for his face bore many scars. He listened to her insistence that she be allowed to see her uncle, then he, too, seemed perplexed. Allora was certain that she was going to be refused, when suddenly the older man looked over her shoulder and let out a glad sigh. "Milord! As the king is engaged and I cannot interrupt him at this time, perhaps you could help me with the lady of the Far Isle."

In the early-morning sunlight, Allora could see a shadow upon the tower wall before her. She spun around quickly and was dismayed to discover that Bret d'Anlou, stripped of all armor, handsomely dressed in vivid blue today, his sword still belted at his hip, stood now before her. He noted the dismay in her eyes at the sight of him and his brow arched.

"What is the difficulty here?" he asked the tower guard.

"I cannot take responsibility for letting the lady in—"

"Ah. Well then, my friend, I will escort her to her uncle, and you will have nothing to fear."

He gripped her elbow and quickly led her past the imposing entrance and into the tower. Her heart thundered as she prayed that he did not intend to stay with her once he had delivered her to Robert. She glanced to his face, noting again his striking coloring, admitting that he was both imposing and compelling, a handsome man in any land.

And young. Young enough to live for years and years. To seize hold of a place, and keep it forever . . .

She shivered. He felt her tremor, and looked down to her, arching a brow again. "Can it be that you are frightened—of me, milady?"

Her eyes narrowed and she shook her head, studying him intently. "All that I could ever fear where you are concerned, milord, would be the terror of holy wedlock. And since you have assured me that you would far rather wed a hedgehog, there is nothing for me to fear at all."

"Perhaps I have changed my mind," he told her after a moment.

She felt the blood drain from her face. "Surely you jest."

"Nay, lady, I do not!"

"But—why?" she gasped, stunned. Truly, he *had* to be joking. Last night he had been more vehemently opposed to the marriage than even she had been! "Why?" she repeated.

He swore impatiently. "Why? Why does one ever marry? For riches, for gain. For your precious, frozen, windswept isle! What difference does it make? Be advised, milady, that I am considering the king's proposal, and am entirely intrigued by it."

"But you *musn't* find it intriguing. You're lying! I know that you do not! If you wed me, you will find it hell—"

"If I wed you, lady, I will tame you, and that will be that."

She gasped again. "How dare—" she began, but he was looking over her shoulder and interrupting her impatiently.

"Yonder, Lady Allora, comes your uncle now! If you seek a word with him in private, there is an alcove there by the fire." He bowed to her, already leaving her even as she spun around to see her uncle approaching the long table where a morning's repast had been set out for the men and women within the tower. Robert had as yet to see her; he was preparing himself a plate filled high with meat and fish.

She hurried over to him, aware now that the tower hall was growing busier as the day began in earnest. More of William's soldiers filled the room; there were a number of the clergy about. Some of these people lived within the tower, she knew, guarding it, cleaning it, caring for it or the king or his royal retinue. She nodded to those who acknowledged her presence, then came to her uncle's side at last, speaking to him swiftly.

"Uncle!"

"Allora!" Robert Canadys turned instantly to her in surprise, a broad, bold, welcoming smile curling his lips. He set an arm about her shoulder. "How kind, lass, to come breakfast with your poor imprisoned uncle!" Balancing his plate in his other hand, he led her across the hall, and straight to the alcove Bret had indicated where she might find a modicum of privacy. Tall-backed chairs were set in a semicircle there, and he quickly indicated she take one, drawing the other as close up to her as he could, and himself sitting. An elderly nobleman, dressed handsomely in a short gold tunic, burnt-brown chausses, and flaring white shirt, walked by them, approaching the table. Then he paused.

"Company, eh, Robert Canadys?" The nobleman's eyes were alight with good humor as he studied Allora. He swept into a low bow. "Milady."

"Now, Michael, the lady is my niece, and 'tis good to have the sweet companionship of a loving blood relation near my side once again—aye, sir, that it is! Now, if you'll be a well-mannered warder, I shall introduce you to the pride of my people. Allora, this ancient creature is Lord Michael Whitten, Count of Newby; he's been assigned the dismal task of guarding me in this place. Yet he's a kind enough fellow, and well-loved of the king, so give him a sweet smile, eh, lass?"

Amused, she offered the older man a very sweet smile indeed, and discovered that he still studied her with pale, very curious eyes, his own smile quite intrigued.

"No more gaping now, man!" Robert warned him. "She came to see her poor uncle, and no other this morn!"

Michael Whitten, Count of Newby, again bowed to her, and then caught her hand. Dry lips touched its back. "Milady. It is the greatest pleasure."

She inclined her head gracefully, and replied in a soft, sweet tone, "Milord, the pleasure is mine."

"Michael, now be a good fellow, have half a heart within that old warrior's chest, and go, eh?" Robert pleaded.

"Farewell then!" Michael said promptly, unoffended, and left them.

"An interesting old man," Allora commented.

Robert shrugged. "We're alone now, niece. As alone as we're going to be, that is. Speak quickly of what's on your mind—that which brought you to me without the eagle eye of my brother upon you so early this morning!"

She leaned toward him as he bit deeply into a wing of some aromatic game bird. "What are we going to do?" she whispered, her voice betraying her desperation. "The king is so determined on my marrying—"

"Then you will have to marry."

She leaned back, staring in utter dismay at the uncle she had counted on for help.

"Nay, nay, lass! I've not betrayed you. I've lain awake the long night, thinking on this myself. And I have the answer. We agree to all that William demands. We—"

"We cannot!" she protested.

"Hush!" he warned. "It's simple enough. Bret d'Anlou's family keeps a town house not far from here down the Thames. If he were to wed, it would certainly be left to him in the strictest privacy for his wedding night, since the main family stronghold is a place called Haselford, half a day's ride from London, I believe. I'm not without friends here, lass. There remain within the city many men not pleased with the yoke of the Conqueror! You need only go through with the words and motions of a ceremony, then let yourself be taken to his town house. From there, we'll flee back to the north."

She should have been delighted that someone seemed to know what to do. She discovered that she was irritated instead. "Uncle, he might well be a very hard man to escape. His sword is always at his side, from what little I have seen of him. This city teems with his men. And—"

"Drugged. Easily drugged!" Robert assured her, waving his free hand in the air. His deep wooden plate teetered precariously on his knees.

Easily? She doubted it. And she had further reservations. "You are forgetting what might be the most important factor in this, Uncle. *If I go through a wedding ceremony with Bret d'Anlou, I will be married to him!*"

"Hush!" he warned her again. "Allora, we can rescue you before the union can be consummated. As soon as we are safe and free from William's despicable grasp, we will set into motion all that is needed to obtain an annulment for you from the pope."

She inhaled sharply, startled that her reckless uncle had thought it through so thoroughly.

She leaned closer to him again. "What if d'Anlou himself refuses to go through with this? Last night I was certain that he would. This morning—"

"You needn't fear," Robert told her quickly. "The Earl of Wakefield came here very early this morning, so the tower gossips assure me. He assured the king that he was most eager to acquire a young and lovely bride with so bountiful an inheritance to bring him. The king was quite pleased, and offered him an exorbitant bonus in gold."

She leaned back in her chair once again, unnerved. "What would have changed his mind so quickly?"

"Perhaps he is worried," Robert said flatly. "His father is not in the country; his mother is a Saxon, and therefore ever suspect in the king's eyes. Perhaps he does not wish to incur the king's wrath in any way."

A breathlessness assailed her. She couldn't seem to get enough air to speak. Terrible things were spinning into motion. And she was suddenly very afraid.

"Alas! Poor old Michael will be disappointed!"

"What, Uncle?"

His eyes were twinkling again. "Lord Michael was, I believe, the king's second choice for a husband for you. He has several grown sons to keep iron fists upon your land—"

"But he is—ancient!" Allora gasped.

"Ancient, yes, but he outlived his last bride, and she a lass of barely twenty-two summers!"

Allora found herself shivering violently, repulsed. Not that he hadn't seemed a kind enough old man, but . . .

"Maybe Michael would be a better choice at that," Robert mused.

"And why is that?"

"Well, he does have to expire *sometime* soon!"

"Jesu!" Allora whispered, looking down to her hands.

"So you will go along with my plan?" Robert said.

She stared at her uncle. At the reckless fire so fierce in his eyes.

"Father will protest," she said.

"I will handle my brother, in time," he assured her quickly. "For the moment, you must agree to the wedding."

"If I suddenly make such a drastic change—" she began.

"Don't worry. I will think of something. And remember, I do have friends in this place. I will keep messages coming to you frequently enough. For now, say nothing."

Allora nodded, noting that his eyes were almost feverishly bright. She bit her lip and lowered her eyes, wondering if her uncle wouldn't steer them all into trouble.

"I barely know the Earl of Wakefield," she warned Robert softly, "yet I wonder if we dare use such a man in our schemes to be free—"

"Would you have me hang, lass?" he asked her softly.

"Nay, Uncle, of course not!" she protested passionately.

"Then they are the ones who play the game," he told her.

"Still, perhaps it is wrong—"

"It is wrong for William to seek to seize our land and make vassals of our people!"

And in that, she thought, he was right.

She rose quickly. "I will go back to Father."

"I will get messages to you when need be," he said, rising, setting his plate upon his chair. His voice rose as he took her into a bear hug of an embrace. "Thank you for joining me, lass, in my dire imprisonment! Yet by God's grace, milady niece, soon enough . . ."

She nodded again. "I'd best return swiftly," she told him. "If Father awakes—"

"Go back," he said, his voice soft again, "and just let your father know that he should agree with all that the king says. We'll worry about actually escaping later."

Well, he might worry later. She was already very worried. But she smiled and turned away from him, and no one stopped her when she hurried down the stairs, past the men in the storeroom, and out to the yard before the tower. She started to head back to the manor house, but she paid little attention to her direction, and soon found that she had wound around the tower instead of coming straight from it. Indeed, she had wandered onto a ledge that overlooked a garden, beautifully green with summer's lushness now. Intrigued, she moved to the stone wall that bordered the ledge and looked down. She gasped involuntarily, instinctively moving back. Bret d'Anlou stood against one of the huge oaks in the center of a circular maze, waiting.

"Bret!" a soft female voice called. As Allora watched, the dark beauty who had watched them both so intently last night came hurrying through the manicured thicket of shrubs and trees to reach him. She flung herself at him, and he caught her. Her arms swiftly twined around his neck; his arm slipped around her waist, then stroked her back as she rose on her toes to passionately press her lips to his . . .

Allora closed her eyes, thinking that she should not be watching this encounter. Yet the dark-haired beauty's words rose softly on the breeze and Allora could not help but hear them. "I go to Wales!" she cried. "I am to become a border bride, wife to Lord d'Este! Bret, they are sending me away tonight!"

"Lucinda!" he said softly, smoothing back her glorious sweep of dark hair. "Perhaps there is a way that I can stop this thing yet—"

"Nay! I would not have you do so!" Lucinda cried, and rose against him once again. Allora's eyes were open then. She was alarmed by the feelings of both envy and passion that swept through her. Watching their intimate kiss, the tenderness in the way that they touched . . .

"Don't, please, Bret. Don't try to change anything. The king is still not convinced that my father was completely innocent of conspiracy when his brother took part in the last rebellion in York. Father is too old to be imprisoned. Nay! I beg of you, if you care for me at all, keep silent. The king may take his wrath out on my family, or yours. You cannot gainsay him in any of this, but . . . oh, Bret! Yet, wed or nay, my love, we might still meet . . ." Her almond eyes were liquid heat upon him. Allora felt a trembling seize hold of her.

Bret d'Anlou eased Lucinda away from him, his hold still gentle, but with something slightly different about it. "Nay, my lady, ever fair! If our courses are set, then we will be honest with them. Rolph d'Este is a good man, a good friend; we have known one another many years. I could not betray him."

Lucinda sobbed softly, burying her face against his chest. "Aye, he is a good man! I've no quarrel with that. It is simply that . . . I love you."

Allora bit her lip, feeling a startling heartache for the woman. Yet, at the same time, it occurred to her that Bret d'Anlou had said that he could not betray his friend d'Este; he didn't seem to care a single bit about the feelings of his reluctant—prospective—spouse!

She had missed something. Bret had spoken softly again; Lucinda had cast back her head and now rose high upon her toes to press her lips against his once again. His arms wrapped around her with infinite tenderness; Allora's heart quivered within her chest. But Lucinda broke from the embrace then, and turned and ran.

She fled through the trees. It seemed that Bret d'Anlou would follow her for a moment, but then he paused and, turning, slammed his fist against the oak. Suddenly, as if she had alerted him with just the light sound of her breathing, he looked up.

She did not back away in time. He saw her there, and his expression turned taut, dark and forbidding. On sheer instinct, Allora pushed away from the wall and started to run. She was desperate to get back to her father; desperate to be alone . . . Nay, desperate just not to be near Bret d'Anlou, the ever-great Earl of Wakefield.

She was impeded by the fact that he knew his way around the tower, and she did not. She thought intelligently enough to steer her course away from the River Thames, away from the busy docks there and the possibility of being cornered, but in choosing to head for the streets of London instead with their bustling citizenry and hawkers and goodwives, she found herself coming down the incline right where the outer trees of the maze edged the road. She began to run again, then came to a dead halt when he suddenly, grimly, appeared before her. Frozen, she kept her distance from him. Not meeting his eyes, she acknowledged him quietly. "My lord, if you will let me pass?"

"Let you pass!" he exclaimed, and the darkness of his tone unnerved her. "So simply! All the tempest that you have wrought, and I should let you pass!"

"None of this is my doing—"

"You stood there not just listening to but watching an intimate discussion."

"I didn't mean to!" she assured him. "I lost my way from the tower—"

"Oh, come!"

"Go to hell then!" she cried to him. "Just let me by!" Determinedly she started to stride around him, but found herself waylaid by the viselike grip of his fingers around her upper arm.

His eyes sizzled with cobalt fire. "Imagine, lady, there are times when I do grow impatient for these nuptials! To have you as lady and wife, beneath my ever-magnanimous thumb! Ah, but then again, *you* can still protest this thing."

She gasped softly, then tried to wrench from him, a furious movement that only brought her crashing against his muscled length. She went still, realizing that her struggles did nothing but add to the tension between them, creating a friction of fire that slowly began to smolder and burn. She tilted her head to his. "I didn't do this!" she reminded him hotly. "*Your* precious king did. And you are the all-wonderful and all-powerful. A man who governs himself. You must stop what is going on—"

"It isn't so simple, as well you know it!" he told her harshly. "You must be aware, having listened in fully to my conversation."

She paled at that, longing to escape his bitter hold upon her. "I'm sorry!" she whispered. "So sorry! But you are the one—"

"What? Do I take it now, milady, that you are no longer willing to protest this marriage yourself?"

She was silent, and he laughed softly. "Ah, so you met Michael!"

"My father would never allow such a thing."

"Your father should have never allowed any of this."

"My father—"

"Ioin tries harder than any man alive, milady. You may rest assured of one thing, I admire him greatly. But he cannot rescue your uncle from each and every one of his reckless endeavors."

She gasped again, wrenching free from him at last. "Milord, you are a monster! You think that my uncle should be hanged—"

"From the time I was twelve, lady, I rode with my father. I seek no man's death. But I tell you this: Robert Canadys has long led your father a merry chase. If your father had remained quietly at the Far Isle, William might never have taken notice of his preference for the Scottish king. Robert Canadys long ago acquired a penchant for wild and reckless rebellion, and will one day be the death of your father, I warrant."

Furiously, she stepped forward to slap him. She moved swiftly, her anger spurring her to a wild momentum, and still he was quicker, catching her wrist before her palm could catch his cheek. "Fair warning, milady, that is all. If you are against this marriage, then stop it. Tell them that you refuse to be a pawn in any man's game—"

"*I* should tell them?" she exclaimed, wishing she had never tried to strike him because she was caught up in his merciless grasp once again. "What! The great knight has become a pawn, but *I* should manage to stop this! You swore that you would rather wed a hedgehog! Can you find no such willing creatures either?"

She thought for a moment that his grip upon her wrist would crack the slender bones.

"Stop!" she cried.

His hold eased instantly.

"*Why* have you agreed?" she asked him in dismay.

He shook his head. "Many reasons, milady. One among them is that the king has his logic. It will be a profitable union for all parties concerned."

"Not for my people—"

"Aye, for your people. For if they do not bend a knee to William, he will, in time, decimate them."

She stared at him, wide-eyed, in anguish. It all seemed the worse now that she had seen him with Lucinda. Such a mockery. Almost as if he read her thoughts, he spoke again, and surprisingly softly now. "Milady, you know where I stand, and that is where I must stay. The decisions are now yours. Be warned—and I mean this with all my heart—I will not play games with marriage. There will be nothing of convenience in this; if you vow to be my wife, know that I will expect you to honor every vow."

"You would rather wed a hedgehog!" she reminded him again, tears stinging her eyes.

"Milady," he said, and bowed slightly, releasing her at last, "I am finding myself more and more resigned to the task ahead of me. Things could be far worse. I might have found myself in a similar position with an elderly dame, or a young one not so gently endowed in face and form as yourself. And, milady, at least I am not quite decrepit—"

"Aye, you might well take forever to depart this earth!"

He was shaking his head. "I shall live long and hearty, my love, just to thwart you!"

"Oh, let me by!" she cried again, but once more, when she would have swept past him, he caught her by the shoulders. And the look upon his grave, handsome features as he stared down into her eyes brought a fresh shiver to her heart.

"The decision is yours!" he repeated. "But again I beg you to heed me! In truth, I would not seek to make you suffer in any way. Neither will I abide your barbs against me. When you say the words, lady, you will have wed me. You will stay with me, sleep with me, lie with me, learn to obey and honor me."

She felt as if she were choking; as if she was on fire from his touch. She was in anguish, and not even sure completely of its cause. He spoke so easily of intimacy when he cared nothing for her, when she had so recently watched him display tenderness to another—watched with a fascination she so desperately longed to deny.

"What of you, milord? What of your vows? If I am to become so obedient and docile—"

"My vows, milady?" he interrupted. "Well, lady, I would honor them as well, and cherish you as my young, lovely, *sweet, tender* bride."

She felt herself trembling furiously, torn between acknowledging some strange truth in his words, and resenting the mockery that tinged them.

"You love Lucinda!" she whispered.

"I had intended to wed her," he admitted.

Her lashes fell, and an aching sense of deepest unease filled her. She played with fire. Robert didn't see it; he didn't want to see it. She played with a slow-burning blaze that could erupt into a wild, destructive explosion at any time . . .

She felt his finger on her chin, lifting her face so that he could study her eyes again. "I have told the king that I will eagerly bow to his suggestion. What comes next now lies with you, milady."

"Please let me pass!" she whispered.

His thumb fell from her chin. He stepped back, inclining his head in a courteous bow.

She hurried around him, and fled.

Chapter 6

❧

"*I* daresay," Fallon said, her blue eyes direct upon her son's, "that the king has had his subtle hand in all this somewhere!"

They were in the town manor, just as twilight claimed the afternoon. Summer was beginning to move into fall and the evenings were damp and cool; she and Bret spoke together in the long hall with the carved tables and chairs, a warm fire burning brightly behind them. Moments before, she had returned to the house with his two sisters, and she had greeted him with warm excitement, throwing her arms about his neck, kissing both his cheeks, and studying him at arm's length, as it seemed parents were prone to do when they had been parted from their offspring for any length of time. Perhaps, for his mother, it was a precious thing to see a loved one again; too many times, the people she had cared about most in life had gone away from her to disappear forever.

Homecoming was always good, Bret thought. Good to see her, good to hold her, good to toss the baby, Gwyn, into the air, and hear her spate of giggles fill the room; good to hug Elysia, nearly eighteen now, and a stunning beauty with their father's silver eyes and deep-red hair that could only have come from their mother's Godwin relations.

But now, the older girls had taken Gwyn upstairs to play and Fallon was all Harold's daughter as she stared at him suspiciously. It seemed that his wedding plans—those he had not even imagined until he had sat at the king's table last night—were the talk of London, and before she had managed to come through the door Fallon had heard that he was betrothed to the border lord's wild daughter. And her first question, after they had all greeted one another and she had implored him to tell her about his father and brothers, was simply phrased. "This rumor—is it true?"

"Aye, madam, it is true," he told her.

It was then that his sisters had caught his eye above their mother's head, scooped up the baby, and departed, Eleanor knowing the exact truth of the situation, Elysia instinctively certain that this was a conversation best handled alone. And so Bret sat before the fire now with his mother, thinking, oddly, of the many times he had gone to battle. First the rebellion in York when he had been very young; the constant skirmishes along the Welsh and Scottish borders; and, more recently, the trouble back in Normandy. Warfare was a trade he had learned by necessity; it had never been one that he had relished. Going forth to battle had never been easy.

Yet nothing in life had ever been so difficult as trying to convince Fallon, Harold's daughter, that what was to come was entirely his choice, something that he was determined to do—nay, hell-bent upon achieving.

"I repeat," Fallon said, "William has had something to do with this."

He shrugged, and arched an ebony brow. "Only in that he had decided the girl would be wed, and to one of his own people."

Fallon winced slightly at that, but did not deny his words. She was not one of William's people, and she never would be. But she had long ago accepted that William was king of England now, that her father could not be brought back from the dead, and that her sons were also her husband's sons and therefore among William's own people. Life had never been anything less than complex for Fallon, for long before William had invaded England she had known both the Conqueror and Bret's father, and their lives had always been deeply entangled.

"One of his own people—you?" Fallon queried softly. There was a glimmer of suspicion in her beautiful blue eyes, a definite query to the tilt of her head. He thought with the deepest affection and admiration that King Harold's daughter was a beautiful woman still, just past forty now, yet still as slim and lithe as a nymph, her jet-black hair betraying no signs of gray, and just the very lightest lines by her eyes indicating in any way at all that the first flush of youth had gone. "Bret, I will have the truth in this!" she insisted.

He rose and went to the chair where she sat, his hands upon the arms of it, and leaned down to brush her forehead with a kiss.

"Bret—"

"I was just thinking that Father must frequently walk into a room and think that you have not aged a day since the two of you met."

"A shadowed room!" she said dryly. "Actually, I don't think that I was more than four when I first met him, so I do hope I have done some changing. And your sentiment is charming but I will not be swayed from what I want to know."

"Mother, it is simple. He offered the girl and the property to me—"

"He has already bestowed the title of earl upon you, after having done likewise for your father so that your brother Robin will inherit such a title as well. Not to leave your other brother out, Philip has been given the title of count and granted lands in Normandy. Considering the fact that William seized the crown from your grandfather and has spent half his life battling your blood relations, he has been uncustomarily magnanimous with all of us, and you especially. But then, I think that though William did not know my father very well, he did like and admire him."

"So did all men—"

"Nay, not all men!" she assured him.

"But William at least. Grandfather fell in battle."

"He was mercilessly slain, but I'll not let you get me started and change the subject! The king has already given you vast lands—"

"Lands that will remain devastated for at least a generation, no matter how hard the people labor upon them."

"I have never known you to be exceptionally eager for rewards or riches, since they seem to fall your way regardless. Not that you haven't earned all that William has bestowed on you."

"I'm intrigued, Mother."

"Oh, really? By border lands? Harsh, windswept places where ice forms readily on the stone—"

"Mother, I have seen the Far Isle. Years ago, when I first saw the place, it fascinated me. It is fantastic, more so than any fortress William can order built, for the lairds of it constructed it piece by piece, bit by bit through the centuries, using all the natural outcropping of rock. It is nearly impregnable! I was delighted that we were not forced to lay siege to the place. I was also pleased to find that Ioin is a fine man—reasonable, temperate, and ready to negotiate with Father. A siege would have cost us dearly in lives. Aye, the wind blows, and it is fierce, but reckless, exciting. The sea is beautiful, seeming to stretch out forever. I have never seen such blue skies as I have there, such magnificence!" He realized, even as he spoke, that what he was saying was true. He'd been very young when he'd seen the place. But the sight of the island castle, rising out of its own shimmering reflection in the water, had remained with him forever. He was startled to realize that he wasn't lying at all. He did want the place.

"And the girl?" his mother inquired with a fine brow arched high.

"And the girl . . ." he murmured. He lifted his hands. "She is stunning. Young. Blonde. Not pale-blonde—burning blonde. Her hair is like a sunrise. She's slim, shapely, graceful—"

"Very beautiful, so I hear," Fallon said matter-of-factly. "And very outspoken."

He grinned suddenly, watching her. "The same could easily be said of you, my lady mother!"

The slightest smile curled her lips as well. "*Touché*, my son!" she murmured. "But I was under the impression that you and Lucinda had all but determined to announce a betrothal—"

"She is to marry Rolph, and travel with him to take possession of one of the castles bordering Wales."

"William is a wily old fox!" she muttered. She leaned back, closing her eyes, appearing very weary for a moment. "And Lucinda has agreed, I imagine, poor dear. She'd be worried about her father after her kin took part in the rebellion. Jesu, that must be half the king's power! Not a man or woman in all England hasn't a relative who hasn't risen at one time or another against him."

"Rolph is a friend of mine," he reminded her. "A good man, a gentle one, a kind one."

Fallon studied her son shrewdly for a moment. "I'm not so sure that you are in any way fond of the Scotsman's daughter, but I am afraid I'm convinced that you were not really in love with Lucinda."

"I cared most deeply for her—" he began indignantly, but then realized that she was maneuvering him right where she wanted him. "Deeply indeed. But perhaps you are right; I was not really in love."

"And what of this Allora?"

"I want her, Mother. Just as I want the castle."

And that, he was equally surprised to discover, was true as well. He did want the Scotsman's daughter. Wanted to silence her rebellion with his lips, cover himself with the silken strands of her hair, see its gold against the bronze of his flesh. He was fascinated by the passion in her eyes, with the swift fury and intelligence with which she fought . . .

"But you do not love her," Fallon said.

He sighed. "Mother, we've met just a few times. And I'm afraid that love has never been one of the real requisites for marriage, not that I've seen."

"Maybe not," she murmured, looking down at her hands. "Though I loved your father when I married him," she said very softly. "I think I loved him long before that, but that is no matter." She hesitated reflectively for a moment, then she too sighed. "I swear, Bret, I would gladly fight the king and fight him strenuously if he is forcing this—"

"Madam, I do not want you fighting the king for me; I could fight him very well myself if I so chose. He would never manage to make me do something that I was adamantly against, no matter what his threats!" he assured her. And once again, Bret realized that he was speaking the truth. Aye, he'd agreed to the marriage partly because he'd been afraid that Fallon would rush to battle for him, all too swiftly.

But if there hadn't been something about the girl . . .

If he hadn't wanted her . . .

Right from the beginning, he would have turned the king down in some way, disappearing across the channel with his entire family, if it had come to that!

"I am dying to see this golden-haired vixen," Fallon said.

Bret arched a brow again. "Then you will come and celebrate my wedding?" he asked her.

She rose, smiling. "Oh, indeed. Wild horses would not keep me away. When do you plan on marrying?"

He shrugged. "Soon, I imagine. William will not let her uncle have his freedom until the ceremony is performed, and since the king is eager to hurry back to Normandy himself, I am sure that he will speed along all the necessary arrangements."

"What then?"

"Her uncle will then be set free."

"And what of you?"

He shook his head. "I will spend some time here, but then follow William to Normandy and hope that I can return home with my father and brothers this time."

"So I pray!" Fallon said softly. She smiled. "Well, you must have this house for your wedding night. The girls and I will return to Haselford immediately following the ceremony."

"Thank you," he said, "but that won't be necessary." He paused. "Thank you. Mother, I will not be taking the house, because everyone will assume that I am doing so, and I would very much like to avoid an overzealous crowd on my wedding night. If you do let it be known that you and the girls are going to Haselford, perhaps any crude merrymakers will come here, and discover far too late that I have chosen to take my bride elsewhere."

Fallon nodded, quickly understanding. In the most noble of families down to the lowliest villeins, public beddings were common, with the wedding guests assembling to strip both bride and groom and see them tossed firmly into bed with one another.

"Don't worry, I shall spread the word, and it will be true. Whenever you and your bride are ready, I will be delighted to have you bring her to Haselford." Fallon kept watching him shrewdly.

"All right, milady, what now?" he asked her.

"Well, it seems that you are willing enough to take part in this move, but what of your bride-to-be?"

He shrugged. "If she refuses, then there can be no wedding, can there?"

Fallon shook her head ruefully. "There's a lie if I've ever heard one! Countless young heiresses have been wed to men of William's choosing, screaming all the way to the altar."

"I hardly see myself awaiting a screaming bride that someone is forced to drag to me."

"No, my dear. You are your father's son—you would do your own dragging, I am quite certain."

"Mother—"

Fallon waved a hand in the air, her eyes twinkling. "Bret, I speak because I can remember too clearly a time in life when things were different. Listen to the chroniclers! They say that the Normans have brought a better standard of building to England, that farming methods have improved, that the Normans will make us a stronger people. They are trying to say that my father seized a crown, when indeed, he could not have done so without the legal blessing of the witan, those wise councilmen who helped to govern us all. In my father's day—and long before his!—women had rights. They owned property, they could make their own choices in where and when they were wed. Aye, noble ladies did wed upon their father's wishes to improve their family's situation. And there are many ways other than the law and sheer brute force to make a damsel wed against her will. But nothing is so absolute as William's Norman feudal system. And many a shrieking, screaming woman has been legally wed to a Norman lord. It is somehow legal for a maid to be wed without ever making a vow—indeed, while cursing her intended—or while being gagged, so that the service can take place with her curses silenced."

He lifted his hands. "Mother, I will make my vows. She must do as she so chooses."

Fallon sighed. "She is from a different people!" she insisted softly.

"From a land claimed—"

"Her heart is Scottish, everyone knows that. And the Scots are different. Largely Viking—"

"Mother! Godwin's wife was Viking—England was ruled by Vikings, Normandy invaded by them just as much!"

Fallon nodded. "Aye, but the Scots remain different! The Romans conquered here; they did not reach Scotland, they did not have the strength or the manpower to tackle the wily chieftains! Invasions have always tended to stop at the border for that very reason. We are conquered here. They are not."

"If I am lord of a land, Mother, it will be mine."

"Ah! There's the Norman in you, my son."

"Milady, are you worried for me, or my intended bride?"

"Both!" Fallon admitted. "What is the lady's name?"

"Allora."

"Pretty enough."

"It fits her," he said softly. Then with a sigh he took his mother's hands in his. "Milady, marriage is a legal bond, one meant to last for life. I intend to be a good husband and lord."

"And father," Fallon reminded him. "I cannot imagine that I might be a grandparent so quickly, yet I find I am eager for the task."

"Indeed, milady mother. I intend to be honest in all endeavors as concern this marriage," he told her lightly.

She studied him, then sighed again. "I believe that you are truly set upon this course of action."

"I am."

"Then I wish you well, my son, and will be delighted to attend your wedding. Assuming, of course, that you do have a bride."

"You seem skeptical, my lady. I'm deeply wounded!" he teased. "Is it so hard to believe that marriage to me might not be the hardship of a lifetime?"

She touched his cheek lightly. "You have been quite the rage of William's court for a number of years now, you and your brothers. You are highly favored of the king, proven in battle, wealthy in your own right, and exceedingly handsome."

He arched a brow, smiling, for naturally his own mother should see the best in him.

"But," she continued, "you are marrying an heiress who belongs to a different people, a people who consider themselves unconquered. And she might not see all the shining qualities that I do."

"She'll be free to answer for herself," Bret assured Fallon.

Again, she gazed at him intently, and then she nodded. "I believe you," she told him, then smiled. "I'd best go see how the girls are faring. Are you staying to dine with us this evening?"

He shook his head. "I'll be with the king. Do you care to join me?"

She shook her head. "I'm very curious to see your lady, of course, but in this you are quite set and have not asked my opinion in the matter, so I'll try not to give it. I shall have to see William for your wedding; that will be enough."

She grimaced and sailed out of the room and Bret leaned against the stone mantel over the fireplace. A cool wind blew down the chimney. Sparks flew in a whirl and he watched them.

Fallon did believe him; in her heart, he was certain, she could not believe that any woman would not want one of her beloved sons—whether she sympathized with the bride or not!

He studied the flames for a moment, suddenly overwhelmed by the full weight of what he intended. Upon Ioin's death, he would be lord over a place where the vassals loathed and despised him as vehemently as—as his own wife. It was his life, perhaps endless long years, at stake here.

He started, hearing a pounding at the front door. He left the hall and started to answer it, waving a hand to the young servant girl who had come rushing forward. He threw open the door to find one of his men there, Jarrett of Haselford, a childhood companion who had grown up with him to serve him first as squire in battle, and then to rise to become one of his most trusted knights. He was red-haired, with somber hazel eyes, and was honest and loyal to a fault.

"Milord!" he said quickly. "I'm so very glad to find you here—"

"Why? What has happened? Come in and—"

Jarrett shook his head. "I'd not come in, not now. I wanted you to know that you are the gossip of the court once again and—"

"The gossip of the court! I care not for wagging tongues, Jarrett—"

"But you must, this time. Word is out that the Scottish heiress has agreed to wed you."

"Ah!" he said softly. Had he been preferable to old Michael after all? Or Ioin had, perhaps, sanctioned the marriage.

Then why would Jarrett be standing there looking so damnably miserable?

"They're saying that she adamantly refused, but that her father beat her into submission."

"*What?*"

Jarrett nodded unhappily. "The girl must have told someone—"

"Indeed, she must have, but if I know Ioin, it's a lie!" Bret said hotly.

"Milord, I am sorry to have come here—"

"Nay, it is necessary that you have come here!" Bret told his old friend. He swore savagely and stepped outside, closing the door behind him and striding angrily across the gravel path to the stables, Jarrett right behind him.

"Milord, there is more!" he said.

Bret stopped and whirled around, waiting.

Jarrett swallowed, his Adam's apple jiggling. "Ioin is at the Tower with his brother and the king. Allora isn't coming, they say, because she is too wretched to do so."

Once again, Bret exploded with an oath. He continued toward the stables, hearing Jarrett behind him, ready to ride with him again, no matter what reckless move he might now make.

"Milord—"

"Lad!" Bret called to the stable boy. "Bring Ajax, and quickly, my good fellow!"

The boy, clad in d'Anlou bright-blue and gold, hurried to the task. He threw the heavy saddle over the huge white horse, but Bret stepped forward to finish the task of drawing the girth himself. He leaped up on Ajax. Jarrett pointed to his own bay tethered to the iron stake imbedded in the muddy street. "Milord, I'll come with you."

Bret reined Ajax in and looked down to Jarrett. "Nay, good friend, I need no one to stand beside me now, for this is a matter I must solve by myself. But I tell you, if this wedding goes through, I will implore you and others to guard my back well! I will make a lord of you yet, Jarrett!"

He nudged Ajax hard, then moved swiftly through the London streets. Night was falling. Torches burned from the carts of the peddlers, now being pushed through the streets as they made their slow way home. William always kept a large number of his men in the city; they walked about alone, in pairs, in groups of three. Bret's own troops were abundant in London now, enjoying the rewards of the king's bounty after their service in Normandy. Some of them called out to him, and he lifted a hand in response, but hurried on through the sometimes crowded lane. He swore when the pitched contents of a chamber pot landed just ahead of Ajax on the street before him, causing the huge war-horse to rear in rebellion. Foul, smoky scents rose from the center chimneys of thatched-roof dwellings—even more foul than that which sometimes rose from the river. Bret spoke soothingly to Ajax, and hurried onward again. Suddenly a group of children burst from their small crowd in the center of a muddied square, and ran to watch his approach on the huge war-horse. Pale faces, grimy, too thin, looked at him in wide-eyed awe. " 'Tis Wakefield!" one of them cried, "the Earl of Wakefield!" And then the whole scruffy lot of them was kneeling before him.

"Out of the mud, my fine lads and lasses!" he commanded. He tossed a handful of coins for them to pluck up from the earth and then spurred Ajax onward, his temper worsening rather than softening.

The children had reminded him anew of his mother's words, and he could not help but wonder what her thoughts would be once she had heard that his new bride had been beaten into submission. They had managed so well all these years despite the tempest of the Conquest. Now all he needed was Fallon in open defiance of William! For Fallon was right, England had changed. He knew it well, for he had been tutored by Saxon as well as Norman scholars all his life, given insights into many different truths by Father Damien, a native priest who had managed to serve both a Saxon and a Norman king.

None of that mattered. Seeing Allora now did.

He came at last to the house where she was lodged. Leaping down from Ajax, he gave the horse the order to wait for him, and then burst through the front door. Joseph came hurrying, his wrinkled face alarmed.

"Where is she?" Bret demanded impatiently.

Joseph's eyes darted toward the stairs; he swallowed uneasily. "Milord, I will inform the lady that you have called upon her—"

"I shall do the informing, Joseph, thank you!"

Two at a time, he took the stairs. He found the center solar empty, tried the first bedchamber, and found it empty, too. He threw open the second door with a vengeance, and there found her at last.

She had been upon her bed, clad in a white nightgown that sat low upon her shoulders and tied with a drawstring just above her breasts. She was barefoot and bareheaded, with the wicked length of her hair streaming down her back in all its golden glory. Her face was flushed, her eyes were brilliant with indignation. Firelight flickered behind her, making the gown very sheer, detailing and enhancing every inch and curve of her lush young figure. Even in his anger, he was startled by the rush of hot desire that leaped into him. In the upheaval of it all, he had not realized until this very moment just how badly he did want her.

Jesu! he railed to himself, more furious still that he could feel such a tempest when he had come to tell her what he thought of her miserable behavior. But so much was visible in the diaphanous gown. The rise of her breasts, the slim length of her legs. The downy shadow at the juncture of her thighs. . . .

His eyes rose to hers. He gritted his teeth hard together and crossed his arms over his chest. "Milady, you do not look too sadly used and abused to me! So your father wretchedly beat you, eh? Consider this then, my love: whatever you might have imagined to have happened to you at his hands, know that it will be doubly so at mine!"

"*What!*" she gasped, stunned, furious.

"Is the effort here to humiliate me, or merely an attempt to have a battle break out in the London streets?"

"I don't know what you're talking about—" she began, but then she broke off suddenly, her face nearly as pale as her gown.

"Ah, so you *have* said you were beaten into submission!"

"Would you please leave, milord Wakefield?" she demanded, fingers passionately clenched into fists at her sides. "Whatever I have said, whatever my reasons for agreement, whatever your own, no wedding has as yet taken place, and you've no right in my room."

"I'm not leaving, milady, until you accompany me."

"But I am not going anywhere tonight! William has what he wants from me, and I want no more of the company of his court!"

"Nay, lady! Better to have his court believe that you are sore and sick and abused from your father's beating to force you into marriage with a dreaded monster!"

"I don't care what your barbaric Norman robbers think!"

"But I do!" he told her, his tone quiet but menacing. "I do! I will not let you rip my family to shreds!" he warned, walking across the room.

"Get out!" she gasped, backing against the wall, certain that he was coming for her.

Yet he did not go to her side. He stopped at the trunk at the foot of the bed and tore it open, finding the cache of her clothing. She protested with a cry when he began to throw shifts and tunics, bleaunts and veils carelessly across the room.

"You are insane!" she said. "Get out of my things!"

When he continued his quest for just the right garment for her appearance that evening, she suddenly pitted herself against him, slamming her palms against his chest. "Get out of my things and out of my room!" she charged him. "You cannot do this! If the rumor about my father beating me has you distressed, milord, think on the words that I will circulate now!" She gripped his arm, pummeled her fists against his shoulder.

He spun, catching her shoulders in his grasp, shaking her slightly and staring down into the emerald fire of her eyes. A subtle, tantalizing scent assailed him when he touched her. She was fresh from her bath; strands of her hair were still damp and carried the sweet smell of some lightly scented soap. The warmth and near-naked shape of her form were warm and flush against him, and he found himself thinking of the words he had spoken earlier that day. *I want her*, he had said. The simple statement was so very true at this moment that it seemed the fires of hell suddenly burst within his mind and body. He wanted to be damned with the wedding and all else, to strip the fragile material from her body and end the fascination that had so suddenly and swiftly brought him to such blazing heights of desire.

He clamped his lips together tightly, staring into the beauty of her face, the defiance of her eyes. He reminded himself that she had sworn him her enemy, and would ever do so. Their wedding *would* take place; they would both bow to the king for their different reasons, though the vows might be spoken with bitterness.

But she would be his wife. And the very fire she created would be recompense for the battle that must be engaged in.

He fought the wild longing to seize her then and there, fought the fury that had brought him to her that night. His tone was cool and dispassionate when he spoke, yet rigid with warning. "You will come to court tonight so that all may see you are hale and hearty, milady. The white gown here will best suffice for the evening, for the sleeves are sheer. It's a pity women's clothing does not allow for bared backs. Perhaps I will suggest to William that the gown be ripped from your back so that all doubting——"

"I will *not* come!" she gasped in a strangled voice. "And they call us wild upon the border! Barbaric!" Her voice shook. "I have met no people cruder, coarser, than you conquering Normans, and I will not dine among such company again!"

"You will dress——"

"I will not!"

"Then I will dress you."

"All-powerful, arrogant henchman of a bastard that you might be," she hissed, struggling against his touch upon her. "You would not dare such a thing!"

His eyes remained coolly upon hers. His fingers grasped the thin linen fabric at her shoulder and began to rip. The cloth tore quickly and easily and the garment began to fall from her shoulder. She caught it, stamping a foot, eyes shimmering with hatred and fury.

"My father will kill you!" she swore.

"I don't believe you seek to have your father meet me with a sword at all, milady."

A dark anguish swept through her eyes. Unconquered, his mother had warned him. Aye, her people were that; she was that. She hated to bend to him in any way, yet now it seemed she would, her chin quivering, but still so very high. "I will accompany you to court, Wakefield. Just get out and let me dress!"

He released her instantly and stepped back.

"Get out of the room," she commanded, her voice still trembling.

"I think not. There's a window there, and I'm quite certain that you would go to any length to defy me. I am weary of this struggle already."

She *had* thought of the window. The quick fall of her lashes against her cheeks betrayed her.

"Then——"

"I will be at the door, milady," he said courteously, with a deep and mocking bow. He strode to it, turned his back to her, and remained there stubbornly without moving, his arms crossed over his chest.

"My uncle will kill you!" she warned him furiously.

"Maybe not today, perhaps not tomorrow—"

"Ah, good. As long as he lets me live through our nuptials."

"God will surely cause you to rot in hell."

"God is not always so accommodating, milady."

She swore beneath her breath, but then was ready with amazing speed.

"We can go!" she told him, and he turned again to find that she had donned the garments he had given her: an undershift of a gauzy material, with sleeves loose and very wide-slit at the wrist, the overshift, her bleaunt, of a heavier material, the neck trimmed in white rabbit fur, the hem likewise decorated. A sheer white veil sat atop her head, a slim circlet of gold keeping it in place. She looked demure and beautiful, young and virginal. And healthy, and not at all bruised or battered. That was the most important factor in her appearance.

"Am I suitable, milord?" she demanded hotly.

He nodded, opened the door, and allowed her to exit. She did so swiftly, hurrying down the stairs ahead of him. He followed her. She did not await him below, but threw open the door to the street.

"Milady—" Joseph called in concern.

"The Lady Allora has decided she is dying to dine with the king after all, Joseph," Bret informed the servant, then followed her out where she was already walking away from the house.

"Oh, no, milady! Back here!" he told her, catching her swiftly.

"It is not far; it is easily walked."

"But I have Ajax."

"Then I will take my own mount."

"And ride your own way into oblivion, I imagine," he said grimly.

"I prefer—"

"And I do not give a damn!" And in a minute, he had her cast upon his own horse, and leaped up to join her. She didn't speak to him again. Her back was stiffer than an oak as they rode, but they very quickly reached the tower, and there he helped her down. Ajax was taken away as they passed among the guards and entered together, coming up to the hall.

The king had already sat down to the meal; his guests, his lords and ladies, were aligned down the table, seated according to their station. One place remained at the head, that next to the king himself.

His hand firmly upon Allora's, Bret led her there. The seat had been his own. He forced his mouth into a polite smile, nodding to Robert Canadys and his brother Ioin, just to the other side of the king. Ioin looked concerned, as if he would rise, and Bret spoke quickly. "Laird Ioin, your daughter has decided to join us after all. The Lady Allora must take my seat here with you, at the king's side."

He could feel the heat of the fury that swept through her as she was left next to the king. But he bowed and departed, hurrying down the length of the table.

"Bret!" came the soft call and he turned. There, just down the length of the table from where sat the highest nobility, next to a young count from the southwest region, was his sister Elysia. The count leaped swiftly to his feet, a little red-faced.

"Milord Wakefield, I would be privileged if you would take my place here."

Bret lifted a brow. The count, a very young man, was eager to please. He shrugged. "Thank you, milord. I will gladly accept your invitation."

As he slid into the chair next to Elysia he stared down the length of the table. There was William, at center. Whether he had been born to be a king or not, he had the look of one, the look of a warrior king. Once he must have been something of a handsome man; he was still striking, a gemstone broach at his shoulder tonight, pinning his ermine-trimmed mantle to his shoulder. There was Ioin to his left, with his wild mane of reddish hair, just as striking in his own way. The wild Robert was at his brother's side, dark, his hair raggedly long as well, so very different from the close-trimmed Norman fashion.

"She looks like an angel, a goddess," Elysia whispered to him. "I doubt that you shall suffer too badly."

He stared at his sister, ready to reprimand her, but she

smiled with swift understanding and he arched a brow
again. Then Elysia continued softly, "Lucinda has already
left for Wales. She is to be married there and travel on to
the Welsh border immediately. I'm sorry, Bret."

He pressed his temples briefly between his palms, then
turned to study his sister with her wide silver eyes and
fire-stream of hair. "Don't be. I have said—"

"You have kept the family from sure disaster," Elysia
said. "But I wonder if your golden angel is aware that she
has done very well to accept you, when her next choice
was a doddering widower."

"Michael does not dodder."

"Perhaps it was an idle threat on the king's part. She is far
too lovely to imagine a life ahead with so ancient a lord!"

"William would wed any of us to toads if it so advanced
his grip upon his kingdom!" Bret murmured somewhat bitterly. He then noticed that, from the head table, Allora's
eyes were on him. His head had been lowered, very close
to his sister's. She stared at him, white-faced, lips taut. Yet
when he returned her stare, she looked quickly away.

A platter of roasted boar was set before him and he
speared a piece with his knife. Eels were passed before
him, great platters of fowl. He gave little attention to the
food on the table, and watched his bride-to-be. William
seemed to be in fine good humor, taunting her, fully aware
that she would be as polite as she could manage while her
imprisoned uncle and her father sat at his other side.

He started to feel a growing pity in his heart.

"It's good that you two arrived here together tonight,"
Elysia whispered. "There was a terrible rumor going about
that she had been hideously beaten."

"Aye, well, she seems to sit just fine, doesn't she?"

"Indeed!" Elysia agreed. Then she stared at him. "Why
are you looking at me so?"

He shook his head with a weary sigh. "Because I wish
you weren't here."

"Bret! I—"

"I mean no offense. William is willing to use us all as
pawns now. You need to stay away from his court, and to
take the gravest care."

Elysia kept staring at him.

He sighed in exasperation. "Elysia! It is a compliment, I swear it! Some young—or old!—swain is going to take it into his head to ask William that you be his reward for some service rendered, and then . . ."

She gasped, flushing. She lowered her head quickly. "Jesu! I thought that Mother was foolish, being so willing to spend a night upon her knees rather than dine with the king! She did not refuse me leave to attend tonight, but she was not at all pleased, either! Oh, Bret! I had not thought—"

"Shhh!" he warned her. "Mother intends to return to Haselford immediately following my wedding. Father will come home soon, I know it. Then you'll be safe, for I do not believe even William would betray a man who has served him for so many years."

"Too late for you?" Elysia asked softly.

But he was staring at his future bride again, and finding that the same fire which had touched him in her room was returning to his limbs once more. She shone like firelight among the men, her hair golden and shimmering beneath her gossamer veil, her delicate features so lovely and perfect, her flawless skin. Her beauty was exquisite; he could find no complaint there. And even the passion within her . . .

He saw her gasp suddenly, nearly rising from her chair at something that the king was saying. William's hand fell upon hers. She sat again, gone pale as snow.

Bret frowned, startled to discover that he was ready to leap to her defense. But William himself stood then, taking Ioin by his one hand, Ioin's daughter by the other, causing them both to rise with him.

"My friends!" he called to the gathering. "Drink with me tonight, salute my mighty Scottish friend, so strong in wisdom, and now my ally! Negotiations, it seems, are complete. Tomorrow night, Laird Ioin's daughter, the Lady Allora, will wed our bravest knight, milord Bret d'Anlou, Earl of Wakefield, and thus fortify our borders and bring peace to our peoples!"

Thunderous noise filled the hall. Chalices were clanked

down on the wooden tables, boots were pummeled against the floor. Bret discovered that half the room had risen. He found himself standing. A number of his own men had come forward from their places far lower down the hall, congratulating him, gripping his hand, slapping his back. In a few moments, he found that the king was at his side. "You must stand a vigil tonight, before the altar in the chapel here," William said quietly, beneath the din around them.

"I do imagine!" Bret returned. "How can we wed so swiftly? What of the Church? What—"

"The Church can be amazingly accommodating under such circumstances." He slipped an arm around Bret's shoulders, lowering his voice still further. "Would you have these wily ruffians be given more time to plan some rebellion before the wedding can take place?"

In that, the king was right. William had spent his entire reign with a multitude of knights around him, men who were ready to defend his life against those who might rise against him. He was an eager warrior himself, too often at the front line of a battle. But he had learned early that he need be forewarned, and he was no fool in this matter.

Aye, Robert Canadys would have friends here. And the more time the man was given, the more he would plot. Perhaps he even now plotted to spirit himself and the girl far from the city before the lady could become any Norman lord's property.

"Are we agreed?" the king demanded.

Allora remained near the head table, father and uncle protectively at her side, well-wishers and the curious pressing around her. His gaze fell up and down the length of her. Recompense! he thought. A bounty of youth and beauty, a woman he had discovered that he did lust for . . .

One who would fight him, he thought wearily.

One who would be his wife in all things no matter what, he vowed. She had been warned.

"Tomorrow night, then," he told William.

And so it would be.

Chapter 7

Allora's hands were folded reverently as she knelt before the altar in Edward the Confessor's magnificent chapel.

She had come to this chapel in the company of women— Norman countesses and ladies—all as kind as could be to her face, and surely entirely critical behind her back. The women awaited her patiently at the rear of the majestic cathedral, having left her at the altar alone to commune in private with God. Tomorrow, she must confess her sins before the wedding mass. Dear God, but she did need help!

She was praying feverishly, even though she had little heart or intent to free her soul from sin, or to humbly beg God through Christ's grace to help her be a good wife and serve her lord in all manners—as a good wife should. She certainly didn't wish to pray for fertility or that she should swiftly bear heirs for a Norman spouse.

There was only one prayer on her lips at that moment, and that was that God should deliver her from them all— father, bridegroom, uncle, and king.

She felt a weight upon the pew beside her and lifted her face from her folded hands to stare at the man who had come to kneel with her. Her uncle Robert was to her left, his hands folded as if in prayer, his eyes serenely upon the figure of the crucified Christ far above them.

"What are you doing here?" she demanded, furious with him. He would manage an escape, so he had claimed! How was he going to arrange such a thing in less than a day? And not only that, but he must have been the one to spread the dreadful rumor that Ioin had *beaten* her into submission.

She loved her uncle, yes; she certainly didn't want his neck stretched or his head severed from his body. But his reckless bid for freedom was now drawing her into a vortex from which it seemed escape was impossible, and the more she knew her prospective bridegroom, the more wary of him she was coming to be. She was going to stand before an altar such as this tomorrow, before a small crowd at the tower itself, and swear before God to love, honor, and obey the man. And then she was going to escape him, and somehow, she didn't think that he would quite ever forgive her.

Because it was wrong.

It wasn't wrong for her!

Robert had been right in one issue—it was the king forcing the wrong upon them. It was wrong for William to demand that the people of the Far Isle bow down to him. So how could it be so wrong for her to escape?

Yet she shivered, thinking of her intended bridegroom. Her escape might well be an offense he would never forget or forgive.

He would not really be hurt in any way. They would have the marriage annulled, and he would be free to pursue his own life again. He hadn't wanted the marriage either, he had only agreed to it, she was certain, to protect his family. So there really wouldn't be anything so absolutely terrible about what she was doing. She was doing what was *necessary*.

She gritted her teeth, for her uncle seemed exuberant. Ah, and well he should! For she was purchasing his freedom, though she couldn't help but wonder at what cost to herself.

Bret. She hadn't seen him since the king had informed her how quickly he had managed to get his church officials to sanction the marriage. She had been watching Bret, in fact, when the king had spoken. His dark head was bent so close to that of the young auburn-haired woman at his side—another great beauty, fawning over him! She'd felt the most curious flare of anger in her heart . . . and something more. They weren't as yet wed, and he was handing out all manner of dictates to her, and then to be speaking so intimately with another woman . . .

What difference did it make? She asked herself in anguish. One moment she wanted to slap him, and the next moment she was praying not only that she would manage to escape him easily enough, but that he would forgive her for the act.

"What are you doing here?" she again asked her uncle angrily.

"Niece! I have come to assure you that I have never intended to desert you, or allow harm to befall you!" Robert protested in a whisper.

"Ah!" she whispered fiercely in reply. "Did you know, then, that my wedding day would approach so quickly?"

"Nay, lass, I did not," Robert admitted ruefully. "But you mustn't fear. I have friends, and we will rally them to us as quickly as we can."

"How can we trust your friends?" she demanded.

He shrugged. "Easily enough!" he assured her. "The English are a conquered people, lady; many of them are bitter that their overlords do not speak their language! Aye, lass! There's enough hatred against William to last many a lifetime! Mind you now, Allora, look to the cross, and not at me! I'd not have those gossips in the back saying as how we Scots had done anything other than look to our Holy God for guidance!"

"I *am* looking for guidance!" she assured him quickly. "And were you not my uncle, I might be looking to Him to strike you down! Robert! How could you have started such a horrible rumor—"

"You said that Wakefield must be convinced of your change of heart," he interrupted with a shrug.

"But to say such a thing about Father—"

"Apparently, all know that it was not true."

"Uncle, I don't like this! It was bad before; it is wretched now. Who are these friends? I must know!"

"Shhh!" he warned again. He cleared his throat, looking away from her and up to the cross above them with a reverent look in his eyes once again.

"There are enough of them!" he assured her harshly. "Count Geoffrey of Ballantyre, Lord Flynn of Eire, the old woman, Sara, who cleans my chamber each day—we've enough friends! Friends to see we've horses ready, friends to help on an easy path to escape. But we've no more time here, lass. So listen to me, and listen well. The wedding and mass will be said by six tomorrow eve, the feast will follow. Most certainly, your new husband will intend on taking you to his family town house here in London on the Thames. There might be a great deal of merrymaking to follow, but . . ." He looked at her as if she should understand something he was warning her about, but then he shrugged. "None of that matters. I know for certain that Wakefield will take you to his family's town house, for the king received word from Lady Fallon, Countess of Haselford, that she will be returning to her husband's lands immediately following the ceremony, along with her daughters. I will see to it that we've a girl in his home tomorrow night. There will be a blue vial by the earl's bed, so no matter how far the guests insist on following in your footsteps, you will not be trapped away from your method of escape."

"Vial? Dear God, Uncle, what are you planning? Sweet Jesu, I cannot poison the man—"

"Nay, not poison him, niece. Merely leave him sleeping through the night, only to awaken to find himself free."

Allora stared intently at the cross once again. She fought the trembling that started within her fingers. She wouldn't see d'Anlou again until the wedding ceremony. He would stay through the night at the chapel within the tower, along with a few of his most loyal men and his personal servants. He would remain at the tower, rest there, await the ceremony there.

She closed her eyes. He definitely had his pride, and his arrogance. He had claimed he would much rather wed a hedgehog. Well, she would only be giving him his opportunity to do so.

"Allora, your father is not happy with my plan, but he is in agreement that we must do something."

Her gaze fell from the crucifix to his face.

"Don't look at me!" he warned her.

She could suddenly hear a soft, beautiful chant. She swallowed as she realized a group of black-clad nuns had come into the nave, and were reverently singing their homilies.

"He is desperate for your happiness," Robert continued.

"And you are desperate for your freedom. And now I am merely . . . desperate!" she added very softly.

"Freedom awaits us all," her uncle said, somewhat angrily. "Have you forgotten where we come from? We are a free and independent people!"

She inhaled and exhaled slowly, lowering her eyes to her folded hands. Aye, she had forgotten that! Yet she wondered even then just what it mattered to her people themselves to whom the lairds of the Far Isle chose to give their allegiance. Life for them was much the same, day after day. Things on the Far Isle were far simpler than they were here in London town. Her father was the laird. His tenants worked the land, following the feudal system. A certain amount of their labor was given over to Ioin, and Ioin used his great strength to protect them. Everyone had his or her place. The smith, the cooper, the fishermen, the shepherds and shepherdesses. The maids within the castle keep, the lads in the stable, the housecarls whose duty it was to support the laird and protect the castle. Life went on. Some of the people never left the isle itself. So what could they care about things in the outside world?

Ah, but they were not conquered! Unconquered, and in that freedom, something beautiful did exist. Robert was right. She was not acting maliciously; she was following the only course of action left to her by the English king's dictates.

"Don't fail me, Uncle!" she charged him.

"I'll not."

"You musn't! We'll all hang!"

"Nay, milady niece. I'll not fail you," he swore. "By the Blessed Virgin, I'll not do so."

He caught her hand, bent low over it, kissed it. Then he crossed himself and rose; turning, she saw that he had been escorted here by a number of William's men, who would now escort him back. She remained kneeling herself, with little tremors continuing to shoot through her, prayers refusing to come to her lips. Then she realized that Robert's place beside her had been taken anew. Her father knelt there, looking as if he had aged a decade overnight. He did not address her. He stared at the crucifix above.

"God forgive us and help us!" he murmured fervently.

Allora ached to see him so torn. He was as fiercely proud and determined as his brother Robert. But he seemed far more miserable with the arrangements than her uncle was.

"Father," she said quickly, "you're upset because you like this man. Then realize this: he will want his freedom as well."

"Is that what you see?" he asked, staring at her.

"It is what I know in my heart!" she promised.

"Then again, I pray that God forgives us all, and that He will ride at our side." He was quiet for a moment. "Indeed, I pray that you are right!"

"Father, we can still stop this—"

"Oh, aye!" he said bitterly. "Then I watch my brother hang, and become a martyr to the chieftains. The way we have planned it, I see my daughter wed in a mockery of marriage with a man who one day might crush us all."

"Then we deny the marriage again, and take another man of William's choice. An old one, maybe a very old one—"

"Aye! And the king would know our scheme, and hang us all. And if he would not, it would not matter. Wakefield has agreed to the marriage, and so have you, and God help me, so have I. That he has chosen Bret d'Anlou to be a part of this is just another curse upon us, for I have always liked the man. Now I must fear him. I cannot imagine that I, Laird Ioin of the Far Isle, have become a part in such treachery!"

Her father's words brought shivers racing down her spine. But there would be nothing to fear. She would share wine with her bridegroom, be pleasant, he would sleep peacefully, she would depart. If she truly dwelled upon it, she could convince herself that the great Earl of Wakefield was so arrogant that he deserved to awaken without a bride. There would be no bloodshed. She and her family would disappear behind the rocks of the Far Isle, find the right churchman to appeal their case to the pope. Bret d'Anlou would be as free as she would, and unless William was willing to sacrifice half his army on a siege against the fortress walls, they would all be back where they had started. Except, of course, for the Lady Lucinda. She would be wed and far away.

"William has caused this!" she reminded her father hotly.

"Ah," Ioin murmured unhappily, "God will be on our side, eh?"

"The side of right."

"Every side is the right one when a Christian lord battles a Christian lord."

"Father, we have no choice!" she whispered.

He fell silent, and bent his large, wild-haired head. Anguish swept through her. She didn't want him aching for her, not with the other burdens he carried.

She reached a hand out to his, curled her fingers around his. After a moment, he rose, and she was left alone.

Her knees seemed frozen to the floor. No prayers would come. At length, someone—a shy, homely, but very sweet girl named Lady Anne—came and tapped her on the shoulder. It was late; she would want some rest and peace before tomorrow came.

Rest.

She was quite certain that she would never rest again.

And surely, she would never find peace.

She did sleep. It was dawn when she did so at last, and she was startled to be awakened by one of the young maids who quickly and breathlessly informed her that she had a bath waiting, that the groom's family had sent the gift of a wedding gown, that she must eat something quickly and prepare; the priest who would wed them, a Father Damien, would be awaiting her confession as soon as she was dressed for the evening's ceremonies.

Allora was surprised to hear a commotion below, and the young maid told her that as she had brought no women of her own to London town, some of the ladies of the court had come to help her bathe. Greatly alarmed at such a prospect, she leaped swiftly from bed, wrenched off her gown, and all but jumped into the bath, nearly scalding herself in the process. She ordered the girl to stall the women the best that she could, determined that she would bathe and at the very least don a shift before the ladies of the Norman court could come and inspect her.

She did not get quite so far, but managed to scrub her skin and wash her hair and wrap herself in a huge linen towel before the women burst in on her. There were only two of them, she was relieved to see, one of them an older, kindly-looking matron with a round body, graying hair, and a sweet, cherubic face. The second woman was far younger, an exquisitely striking woman with raven-dark hair and shimmering blue eyes, a slim form, and a very quick and somewhat mischievous smile. She came forward and greeted Allora with a slight bow first, then a swift kiss upon the cheek. "God's blessing on your coming marriage, my dear," she said, and then, without introducing herself or the older woman, she put her hands upon Allora's bare shoulders, sat her upon the trunk at the foot of her bed, and began to comb through the length of her hair. The woman didn't comment on the coming wedding at all, but quizzed Allora about the Far Isle, and Allora found herself painting a picture of her homeland as best she could, feeling remarkably relaxed given the circumstances.

The dark-haired woman continued combing Allora's fresh-washed tresses, toweling them as she went, until she was satisfied with her work, then spun out from a trunk the gown that had been brought that morning, a stunning creation of gossamer silver material. "A silk acquired straight from the Byzantine empire!" the woman told her. "Do you like it?"

Allora realized for the first time that the black-haired lady who had so charmingly taken charge spoke Norman French with the slightest accent. "Are you English then, milady?" Allora asked her curiously.

The words caused the lady's eyes to sparkle humorously. "Oh, indeed, very. But come, tell me, what do you think of the material?"

She touched the gown. "It is very beautiful."

"Let's get you into it."

The undertunic came first with its lighter-than-air sleeves. The bleaunt that came next was of a slightly heavier weight.

The veil that crowned her hair was all but nonexistent, and the circlet of gold that held it upon her head was delicate and intricately wrought.

The dark-haired woman stood back, still smiling with her charming air of slight mischief. Allora indeed found herself inspected, but it was a pleasant enough feeling, for the woman seemed to approve of her greatly. "Magda," she said, addressing the older lady, "you must hurry down and inform them that the Lady Allora is ready to be taken to Father Damien."

"Oh, indeed, I shall hurry right along! What a bride our Lord Bret shall acquire!" she said with pleasure, then left the chamber.

Allora felt a flush rise to her cheeks. The dark-haired woman added warmly, "Indeed, Bret is acquiring quite a bride. He told me that you were very beautiful. Yet I cannot help but be blunt and curious. Are you really eager for this marriage, milady of the Far Isle?"

She didn't dare tremble or shiver, or give away a thing. "My father and the king have advised it, lady."

The woman laughed outright, a pleasant thing. "Methinks you have been coerced on behalf of that rogue uncle of yours. But never mind. As long as you are not against the match."

Allora was dying to ask the woman if she might have intended to help her escape if she had been opposed to the marriage. But she had to be so very careful! Everything was in motion now.

"It is my understanding that the Earl of Wakefield is a powerful man from a powerful family. He is young and certainly handsome enough. Don't you think so?" Allora asked curiously.

"Oh, yes. I think so."

"Then what, milady, would there be for me to protest?"

The woman smiled. "It had simply occurred to me, my dear, that you might not have wanted a Norman marriage."

Allora shrugged. "Men are much the same in essence, aren't they? Two arms, a head, a neck."

The woman laughed very softly. "Aye, and a rogue is a rogue from any nation, and a good man a good man, no matter what his country of birth. Milord Bret d'Anlou, Earl of Wakefield, is indeed young, and is, in my opinion, an extremely fine match for the loveliest and most noble of young ladies. He is many fine things. He is also very proud, very determined, and extremely *Norman* in his ways of thinking. His will is a powerful one; what is his, he will keep. What he claims once, he will never let go."

Allora felt herself shivering. What was this speech she was receiving? The woman was older than Bret, but so beautiful and arresting. Was she someone else from his past? Perhaps a widow left too long alone, seeking not a husband but a lover? In annoyance, Allora wondered why in God's name she must keep feeling such fierce jealousy over a man she meant to escape the very moment she could. Yet something in her heart had ached when she had seen him with Lucinda; the pangs had been there again last night when she had watched him at the table with the very lovely young redhead. And even now, she felt a pang of jealousy over this woman who spoke to her with a pleasant humor and good nature, seeming to truly wish her well in all things.

"You seem to know him very well," Allora commented softly.

The woman shrugged, her eyes touched with humor. "I should. I am his mother, my dear."

Allora gasped, quickly coloring, amazingly relieved on the one hand, deeply embarrassed on the other.

"You—you should have told me!" she whispered.

She felt that she might just be sick. Or pass out. Jesu, this was getting worse and worse! Allora liked this woman, liked her very much, and even as they stood here, she was planning the greatest treachery against her son. Allora had been so convinced that Bret d'Anlou would want his freedom! But it seemed that once he had determined on his course, he was taking the marriage very seriously.

"I'm sorry," Fallon said softly, eyeing her pallor in concern. "I could not resist getting to know you without an introduction. I wanted to see for myself that you were not being coerced into this."

"But milady, you are obviously quite fond and proud of your son," Allora murmured uncomfortably. "Why would you think—"

"I think that my husband and my sons serve the Norman king of England, and that is not always agreeable to others," Fallon said swiftly. Then she stepped forward, catching Allora's hands. "I have been very glad to have this time to meet you. Now you must go; Father Damien is below. You are to be wed by a Saxon priest, a very dear friend of the family—if that is any consolation to you for the speed of this affair and the fact that you are so very far from home. God bless you, my dear. And welcome to our family. We are deeply glad to have you."

She smiled again, squeezed Allora's hands, and turned to go with a whisper of her skirts. Allora stood stock-still, watching her depart. Her fingers dug into her palms at her side, and for a moment, she actually hated her uncle. If he hadn't been so determined to fight! He hadn't even been captured fighting on his own side of the border; he had been helping in an English rebellion. And now . . .

Now she still didn't have any choices! she cried inwardly. Before she could think anymore, she hurried out the door of her chamber and raced down the stairway.

So much of the rest of the day seemed to pass in a blur! Her father brought her to the tower, and for his sake, she tried to appear serene and completely confident. She saw the priest, Father Damien, for confession, and she wondered if there could truly be a hell worse than those created right on earth by men, and if so, was she now definitely doomed to burn within it? She told herself that as yet she hadn't done anything, so there was nothing to confess. Yet when she looked at the priest, she felt as if he looked right through her in return. He had snow-white hair and an eagle's eyes. Even as he absolved her, she felt that he was wary of her.

Indeed, that he might know exactly what she was up to.

She was given a chamber in the tower to await the final preparations. She paced and prowled the space, like a caged cat. Then, suddenly, too soon, the door opened and her father stood there.

Her heart seemed to catapult, and then go still. She stared into his worried eyes, at his worn and haggard face, a face dearer to her than any other. Come what may, she would do anything to erase the cares that so creased and aged that beloved face.

"It's time," he said, his voice pained, gruff.

She forced herself to smile with tremendous confidence. "We are all nearly free!" she promised him, kissing his cheek.

"You're not afraid?"

She shook her head, holding his arm warmly and firmly beneath her own. "We are the unconquered!" she reminded him. "And I am not afraid of anything."

Oh, she lied, she lied! For her heart, which had been so very still, was suddenly beating out thunderously.

She had never been so afraid in all her life.

Chapter 8

$\mathcal{S}$he came with her father from the room and along the hall. As always, William's tower guards lined the walls. When they came to the rear of the chapel, Allora saw that it was full.

Yet the people all seemed to fade away in a roar as she saw her bridegroom awaiting her at the altar, the king himself at his side, serving as witness. Yet she scarce saw the king. She only saw *him*. His head was bare; his ebony-dark hair had been trimmed, yet it was still longer than the customary Norman fashion. He was in the yellow-gold and royal-blue that were his family colors, extremely tall in boots nearly as black as his hair, broad-shouldered, imposing. The fierce blue of his eyes touched upon hers, and she seemed to hear a rush of warnings in her head. *If she agreed to this, she must be willing to be his wife. If she agreed to this . . .*

Her eyes slid down the length of him and she noticed his hands. They were large, with very long fingers, and clean, clipped nails. They were at rest, folded before him. She could almost feel them . . .

Around her throat.

She couldn't do this. She couldn't. He had warned her. If something were to go wrong . . .

She nearly bolted. She nearly stopped dead in her tracks to turn to flee in the opposite direction!

But where was there for her to go?

Nowhere. Nowhere at all.

She willed her fingers not to tremble upon her father's arm. The priest with the too-knowing eyes, Father Damien,

117

awaited her at the altar. In a ringing voice he asked who had come to give Allora in marriage to Bret, and her father brought her forward, his voice shaking when he said that he, the lady's father, did so.

Then he placed her hand into Bret d'Anlou's. Once again, Allora felt a wild rise of panic. She nearly bolted, nearly screamed. There seemed an awful heat in his touch, a staggering force, a power. She felt his eyes on her, but could not look his way. She knelt beside him, heard the words said above them. Bret gave his vows, his voice very strong and sure. The priest demanded the same of her. She couldn't breathe, she couldn't speak. Once again, she was afraid that she would pass out . . .

She didn't, of course. His fingers wound around hers in warning and the pain almost made her scream. She blurted out the proper words, then gazed at him at last with narrowed, warning eyes.

He surveyed her with his customary hard stare, and she was certain that neither of them heard the words then as the priest droned on. Maybe Bret did hear what was being said because he was suddenly taking her hand and slipping a band upon her finger. It was a little snug, and she felt a tremor in her heart.

She wasn't going to be able to get it off! She wasn't going to be able to get the damned thing off!

"What's wrong?" he whispered, his head bent as if he were very deep in prayer.

"It's tight!"

"Ah, lady, marriage itself is such a fit!"

"Imagine marriage then, milord, with your precious hedgehog!" she hissed back.

"I think it will be tight enough as it is."

"Go to hell!"

"I love you, too, milady."

"Do so from hell, milord."

She sucked her breath in hard, praying that her words had not been heard by the wedding guests, for the priest had suddenly stopped speaking in the middle of his prayer and looked at them both with an arched brow. "Is there a problem, milord, milady?"

"Nay, Father! Please proceed," Bret advised him, his voice ringing clearly.

Her head seemed to be swimming. She tried to remind herself that she was supposed to be charming, so that none might suspect she was anything other than the resigned bride if not the anxious one.

She received communion, sipping from the cup first, seeing his lips touch where hers had been. Her stomach constricted. It was one thing to break a contract with William. It was another to do so against God, even if the king did seem to think that he was both at times.

She quite suddenly felt Bret's hands upon her, drawing her to her feet. A taunt filled his eyes; a reckless, mocking smile curled his lip.

And she found herself crushed very hard against him, his arms encompassing her. His lips fell upon hers with a sure and easy command. His fingers at her nape held her still to this marriage kiss, one that seemed to sweep fire into her body and soul, to sweep her breath and nearly her very life away. She wanted to pound against him, hate him. She didn't want to feel the spreading warmth, the weakness that brought a new trembling to her. The sudden promise of something more in his arms, something hinted, something that tantalized . . .

Cheers and shouts went up around them. She heard the sudden strumming of a lute, and Rupert, one of the king's musicians, began to cry out. "Ah, and there, my fine lords and ladies, is a kiss!"

It was a rowdy crowd, ready to rise to the occasion, and others began shouting.

"Indeed, a fine beginning!" someone else cried, somehow making innocent words indecently suggestive.

"A Norman kiss, the conquering kind!" Rupert chimed in again.

She froze, the heat in her veins fading. Her body stiffened against his. His lips rose from hers at last. The deep searing blue of his eyes still seemed to impale her.

Tears stung her eyes. "You'll not conquer me!" she promised him in a rush.

"They were not my words, milady," he told her, and

he spoke softly, with a gentleness she had not expected from him.

"They are the same as those in your heart!" she accused him swiftly.

"Marriage is a tight fit, lady, and one not made warm and comfortable by conquest. Still—"

"Still, you are the Lord Bret, Earl of Wakefield. And at my father's death, lord of the Far Isle. And you would rule in all things!"

"I manage what is mine, milady, yes!" he muttered, suddenly fierce.

"And I will not be managed."

"We shall see."

"Indeed," she promised him, her words bold, her feelings so desperate, "indeed we shall." The guilt still plagued her but her fear outweighed it. She had to escape. She prayed that she could do so soon.

"Hush!" he warned her on a harsh note. "Or are you anxious for all our arguments to be public, milady?"

The crowd in the chapel was beginning to surge toward them, well-wishers determined to congratulate the bride and groom. She fell silent, startled to be so suddenly buffeted by the crowd of elegantly clad nobles around her.

They were suddenly drawn apart. She felt her uncle's kiss upon her cheek and saw his brilliant eyes, his flushed face. Then the king embraced her, boisterous, glad, exceedingly pleased. The beautiful Fallon, Countess of Haselford, swept Allora into her arms, hugging her tightly. "I have always loved my sons, and cherished my daughters!" Fallon told her. "Now I shall cherish another."

Allora wanted to sink beneath the red carpeting laid out on the chapel floor. Then she found herself in her father's giant bear hug, his arms trembling. Lying came so very hard for Ioin. Robert embraced her once again, his arms so strong, as if the taste of freedom that lay ahead had given them greater power. He was alive now. He was ever ready for the battle, the rebellion. Next came her husband's men: Etienne, Jarrett, Henry of Greenwald, Jacques, and, so many more, all greeting her so charmingly. Father Damien wished her well, and she saw him whispering to Bret, and wondered just what the good priest was saying to the lord it seemed he served so faithfully. What dire warning did he give Bret about her?

Bret was with her again, his forcefully guiding hand upon her shoulder. She signed the proper documents, saw his powerful flourish next to her own signature. Her father signed the paper as did the king, the Lady Fallon, and the priest, Father Damien.

"Ah, we are well pleased!" the king proclaimed. "How often is it, Ioin, that a ruler can see such strength and beauty joined? A striking, wondrous means to an excellent end!" William took her hand, kissed it, and assured her that she had brought about peace for a great many people . . .

She felt chilled, as if a cold wind blew. "The feast! The feast!" Rupert, tall, thin, gawky, the perfect leader of the festivities, cried out. Where he led, the guests followed, and the crowd moved from the chapel and out to the hall where their wedding feast waited. She was hurried along in the midst of the crowd. Knights caught hold of her and stole swift, chaste kisses. Then she gasped with dismay, for she found herself in the arms of Jan de Fries, the Norman who had all but assaulted her in the shadows of the alcove. He gripped her hard against him, and his kiss was not like the light easy kisses she had received at the gentle hands of the others. Like her husband's at the altar, this was too long. Forced. She felt as if she was suffocating, and she struggled against him. She suddenly found help as her new husband caught hold of her shoulders, pulling her into the protective custody of his arms. She was shaking; no more so than Bret.

"Mind yourself, de Fries!" Bret warned. His tone was low. Quiet. Yet it seemed to still the entire room.

" 'Twas a kiss for the new bride, and nothing more!" de Fries said defiantly. His face was flushed; clearly he'd already been enjoying wedding wine. He bowed deeply to them. "The prize is yours, milord Bret! As always." He raised a chalice to them both. "To the earl and his countess, God bless them both!" At his words, the crowd cheered, and the sounds of laughter and conversation rose all around them again. But de Fries kept staring at them. "Perhaps you have not fared so well in this endeavor, milord! For there are a multitude of pricking thorns around this Scottish rose. She can be treacherous—ah, beauty can be that! And she can hurt, milord; perhaps it is you she will hurt!"

A fierce chill seemed to take hold of Allora as Jan de Fries stared at her.

"One more comment about my wife, de Fries, and I will slice you to ribbons here and now!" Bret said, and it was not a warning, but a statement of fact. De Fries again bowed deeply, then stepped quickly away.

And still, as they entered the hall for the feast, Allora could feel his eyes burning into her back.

Dear God, but the drunken fool was right about her!

"Ignore him!" she heard, and, turning swiftly, she saw the redhead who had been with her husband down the table, just the night before. The words should have been reassuring, but somehow, they were not.

She found herself seated next to Bret, forgetting the strange incident with de Fries as more and more people came to her and Bret, wishing them well as the wine and ale began to flow, as endless trays and trenchers of food were brought to the tables. She saw Bret smile, laugh, the handsome flash of his white teeth against the bronze of his flesh, his temper eased as he too forgot the incident. She herself smiled at someone else, an instinctive reaction. She reached for a chalice, suddenly desperate just to drink down a chalice full of wine.

Her fingers touched his. She met his gaze again, one that seemed a little perplexed. She drew her fingers back instantly. Jesu. She had done it. She had married him. Before God, she had sworn to be his wife . . .

And even if she didn't intend to hurt him, she would betray him.

"What?" she cried softly.

"Milady?" he inquired politely.

"What is that look?"

He shook his head. "I am just pondering just how—er—how I will manage you."

She snatched the chalice from him and drained its contents. Ah, such a mistake! She hadn't managed to eat during the day. Her head swam.

"You shall not—"

"Shhh," he said, and took the chalice from her hands. "Perhaps we should start over, Allora, since this has now come about. You *are* very much like an elegant red rose, deep within the leaves of the bush, so visible and tempting, yet defended so staunchly by such an array of thorns! I do mean to get through the thorns, milady."

She stared at him, swallowing hard, wondering if his words were something of a compliment, or merely another of his warnings. She turned swiftly from him, having no reply, and none was needed then, for someone was suddenly behind her new husband and he had risen, turning from her as well. She heard a soft feminine cry and bit her lower lip, but then found herself unable to resist the temptation to see just which woman now claimed his attention. It was the redhead again, and the young woman hugged Bret fiercely, kissed his cheek, and started to speak, but then someone called to her and she released Bret, promising to return swiftly. He took his seat beside Allora again. She wasn't sure what he read in her face, but he was suddenly amused again, so it seemed.

"What now, milady, is that look about?" he asked her.

Allora shrugged, pretending that there was nothing about him that could really be of any import to her. "She is quite lovely," Allora said dispassionately, inclining her head to indicate the girl who now talked animatedly with someone behind them. "Much prettier than any hedgehog. Imagine, had you really been a power unto yourself, you might have defied the king and married the lady."

"Oh, I don't think so," he informed her.

"Oh? Is she married already then?"

"Nay, that she is not!" he said lightly, his eyes sparkling.

"Then—"

"She is my sister."

"Oh!" Allora murmured, looking to her plate, feeling a renewed surge of anger against him. By all the saints, just how many relations did the man have? She willed herself to curb her temper, trying to remember that there were more important things at stake, then she turned to him, trying to keep her voice level. "Have you any more siblings or other relations running about the hall?"

He smiled, leaning back, muscled arms crossed over his chest, eyes sharp upon her. "Fallon said that she could not resist the temptation to meet you this morning, away from the court, before you had been formally introduced. I don't believe, however, that Elysia made any attempt to deceive you in any way on purpose."

"I repeat, are there any more?"

He nodded gravely. "Indeed. Robin, my father's heir, remains with him in Normandy. Philip, two years my junior, is with him also. The young woman coming toward us now, the one who looks so very much like a younger version of my mother, is Eleanor. And there, with Fallon, see the little urchin patting the hound? That is my sister Gwyn, who is two, and the true ruler of the household, so I believe."

She barely had a chance to see the pretty toddler playing with the hound before the girl with the raven hair reached them, hugged Bret, then anxiously waited to be presented. Allora found herself rising, and then being hugged by the girl as well.

"Mother said you were absolutely stunning, and I can see that!" Eleanor whispered. "Oh, the tales one hears are always so untrue! Why, it was rumored you had but one breast—"

"Eleanor!" Bret said firmly. His sister grimaced, but went on. "I'm sorry," she said. "I mean, I can see that you have both. Well, at the very least it appears so—"

"Eleanor!" Bret snapped, even more firmly.

Eleanor winced again. "Anyway, I'm delighted to see that you are so perfect and lovely. You see, I consider my brother to be quite perfect. He is built like Adonis, and is surely a better military commander than Alexander the Great. Even my father has said so. He really is perfect—"

"Eleanor!" There was a pained note to his tone.

"Even if he does like to dominate the situation and can be quite overbearing at times."

"Eleanor," he said yet again, warning in his voice. He

leaned close to her ear; still Allora heard the hissed whisper. "I will wed you to a toad in Father's absence if you don't behave this second!"

Eleanor smiled. "Excuse me!" she told Allora. "All best wishes!" she added, made a face to her brother, then obviously deemed it wise to depart as quickly as possible.

Allora stared after her, feeling a flush rise to her face. One breast? What did these people think of the border lairds and their offspring?

"She is very young, and far too talkative!" Bret murmured of his sister, still watching her depart.

Allora sank back into her chair. The wine chalice had been refilled. She drained it quickly once again, then felt his fingers curling around hers. "Enough, I think. For the moment."

Her breath seemed swept away as she felt him so close to her. His scent, clean and masculine, seemed to wrap around her. She wanted to scream as she felt the touch of his eyes upon her face.

"I'll not be told how much wine—"

"And I'll not have a bride retching throughout her wedding night," he said firmly. And she felt the touch of his whisper, warm, sending cascades of molten fire throughout her. "You were definitely forewarned, my lady. I have planned the most intimate of wedding nights."

Jesu!

She tried to ease her fingers from the chalice. They seemed frozen there. The room was suddenly overly warm—spinning. She looked around. Norman tapestries lined the stone walls of the fortress hall. Fires blazed. The brilliant colors of the nobility's dress seemed to meld together. Servants hurried from table to table. Ladies, with headdresses askew, leaned around their lords to speak with one another. Laughter rose as men and women reached for wine chalices together. Smoke rose from the hearth, creating a mist within the room. Rupert was playing his lute now, and it was amazing that the fool's voice could be so beautiful and plaintive as he sang a love ballad.

The walls seemed to be closing in on her . . .

Not for long! Not for long! she cried to herself.

He had just claimed to have an intimate night planned for her . . .

She lifted her chin, managing to meet his eyes. "Have you now?" she replied at last. *Nay, my lord!* she thought. *You shall sleep through your wedding night, and finally, I will have escaped you and this . . .*

Ah, *this!* This strange wild tempest in her blood he so swiftly created, the anger . . .

The passion.

He was studying her again. Jesu, Lord above her! She musn't give herself away!

"Indeed, my lady!" he said very softly. "As you will soon discover, Allora," he added. "In truth, I have done what I can to see that the night is made as comfortable as possible for you. Private. I bear you no malice, milady, and there are times when I do see beneath the thorns, and I am sorry that you were forced to be such a pawn."

"You, too, milord, are a pawn."

"But I chose for the play to be made for very specific reasons. So let us begin in peace, shall we?"

She leaped up, unable to bear sitting beside him for one moment longer, certainly unable to answer him. "My uncle!" she gasped in a swift excuse. Jesu, what if he tried to stop her from leaving him now? But he did not touch her. He watched her with his endless blue gaze and she stammered quickly, "I see him—my uncle, that is. Ah, I must go for a—for a moment. He—he beckons to me. Excuse me, I beg you . . ."

He caught her arm and she stared at him, alarm triggering her heart to a rampant beat once again.

"See him, lady. But remember this—you must come when you are summoned. And come quickly, else we shall both find ourselves greatly distressed."

She didn't have the least idea of what he was talking about, but she nodded vigorously.

She would have sworn to consume a bucket of living rats, anything, just to escape him at that moment.

She tore past him, hurrying to stand near the hearth where her uncle had been deep in conversation with his elderly friend, Lord Michael. Michael kissed her cheek, and wished her well. Robert cleared his throat, waving his wine chalice in his hand.

"I beg you, a word alone with the lass, Michael! Ah, but she's a great countess now, isn't she?"

"That she is," Michael agreed, bowing, leaving them very politely.

Robert lifted his chalice high then, as if he wished her the best for years to come. His voice dropped until she could barely hear it herself, yet she hung on every word. "The vial is by the bed. The town house is laid out simply, foyer and great hall downstairs, a door to the alley out back behind the kitchen in the rear. There is where I will find you. I will come there alone, from the moment you have departed the feast, and wait there with a horse. We will join your father just outside the city—"

"Why isn't Father going to be with us?"

"Because he is too damned noble in his own mind—he is best out of the city ahead of us. I fear for his safety if we are approached. You mustn't worry; we will find him on the old Roman road north. Then we will take to the forests along the lesser-known roads, but you mustn't fear, I know them all well." He came closer to her. "William is determined to head to Normandy immediately to attack some castle there. He must command that Wakefield accompany him, for he will need Wakefield's military expertise in the area, and also the number of men that he commands. We will be gone; they will have to hie to Normandy. All will be well. Don't forget! The vial is by the bed; I will wait with the horses in the alley!"

"Be there!"

He kissed both her cheeks, as if congratulating her heartily on her marriage.

And himself on his freedom.

But he whispered once again. "Allora, you must be there, niece! You mustn't falter. The man would not hurt you. Plead that he must drink wine with you before you can manage any marital duties." She felt her cheeks redden. "Take care that he does not see you slip the contents of the vial into his chalice. *Most important, Allora, be where I have told you to be!*"

Then he turned and left her swiftly, joining a group of lords who talked next to the hearth.

She looked around for her father but could not find him. In searching for him, she realized that neither could she see her groom, his mother, or his sisters. The hall was large and crowded with the curious; with King William's nobles, and her new husband's men. Too many of them, and all of them tried-and-true warriors, battle-scarred and heavily muscled. The din in the room grew louder. The guests by now had partaken of the feast, and of William's wine. The men grew louder, gruffer. The women grew more shrill. They seemed to be all around her, laughing too loudly, casting sly glances her way . . .

Suddenly, she felt a tap on her shoulder. She saw a face she knew, a sober face. Slim, handsome, earnest. She had met him earlier; Bret had introduced him as one of his closest companions, one of the best men in the Christian world to have as a friend, in battle or in peace. His name was Etienne, and he was dark-haired with lively hazel eyes. "Milady!" He caught her hand and pressed a kiss upon it.

"Countess!" said another man at her left. She whirled and saw that it was the knight Jarrett. She was caught between the two of them.

She didn't dare be rude, not at this point. She had to be so very careful now! To play everything perfectly. To be charming even to Bret, see that he drank the wine she poured for him.

"Your bridegroom has a gift for you, milady," Jarrett said. "If you'd be so good as to accompany us, just down the stairs to the courtyard below."

She frowned uneasily. Where was Robert? She couldn't even see her uncle anymore. Nor could she see the king, the Lady Fallon, or even Bret's sisters. She didn't see Bret himself. They had all disappeared. Norman knights she had barely met talked by the fire, hounds sprawled at their feet. Flames rose high on the hearth. From somewhere, a lady, one grown very tipsy from an abundance of wedding wine, began to laugh on a high, jarring note.

Where in God's name were her people?

"My lady?" Jarrett reminded her of his presence politely.

"I'm afraid I don't quite understand. All the property and settlement arrangements for the marriage were made among the Earl of Wakefield, my father, and the king. If a lord would have any gift for his bride, he would give it to her the morning after the wedding, I believe," she told them nervously.

She sought through the crowd for her uncle's form but he wasn't to be seen.

"Milady, your husband is a courteous man, and seeks to give you something very special tonight. We just need to reach the courtyard below."

"I must speak with my father—"

"After the gift, lady. It awaits us below. Milady, I swear that this is something the earl has insisted upon for your comfort and ease!"

She bit her lip, thinking that perhaps Bret d'Anlou had thought to give her a horse as a special gift with which to begin their marriage. How could she explain refusing to see what he might want to give? She had to be so very careful!

"Aye, then, sirs, if you must, show me this wondrous gift!" she said, offering them both a charming smile.

With her between them, they hurried for the stairs with what might seem an inappropriate speed for such an occasion.

"Wait!" she murmured, alarmed. She was the bride, the guest of honor for this feast. But the king's guards gave way quickly, as did the rest of the men wearing her bridegroom's colors. Before she knew it, she was being rushed down the full length of the stairs to the courtyard below, where saddled horses awaited them.

"I don't know what you two think that you're doing, but I will not be dragged about by you barbarians. What—"

"Lady, your husband summons you."

"My husband is somewhere above us—"

"Nay, he has already slipped out, and bade us help you to do the same."

"I can't slip out. I have to see my father—" she protested.

"Lady, you must quit making such a fuss. I'm already afraid we were noticed leaving. I swear to you by God above us! We are charged with helping your escape from this place by your husband."

"What?" She went stock-still. Escape? Were they friends of her uncle? No, no, they meant to escape the tower and the merrymakers.

"I can't come with you!" she cried in alarm. "Wait! The town house—are you taking me to his family's town house?"

"Nay, lady, that was the ruse! You'll not be followed now, you'll spend your night in peace."

"What are you talking about?" she demanded. She tried to jerk free from the light hold Jarrett had on her arm. "I can't come with you—"

"Jesu, lady! Cease your screaming! I've no desire to harm you, I swear it!"

"Then let me go."

The men looked at one another. "He said that we were to bring her immediately!" Etienne said unhappily.

And they meant to bring her. One way or another.

"No!" Allora cried, and she turned, ready to flee back to the tower. She had to reach her uncle!

But she had barely taken a step before she was suddenly blinded. A heavy cloak had been thrown over her head.

"I don't think he meant that we should deliver her in such a fashion!" Allora heard Etienne say with a groan.

She tried to assure him that he was quite right, but her words were garbled and muted. She struggled against the encompassing cloak, but she only managed to wind herself further within it. She kept twisting wildly, trying to shout and rail against them, trying, at the very least, to warn her uncle she could not be where the precious vial was to be awaiting her . . .

"Milady!" She could hear Jarrett's pleading voice. "I swear that you will be grateful to leave here and swiftly!"

He didn't understand! She struggled anew. She tried very hard to tell Jarrett that she would see him skewered on a stake.

All to no avail. Wound into a cocoon, she was lifted into someone's arms.

"Milady! You'll kill us both!" Jarrett pleaded. "Please, stop! Trust me, countess, 'tis for your own good!"

Tears stung her eyes. She let out another spate of muffled cries and dire warnings as she began to ride, blinded and bound by the cloak.

None of her threats seemed to matter to her husband's men.

The great Earl of Wakefield had spoken, and they had obeyed.

And now . . .

She galloped toward disaster.

Chapter 9

Bret stood before the fire, sipping wine, staring at the flames, and gravely contemplating what he had done. The hunting lodge had been well prepared for his evening's tryst with his new bride. Fresh linen sheets covered the bed, the pillows were huge and plump and made of the finest down. A warm coverlet of snow-white rabbit pelts lay over the foot of the bed, ready to enwrap a pair of laughing lovers. *If* there was ever to be laughter tonight.

A huge wooden tub, encircled by shiny brass fastenings, had been brought in and filled with steaming water; in the rear of the wide hearth, water remained in a kettle that still steamed and hissed, to be added if the tub cooled too swiftly. Wine had been left, as well as sweet Mediterranean grapes, brilliant-colored oranges, tiny bites of cheese, and twin loaves of bread, wrapped in linen cloths to keep them warm. There was little she could possibly find to condemn in the chamber where she was to spend her first evening of wedded bliss—other than the husband fate had cast her with whom to share it.

Brooding, Bret watched as a log burned within the blue center of the blaze. She had seemed to accept the marriage—even if she had stumbled somewhat over her vows. And she had seemed to burn like the log within the flames when he had drawn her into his arms and kissed her before the assembly in the church. Thinking of it now warmed his very blood, brought the fire into his limbs. He hadn't wanted to marry her, he hadn't wanted any part of her great inheritance, and he certainly hadn't wanted anything to do with hostile Scottish people. But in the days that had passed, with all his taunting and his determination that if he were to be saddled with a bride he would make her his true wife, he had learned that he did want one thing. Her. The Scotsman's daughter. With her wild tangle of incredible gold hair, her emerald eyes that betrayed so much: fury and fire, contempt, laughter, pity, sorrow . . .

"I will try!" he vowed softly to the leaping flames within the hearth. "By God, I swear that I will try to be patient and *not* let her run my temper ragged!"

Yet even before he heard the sudden, fierce pounding on the door, he had the intuition that this promise would not be an easy one to keep.

"Milord!"

Frowning, he hurried across the room, thinking that this thunder of fists against wood might waken the very dead all the way back in London. It was Etienne calling—he knew his man's voice well enough—and he quickly threw open the door.

It was indeed Etienne, along with Jarrett, and between them they were having a great deal of difficulty holding on to a squirming bundle within the confines of an encompassing brown cloak. Bret raised a brow, eyeing his men, who were clearly quite worn and frazzled. "Etienne, I believe my order was that you *ask* the lady to accompany you—"

"Milord," Etienne exclaimed with a sigh, "I do beg your pardon, but she—" He broke off, his feet shifting as he continued to struggle with his bundle.

Jarrett, more aware of the true circumstances of his marriage, spoke up bluntly. "Milord, your lady wife refused to come with us of her own accord. She was anxious to join her own brethren, yet I did not think that you would be anxious for anyone else to be informed of your whereabouts."

"Ah, so she would not come of her own free will?" Bret asked softly.

Etienne unhappily shook his head. Then he smiled with the eagerness of a loyal hound. "But she is here now, milord! And if you'll just—"

"Everything is fine," Bret said evenly. "Just set her down, my friends, and leave us."

"Aye, milord!"

Only too happy to comply, the men quickly set their bundle on the floor.

And just as quickly left.

The door slammed behind Etienne and Jarrett and Bret looked down at the squirming, swearing bundle that had been set before him.

Her head and arms flounced out of the cocoon, her eyes fiery, her golden hair a wild, tousled halo about her. Her chin was very high, quivering with rage and indignation.

"How dare you! Oh, how dare you!" she gasped, still entangled with the cloak and hunched upon the ground. "How in God's name dare you do such a thing, you horrible, wretched, pigheaded, serpentine, Norman . . . *creature!*" she snarled, struggling to free herself from the cocoon of wool wrapped about her feet.

"Allora," he began. He reminded himself he'd made a vow of patience, and he kept his voice soft enough, his determination at that moment only to explain. "I bade them ask you to come, and to tell you why." He stepped forward to help her, but her gasped "No!" brought him to a halt.

"No, don't *you* touch me!" she cried.

Bret held on to his temper and shrugged. Fine. Let her untangle herself, he thought, and he kept his distance while he waited for her to stand on her own power.

It was going to be a long night. He should have warned her vigorously that they needed to slip away without being seen, for if they did not, they might find half of the wedding party in the marital bed along with them. Maybe she would have understood. As it was now, she was outraged and furious.

And it did not bode for a good evening.

"Allora, come now. Let me help you."

"I told you not to touch me!" she cried, and finally freed herself from the material and stood. Yet once she was on her feet, she was suddenly not so loath to touch him.

"Bastard!" she hissed. And she flew at him, her fists flying with a wild and reckless will. She was amazingly powerful in her fury, and just as incredibly quick. She managed a solid strike against his cheek and several good blows against his chest before he caught hold of her arms, pinioning them to her side.

"Enough!" he roared.

She struggled anew, trying to free herself from his hold. Then she seemed to realize that her exertions were binding her to his body and she went still. "Let me go!" she charged him hotly, and her mere tone would have kept him in position even if releasing her had been promised to him as the sure road to heaven.

Then her tone changed. "Let me go—*please!*" Now there was a desperate note to the words, and as he really didn't want to start the night out with any more anguish than possible, he eased his hold on her. She spun from his arms quickly and stood near the door, like a slim golden bird about to take flight.

Bret stared at his reluctant bride with pure exasperation. She gasped for air, her breasts heaving beneath the beautiful silver wedding gown she wore. Her veil had torn free along with the gold circlet that had held it in place and lay on the woolen cloak that had engulfed her earlier. Her hair, rippling waves of pure gold, fell long and luxuriously down her rigid back. She shook, she trembled; her eyes were as feverishly bright as wildfire, never before so brilliantly emerald in their color. She was obviously so furious that she couldn't seem to find any more words to convey her complete loathing for him at the moment. Yet it seemed to be more than simple fury. A glaze of tears had given her emerald eyes that fantastic color. She was afraid of something. Him? She obviously hadn't relished the thought of this night, but he hadn't thought that she had ever been afraid of *him*. No matter what dire warnings he had given her, she had tossed her head and assured him that he was of no consequence in any way, no matter what he thought of himself.

"How dare you!" she cried furiously once again.

"You little fool!" he told her very softly. "I'd planned this escape for your benefit. Did you wish a public bedding?"

Perhaps she had never envisioned such a thing, for even as his words lay upon the air between them, her cheeks took on the color of new-fallen snow.

"Knowing your feelings regarding any of the intimate commitments of our marriage, my love, I meant every kindness in seeing that we both escaped those guests made lascivious by too much wine—and those made lascivious by nature—before they could too eagerly help us along the way in the consummation of our vows."

She remained very pale. Perhaps what might have happened had not occurred to her before, but she had very quickly grasped hold of a vision of how awful it could have been. And still a swift and startling cry of dismay escaped her. "But we are not where we are supposed to be!" she gasped.

He frowned, wondering what difference it could make to her where they spent the evening. He couldn't see how he could possibly have been more palatable to her at the house in London than he would be here.

Then it occurred to him that perhaps she had agreed to the wedding for one reason, and one reason only.

She had never meant to honor a single vow she had taken.

If it had been arranged that someone would come to her rescue, her refusal to come to him—one so strenuous that Etienne and Jarrett had all but abducted her—would make sense . . .

She had been anxious to get to her kinsmen.

A searing rage seemed to blind him for a moment. So much for patience. He had committed himself to the marriage, turned his back on the life he had planned, aye, even turned away from another. Aye, he had done it for his own reasons, just as he had known she had agreed to the wedding for her own advantage.

He had not imagined that she had intended treachery as part of her advantage.

Ah, lady! he thought. *You stood in that church and you made the vows! So help me God, but you will keep them!* He was glad that he had warned his men they must keep guard through the night. He would not be interrupted with a knife in his back even as he set himself to the evening's . . . rewards.

"Milady," he began, fighting the dark emotion that had washed over him, fingers clenching into his palms at his sides as he vowed he would not let her know this night that he was well aware of her intentions. "I planned the night at this gentle place with nothing but the utmost concern for your tender innocence! Indeed, I intended to make life as pleasant and easy for you as it might be. See, the fire burns, the room is warm, the rushes are strewn with flower petals, and all is sweet-smelling. The very best wine awaits us—"

"I don't want any more wine!" she snapped. "I want—"

"Trust me," he assured her, walking to the small, leather-covered three-legged table where the carafe and glasses awaited them, "you *do* want wine." He filled a glass and lifted it to her, smiling pleasantly. "You're going to need it." There was no threat in the words. Merely a deadly promise.

Allora, watching him, felt the wildest sensation of fear she had ever known shoot through her; it was as if she had been struck with a burning arrow and the flame was taking root throughout her. She had somehow betrayed herself, she knew. He had never made his intentions anything but clear, and now she realized that she had incited a depth of anger she had not seen in him before. He knew. She had betrayed herself so foolishly in her despair. She met his eyes, the cobalt command within them, searing as ice now. He stood some distance from her, striking in his fine attire, his shoulders broad beneath his silk shirt and tunic. He had never seemed such a threat before. What a fool she had been. Robert's plans would be to no avail tonight, his friends could not help her now. And the way that her new husband looked at her seemed to cause her blood to boil within her, a staggering weakness to assail her limbs. He had warned her. She should have heeded his warnings. Robert, her reckless uncle, was free. And now she was alone and would pay the price of that freedom.

Bret knew that she had intended to escape him. He hadn't made a move, yet his eyes seemed to slice through her, pierce her, condemn her. She was afraid of him, aye, afraid of his passion, his tempest, his anger. Afraid of the way that she had felt when he touched her, afraid that she would never be able to forget it. She couldn't forget the feelings that had assailed her when she had seen him engaged in a tender embrace with another, the shaking sensation of something like hot oil cascading through her body and limbs. And what now? Oh, Robert had erred, erred so greatly! It had been pathetically foolish to imagine that she could draw this man into their web of intrigue and think to escape him! He had agreed upon this path they were to take together. She had been given to him.

And even if he despised her, she thought desolately, he would not let her go.

Nay, there would be time to escape him later! Not tonight, but in the future, surely . . .

Yet, surely, what good would that do her? For her greatest fear of all was that, after tonight, she would sleep with him forever *in her dreams*. She would have felt those long strong hands upon the length of her. She would have known him, slept with him . . .

Desired him . . .

She let out a soft cry, and blindly, wildly, spun away from him again. No, she was doing this all wrong! She needed to turn back, to be sweet, humble, beg him give her time to come to know him before . . . before becoming his wife in truth.

"Allora!"

The tone of his voice brought her turning back to face him. She stared at the determined lord, *her husband now*, and felt again a sense of wild panic. His presence, his energy, was the greatest power in the room, and his brooding eyes focusing so intensely upon her caused a shiver of fearful anticipation to run through her. Dark, handsome, striking. Compelling by the very force of his command, and ever alluring despite her staunchest vows. She was coming to know him so well. Indeed, she knew the steel of his muscle, the raw vitality and force within him. Hardened in too many battles. The Conqueror's man.

He'd wed her; he would have her.

"You'll not leave me tonight, my love!" he warned very softly.

Apparently, Bret thought wearily, she didn't believe him. Emerald eyes touched his with their gemlike fire, and then turned away from him again; she whirled, spinning in her gold and silver cloud of beauty, as if she might escape him by simply running out the door. Perhaps she hadn't realized that his men would not have left him so completely, and that if he didn't manage to retrieve her swiftly himself, she would be scooped up again by Jarrett and Etienne. Yet before she could touch the door herself, a thunderous knocking sounded again, and the door burst open upon them.

Etienne stood there. He looked quickly from Allora to Bret. "They're coming, milord."

"They?" Allora gasped, stone-still and pale now.

What "they" did she think?

"How in God's name did they find us?" Bret demanded, deeply irritated, for being grasped and mauled by a drunk and sodden crowd was not something he had relished himself. Yet it was something that was simply done in Norman societies, in old English societies, in marriages blessed in Druidic days, Norse days, and Frankish days. There was even something so heathen as the *droit de seigneur* that could spill into a wedding, and that was the right of an overlord to claim a bride of his vassal on the first night of their marriage. As William was his only overlord, he was assuredly safe on that score, and it was a custom only claimed when the lord was an all-powerful one; the Church, of course, was staunchly opposed to it.

Yet public beddings . . .

They were considered good fun. A bride could prove her perfection and beauty. A husband his prowess.

He was definitely opposed to these things. He had tried to spare them both.

But then again . . .

Maybe his bride deserved what she was about to get.

"I think, perhaps, the disturbance when we left might have alerted someone—the countess was rather difficult to subdue, milord. Perhaps we were followed. The king's musician, Rupert, heads the group," Etienne warned. "Yet the king is one of the crowd. At least twenty are with him. They come even now!"

As Etienne spoke, Bret heard the noise of the merry-makers. Allora spun around, looking from Etienne's face to his. A startling pity seemed to seize him, wrapping tightly around his abdomen. She looked to him as if she sought help. Safe harbor. A protector.

A shame. There wasn't a thing he could do for her now.

"Make way!" Rupert, indeed leading the crowd, cried out merrily. Etienne was thrust forcibly into the room. Allora tried to back away from the doorway, seeking a defense somewhere, but several of the women had made their way in behind the musician, and she found herself quickly engulfed. She shrieked out a protest, but the women's laughter rose above the sound. She struggled, but they didn't seem to realize, or care. Bret was surrounded by the king's men himself, all of them pulling at his clothing and accoutrements.

"A toast! A glorious toast to a glorious pair!" Rupert cried out from the center of the chamber. He lifted a chalice high. "May their marriage be long and happy and fruitful, from this night forward!"

Bret's bride was obscured from him as the king's men— good-natured fellows deeply gone in their fine wine—raised him up and then laid him upon the fur-covered bed, divesting him first of his scabbard and boots, then wrenching from both ends his shirt and tunic and chausses. He heard a soft cry, and when he was jovially lifted back to his feet, he saw Allora at last through the sea of bodies that parted them, the men red-faced and laughing, the ladies with their headdresses and veils askew. And within them stood his bride, stark-naked now, shivering, her eyes wide and shimmering, her face as pale as ash. Her hair streamed over her body, enhancing rather than hiding any of its supple perfection. Bret caught his breath; he'd never been aware himself of just how exquisitely perfect she would be. Her flesh was flawless, alabaster and cream. He caught glimpses of legs that were long and slim and yet wickedly shapely. Her waist was tiny, her abdomen flat. Her breasts were beautiful, full and firm and round, peeking out with pink-crested nipples from the golden fall of hair around them. Left alone at last to stand there without the less-than-gentle feminine hands upon her to divest her of her clothing, she crossed her arms over her chest, hugging herself, then sank to the floor to cover more. "Nay, lady, nay!" one of the women, Lady Margaret Montague, cried, catching her arms and drawing her to her feet. "You would pluck the finest lord from the field, my dear! Look yonder at your groom, virile in all manner, lady! Take pride, and show all what grace and innocence and beauty you would bring him!"

Margaret had been one of Lucinda's very good friends, Bret thought, and she was resentful of the wedding that had forced Lucinda far from London; he was sorry for her, but this had gone far enough now. Allora looked stunned and appalled and already violated. Once she regained her wits, she might well assault Margaret, Bret thought. And even if she didn't, this had gone far enough.

Naked he strode through the crowd, sweeping the brown cloak from the floor and throwing it around his bride, pulling her into the shadow of his arms, thus hiding her nakedness, and his own to some extent.

"Enough, good friends! I beg you!" he entreated.

"Ah, but milord, you and your lady are not yet abed!" Rupert charged him quickly.

"Enough!" he repeated, and the word rang out in the room, a command that stopped all laughter and movement.

The king stood at the rear of the room. He had taken no part in any of the festivities; he had merely watched. Now he met the demand in Bret's eyes. The wedding was complete; the bedding nearly so.

"Aye, milords and ladies," the king cried, "we've set them off along their way merrily enough. All have seen the beauty of the bride, the power of the lord. Let's leave them to it, eh?"

He turned and left the room. It was a command to the others. One by one they trailed out, each calling "*Salut!*" as they departed, Rupert the musician performing agile somersaults out of the place as he did so.

At last, the door closed behind them.

To his amazement, Allora did not immediately fight him. Her knees seemed to buckle beneath her and he swept her up, grabbing hold of the chalice of wine he had been drinking before the invasion upon them, and carried her to the broad chair before the fire. She sat still in his arms, fighting tears, shivering, and accepting the chalice from him. If she had denied her need for wine before, she did not do so now. She swallowed down the contents of the chalice in a matter of seconds.

He sighed. "I tried to spare you that!" he reminded her.

She shuddered fiercely. Then she spoke softly and slowly. "Indeed, you sought to spare me. Find an even greater kindness in your heart for me and spare me just this night—"

"Nay, lady!"

Her eyes rose to his, her frustration apparent within them. Perhaps it was good, he thought, that she had been deeply humiliated by all that had occurred.

Now she grew angry again.

He held his arms tightly around her despite her sudden struggle against him once again.

"No, Allora," he told her. "You are wed to me. I've no desire to hurt you, but neither will I play games, or be anything other than your husband and lord."

"And master!" she charged.

He was silent for a moment. "If that is how you wish to see it."

Some sense of pity for her stole into his soul again as he saw the delicate rhythm of her heartbeat thunder swiftly within a blue-veined pulse at her throat. His mouth felt suddenly dry, for he realized again the extent of the beauty he held, for the Scots laird's daughter was a treasure infinitely fine in face and form. He had thought it before tonight; thought it again when she had stood naked and trembling before those determined to see them not just wedded but bedded, and he thought it again now, even as the encompassing cloak hid much of her glory from his eyes.

He suddenly lowered his lips to hers, seizing them quickly when she saw his intent and would have twisted away. She started to struggle, but discovered her arms caught within the cloak. He threaded his fingers into her hair, holding her face still to his, allowing her lips no quarter. He tasted the wine upon them she had so recently drunk. He tasted more. The sweetest honey, the wildest heat. Even knowing that he desired her, he was startled by the blaze that seared though him as his lips formed over hers, his tongue thrusting them apart, demanding entry. Some small whimper sounded in her throat. He gave it no heed, parting her mouth, tasting deep within it, his tongue seductive, his own hunger growing. He didn't know how long he tasted the sweetness, how long he sampled the heady innocence and beauty he discovered in her lips. He only knew that she ceased to struggle, that she lay slack in his arms.

He eased his hand from her hair, slipping it within the cloak. He rubbed his palm over the swiftly hardening peak of her nipple, then closed his fingers gently around the fullness of her breast. She squirmed again, but was caught within the folds of the cloak when she would have shoved his touch away. He lifted his lips from hers and stared into her eyes, grown brilliant now, the pupils dilated.

"You have not been cast into hell, my lady, nor am I a demon created from its fires," he told her.

Her eyes closed. "But aye, you might as well be!" she exclaimed softly, yet went silent when she might have said more, shaking her head.

Then her eyes opened to his again with a certain alarm painfully visible within them, and he realized that she had suddenly become very aware of the extent of his arousal, for though she was encompassed in the cloak, he remained naked. He stood with her, saying nothing, walking with her to the side of the bed and setting her down there. He turned from her, striding unself-consciously back to the small table, and poured her another goblet full of wine. He walked back to her. Her eyes fell to his lower torso, rose swiftly to meet his, her face feverishly flushed. "Take it," he said, offering the goblet.

"It will not help!" she prophesied huskily.

He shrugged. "It might."

She shook her head vehemently. "I need—time. I will fight you, I swear it. Fight you until hell itself should freeze—"

"Fight me then. Take the wine."

Her fingers curled around the chalice. She tossed her head back and drank deeply. She handed him the chalice, and he strode to the table to replace it there. When he turned back, he met her wild emerald eyes one more time. They fell against his length. Met his again.

Then she bolted. She leaped from the bed with nothing but the cloak about her, and raced wildly for the door.

Chapter 10

He caught her inches before she could reach it and swept her up hard into his arms, his hold upon her firm when she would have struggled.

Her eyes were liquid, she lay panting and breathless in his arms, and, for once, silent.

"Lady, lady!" he whispered softly. "You know I cannot let you go!"

She trembled. Her lashes fell to shield her eyes. Then they rose, and her gaze was full upon his once again. "It should not have come to this—"

"From the moment I said we would wed, I warned you it would be no other way."

He laid her down upon the bed, stripping away the cloak as he did so. She shivered; he quickly covered her body with his length, yet he did not think that she was cold within the fire-warmed room. She lay stiff in protest. He kissed her again, holding her within his arms, feeling the wild beating of her heart. He heard the snap and crackle of the fire, felt its warmth become one with them. At length, she eased against him. The wine had been potent. His determination was more so. She did not struggle against him, did not raise a fist to him. He rose slightly above her, cupping her delicate cheeks within his hands, finding that he trembled a little himself when he touched her. She exhaled on a shaky sigh, her eyes tightly closed. "Do it then!" she whispered suddenly, fiercely. "Be quick, dear God, be merciful!"

Startled, he held his weight upon an elbow and looked down at her, perplexed, a smile curving his lips. "Madam, I am not about to slit your throat, you know."

Her eyes opened. "I . . ." she began. But her words trailed away. She moistened her lips.

"Quick and merciful are most certainly not always the same!" he assured her with a trace of amusement. Then his amusement faded with the hunger and passion that filled him anew. "Quick? Never! But aye, lady, merciful! That I do intend to be!"

He slid his length against her once again. Captured her lips. Fire seemed to burst and blaze in all directions within him. Perhaps he would be quicker than he thought. He felt the thrust of her breast against his own nakedness, felt the softness of her thigh next to his sex. He stroked her throat and cupped her breast once again, and his hand strayed farther still, sweeping over her abdomen, sliding between her legs. He lifted his lips from hers, met her eyes briefly, then brought his liquid caress down the length of her throat, to the valley between her breasts. She shook beneath him. "Nay!" she cried softly.

"Aye," he promised against her flesh. His mouth closed gently upon her breast, tongue playing wickedly over her nipple, sweeping it again and again, sensually playing upon it. Her fingers fell into his hair. They tugged upon it, then eased. Dear God, but she was perfect. He hadn't wanted to wed her! he reminded himself. But now she was a fever within him, a longing so fierce it was unbearable. From the emerald of her eyes to the fullness of her breasts and the taut curve of her buttocks, she was beautiful and sensual. From the taste of her lips to the sweet musk of her flesh, she was erotic and arousing. He wanted more. More of this sweetness that seemed to drug his very senses. He rose above her. Her eyes were closed. She was still, and pale. He caught her finely shaped legs, parted them, and slid his length between them. Her eyes opened again, now with a shade of alarm. He held himself above her on his knees, the weight of his body blocking any chance of her twisting away from him in sudden denial.

Never quick, but merciful, aye . . .

He touched her lips lightly with his own, circled the shape of them with his tongue, plunged within the fullness of her mouth once again. His kiss then trailed the length of her slowly, teasing here, demanding there, touching one spot gently, tugging with a greater passion upon the delectable peak of her breast. Her hands fell upon his hair again, not tugging now. She twisted restlessly beneath him, her breath catching, then expelling violently as if she kept holding it. He sank lower and lower against her, creating a havoc and a tempest within his own blood, yet either some angel or some demon drove him on, and no matter what the rigor and agony within his own searing body, he was determined that his wild Scottish bride would not be able to look back on her wedding night and claim in her own heart that she was anything but willing at the final moment. His fingers played over her abdomen; the hot, damp trail of his tongue followed behind. He touched her lower, his fingers brushing first the golden triangle that guarded her innocence, then delving intimately there, parting her, stroking her. She twisted violently, a strangled sob escaping her, yet she gave him no coherent protest. And in seconds he felt a warmth within her, a dampness. He touched and touched, then gripped her hips firmly while he brought a liquid and searing caress to the tender bud of her awakening desire, seeking not only to arouse her, but ease the necessary pain of what was to come. Yet with each new determination to seduce her, he found himself newly hungered, his body tensing, muscles bunching, loins near screaming in protest. The sweet feminine scent of her, the way she twisted so wildly, arched, writhed . . .

At last, she arched high against him. She seemed to cease to breathe. He laved her once again. Teased her with just the tip of his tongue . . .

Her fingers were entwined in his hair. She twisted to the side, crying out, dazed. Stunned, still. Now the sweet liquid heat spilled from her, and a startling pleasure filled him. Aye, their marriage could work, he could indeed seduce his bride and . . .

Hunger for her. He could want her now with a force unlike any he had ever known before.

He rose above her. Her eyes were closed, her alabaster flesh was pale. She lay as still as she might in death, surrounded by the wild golden mane of her silken hair.

He did not hesitate, but lowered himself on and into her, feeling first the welcoming wet warmth, and then the barrier he had never doubted in Ioin's proud young daughter.

She didn't cry out. Her eyes remained closed; her head twisted violently to one side. He moved as slowly as he could, cursing himself silently for wanting her with such fierce desire at this moment.

"Lady—"

"Nay, don't talk!" she cried hoarsely, but her eyes met his briefly, glittering with the tears she fought back, and he had to wonder if she cried from the pain, or from fury with herself that he had managed to excite her to climax before claiming her innocence. She squeezed her eyes shut again swiftly, and set her jaw, still so pale, so determined not to cry out her pain.

"Allora . . ."

He locked his fingers with hers, allowing her to grip them with her agonized force. He began to move, a slow stroke, and her eyes flew open to meet his once again. He lowered his head, his lips touching hers, forming over them, gently, slowly. He kissed her with all the tenderness he could manage, filling her surely with himself, until he could bear it no longer. He moved within her, gloved by her, his invasion completed at last, his conquest nearly complete. Yet when he felt the fire ripping and burning in him raggedly, so ready to explode, he gritted his teeth and willed his hunger to abate, seeking to bring her with him once again. Her fingers dug into his back, her face lay buried against his sweat-sheened throat. She lay so tense and still then beneath him . . .

Yet a muffled cry suddenly tore from her throat. She arched violently, her fingertips tearing into his shoulders, then she lay stiff and trembling. A roaring tempest seemed to rush into his ears and burst into a volatile, violent climax himself, his body filling hers excruciatingly, the very life of him itself seeming to spill out of him and into her. After-tremors seized him, gripped him again and again, until at last he groaned, sweetly amazed, incredibly replete. He fell to her side, struggling back to sanity from the blinding sun-burst of pleasure he had discovered with his hostile bride.

"Oh!" she moaned, and turned from him, curling away, her knees drawn to her chest. Bret frowned, longing to linger awhile in a sensual mist, yet growing ever more irritated that she turned from him now as if he had taken her with some awful brute force.

He rolled himself, hiking up on an elbow, his chest nearly brushing her back. All that golden, glorious hair of hers was tangled around the both of them, and he eased a lock of it from beneath his elbow, then studied the woman who bit her lip and so determinedly looked away from him.

"I did my damnedest, lady, to ease this night for you. And lie all you will—"

"I never lie!" she cried. "At least, I never did. Oh, never mind—"

"Then if you do not lie, fair princess of the Far Isle, Norman *creature* that I might be, you will admit I did teach you far more than a maiden's loss this night! And if you intended to fight me until hell itself froze over, then Hades must be a frigidly cold place at this moment."

"How wretched, milord, that you should mock me in such a way—"

"Nay, lady! I mean no mockery, for I have been deeply pleased with not just your beauty, but your warmth."

He touched her upper arm gently. She jumped. He gritted his teeth, and eased his fingers up and down her flesh, noting now with a new and fantastic pleasure each subtle nuance of her beauty. Her breasts were wonderful, so full and taut, her waist was so very slim. And the feel of her naked flesh . . .

"Quit hating me and admit that it was not so terrible!" he demanded in grating tones.

She did not answer, and he rolled her to him. Her lashes veiled her eyes.

"Look at me," he ordered.

Her lashes rose at his command. Her eyes were all emerald-green defiance.

"I warned you, Allora," he told her softly, "before we wed—several times!—that I would take no bride in name only for convenience's sake. I crave sons, lady. No man serves so long in warfare and rebellion to earn titles and lands who does not look to the future for heirs to claim what he has gathered by his sweat and blood!"

She trembled beneath him, despite the wild look in her eyes. Her lashes fell again.

"Then hate me!" he snapped suddenly, harshly.

Her gaze rose to his. "I—I do not hate you!" she whispered, the words soft and pained. Then more of them spilled from her lips, honest words, still so softly spoken. "I was grateful for your kindness to my father, and admired you for it. You must understand. It is simply that you are—a Norman."

She might have been stating the sad fact that he was a leper.

"You will bear Norman offspring, milady," he warned her, stroking her cheek once again. She paled once again, seeming to take on the color of new-fallen snow. He laughed lightly, leaning back against the pillows and hardwood headboard, and scooped her resisting form up with him. His arm lay around her then. Her head rested upon his chest. She tried to fight his hold but once, then lay against him wearily, her cheek against his flesh, her hand resting lightly upon his ribs.

"There's not so much to fear as you might imagine," he told her. "I know that once, long before the Conquest, when my mother was but a child, she told some village children that Normans had horns and tails. My father and a number of men in his party heard her words, and someone reported back to William. When I was young myself I can remember how William teased Mother, telling her that he hadn't seen a tail sprout out of a one of us yet."

She pushed up suddenly, seeking out his eyes. "Your mother knew!" she charged him softly. "Even before the Conquest, by your own words, your mother knew that Normans were demons!"

He sighed with exasperation, pressing her head back down again. "Lady, that was not the point of the story!"

"Then what was?"

Did she tease him? Or taunt him? He threaded his fingers into the tangled mass of her hair and drew her face back to his once again. "The point is, milady, that you will bear fine, beautiful children."

"You are quite something, milord!" she responded with her chin high and eyes challenging once again. "If you seem so powerfully confident that one . . . experience together will guarantee you a child!"

"One?" He arched a brow. She saw her mistake. Her eyes quickly darted from his and down the naked length of him, seeing that he was most assuredly aroused once more, and back again.

"But—"

"Alas! You've shattered my confidence completely. I shall need numerous experiences to believe in my ability to sire a child now!"

"Nay, Bret!" she cried softly, using his given name at last. Her head tossed wildly. "Nay—"

"Allora, I am neither a fool, nor inexperienced," he told her gently. "I know that you reached some pinnacle of pleasure when I touched you!"

She flushed at his words, not denying them, but shook her head. A soft glaze of valiantly fought tears seemed to shimmer within her eyes. "Aye, there was . . . pleasure!" she whispered. "But milord, agony, too!"

"Ah!" he murmured. "But I swear, Allora, there will be no pain this time. I promise you."

He pressed her back into the soft bed amidst the down pillows, cupped her cheek and kissed her. Her heartbeat raced frantically beneath his hand as he caressed her breast, exploring again its fullness and contours and the pebble-hard crest. His initial desire slaked, he could truly take his time, letting fire and passion build within them both. He still asked nothing of her. And at first she did nothing but shake beneath him. Yet subtly she began to change. Her fingers soft upon his hair, stroking over his shoulders, nails grazing them. Having her had done nothing to ease his fascination; rather he found it increased. He tasted and stroked the length of her, pressing kisses behind her knees, upon the arches of her feet, stroking her calf and thigh, making love to her all around the point of her greatest sensitivity, then parting the golden down with the thrust of his thumb, finding her heat, her liquid warmth.

He looked to her face; saw that she lay with her eyes closed. "Look at me!" he charged, but she shook her head from side to side, golden hair flickering in the candlelight with each wild movement. "I cannot!" she cried, and he did not press the issue then, but rather pursued his course, parting her, stroking her, bringing wildfire with his hot liquid caresses and demanding strokes. When he rose above her again, he paused briefly, very softly commanding, "Now, lady, look at me." She did so, eyes so beautifully glazed. For once, for that moment, he thought, she was his. He was not the Norman, she was not the princess of the Far Isle with a host of people she would ever fight for. For this precious moment, she was his wife, he was her husband— but perhaps that was not even the point. She was simply his, as any woman might be a man's, and what passed between them was theirs only, and would be burned within some shared and mutual memory.

He smiled at her, seized hold of her lips tenderly, then spoke softly above them. "No pain, lady, I promise you."

And there was none, he was quite certain. For when he thrust within her, a soft gasp caught within her throat. Her arms wound around his shoulders.

And within seconds, she moved with him, fluid, graceful, incredibly arousing and exciting, her arms, her body, gloving his . . .

Again, within her, he reached a fantastic climax. He waited until he felt her body strain wildly and give, then allowed free rein to his own passions, and when he was spent, he lay back, soaked, exhausted, and amazed.

He had never imagined that he could discover such a sweet-tasting ecstasy with her.

"No pain?" he whispered softly.

"No pain," she admitted, and he drew her to him, her back resting against the length of his chest and body, his arms protectively around her. In time, they dozed, but he awoke later and discovered that he had grown hard against her, that her back was as arousing as her front. She slept, but he stroked her flesh up and down her spine until she writhed within her haze of sleep, then he awoke her, sliding within her from behind, pulling her hard back upon him. He heard her gasp, yet not a whisper of protest, and even as the surcease of climax came upon him, he heard the softest cry escape her, and he buried his face within her hair, incredulous once again, amazed to have discovered such a prize when he had been so very determined not to have her.

He held her in silence, then rose, discovering he had acquired an appetite. He thought she slept again, but she asked softly, "Have we water? The wine is certainly potent and good, but I am not accustomed to it, and pray that I'll not have a pounding head tomorrow."

"Good English ale, eh?" he inquired.

She shrugged. "Nay, sweet, clear *Scottish* water."

He smiled, not replying. She was sitting up, the linen sheets pulled to her breasts, her hair spilling all around them. "Water, my princess, indeed. Whatever you should desire." She flushed slightly, but offered him a tentative smile, and he brought her water and a tray with food. He sat at the foot of the bed, slicing the bread and cheese, offering her the first cuts. She took them from him hesitantly, then seemed to discover that she had acquired an appetite herself, and she quickly, if still delicately, ate what he had given her. She leaned forward, reaching for a grape, lost her sheet, flushed, and grasped at it once again. He might have told her that there was no longer anything she could hope to hide from him, but he held his peace, plucked up a grape, and held it before her mouth. She hesitated again, but then took it with her lips, her eyes falling as she chewed it. He rose again, restless, and noted the bath, grown cold now; but the kettle still steamed above the fire. He poured the hot water into the tub, then stepped into it, sighing as the heat burned into his muscles, closing his eyes to luxuriate in it. He opened an eye to her then, and found her watching him. "What is it, my love, that you're thinking behind those emerald eyes? Did you agree to wed me for just such an opportunity as this to slice open my throat?"

She seemed to choke upon her water, and her flesh took on a flush now that somewhat alarmed him. But she shook her head vigorously. "I would never intend to murder anyone, milord!" she denied hotly.

"Ummm," he murmured. "Poor lass! You did wed for one reason, and one reason only!"

"You had your reasons," she reminded him stiffly. "Even if they were not so clear."

He opened his eyes fully, arching a brow. "Come join me. I'll explain my reasons."

She shook her head. "I think there is safety where I am."

She let out a startled cry as he rose, dripping wet, and swept her from the bed and back into the tub with him. The water did not quite cover her breasts as she faced him across the circumference, and she crossed her arms as nonchalantly as she might. He lowered his head, smiling, teasing her buttocks with his toe, and received a dark scowl for his efforts. He laughed aloud, catching her arms, kissing her lightly. "Lady, lean back. Relax. There is naught that you can keep from me."

She bit her lip, not moving. "You said that you would explain your reasons. I heard rumor that there was something to do with your mother. Yet I cannot imagine you commanded by any parental dictate, though I know that she is a Saxon, and therefore I believe you fear for her sometimes where William is concerned. Still," she murmured, and the words were somewhat bitter, "since you are his great warrior and champion just as your father, one would think that her birth would have come to mean very little to the Conqueror."

He arched a brow again, watching her. "My sweet innocent!" he said very softly. "My mother is not just a Saxon."

Allora frowned, having at last seemed to have forgotten that they shared a tub, naked. "Then—"

"My mother is Fallon, from the house of Godwin. King Harold Godwinson's daughter. Aye, and lady, I can promise you this! If you have difficulties with many things Norman, you can well imagine that hers have always been tenfold!"

She stared at him, stunned. "You are Harold Godwinson's—grandson?" she demanded in a whisper. "Why did no one tell me?" she asked with dismay.

He shrugged. "I assumed you knew. Yet how my Saxon lineage would make anything worse—"

"Oh, God!" she breathed, staring at him.

"What is it?" he demanded, leaning forward.

Though she still seemed distressed, she shook her head vehemently.

"Actually, milady, think on this—your children, in truth, will not be so very Norman. They will be half Scottish, a quarter Saxon, and but a fourth Norman as well."

She nodded, but her features seemed tense and pained.

"For the love of God, Allora, what is it?"

"I am surprised, that is all. But my God! How could she live with it, with your father, with William . . ." Her voice trailed away and she bit her lip.

"William has always claimed that England was his by the word of Edward the Confessor himself. Mother saw her father swear an oath of fealty to William, even if that oath was forced, since she and Harold were his prisoners. She has never really surrendered. But she knew my father long before the Conquest, and she loves him. They made their own peace."

She stared down at the water. "William claims England by inheritance, by right!" she exclaimed suddenly. She looked back up to him with her eyes blazing in challenge. "So by what right does he try to claim his little bits and pieces of Scotland?"

"The lords of the Far Isle," he said patiently, "whether they called themselves jarls, earls, kings, or lords, long ago gave their fealty to England."

"But they give it to Malcolm now—"

"Alas, William believes that what was once English will remain English, and that is that."

"But—"

"I'll not argue this tonight!" he told her.

With effort, she bit back her words. He leaned forward once again. "I am still confused as to why my mother's royal Saxon lineage should so disturb you."

She shook her head. "It does not!" she vowed. She lied, he was convinced.

"Allora—"

"Milord, but I have grown so cold!" She shivered suddenly, fiercely. Instinctively he rose to his feet, scooping her up into his arms. He stepped from the tub, set her upon the floor before the fire, and reached for the linen towels that awaited them. He wrapped her swiftly in one before drying himself with the other, still not quite certain how she could be so cold, for the fire warmed the room well.

"Lady—" he began again.

"I am still so cold!" she said, and she stood there, bathed in the firelight, her skin glowing softly, her hair as radiant as the sun. He cast aside his towel and took her within his arms. "I will warm you," he promised her. Her eyes met his. Her fingers entwined behind his neck. She lifted her lips to his, parted them to his kiss.

It was later, much, much later, when she lay sleeping beside him again, that he looked to the ceiling and sighed, gritting his teeth.

Women learned so swiftly.

When he had sought an answer from her, distrusting her protests, she had used a power she had so recently discovered. Her kiss could waylay his questions; the sweet, erotic rhythm of her hips could make him forget that he had ever voiced them.

Perhaps it was not so important. In all, the night had been incredible. He looked at his sleeping bride once again and felt a fierce tension seize hold of him. He had not imagined that any woman could create such a desire within him in one night, could arouse such passions, such a deep tempest. She covered nothing now, but slept against him naked, her hair splayed over him, her slim white hand upon his bronzed flesh, just above his abdomen.

Well, she was his wife. The vows were spoken, and fully consummated.

Then why this irritating doubt that ran cold along his spine?

He didn't know, and he no longer cared to wonder through what was left of the night. He curled against her, holding her tight.

And at last, he slept as well.

Chapter 11

She awoke strangely, as if she had come, perhaps, from the depths of an encompassing dream, and at first, she couldn't quite discern where she might be. She felt warmth at her back, the smooth feel of the linen sheets beneath her fingers. She slowly became aware of the arm around her, and that the warmth at her back, alarmingly comfortable and secure, came from the length of the man who cradled her in his arms as he slept. The man she had married.

Then she dared not move. Her hair was caught beneath his shoulders, his leg was cast atop hers. Looking down to her hip, she could study the fingers splayed atop it, long and very dark against the paleness of her flesh.

She wasn't supposed to be here. She was supposed to be on a horse, running north, running free and far from here. And instead, she was hopelessly entangled, with no way out. And the worst of it was that a certain part of her no longer wanted a way out.

She had heard so many things about marriage, of course, but she'd never imagined just what it could be. And she'd never imagined Bret could be so tender, or so determinedly seductive. It seemed absolutely amazing, the difference that a night could make. She had wanted to hate him— it had always been so easy to be angry with him! Maybe even, once trapped, she had wanted the night to be a wretched misery, something from which she could easily run away.

But it hadn't been miserable. Lying awake, afraid to move, she suddenly closed her eyes tightly, wanting to hold onto the moment. She couldn't remember ever feeling so strangely peaceful. She had never been held so securely. She had never begun to imagine the magic that she could feel, and if she was afraid of anything, she was afraid that she might never come to a place in her life again when she could know such sweet and soaring pleasure, to rest again in such secure comfort. Eventually, she would have to move, have to awaken. And somewhere out there, the world would intrude again. She could not forget who she was, or that she owed her father and a whole nation of people a different loyalty. And then there was Uncle Robert, of course. A free man now.

She shifted slightly, then realized that Bret was awake. She turned slowly within his arms and met his eyes, and found that he had probably been awake for some time. His pillow was more highly propped than her own, and he had easily been able to study her face. She flushed slightly, wondering at his thoughts, her lashes falling quickly lest she give away any more of her own.

Then she wasn't wondering at his thoughts anymore; she felt his body tense and tighten next to hers, felt the cup of his hand upon her cheek, and before she could speak, his lips touched hers, forceful, seductive, denying any chance of protest. In moments, she didn't care. There was nothing to be lost now. She allowed herself the freedom to touch him in return, finding a curious thrill in the hot feel of his flesh beneath her fingers, the great, rippling expanse of muscle upon his chest and shoulders. She closed her eyes and savored the sensations that swept through her, until they burned anew, and she reached for surcease, and rose there at last on a sweet pinnacle of wildfire. She drifted down slowly, felt again the security of his arms around her, and she thought, *if only . . .*

She found him on an elbow studying her again, and again she flushed, instinctively pulling the sheet to her breast, her fingers moving nervously over it. He didn't stop her, but when she looked into his eyes again, they were still grave and intense. "What?" she asked in some dismay.

"I'd give so much to know what was going on in your mind," he said lightly.

She felt another soft red wave color her face, and her lashes covered her cheeks. And then she decided simply to tell him the truth.

"I was wishing that you were not a Norman," she told him.

He sighed. "Hasn't my mother's ancestry somewhat redeemed me from being entirely a monster?"

She still couldn't quite look at him. "Many things have redeemed you from being entirely a monster," she admitted softly.

He laughed and sat up, suddenly sweeping her into the circle of his arms. She didn't struggle, and was startled to see the tenderness in his eyes when they touched hers. There was still amusement within them, but it was a gentle humor now. His eyes had never seemed so light a blue, so sky-like; she had never seen such a curve to his lip. His hair was tousled and a rakish black lock fell over his forehead. She didn't think that she had realized his youth before, that he wasn't really so very many years older than she was. He was always the ultimate warrior, cast into William's world of battles and power so long that he seemed too assured, too confident, too powerful, to ever be really young. She had not thought that he could be charming as well as striking, nor had she known that he could laugh so pleasantly.

And certainly, she had never imagined that he could look at her as he did now, with that laughter in his eyes. A look so very close to tenderness.

"I admit, my love," he said softly, "I must take back a few of my own words. You are infinitely superior to the very best of hedgehogs."

"My lord! Such flattery will swiftly turn my head."

"My lady, I'm quite certain that young swains filled with flattery have been turning your pretty head for years. I dare not take such matters too far, for I wouldn't want you to grow too confident!" he warned her.

Within his arms she gazed curiously at him, then found that, despite herself, she was smiling slowly again.

"You fear my confidence, milord?"

"Indeed I do. For I wouldn't want you to think that I was so besotted I might grow careless."

"You are assuming I wish you to be careless?" she challenged him, but in spite of her very best efforts, her lashes fell, and her voice was breathless.

"I do," he said lightly. His hand stroked her hair and she looked to him again, entranced again with the handsome planes of his face, the cobalt sizzle within his eyes. "The fact that I find myself well pleased with my marriage this morning does not change the fact that you are convinced you are wed to the enemy."

She flushed, wishing that she did not give herself away so quickly in this manner she could not control.

"And there's the truth!" he whispered softly. But he smoothed his fingers over her cheeks, reflective for a moment. "But a truce for today, I think."

"Today?" she murmured.

"Tomorrow we will return to my family's town house, as I cannot keep so many men out here idle."

She stiffened, ready to jump away from him, her eyes suddenly searching out the nooks and crannies of the place.

"They're not in here, milady!" he assured her humorously. Then reminded her with a light tone of reproach, "I tried to spare us both the audience we acquired last night!"

"Then—" she protested.

"They are outside, my lady."

"Why?"

"So that your wretched uncle does not have a half dozen Scots breaking in to murder me in my bed, milady."

She lifted her chin. "My uncle would not do such a thing."

"Your father wouldn't; your uncle would."

She almost told him that in certain circumstances, he must not be so assured about her father. But she stared down at her fingers, clutched against his bronzed arm, and held her silence for a moment. Then she asked him, "What on earth could my uncle do, milord? We are outside London town. Within the shadow of William's mighty tower, surrounded by Normans!"

"Lady, never underestimate your uncle!" he warned her, and she was startled by the chill that seemed to snake down her spine, even with him holding her. But he was moving suddenly, setting her upon the pillows, then leaping up naked to stride toward the door.

"Wait!" she gasped, aware that he meant to open it.

But he glanced at her over his shoulder and continued as she dived beneath the covers. But he barely cracked the crude wooden door and spoke with someone just outside of it. Nervously she watched him as he returned and slid beneath the covers once again, his flesh now very cold from the chill within the room.

"Have you invited an audience now for the morning after?" she demanded, then felt the coldness of his feet against her own. "Oh! Get them off of me, they are freezing."

"Aye, and aching to be warmed. We need a fire," he told her.

"Aye, and perhaps you should be building one."

"Perhaps I will!" he told her softly. He kissed her forehead and left the bed again, deftly building up the fire again with thatch and kindling and logs, and crouched there before the golden blaze, the fire coloring his body, enhancing the hard-muscled sleekness of his form. A moment later, there was a light tapping on the door. Bret found the cloak that had enwrapped Allora the night before and threw it around his own shoulders before opening the door. His man, Jarrett, was there, offering him a covered tray. Bret thanked him, and the door closed again.

She could instantly smell the fascinating aroma that wafted from the tray. She assumed that he would bring the food to her, but he didn't. Rather, he set the tray before the fire, wrenched a fur from the bed, and sat upon it, lifting the cloth that covered the food to keep its warmth. The delectable scent of roasted meat was nearly more than she could bear. She had eaten so little in the past few days, and now she was ravenous.

"Over here," he told her, patting the fur by his side. He had already sliced and picked up a portion of meat with the small sharp knife that had protruded from the haunch of venison there. He nibbled at it hungrily, sucking the juice from his thumb as he watched her and waited.

"Milord, I thought it was customary for a man to gift his wife upon the morning after their wedding—"

"Aye, lass! It is also customary for a woman to serve her lord! Then again, perhaps I have been well enough served." He leaped easily to his feet. She gave a little cry as she found herself scooped up with a wrap of fur herself, and brought in his arms to be set before the fire where he joined her again. He sliced a piece of meat and she took it delicately with her fingers, then nearly swallowed it whole. He laughed and cut her more, and poured out chalices of cool water for them both. When they were done with the food she found herself leaning back against his chest, encircled by his legs, while they both watched the flames. "I do have a gift for you, you know," he said softly.

"Aye?"

"A manor in Wakefield. The title is free and clear. I remain the overlord, of course."

"A manor? And I have given you an entire island?"

He laughed. "The isle remains your father's, milady, I would remind you. And I do honor that good man, and pray that he lives on for many, many years. I would only seek to claim it at his death, and perhaps my own could precede it!"

She shivered, then cast aside the unease she had suddenly felt. He was right. Her father was a healthy, vigorous man. And in truth, Bret had never claimed any great interest in possessing the Far Isle. His visions, she knew, had encompassed far different lands.

And a different wife.

She threw off that thought too, and, lifting her chalice, though it carried nothing but cool water, she said, "To my father's health."

"Indeed," Bret agreed. "And would you drink to the king's health as well, my lady?"

"Only if he were here with a knife at my throat promising to slit it if I did not."

He was silent for a moment. She felt his breathing, felt his heart beat at her back.

"Bear in mind that your Malcolm is the same as any other king, my lady."

"Malcolm gave support to Edgar Atheling—"

"Malcolm is wed to Edgar Atheling's sister, who has considerable will of her own, and certainly, Malcolm would have been happiest with Edgar as king of England. But it isn't going to happen. Anyone can see that. William remains a powerful man; his sons already squabble over the vast properties he will leave them. William came here and found villages of wood and daub and thatch, and he built great castles of stone. Things are not going to change, milady."

"You're talking about the exact things that frighten me!" she told him. "The Norman way is different! Before William came, men were not so afraid. They did their duty for love of one another rather than fear for their lives. They were never so subjugated. You must try to understand my people, too. Family is everything. Father heads ours now; Robert will head it at Father's death. Neither you nor I ever will, even if I were to rule the fortress. My guards were the children of sheepherders and farmers; men could prosper to become either warriors or to hold and work their own land. Now, they are forever bound to service, as is William's way! I don't see how your mother ever managed to endure your father—" She broke off, wincing. She hadn't meant an insult at the moment; she had just been trying very hard to explain what it seemed that Bret had missed.

But he wasn't offended; he laughed, and his arms locked nonchalantly about her as he said, "There's still a fierce battle that ensues upon occasion, of course. But, my love, my mother knew William and my father long before the Conquest. My father was a good friend of my mother's, even if they did fight for different causes. It's been a good union, I think. William and his half-brothers have spent a great deal of time in Norman affairs, and, except for the last few years, my father has remained here in England, fighting Harold's battles for him, in a way. My father has urged William to recognize some English law, and English rights."

She twisted at that, arching a skeptical brow.

He smiled, nuzzling the top of her head with his chin. "It's the truth. Aye, William has done damage here in his revenge against some of the rebels. Malcolm has done the same, all but creating a no-man's-land south of the River Tweed. But—"

"Aye, there's truth enough of the king's destruction!" she interrupted passionately. "I've heard that he is not even counting the four northern counties of Northumberland, Cumberland, Westmorland, and Durham in his great 'economic census,' his Domesday Book!"

"As I said," Bret told her, his tone even and firm, "your wondrous and wily Malcolm is equally responsible for the destruction of the land there. And since we began this discussion with your censure of my father, I would have you know that there were numerous times when he prevented destruction when destruction wasn't warranted. He kept many villages from being pillaged and burned."

"So your mother has tolerated him for his strength, and made a decent-enough marriage of it!" Allora said softly.

"No," he said, "my mother loves him, and he loves her, and that is why they have made a very decent marriage of it."

She couldn't see his face then, but she felt the simple truth to his words, and wondered what he thought of his own marriage at that precise moment.

"She must have just adored him when he arrived on her father's shore with a conquering army," she remarked dryly.

"Well, I've heard the story a few ways," he said lightly in reply. "He came ashore, won the battle, seized my mother, raped her, and that was that. Then there's another story in which my mother threw herself upon my father's mercy, and he was completely beguiled—and that was that."

"And which story is true?"

"Well, my mother is not the type to beg for mercy, but then, neither would my father have been beguiled beyond duty by any woman. And so I imagine the truth of it all lies somewhere in between. They had always cared for one another. Once Harold was dead and William had come, my father was given the lifelong task of keeping a distance between William and my mother, since there never was going to be a truce. Perhaps he did seize her, but he saved her life. He didn't marry her at first—in fact, I believe my brother Robin was just hours away from entering this world when they were legally wed."

"Ah!" Allora said softly.

"You are condemning my father again."

"I'm sorry. He *is* the one who made you a Norman."

He ignored that. "They're very lucky," he said after a moment. "They are among the happiest people I know."

She pulled away from him for a moment, drawing the furs to her chest, studying his face. "Life must be good for you. You grew up beneath the Conqueror's very wing, beloved of both parents and of both peoples—the Saxons who are grateful your forces don't pillage them, and the Normans who upon occasion let you sway them to be moderate in their rape and murder."

"The battle of Hastings was fought before either of us was born, milady!" he told her, and there was a note of warning in his voice once again. "And life is what we make it," he told her after a moment, then added softly, "princess! For I hear that's what you've been called. The princess of the Far Isle! Adored by all who come forward to cast their gifts at her feet."

"Life is what we make it!" she reminded him.

"And you have made yours by studying your uncle's view of history—"

"I should have studied William's?"

"You should not be asked to fight Robert's battles for him. Especially when he is ever ready to risk your neck— or your father's—in his endeavors."

She stood in a sudden fury, feeling the bitter sting of tears behind her eyelids. She had been a fool to feel such comfort and security. He was right. She was his enemy. She could not help but be so.

"You've no right to speak about my uncle like that! Just because everyone else gives up—"

"Gives up! William has fought down rebellion after revolt after rebellion! The Welsh have risen, the Danes have come and taken their turns, the Northumbrians and the Yorkists have all taken a turn. What you don't understand is this: William has taken hold of England. It is his by conquest, and, according to many, by right. He has made no claim on Scotland; the border lairds so determined to fight him on English soil will wind up with their necks stretched!"

"The Far Isle bows to Malcolm!"

"And before that, to a heathen Viking!" he said.

She swung away from him, longing to run somewhere, anywhere, but if she did run out into the cold, he would merely bring her back. And his loyal men would wrap her up in some other garment and see that she was duly returned. She walked across the room in silence and turned her back on him, staring blankly at the wall, wondering just what would become of her now. She felt his touch upon her shoulder and jumped; she hadn't heard him move.

"Let's go riding," he said.

"What?"

"Let's go riding. In the woods."

"What if I outrun you and escape?"

"You will have to run very, very fast," he warned her.

"I have nothing here," she reminded him. And fingers suddenly seemed to curl with a painful squeeze around her heart. "I never knew we would be here last night. You neglected to tell me how courteous you were planning on being."

He ignored the slight taunt in her voice and turned from her, walking to the rear of the room where there was a leather trunk set in the shadows.

"Milady," he replied, casting the trunk open and crouching down before it, "I did plan well, the only flaw in my plan being my unawareness that my bride would refuse to come to me."

She fell silent at that and waited. A moment later he had found what he wanted, and he returned to her with a handful of clothing. She found a man's chausses, a warm shirt and tunic, and very soft doeskin boots. She looked over at him but he was already halfway dressed, and so she turned away from him and quickly donned the clothing he had brought her.

He stretched out his hand to her. "Come on."

She hesitated, then joined him. Outside, tethered near Ajax at a tree, stood Briar, and Allora couldn't help but think that if her horse had been brought here, her father now knew where she was—as did Robert. Anyone might know where they were by then, because they had been seen leaving last night, and the king's party of merrymakers had followed them here.

Her uncle, the man who had been so convinced that escape would be so easy, had not tried to reach her . . .

He couldn't have reached her. Three of Bret's men—Jarrett, Etienne, and a slim, wiry Frenchman called Gaston—were all seated around a fire they had built in the small clearing before the crude little house. She was certain that more of his men would be nearby.

The men at the fire rose when she and Bret came outside, awaiting his orders, nodding their heads in a cautious manner toward her. Bret waved them back to their seats upon the earth and swiftly lifted Allora atop her horse.

"Aren't they following us?" Allora asked Bret.

"Should they be?" he asked her, mounting Ajax.

She ignored the question and took hold of her reins, and, seeing the trail before her, took flight upon it. Briar was a wonderful mare, small, yet beautifully sleek and powerful. She could run like the wind, and she was doing so now, giving Allora the sweet feel of the air hard against her cheeks, the whip of her hair about her face, the feel of thunder beneath her as she raced. Even the sting of tears from the sudden wild wind felt good.

Could she outrun them all? she wondered. Race and race, until she had outdistanced every one of them?

Briar was swift, but Allora quickly realized that no matter how fast the little mare was, she was no match for Ajax. Her husband's mount was quite remarkable, reminding her of the eight-legged creature that bore the Viking's god Odin across the storm-swept skies. She heard Bret and Ajax coming behind her, and slowed her gait.

He rode next to her. "There's a stretch of field beyond the next bend," he told her.

And passed her by. And she found herself laughing and following hard after him.

The afternoon passed that way. Each of them overtaking the other. If his men had followed them, she did not see them.

If her uncle or his friends were anywhere about, she did not see them either.

At last they came to a huge oak and when Ajax had over-taken Briar, Allora slipped from her mare and went running quickly around the tree, only to discover Bret already on the other side. She found herself locked within his arms, caressed by his eyes. He brought her down into the soft leaves of autumn and made love to her there. She listened to the wind, and felt a new thunder that seemed to rise from the earth, and when it was over she stared up at the sunset for a moment, watching the dazzling colors in the sky. She closed her eyes. And slept.

When she awoke, he was dressed again, standing by Ajax, staring out into the darkness. She rose quickly and gathered her things, dressing, aware that he watched her. When she was finished he walked to her, kissed her fore-head, and swept her up to set her on Briar's back.

"What now?" she asked him softly.

"Now we go home."

"To the cottage—"

"To the town house. Tomorrow, I have business with the king."

They arrived late, but Allora was strangely impressed with the place from the moment she saw it.

It was very much a town house, set upon the River Thames, with a barge in back, should swift travel to William's White Tower be necessary. There had been some kind of manor here, before William had come on his Conquest, and it had been built the English way, of wood and thatch. But in the last twenty years, it had been enlarged and rebuilt, and there was a striking stone entry in the front. When she was ushered in, she instantly felt the warmth there. The place was sweet-smelling, with clean rushes strewn about. Great hounds rushed out to meet them. She thought of her home, the keep on the Far Isle, and though she had come from a castle that ruled an entire isle, there was nothing nearly so gracious in all of it that matched the beauty and warmth here. The walls were hung with huge tapestries, the fireplaces were fronted by stone masonry.

The house was very much like Robert had said it would be, the entry being something of a hall itself, leading to the stairs and to the hall on the left with the massive table and richly covered chairs. Beyond the dining hall was the kitchen, and though she didn't enter there, she was certain that there would be an alley behind it—just as Robert had said there would be.

Though they arrived late, the servants were quickly there to greet them: Tim and Tad, brothers, who tended the stables; Arthur, who managed all household affairs; Griff, who managed the stables and oversaw any construction or repair work, and saw to the tending of the vegetable gardens in back, and to the curing of any meat that was brought in. Under Arthur in the house were Peg, Susan, Mariah, Pete, and Jamie, all young, fresh-faced country lads and lasses. And all, it seemed, of Saxon descent rather than Norman. They all bowed and bobbed before her, and she realized for the first time that though she had always been incredibly proud of her own lineage, she had married an earl—one whose title had been invented and bestowed by a conquering king—but a premier lord of the realm nonetheless.

They hadn't come alone; Etienne, Jarrett, and Gaston were right behind them, and after Bret had formally brought her into the house and very courteously performed all the necessary introductions, he was drawn back into the hall with his companions; he commanded Arthur to see that she was shown his chambers, and made comfortable there.

The upstairs of the place seemed huge, with numerous doorways, but she remembered that it housed not just a big family but a powerful one as well, one which no doubt often offered its hospitality to guests. Arthur, very tall, very thin, and yet with a wondrous strong voice that no doubt kept those servants beneath him in ready line, directed her to the left, a candle held high in his hand, and at the third door, they entered.

Arthur set the candle on a stool by the bed, and Allora quickly surveyed her surroundings. There was a skeletal steel figure in the far corner holding one of Bret's massive coats of mail. There was a long flat table next to it at the far wall, and upon it lay his steel-knuckled gauntlets and the helmet that had so fascinated her with its curious design of the stag horns. She studied it for a moment, then turned to survey his bed. It sat upon a platform in an alcove against the opposite wall, with a tapestried curtain lashed to the far post of the alcove, ready to keep out the chill of a cold winter's night. She looked away from it and saw another table before the windows, and numerous trunks placed against the walls and at the foot of the bed. Near the bed was a small table, and upon it she saw a carafe of wine and two golden chalices. She swallowed hard, seeing that the vial Robert had promised her was next to the chalices tonight. Had it sat there all this time? Perhaps—for once this room had been readied for its occupants' wedding night, what need would anyone else have to enter within it?

She wondered if Arthur saw the vial as well.

"Is there anything you need, milady?" he asked her. "Anything at all?"

She shook her head. "Thank you. There's nothing." Nothing, she thought, but a burning desire to be alone.

He inclined his head in a deep bow to her, then exited the room, closing the door behind him. He was barely gone when she heard a noise, like a stone striking the walls of the house. She raced to the window and looked down, discovering the alley that lay at the back of the house.

Robert was there, hands on his hips, looking up at her.

" 'Tis sorry I am, lass, to be so late!" he called.

"Late!" she cried. "You must be mad! He has men with him, someone will see you there—"

"The vial, girl. Use it tonight."

She suddenly felt a chill sweeping through her. "Robert, he might have been with me!" she called in warning, dismayed and alarmed. "Where is my father?"

"With the king for the next hour or so. I will be down here at midnight. See that he drinks the wine, for we must have a good four hours' head start if we hope to escape the long arms of the Conqueror."

"Damn you!" she cried. "What good is this now? Last night, you could have still sought an annulment—"

"My God, Allora of the Far Isle afraid now of the great Norman?" he taunted.

"I'm not afraid, it's just that—"

"Lass, I'm grateful for your sacrifice, grateful for my life. But you cannot forget who you are, or what your people are! Free from the yoke of William the Bastard, who thinks he can grasp his hands around anything!"

"Robert—"

"Norman rule will destroy your people, and your father! By God, niece, you've got your duties to us all!"

She inhaled swiftly, staring down at him in silence.

"Midnight, milady. When the darkness is very deep and the full moon rises above you, I will be waiting. And in swift time, you shall see, all here will be forgotten."

She was suddenly aware of footsteps on the floorboards and she brought her head inside. Her heart was beating wildly when Bret entered the room; her breath was coming far too quickly. He stared at her as he came in, sweeping his mantle from his shoulders to cast it upon a peg on the wall. "What's wrong?" he demanded.

She shook her head. She couldn't seem to think. "I'm—chilled," she murmured. "I think I shall have some wine."

She hurried to the carafe, putting her back to him. She found the vial, and gritted her teeth very hard. Was it too late to run?

Dear God, what choice did she have? Her father was awaiting her, her uncle. Bret never denied being what he was, one of the Conqueror's men, and she had sworn that the Far Isle would not fall beneath that heavy yoke.

Her fingers were trembling. She had to drop the contents of the vial into the wine. If he slept, she would at least have the time to think without being influenced by his touch. And she had to hurry or he would wonder what in God's name was taking her so long.

She dumped the contents of the vial into his chalice and secreted the empty vial in the small pocket of the tunic she wore over the masculine garb he had brought for her to ride in. Then she turned quickly, perhaps too quickly, and walked over to him with the wine, offering the drugged chalice to him.

Her heart slammed, and she wondered what she would do if he insisted on the other chalice. But he did not. He took the wine she offered him, and lifted his chalice to her. She smiled, and sipped wine from her own chalice. Suddenly he took the wine from her hands and set both chalices down on the long table by the far wall. He pressed his palms to her cheeks. "You *are* cold, my love. So very cold," he said softly.

Her lashes fell.

"One would think you'd had half your body out the window," he commented.

She looked over his shoulder, anxiously studying the way he had set the chalices so that she could easily retrieve her own. "I did look out the window," she said. "Alleys intrigue me. Cities intrigue me. I am a border barbarian, remember?" she asked lightly.

His hands fell from her cheeks. He was still watching her, and she cursed herself for being so inadequate in the pursuit of deceit. This had to happen quickly, she thought, and she went for the chalices once again. She handed him his and took her own, then walked to the large hearth in his room where a fire quietly burned, and crouched down by it. She watched the flames, then remembered the way they had sat that afternoon, and wondered if she would ever see a blaze again and not recall his face, his touch, his scent.

He came beside her, crouched alike. He drank deeply from his own chalice, his eyes touching hers over the rim of it. She felt breathless once again.

"What are you planning, my love?" he asked softly.

"What?"

"I asked you what you were planning."

She nervously took a very long swallow of her own wine, then felt his hand curled hard upon the chalice, wrenching it from her grasp. He threw the portion of wine that remained and the chalice itself straight into the flames and she cried out in fear at the violence of his motion, leaping to her feet.

"You little idiot!" he cried harshly, catching her wrists and drawing her to him. "You just drank whatever foul potion you had concocted for me. Tell me the poison so that we can combat it!"

It was fast, so fast-working! Even as she stared at him, the room began to spin. Her knees were buckling. She started to fall.

He caught her, but offered no welcome comfort. As the world began to dim to black, he shook her. She managed to cry out a protest as a cocoon of darkness and peace seemed to await her. He kept shaking her, and she could hear his voice again and again.

"Not poison!" she whispered. "Just a potion to . . . sleep."

She tried very hard to open her eyes. She met his. They were cobalt and searing, so condemning. But she didn't have to see them, feel them, burning into her. She was sinking again into darkness.

And not even his touch upon her could keep it away.

She heard him speak but once again.

"Jesu, lady, I pray that you are right!"

Then there was nothing else but the darkness . . .

Chapter 12

⤜⤛⤚

The sweetness of the void did not seem to last very long, and she was soon heartily sorry, for she dwelled in some nightmare land where people came and went too swiftly, where they all seemed evil, where her head and stomach hurt as if knives were thrust into them. She saw faces in her dreams. Robert's face as he stood upon a cliff, swearing that she cared not for her family or heritage. "Traitor!" he shouted to her. "Traitor!" Then Robert would be gone, and she would see her father, and she longed to throw her arms around him and tell him that everything was all right. She would see the strange priest, Father Damien, wearing the robes he had worn when they were wed, and he would stare at her so very gravely, reach out, touch her forehead, whispering to her. "It will pass. Don't fight so, it will pass."

She had lied to God, and so she was dying . . .

"Nay, milady, you'll not die."

He forced her to drink something green and horribly vile, and knives sliced through her. She screamed out loud with the pain of it.

"Jesu, Damien, you will kill her yourself!" Bret warned. Bret. Aye she was held, locked within his arms. He held a cool cloth and pressed it to her forehead and cheeks, down to her throat and over her shoulders. She was naked in his arms, she thought, her only covering the sheet he had drawn around her. But it was a dream, and it didn't matter.

Ah, the dream had become too real, for she could feel Bret's strong arms around her shoulders, then twist and see his face, the eyes so dark, features so stern and relent-

174

less. She turned back and cried out, longing to protest that look . . .

Yet she had meant him to drink the wine. And she hadn't even drunk very much of it.

"Would you have her well?" she could hear the priest reply from some very deep and distant fog.

"Aye, make her well! Make her well that I may throttle her in good health. The fool girl!"

His voice faded. The knives seemed to come again, yet not so piercing this time. Yet still a sound of anguish escaped her.

"She is worse!" Bret cried. She could feel his arms around her as he faced the priest.

"Milord, give her over to me, and leave me to my business."

"I swear, if she dies—"

"I've told you, she'll not die; she has not been in mortal danger, she is simply very sick. She didn't drink enough of the wine to be in so grave a danger. Give her over to me; let me tend to what I know—"

"You are supposed to be a savior of souls!"

"And you sent for me. Go. Just for a few minutes."

Moments passed. Days? Maybe forever, maybe a few seconds. The dream was suspended. Then Father Damien was with her, making her sip his foul green liquid once again. She fought wildly, knowing she was going to be wretchedly sick. Yet he was prepared, with a pot upon the bed, and he smoothed his hands soothingly over her back until the spell had passed. Then he was with her still, bathing her face, her hands, her throat, her neck, all with clear cold water. The pain was gone. All gone. She could see him for a moment. It was a dream, but she could reach out and touch his face.

"It wasn't poison, Father, I swear, it wasn't poison."

"Sleep now," he told her, and pulled smooth linen covers over her nakedness. She closed her eyes. It was wonderful this time. The sweet blackness came again . . .

She opened her eyes slowly, painfully. Light poured into the room. Something glittered, and she blinked and focused and saw that she stared at the form of Bret's mail, hung atop the steel frame in the corner of the room. She blinked, and realized that her throat was as dry as the land William had razed and left barren. It hurt. She could see her hand lying upon the sheets, and it looked too pale, too white. She hadn't the strength to lift it.

She tried to shift her eyes. A thousand lights seemed to pierce her head in agonizing flashes. She closed her eyes again, fighting the wave of nausea that seized her. After a moment, she tried opening her eyes again.

She saw the glittering mail again, and realized this time that it was not on the form in the corner of the room, but rather on Bret himself. He was clad in heavy leggings and boots and the mail, a purple mantle cast over his shoulder, his scabbard belted at his waist. He was seated with his back to the fire, his eyes upon her, his hands folded prayer-fashion, forefingers tapping against his clean-shaven chin.

"So you are with us once again, milady!" he said softly. She didn't like the sound of his voice. It was so cold it brought icy rivulets down the length of her spine. She felt too weak to fight. Tears burned beneath her eyelids, and she lowered them quickly, then cast her arm over her eyes, as if she shielded them from the light.

But he stood and crossed the few feet to the bed, drawing her arm away. Then she saw that they were not alone, and she almost gasped when she saw the strange priest standing there, just beyond Bret. She had thought that she had dreamed his presence, yet he was there. And he spoke then, offering her a moment's respite.

"She needs water, milord," he said, pouring water from a pitcher by the bed into a goblet, and giving that goblet to Bret.

Allora did want the water, desperately. She tried to rise, but she hadn't the strength, and Bret supported her to drink from it. She longed to drink the whole of it quickly, but Father Damien warned Bret, "Take care! A little at a time." Bret allowed her only a few sips; his fingers, supporting her head, tugged upon her hair when he thought that she'd had enough.

It was scarcely a gentle touch . . .

She lay back upon the pillows, exhausted from the simple act of drinking.

Father Damien came around the bed and smoothed her damp hair from her forehead, studying her eyes. "She's completely out of danger. I will leave you two alone then," he said.

Allora tried to struggle up, amazed to discover that she longed to stop the priest from leaving, that she loathed the idea of being left alone with Bret. But she couldn't have stopped the priest if she'd had the strength to reach for him, she thought, yet still she called out to him.

"Father?"

He paused.

Don't leave me now when I may well be in mortal danger! she longed to cry. But she whispered only, "Thank you!"

And he nodded gravely to her and left, closing the door firmly behind him.

"Well?" Bret said after a moment.

She closed her eyes. "I feel terrible!" she whispered, and it wasn't a lie. "My throat . . . I can scarce talk. If you could just give me more time—"

"Lady, you have lain here two nights now, and I am out of time; the king has summoned me to service, and given me leave to wait only until I saw you out of danger. And indeed, my sympathy might be far greater had not the entire draught of that poison been intended for me."

"There was no poison—" she insisted in a husky whisper.

"Aye! And is that why you were so desperately ill."

She shook her head, her eyes still closed. "I swear to you, I did not seek to poison you!" she told him with all the vehemence she could muster.

"Lady, I saw you in the act, and found the vial within your clothing."

She opened her eyes, meeting his again. "It was to make you sleep, nothing more."

"Aye, the full glass of wine, milady, and I'd have slept. Forever—the sleep of the dead."

"There is some great mistake—" she began.

"Aye, lady, and that there was!"

She lowered her lashes swiftly. Aye, he was thinking that no matter how good his reasons, he should never have wed her, that he had invited nothing but trouble into his life.

"If you would just listen to me—" she tried again.

"Nay, lady!" he said, leaning toward her. "You listen to me. I'll not live my life wary of my every footstep in my own house. If there is ever any such attempt made against me again, you will find yourself residing as a prisoner in a tower—a remote tower! If you think that I'll let go my hold, lady, you're mistaken. If you're not guilty of the intent of murder, then your all-mighty uncle is, and you're more the fool if you don't see it!"

"You have no right! You hate my uncle for seeking freedom from the shackles of a bastard conqueror. You don't understand—"

"Your uncle loves war for the very sake of it, and your father's great weakness is his love for your uncle!" he told her, then he was up, and striding to lean against the mantel, highly aggravated. He swung around to stare at her. "Take care in my absence, lady! Had I died, William would have found a rope for you and half your kin, and I warn you, my father and brothers would have bested any fortress in their vengeance. You've refused to believe me, but others in the king's court would not be slow to seek glory in the Conqueror's eyes through the death of one seen as a traitor."

"I swear to you—"

"Spare yourself. Don't swear, milady."

She felt the fierce burning of tears teasing her lashes once again and blinked furiously. He would never listen to her. She longed to get her hands on her uncle and shake him viciously. She still could not believe Robert would have lied to her so, risked her so—with poison! Yet he was reckless, careless, heedless in his determinations, and now, he'd involved her.

And still, Bret despised Robert already. She didn't dare try to tell him that her uncle had never warned her that the vial had contained poison.

Bret continued to stare at her; she could feel the fire of his eyes. She looked to him at last, stiffening her spine. He wasn't going to listen to her. What she said didn't matter.

"I told you we were enemies!" she said softly.

He walked to the bed and sat by her side again, not touching her, but leaning close. "And I'm telling you now, milady, we are wed. If you crave the least bit of peace, send your uncle and father home. When you are strong enough, go to my father's house in Haselford and await me there."

"But—"

"If you don't, my love, I will know that you are my enemy in all truth. And when I come after you, I will come after an enemy. And I will break down any wall to reach you, fight any man, any family, any clan—any king, any nation. Lady, be forewarned."

He still hadn't touched her. But he leaned toward her suddenly then, his lips touching like a brand upon her forehead. "Your father has been asking for you, greatly worried, and he has been informed that you are not in any danger, but will travel immediately southward as soon as you are able. Being with any of your kin seems to be a great danger," he informed her harshly. "I told the king that I thought you must have eaten something foul after the wedding, so no one is aware of the truth of the situation—except, of course, the person who supplied you the poison. Someone within my own household was obviously involved, and I will find him—or her—out, you may rest assured."

"My father—"

"Your father is welcome at Haselford at any time. Alone."

He stood and turned, the sweep of his mantle falling gracefully behind him as he strode for the table by the wall, and his horned helmet, which he took up swiftly in his arms.

And with long, sure, angry strides, he left the room then, without ever looking back.

She listened to the door slam, heard its reverberations. And suddenly the stinging in her eyes was too much to bear, and the tears slipped from beneath them unbidden. She wanted to close her eyes again and find some relief from the anguish that plagued her in sleep. But sleep eluded her, and she hadn't the strength to rise on her own.

But she wasn't left alone for very long. Father Damien returned quietly and she gathered her covers, trying to sit up, watching him. In his youth he must have been a handsome man; he remained a striking one. She saw that he had brought a satchel with him and he sat at the edge of the bed, produced a piece of bread from it, and handed it to her. "Try to eat this. It will help you regain your strength."

"Could I have another sip of water first, please?"

He obliged her, and she was careful not to drink too much too quickly. Then she began to nibble on the bread. She had thought that it would never stay down; it did. And to her amazement, she ate the whole of it, and when she was done, she felt much better.

He studied her still. She let her eyes fall.

"Thank you," she told him simply again. He still watched her. She looked up at him quickly. Unbidden, the tears were stinging her eyes again. "I didn't try to poison him—"

"I believe you," he said.

"But he does not."

"No."

Father Damien believed her, she realized—but he also believed that someone in her family had meant to poison Bret. To death.

Robert.

"This was all a tragedy on the king's part!" she cried. "We are different—"

"I have seen people change," Father Damien said.

"Then let *him* change!" she said softly. "Let him disavow his own king and join with another people!"

Father Damien leaned forward. "Perhaps you should remember this. Someone among your people risked your life, for you are the one who sipped the wine. Your enemy— your husband—was the one who stood over you night and day, nearly becoming violent with me that I did not end your suffering swiftly enough."

She fell silent, wincing. Indeed, it might have been better for Bret if she had perished!

Father Damien rose and smoothed back her hair. "Change comes from within, milady. I can stay no longer now, as I am to accompany the party to Normandy. There's a trunk of your belongings at the foot of the bed, and water on yonder table when you've the strength to wash. You'll still be very sleepy. Rest tonight. By tomorrow, you will be grateful to be living again."

He smiled at her, and she smiled in return. Then he left as abruptly as Bret had, and she was again alone with her thoughts.

They were painful ones. He had ordered her to Haselford. He had denied her leave to see her father . . .

She tossed for a few moments, then braced herself and found the strength to rise. She shivered fiercely as she walked across the room, found the water, and washed; then she tested if she still had balance and strength, and dug into her trunk for a long-sleeved shift to slip over her still-shivering body. She walked and sat before the fire for a while, yet flames would always remind her of the time she had been with him in the hunter's cottage in the fire. She rose at last, and went back to bed. She couldn't even think; everything seemed to be such a terrible tempest. She wanted to shriek and scream at Robert, but she also longed for her father with her whole heart. It seemed incredible that Bret would be so cruel as to not let her see Ioin, but then, she reflected, he had gone from finding her a nuisance to discovering that at least he did want her—and then finding that he despised her.

She bit her lower lip, wishing that his feelings toward her did not hurt so badly. In the end it was true; she did have a duty to her people, and he couldn't see it. He was the Conqueror's man, and he had left her at the Conqueror's bidding, with no word of when he would return. He had denied her Ioin's company, and then he had left her . . .

He had stayed with her until she was well.

She tried to tell herself that she had to stay awake, that she had to think, and she had to make decisions. She could never trust Robert again. Bret would never trust her. He might well not come back, or if he did, he might never come for her. He could conceivably choose to leave her far from home for years, and seize hold of her inheritance if her father were to die.

Despite the tempest raging in her heart and mind, she found that she slipped easily into sleep. And once there, she slept deeply, very deeply.

She awoke with a start, stunned to realize that she was being carried. Tenderly carried in strong arms. Alarmed, she struggled against the arms, then looked up into her father's tormented eyes.

"Father!" she said.

"Hush!" he warned her.

She was still in her room, she realized. Nay, Bret's room within his father's London town house. And Ioin was swiftly taking her to the window where the tapestries were drawn far back. "Slip easy from my grasp, daughter. They'll catch you below. Your uncle has a cloak to warm you, and all else we can leave behind."

"Wait, Father—"

She suddenly felt the huge tremor that seized him. "I will kill that young fool for what he did to you!"

"What?"

They had come to the window. Ioin leaned his great bulk out of it. She grasped his shoulders instinctively, for the ground was many feet below. But her uncle Robert was there, waiting to catch her.

Robert! Waiting? Or ready to move to let her drop to the ground?

"Come, girl, leave hold of your father!" he called to her anxiously.

"Wait—" she cried, but Ioin had hefted her out and she was falling at a furious speed, and it was all that she could do to keep from crying out.

Robert did not drop her. She landed heavily in his arms, but he was a supple and wiry man and gave a little with the fall, then straightened.

"Uncle, damn you!" she cried to him softly.

He stared at her in utter disbelief, then warned her, "Damn me if you will, my fine lady, but keep your peace for now! We've come to your rescue and Ioin Canadys will hang right along with the rest of us if we are discovered now!"

He turned with her quickly, and she found herself sud-

denly seated atop a dark horse in the middle of the alley.
She turned, gasping, as she heard hoofbeats, then saw that
her uncle had brought help from their own home. David
was there—her David, the man she had always thought of
as her David—clad darkly as were all the others; but his
light hair caught the moonlight, and the look in his eyes
was one of such concern and torment that she caught her
breath, and could not protest when his horse came to hers,
when his arms reached out, when he held her briefly, then
released her before she could topple from her horse. David
wasn't alone; his half-brother Duncan rode behind him, and
behind the two of them came Sir Christian, captain of her
father's guards upon the Far Isle.

"Lady!" Sir Christian called in gentle greeting.

"Ioin!" Robert called, staring up at the windows. "Brother, we need make haste from this place!"

Then they all fell silent and still, for even in the alley,
they could hear a soft, feminine voice calling out Allora's
name, and then there was a knocking at her door.

"Ioin, for the love of God!" Robert whispered vehemently.

"Father!" Allora cried softly.

But then they heard a swift gasp that promised to become
a full-blown scream in seconds.

But it did not. Ioin appeared at the window, now carrying
another woman. Allora inhaled sharply, seeing the still and
silent form of her sister-in-law, Elysia.

"Help me, man, fast!" Ioin ordered, and it was David
who rode swiftly forward to catch Elysia as her form fell
gracefully from the window with a trail of soft linen and
fire-red hair.

Ioin wasted no more time, leaping from the window to
his horse with uncanny precision. Allora stared at her father
in dismay.

"Ride!" he commanded her.

Robert's hand slapped down upon her mount's haunches,
and they started off wildly through the alley.

It was very late, it seemed, and a full moon, still so
very full, rose high in the heavens. The streets—even the
bustling streets of London town—were quiet and darkened,

with occasional lanterns casting the only glow upon the earth. They turned a corner. An army of rats suddenly scurried before them and Allora's horse reared. She gained control, and even as her father called out her name, she was riding again.

Robert had studied his route well, Allora realized; they were very quickly out of the city and into the surrounding countryside, and they hadn't encountered a single one of King William's men.

Grouped in the shelter of some heavy oaks, Allora tried to reach her father and David, anxious to see that Elysia was all right.

"Father—"

"Lass, I gave her a sound bump upon the head with the handle of my sword, and that was that. She'll come to soon enough, I promise you!"

"And then there will be hell to pay!" Allora whispered.

"I had no choice!" Ioin told her. "Even if I had slipped from the window before she had seen me, she would have discovered that you were gone. An alarm would have been raised."

Robert urged his mount up between the two of them. "We haven't time for this now—nor for any reproach from you, niece!" he said sternly. "We must use the darkness to get farther and farther north. We ride now!"

"We wait one moment!" Allora responded furiously, and she slammed her heels against her horse's haunches, forcing her uncle's mount to give way to her own, and she moved quickly toward where David held the still-pale Elysia.

"David—"

"She is breathing, Allora, I swear it. Her heart pounds regularly. She will awaken soon, so I suggest that we do ride."

Allora nodded, knowing that David told her the truth. Knowing, too, that they could not release Elysia. Not yet. They had to flee the city. Yet she was pained to see her, for none of Bret's family had ever shown her anything but courtesy and kindness, and she was certain that Elysia had arrived when she did only because she had heard that her brother was gone, and that Allora had been ill.

"Ride then!" Ioin commanded, standing tall in his stirrups and waving his sword, gathering their party to begin again. "Ride again, and hard!"

And indeed, they did so.

Now, Allora was certain, they all rode for their lives.

Chapter 13

❦

Allora didn't know how far they traveled. They didn't stop again, not to exchange any words, not for anything, not until the sun began to rise. By then, at Robert's determined urging, they had come at least thirty miles from the city, David was convinced.

They had stopped at last by a small stream far off the old Roman road they had been traveling to reach the north. Allora drank deeply of the water then, still feeling as if her throat had been made of burnt material. Elysia lay by the stream, very much like some legendary princess, hair strewn well out behind her, eyes closed, her beautiful face still so pale that it made Allora very nervous. She knelt down by Elysia, lying her head upon her sister-in-law's chest, listening to the deep, rhythmic breathing. "She's a very beautiful girl," David said from behind her. "Is her brother, *your husband*, much like her?"

The anguish in David's voice brought her eyes quickly to his, and she was sorry, deeply sorry. They had been all but betrothed; that they would be married had simply been assumed by everyone, since Ioin was not the father to command a daughter to wed to add to his riches. David was one of them, a border lord, and that was what had counted in their world.

Not only that, but he was a good man, a gentle one, who seemed to deplore the battles they so frequently fought, yet went to them all with silence and fortitude.

Serving her uncle.

"David, this has not been my doing," she reminded him quietly. She looked past him. Near another oak, her father

186

and Robert were deep in conversation with Sir Christian and Duncan. "My uncle might have died—"

"Aye, Allora!" David said softly, but with passion. "I don't blame you, my love, for anything that has passed. Yet I feel a tear in my heart, and the blood that spills from it is for the both of us!"

She lowered her head quickly, once again feeling a tempest of emotions. She'd cared for him so deeply for so many years. And in such a strange and short period of time, everything had changed so completely. She still cared deeply for him, but she couldn't forget the feel of sitting before the fire, watching the flames, and knowing that her harsh Norman husband sat behind her.

"How touching!" she heard suddenly, and jumped back, for Elysia had come to at last. Her wide gray eyes were focused like twin daggers upon Allora and her expression was furious.

"Elysia—" she began, determined to tell her sister-in-law how sorry she was, that she would be freed as soon as possible. But Elysia wanted no part of it. She leaped to her feet, far from Allora's outstretched hand.

"We tried to make you feel welcome!" Elysia cried vehemently. "Sweet Jesu, I am here because I thought you might be ill! Your whole family of wild border wolves will hang for this now. They might just up and hang *you!*"

"Quiet, else find yourself gagged!" David cautioned her swiftly in Allora's defense.

But Allora didn't want anyone defending her. "You'll go free as soon as possible, Elysia. No one meant to abduct you, surely you know that. They were forced to do so. And just as soon as we've gotten far enough north, we'll set you free."

"And maybe we won't," Allora heard Duncan say from behind.

She swung around to face him. "What are you talking about?"

"The daughter of the Earl of Haselford, Count d'Anlou! Sister to the magnificent Earl of Wakefield! What a wonderful hostage she makes. There may come a time when we might need her in our negotiations."

"There may not!" Allora cried furiously. "Duncan, she is no part of this!"

"And what part were you, niece, in William's schemes?" Robert demanded heatedly from behind her.

"You!" she snapped to her uncle, spinning to face him. "You tricked and deceived me as well as others. You might have cost me—"

"Nay, lady, you're wrong!" Robert said swiftly. And she realized then that her father hadn't had the least idea that someone had added poison to the sleeping draught intended for Bret. But then, she had always known that her father would never condone such a thing.

And now she knew that her uncle was willing to go to any means to reach his ends. Any deed was a respectable one, if it was done in honor of his cause.

"You bastard!" she hissed softly.

"Allora!" her father interrupted her, shocked. "All of you! I am the head of this family, as long as I draw breath. We've not the time for this now. We've got to ride again." He bowed to Elysia. "My lady, I am heartily sorry for any ill I have caused you, and am deeply distressed that your brother was swept into William's wretched trap to seize our isle. But lady, for the lives of all here present, we dare not let you go. Now, to all of you! We will ride. And when we've reached home, then we can sort through this disaster!"

All around him, everyone fell silent, Robert and Allora staring warily at one another, Elysia looking as if she would gladly hang them all herself.

Ioin turned, striding for his horse. The others followed suit. Allora mounted.

"I'll not ride with that barbarian again!" Elysia snapped.

Allora inhaled deeply, thinking that she would dismount from her horse and ride with David herself. Then she met his eyes, and he shook his head. It would not be a wise move for her to make.

"Lady Elysia, you will ride with me," David assured her. And in a minute, despite her protest, she was thrown up on his horse before him, and they were starting out through the forest once again.

They rode hard through the day, then paused in the woods in the afternoon and shared what food Allora's rescuers had brought in their saddlebags. There was wine, which Allora still could not stomach, but there was also plenty of fresh sweet water, and she found that she was ravenous and that the cheese and dried meat they had brought tasted delicious.

She told her father that she needed to talk to him in private, but before they could have time together, her uncle found her rinsing her face and hands and throat in the stream by the copse where they rested. Hands on his hips, he accosted her.

"The wine was never meant for ye, lass!" he assured her.

She gritted her teeth and rose. "You meant to poison him, to kill him. Dear God, Uncle, have you no sense? Are you so determined on your course that you don't care if William comes in force to kill us all? Robert, you didn't even warn me! Dear God, if Bret hadn't knocked that chalice from my hand, I might well have died the death you planned for him. How could you?"

"Don't you dare judge me, lass!" he warned. "I did what I had to do to set you free! You came to me for help, Allora! You came running to me, desperate to escape the ropes William planned to tie around you—and your great Norman lord!"

"Poison, Uncle? Sweet Jesu, what are we stooping to? And you did not come when you should have come, Robert! There should have been no wedding night. You do not know what you have done to me."

"Jesu, lass, if he was cruel or brutal—"

"Oh, my God! You don't understand at all!"

"I understand that it seems you have all but turned traitor, niece. You forget who you are—you forget who *we* are!"

"Indeed. You forget that my father runs the family!" she cried.

He strode suddenly to her. "Don't you go running to your father with tales, my fine lady!" he warned her. "You—"

He broke off as they heard a wild scream. Both of them turned from the bubbling water and went tearing swiftly back to the copse of trees.

And there, coming back into the midst of them, was David with a wildly fighting Elysia in his arms.

"You will pay dearly!" Elysia promised.

"Indeed." David, customarily so very courteous, dumped his human bundle flat upon a bed of leaves beneath an oak. He looked to Allora with exasperation. "Can anyone shut her up?" he demanded.

"Bind and gag her if she tries to escape again," Ioin said wearily. He had been sitting before one of the giant trees, whittling upon a stick. He rose. "We'll have to ride again. Her screams might have been heard."

With too little rest, they were mounted again.

The journey grew harder. They traveled rocky hills in wretched wind, and kept far away from the cities and towns.

Elysia kept looking for any chance to escape.

In a quiet glen with the autumn leaves falling all around them and an icy brook bubbling and trickling behind them, Allora at last spoke with her father, but when she did, she discovered that she couldn't quite tell him that his brother had very nearly poisoned her to death. She did tell him that Bret had never hurt her, that he had never been cruel in any way, and that she admitted that she had not been at all desperate to be rescued. He listened to her sorrowfully.

"Ah, daughter! I didna know! He wouldn't allow me to see you, and Robert grew so anxious, I became so sorely afraid myself! Ah, the plans we make! It was not so wretched a thing to snatch back my daughter before she became a man's wife, but when Wakefield did not bring you to his house that first night, I was sorely afraid for your heart and soul."

"Father—"

"When we've reached home, I will write to your husband, Allora, if that is your choice. If you wish your freedom from the marriage, I will fight for you until it is achieved. If you don't seek that freedom . . . then I will give all I have to see that this may all be righted."

She slipped her arms around him, hugging him tightly. "I don't know what I feel anymore."

"I have always found Bret a fine man, lamentable only for being among William's men."

"Indeed, a Norman."

"And Robert will fight me, as will half the family, if you choose to honor the marriage," Ioin said. "But that is what we all are, isn't it?" he added suddenly. "A bit of this, and a bit of that. Danish, Anglo, Saxon, Pict, Scot—Norman. But first, home. To the strength of the fortress to negotiate."

She smiled, and when they rode again, she was ridiculously happy.

Until she found Elysia watching her, and she cursed inwardly for the ill luck that had brought her sister-in-law along with them on this wretched flight across the length of a country.

There was nothing she could say that Elysia would believe right now, and she knew it. She held her peace with Robert and even Duncan. And she had little difficulty with David because he was so preoccupied with Elysia, who was so constantly causing all the trouble she could manage.

Despite Elysia, they traveled swiftly, a ragtag party by now. Allora's white gown and dark mantle were covered in mud, both garments torn and ragged. She had come with no shoes, and David had stolen her a pair from a poor village farmhouse, leaving some coins for their replacement. But they were rough shoes, and they created blisters on her feet.

They had no trouble at all until they passed York. Duncan had made a careful foray into the town, seeking news.

He strode back into their camp in the moonlight, eyes narrowing upon Allora as he quickly told Ioin all that he had learned. "The Earl of Wakefield was swiftly sent from the south of England to Normandy. Apparently, he didn't learn until he arrived that Allora had fled the city of London. He ordered that his wife was to be allowed to return to her home with her family, that he would deal with her—and the wretched Scots—as soon as he was able, and that all should be forewarned."

"Then we are safe—" Allora began.

"Nay!" Duncan advised her sharply. "For King William was furious, so it is rumored, and so many of his knights are on the lookout for us, determined to produce a few heads for the king and seek out a reward."

"Then we must make even greater haste," Ioin said.

"We are scarcely a day away from the Far Isle," David reminded him.

"And we have rested long enough."

So they began again, pressing hard, yet traveling easier here in the north, where so many people were still hostile to the Normans. They rode relentlessly, covering nearly fifty miles before the sunset the following night.

Almost there. As the sun fell in a crimson arch and the moon rose like a pale shadow in the twilight sky, Allora stood on a ridge with her father, and they could see the Far Isle in the distance. The sun shone on the natural stone that comprised so much of the wall of the castle. The main keep tower, slightly higher than all the others, also seemed to glimmer in the sunlight.

"We are there, daughter! We are all but there!" Ioin cried delightedly.

And it was then, even as he said the words, that Duncan came bursting out from the trees upon them.

"Horses, Laird Ioin!" he cried. "A large body of them, with mounted men armed with bows and arrows, heavy mail, swords, and pikes. They're near upon us!"

"Come!" Ioin warned his daughter.

And she raced with him through the high grasses and the harsh wind until they came to the horses, and leaped upon them. They started straight downhill, shrieking out their cries of greeting to those in the castle of the Far Isle as they came. The tide was changing quickly; they had only moments before the sea would cover the damp sand over which they might now race.

Yet they were pursued, and hotly so. She saw an arrow fly by her and leaned low against her horse's neck, and she thought that no, Bret would not have ordered this. He might long to hang Robert by his toes, but he would not endanger his sister's life, perhaps he wouldn't endanger hers . . .

Perhaps he'd want to throttle her himself.

"Sweet Jesu!" her father suddenly cried.

She turned to him, and saw him rigid in his saddle. Then she cried out, horrified to see that the long shaft of an arrow protruded from his back.

"Stop!" she cried.

"Nay, ride, ride!" he ordered, slumping over. "Ride hard, harder, harder!"

They were upon the sand. Allora twisted in her saddle, near-blinded by the windswept sting of her hair. They were still pursued by a group of knights, perhaps thirty well-armed men.

"The gates!" Robert bellowed as they came upon the fortress over the wet sand. "The gates!"

The gates stretched open before them. The men upon the walls of the fortress began sending their own hail of arrows down upon their attackers. Jesu, they could come no further, not such a party! They could not hope to breech the walls of the Far Isle.

Nor survive the tide which would any moment roll in.

They reached the courtyard of the castle, the seven of them riding in hard.

"Close the gates!" Robert called swiftly, and he was quickly obeyed.

Allora leaped from her mount the moment she reined in, rushing for her father's horse. Robert was there ahead of her, helping the slumped Ioin down. Even as Ioin fell into his brother's arms, Allora saw the way that the shaft of the arrow, now broken, yet so deep within his flesh, protruded from his back, and she knew instantly that his wound was mortal.

"No!" she shrieked, rushing forward herself, nearly blinded by the tears that flooded her eyes. "No!"

Robert obviously knew too that the wound was mortal. He didn't try to take Ioin into the keep, but came down upon his knees with him there in the courtyard. Allora dropped beside him, taking her father's shoulders into her lap, cradling his head there. "Father, Father, oh, my God, Father!" she cried desperately. She leaned forward, kissed his cheek, willed his eyes to open.

They did so. He offered her the gentlest and most serene of smiles. "Rule wisely, sternly, and with mercy!" he commanded her. "I love you, daughter . . ."

His eyes closed again.

"No!" she cried. "No!" She leaned over, laid her ear against his chest, and found no heartbeat. She raised her head and touched his lips with her fingertips, but felt no gentle breath escape between them. Ioin's eyes were closed as if he slept. "No!" she shrieked again, and she cried out the word over and over again, holding him to her, rocking him. She held him tightly as the tears poured from her eyes, bitter, agonized tears. Closer and closer, as if she could instill him with her warmth—with life once again. "Oh, Father!" she whispered at last, aware that everyone was gathered around her. Still now, so very still. None of their disparate party seemed to have anything to say.

She closed her eyes for a moment, and thought that her greatest agony was realized. Of all the people in her life, he had been the one she had loved purely and simply, and with all her heart. He had been quick to laugh, slow to judge, eager always to find truth. He had loved peace, but he had never shunned what he saw as a righteous battle. He would have risked himself for any of his kin.

Over and over again.

She clenched her teeth, fighting the overwhelming pain that seized her. Of all of them, he had been the one who shouldn't have died. And he was lost now, lost to all of them.

"Allora—" Robert began gently, reaching down to her shoulders as if he'd help her rise.

But she couldn't bear his touch, not at that moment. She leaped to her feet with her eyes burning brightly with her tears and passion. "Leave me be, all of you just leave me be! Sir Christian, find our good priest and let him know that Laird Ioin has left us tonight, and that his soul must quickly be commended to God. Have Father taken to the chapel by men who loved him, for God forgive me, it is a task I cannot do myself."

"Allora!" Robert cried, trying again to come to her. But she backed away from him. "You are head of the

Canadys now, Uncle. But I am lady of the Far Isle. Sir Christian," she charged her father's favorite knight, before he could go about the tasks she had already alotted him, "I want Lady Elysia escorted south and on to York with safe passage."

"Nay, Allora!" Duncan cried angrily.

"I have said that it will be done!" Allora cried. "That is all," she told Sir Christian. "Except that I will be left alone in the chapel tonight with my father. Anyone else with complaints may speak with me after my father's body is laid to rest!"

She gazed around the crowd through her haze of tears. What travesty this! For once, they were all silent. Robert, Duncan, David—all staring at her, David's eyes so troubled, Duncan's so rebellious, Robert's narrowed now in speculation.

Only Elysia remained upon David's mount, looking down at the group of them. Her eyes touched her sister-in-law's for a minute, and Allora was startled by the sympathy she saw within them. She bit her lip, trying to fight another wash of devastating tears.

Beyond them, the fortress seemed unbearably silent. De Fries and the pursuing archers who had killed her father had apparently seen the flood of the ocean and the rise of the bridge. Her father's men—housecarls, soldiers, swordsmen, tanners, blacksmiths—all lined the parapets upon the walls, and all stared down now in silent horror. Then Allora heard a ragged gasp and a soft cry, and she saw that the servants had come even from the main tower, the castle keep, and Mildred, one of the cooks, was softly sobbing now; the sound broke the awful silence that had fallen. More and more sobbing could be heard, until the sound rose to a wail. Allora could not bear it, and she spun about, hurrying toward the entrance to the castle where she had lived all her life.

With her father.

She burst into the ground-level great hall, and hurried to the fire and stretched out her hands. She could see her father's blood upon them.

Someone came in behind her. She spun around, and was amazed to see that it was Elysia.

She stood there in the doorway, not entering further. "My brother will come after you, you know. He will crush you all!" she warned. "And it will not matter that you have now chosen to set me free."

Allora wanted only to be left alone. "William is an aging king, and one who fights battles still on all fronts. We are a distant place, and hard to conquer—and to some, not worth the effort."

"The effort will not matter," Elysia said.

"If you wish your freedom," Allora suggested in return, "you might, perhaps, want to leave now. Before all those men lining the walls decide that the only decent Norman blood is that which flows freely upon the ground."

"You wouldn't dare threaten my life!"

"I never wanted you here to begin with! I didn't want so many things—"

"But you have set them into motion."

"I have been cast into this travesty of fate!" Allora cried.

"You could have stopped it."

"Oh, aye! And yet you tell me that your great and mighty brother would not have pursued us so, that he would never seek to slay my father. Somehow, the wondrous Earl of Wakefield had no control over what has happened."

"You know that Bret admired your father—"

"I know that my father is dead at Norman hands, Elysia. And that is all that matters to me tonight. Now I am going to him. And I suggest that you leave, and swiftly." She stared at her sister-in-law, so like her in age, and in so many ways! She stood where the great doors opened, the blackness of the night beyond her, her tunic worn and ragged, her red hair wild and streaming free down her back, her face pale, but her chin high and her eyes blazing.

"Please, Elysia, go!" Allora insisted. "Before God, I pray you swift journey, and a good life!"

Elysia paused just a moment. Then she said quietly, "I pray for you, Allora. I pray that you survive the fires from hell which will surely come your way. In truth, I too wish you well." She turned and left, graceful, regal. Allora winced, thinking of her words, of the way Elysia had looked at her.

Like Bret had when she had awakened from her drugged and poisoned dreams . . .

She shook her head, and great tears again streamed from her eyes. None of it mattered. None of it, nothing. Not tonight. Her father was dead. Great Ioin lay cold.

And her heart, as well, seemed like ice.

She walked away from the fire, ignoring the blood on her hands, heedless of her own torn and muddied clothing. She left the keep and kept her shoulders squared, her head high as she walked among her people again, saying nothing. Everyone parted way, and she crossed the courtyard to the southernmost tower and the chapel there on the ground floor. She entered and found her father laid out on a stone, his sword now set into the grip of his folded hands.

She stared at his dear face a moment longer, slipped to her knees, and cried again.

And again, and again . . .

And all throughout the night. She kept her vigil in a lonely agony.

And when morning's light came once again, she thought that she would never cry again.

Chapter 14

*B*ret had sailed already from Dover and had scarcely touched a foot down on Norman soil when he received the message from William warning him that his bride and her family had disappeared swiftly from London in the middle of the night.

The waves crashed on the shore behind him and he tried to listen to them, to hear them, and fight the blinding red fury that settled over him. Since he had walked away from the London town house, he had lived with a raging tempest in his heart, for he could still grow both incredulous and irate every time he remembered that she had tried to poison him to death. And despite the fact that the wine had been meant for him, he had been crazed when he'd thought that she might die herself; and no matter what William's dictates, he had been determined not to travel until he had seen her safely from the grip of the stuff. It had agonized him to watch her suffer, even though the dull question remained within his mind as to quite why it did. She had willfully tried to kill him, yet he couldn't forget her pained whisper, denying that there could be poison, and of course it was insane that Robert, or whoever was masterminding things, would have risked *her* life in pursuit of him. But perhaps she didn't know, because she had drunk the poison. And he thought that he had suffered agonies as great as her own as he had watched her twist and turn and convulse, helpless until Damien had arrived and purged the poison. Life could be so very strange. He had found her beautiful when he had met her—what man would not, for she was slim and graceful and sensual in her form and movement, with the sun-gold cascade of hair down her back, the perfect softness of her skin, and those emerald-green eyes that challenged and tempted, warned and compelled. Yet she had irritated him with her absolute independence and her youthful dreams, and he hadn't known until their wedding night that she would become an obsession with him.

And yet, after everything, he had not expected this. Sometimes when she had looked at him with those emerald eyes, he had believed in them, believed that something had been born, created between them, that had the most curious touch of magic. She hadn't found him such a monster. Her fingers had curled into his hair, her lips had parted swiftly to his kiss. She had reached out with fascination, and touched him in return, and there had been the sweetest moments of greatest tempest in her arms, and then absolute peace.

Yet she hadn't lied. She had told him often enough that her people were free from William's yoke. She had cried her independence again and again. She had escaped him the first chance she might.

He gritted his teeth, furious once again with his powerlessness. The king was in a fierce mood, frightened on all fronts, a different man from the genius Bret had known when he was young. But William was aging now, and perhaps he'd been fighting so long he now saw danger sometimes where it was not. He had gathered his own men and a great number of mercenaries in 1085 to repel a threatened attack from the Norse army of King Sweyn, but the attack had been aborted before it had begun, for King Sweyn had been plagued with his own dissidents. William's troubles had begun anew in Normandy, for many of his allies had died, and Philip of France was always encroaching upon Normandy; and Robert, heir to Normandy, had sometimes fought against his father with the French king. Matters were never easy here. At the moment, they were in a rare state.

Bret stared at the messenger, trying to feel the wind again, to hear the surf surging behind him. He kept his voice even and level as he spoke to the man. "If my wife chooses to bide her time with her father, then let her go with him. I still have a great faith in Ioin Canadys, and

I will negotiate with my father-in-law and tend to matters myself when I am free from William's affairs."

He strode away, his anger well-leashed to all appearances. He headed into Rouen, already planning battle tactics against the Far Isle, for it would be a near-impregnable fortress to assault. He tried to tell himself that there truly might be no need for the warfare, and he hoped not, for a battle could make him hated for his lifetime by the very people he would rule. Ioin was a reasonable man, a fair man, and Bret was certain that only Ioin's brother's influence—and Bret's own foolish determination to keep the man from his daughter!—had prompted the flight north, and the situation might still be remedied if they had a chance to meet.

Bret reached his father's house in Rouen late at night, but his father and his brothers still awaited him, and greeted him warmly. They demanded details of his sudden wedding, and of the very swift disappearance of his new in-laws the moment he had vacated the city. Alaric d'Anlou, with threads of silver now touching his dark head, matching the steel color of his eyes, listened gravely.

"You agreed to this marriage for your mother's sake," he said sternly.

But Bret, seated with his back to the fire, his legs propped up, a goblet of wine he wasn't afraid to drink in his hands, shrugged. "Aye, at first," he admitted candidly. He looked at his father. "I'd not have wed her if I hadn't been intrigued with the possibilities."

Bret's younger brother, Philip, grinned. "If you have been too busy to hear gossip as of late, Father, my brother's errant heiress is reputed to be one of the greatest beauties of our Christian world."

Alaric arched a brow.

Again, Bret shrugged, casting Philip a hard stare. "I have said I was intrigued with the possibilities."

"And now?" Robin, more serious, very much like their father, demanded.

Bret lifted his hands in frustration. "And now I am in King William's service here in Normandy, and she is most probably behind the walls of her castle, and you have all seen how it sits on its mound of rock. I will need an army myself to take it. But equally, Father, you know Ioin Canadys. While he lives, there is hope of a peaceful settlement to this situation, and thus I have let it known that I do not want the rebels stopped, that I will tend to my wife and her kin when I have returned."

"It's the best decision," Alaric agreed. "Let's pray that William's affairs may be quickly dealt with here! He is at grave odds with Anjou, determined to bring Maine back into the fold, and above all, he is in a rage against the French king." Alaric shook his head. "I have known him since I was a boy. I have seen his great genius, I've seen his rages, I've seen his mercies. But I fear for him now. With his oldest son always in rebellion and Mathilda now gone, his military abilities are not what they were. Come," he told Bret. There was a huge map spread out over the table, and Alaric pointed out to Bret where they were now ordered to hold knights from Flanders at bay and to raze their border towns, for the Flemish knights had been invading the Norman borders, plundering, murdering, raping, and driving deep into William's territory.

For the moment, Bret managed to press the memories of his bride into a corner of his mind.

He did not forget her.

Things quickly became worse, for before they could gather and equip the army they were to lead, another message arrived for him, and this, though written by a scribe, was signed in the king's own hand.

Elysia had been abducted during the Scots' escape.

Bret raged, damning the king, promising an instant vengeance against the Far Isle. "Not a stone of the place will stand, not a man will live!" he swore violently. He had no choice but to tell his father and brothers the news, and as he had expected, they were all equally appalled, and they were all determined to defy William, to leave the constant clash of border skirmishing in Normandy *now*, and travel instantly, swiftly, north to have Elysia back. Charts were strewn over the table again, and they drew up a likeness of the castle and the land around it, and each man gave his opinion on the best way to assault such a fortress.

"Ioin may yet surrender," Bret said. "I don't believe that he took Elysia with any evil intent, or that he would let her be harmed."

"He might be attempting a trade with you, Bret," his father warned him.

"We get Elysia, he keeps his daughter," Robin agreed.

"His daughter is legally wed," Bret said. "So what does he gain?"

"I imagine that all the border lairds and the family Canadys will be extremely anxious to seek an annulment," Alaric replied. "They have kept up their defenses of the area through Malcolm at their back, and the sheer power of the fortress of the Far Isle. They keep close, and though they war with one another when there is no one else to fight, they have maintained their fierce independence by keeping all power among themselves. Clan Canadys will be very intent on freeing the lady from you."

"How in God's name can they get an annulment?" Bret demanded. "Perhaps . . ." He broke off, laughing bitterly. "It was the plan to begin with, it's why my bride was so distressed to find herself in a hunter's cottage instead of Father's London town house. But she didn't manage to escape then, so the marriage has been consummated."

Alaric shrugged, rubbing his clean-shaven chin. "You cannot imagine just how powerful the Church, or man's belief in it, can be. After all these years, I am convinced that Harold lost England to William not because of the Conqueror's strength, but because of Harold's own weakness once he saw that William had been granted the papal banner. It was more powerful than any weapon we carried. If Ioin's family is determined on such a case, they will very swiftly be sending to Rome."

"Then we must send our own men to Rome quickly as well."

"Father Damien will go," Alaric assured him.

Bret nodded, and turned back to the chart they had drawn.

"We will need an army, Father! My outrage is so great that I'm ready to go alone and pit nothing but my own weight against their doors—"

"And that is exactly what those wily Scots will be thinking," Robin put in.

"Aye, Bret! They'd be pleased to see you make an unprepared assault," Philip said.

"And your death would free your wife equally as well," Alaric warned.

"They have Elysia, so we go, and with whatever army we can manage," he said evenly. "Were it not for my sister, then, aye! I'd be willing to wait. And if I went against the fortress then, with a solid army of seasoned knights, if Ioin were to refuse me, I swear it would fall!"

"Then perhaps we should study the possible tactics again," Alaric told him, and again, they returned to their chart on the table, again seeking weaknesses within the fortress.

Yet even as they began making swift preparations to sail home and start the long ride north, Fallon herself arrived on Norman soil, a rarity, for she had shunned Normandy itself with a greater ferver than she shunned the king, and she hadn't stepped foot on land here since Mathilda had died. Her sons and her husband greeted her with the greatest surprise and pleasure and curiosity—after she had spent her first few moments in her husband's arms—but then she had quickly set aside their questions, and told them the latest news. "There is no need to abandon all and risk your necks with the king for Elysia, for she is free. The Scots returned her to York, Malcolm himself is sending his apology to King William, and to you, Alaric. Elysia will follow me here with Eleanor and Gwyn as soon as she has had a chance to reach home and ready them all for a stay in Normandy."

"They seized my daughter, then give her back—and thought that nothing would happen?" Alaric said incredulously.

"Father," Bret said evenly, "there is no one longing with a deeper passion than I myself to storm and take the Far Isle. But I do not intend to lose. I tell you again and you know well, we will need quite a force to take the Far Isle. We haven't that now, not with William demanding that so many men be here. I swear to you, I will see that Elysia's abduction does not go unpunished. If Ioin himself is guilty, then Ioin himself will pay." *As will my sweet wife!* he added in bitter silence to himself. "We had best hurry Damien onward as our emissary to the pope, for I'm quite certain that the Scots will seek an annulment of the marriage, Father, as you have suggested, and take away the right by which I demand surrender from Ioin, else storm the castle."

Fallon nodded gravely. "Aye, Bret, Damien must hurry. But Ioin cannot surrender to you nor negotiate, nor can he be made to pay for anything. He is dead."

"What?" Bret said, stunned.

"There were Norman troops who followed them. Elysia wrote me that her own greatest danger came when Norman archers, under your old friend Jan de Fries, pursued them to the castle. Apparently, de Fries had led a small band straight from London when word went out that Ioin and Robert had left with Allora—and Elysia as well. Elysia swears that Ioin is dead; she saw it all herself."

"Dear God!" Bret breathed. Jesu! The waste of it all. That damned fool de Fries! Always seeking the king's favor, never caring how he might acquire it. He recalled swiftly the night in the king's banqueting hall when de Fries had been so intrigued with Allora, and Allora, outraged, had injured de Fries, and his pride. Then he had stepped in himself and demanded the apology.

And now Ioin, the most reasonable man on the border, was dead. With his love of writing and reading, his great knowledge and gentle spirit. Dead.

And Robert Canadys now left as family head!

"All is lost then! It will be warfare, with no negotiation or surrender. Robert Canadys will see them all dead and rotting in hell!" he cried angrily. "Damn de Fries! Damn him to a thousand wretched hells!"

Fallon set a hand upon his shoulder. "There's nothing you can do now but wait, and be glad that Elysia is free. De Fries is in England, and none in power there will punish a man who has gone after a pack of rebels. What lies between you and Jan de Fries is personal, and Bret, somewhere in time, it may come to the fore. Ioin is dead. That cannot be changed, and yet it changes everything. Bret, again, think. Elysia is free and unharmed."

"Aye, Mother. I'm glad. Jesu!" He slammed a fist hard against the table.

Wait . . .

He would burn to ash in his own anger while he waited.

But Fallon was right. There was nothing else to do. He looked from his brothers to his father, and then nodded at last. "Aye, I will wait until I can take my men and forces with me. But I swear to you, I will take the Far Isle. And my wife will receive her just due!"

Fallon watched him for a moment and then sighed softly. "Actually, I was rather in sympathy with the bride— until, of course, those reckless wild men made off with my daughter. I do feel much better now, knowing that she is safe, and that she was never harmed. And perhaps . . ."

"Aye?"

"Perhaps you shouldn't judge Allora too harshly."

"No, Mother," he said with quiet bitterness, "I'm not so sure it would be possible to judge her too harshly now." He turned his back on his family, squaring his shoulders. Patience, he'd have to learn patience. It had never been one of his virtues.

But it was one cast hard upon him now, for by the end of the week, he was riding on the Angevin border, engaged in the siege of a castle taken by one of William's enemies.

The clang and clash of steel should have somehow expended the depths of his fury.

They did not. Each battle simply fed the fire, and in his dreams, he saw her. Saw her scorned, saw her beaten . . .

And saw her eyes when they made love. Imagined he felt the softness of her flesh. Saw her coming to him, thick lashes sweeping low over emerald eyes.

And he would toss and turn.

And awaken with his desire to reach the Far Isle burning ever more brightly within him.

The time would come, he swore. Aye, the time would come.

Christmas was nearly upon them. Allora stood in the great hall in the castle keep, the largest of the fortress's towers. The wind had been blowing fiercely for days now, and the keening of it seemed to tear through the stone walls. Now, the wind ebbed and darkness fell, lightened by a golden, glowing moon. Snow was falling. In fragile flakes it fell upon the courtyard and bailey and she stood, hands braced against the wall, and watched it through one of the slender arrow slits. Her father had always loved it when the snow fell. It didn't stay too long upon the ground, for the Far Isle was so closely embraced by the sea, and though the wind and cold could be staggering, snow never stayed long on the isle.

Christmas. It would be her first Christmas without him, she thought. She didn't cry. She stood in silence and wished that she still could cry, and that the crying would ease the pain of his loss.

And the strange emptiness in her own heart that went even beyond it. They had been wrong. Ioin would have said it, had he known all the truth. They had been so very wrong in what they had done.

But it didn't matter. Ioin was gone, and she was left with the responsibility for all that he and she and Robert had done together. She was responsible for everyone here, no matter how her uncle tried to assume both the responsibility—and the power.

"Milady!" Mary, her maidservant, a very pretty young dark-haired girl, called to her softly. Allora turned to see that Robert had arrived, along with David and Duncan. She had been waiting for the meeting, and was ready for them.

"Uncle!" She kissed Robert's cheek, and then politely did the same with David and Duncan. In the weeks since they had been back, Robert had never once let up on her, demanding that she send someone to see the pope and convince him that there must be an annulment to the marriage.

David, her uncle's obvious intended choice for her, had shown his customary gentle courtesy, and though she had been pained to realize that the feelings of love and infatuation she had toward him had faded, she cared for him ever more deeply as a good and trusted friend. And she thought that he *was* that, even if he was too often influenced by his own reckless half-brother, Duncan.

"There's wine and ale on the table," she invited, taking nothing for herself and sitting at the head of the table. Craig, her father's seneschal, entered the room quietly and waited, leaning against the wall. He was not one of the border lairds himself, but as the one accustomed to the day-to-day running of the fortress, of seeing to the necessities of the knights and fighting men within the household, as well as any guests who might arrive, Allora thought that he must hear anything that they might have to say in this gathering.

Robert had requested the meeting, and now he sat at the first chair in the lengthwise section of the table, taking Allora's hand in his. She almost wrenched it away, and wondered how she could still love him for being the uncle who had been with her so closely for all of her life—and yet harbor such fury toward him for the things he had done.

"This waiting is dangerous, Allora! We must have your letter, a heartfelt plea to the pope. He can see that there will be an immediate annulment."

Duncan sat across from Allora, swiftly pursuing the point. "By the saints, Allora, we can wait no longer. They claim that your Norman husband was in a rage, swearing that he would raze the fortress and see you shackled and imprisoned until the day that you died! Robert he would clearly long to murder, and the rest of us would be debased just as the Saxon nobility was! He wants us all to become swineherds! We are all in danger while you wait on this annulment!"

She listened to them both in silence, then looked up at David, who remained standing, his eyes level upon hers. "And what are your thoughts on the matter?" she asked him.

"You must do what you see and feel in your heart as right, Allora," he said simply, and she smiled, lowering her lashes. She did have one friend among them.

But Robert slammed a heavy fist upon the table. "Haven't you listened? If he comes here, niece, *you must fight him.* Do you understand that? By every man, woman, and child, each tenant, each freeman, each serf, you must fight him. Or seal the doom of us all."

She rose and walked over to the fire, warming her hands there, wishing that her husband's face would fade from her mind, or that she could look into the flames and not see him there. Well, they were right about one thing. He would surely never forgive her. In his eyes, she had attempted to poison him. To death. And she had abducted his sister, and that was probably equally as atrocious a crime. She had practiced deceit from the very start.

"If he comes," she said quietly, "I will not go against your wishes. We will fight a Norman force. But perhaps you are wrong. It has been some time. He has not come yet."

"William has the majority of his men in Normandy, lady, there is no secret to that. To fight the Danes when he was afraid they would assault England at last, he brought back an army from Normandy. Now he takes even Englishmen to Normandy in his greedy determination not to lose one square foot of his bloodstained land," Duncan said disdainfully.

"If he would have come swiftly, we just might have bested him by now," Robert said irritably. "We should have never let that wretched girl, his sister, go! He would have come then, reckless and hot, and we would have slain him with ease."

He was wrong; Allora was quite certain he was wrong. They might have slain Bret—but never, never with ease.

"If he comes, we will fight him," Allora said. She stared hard at Robert. "But there will be no annulment."

"Allora—"

"There will be no annulment, Uncle, because I am going to have a child."

"What?" Robert said, standing, rigid with anger and dismay.

"I am quite certain, Uncle Robert, that I am going to have his child. But mine as well. My father's grandchild. And I will not make this babe a bastard for you, or for any man or woman in this place."

"Jesu!" Robert cried, frustrated. He came around the table and approached her, grasping her shoulders. "Allora, this child will be his heir—and his steel binding to the fortress! You must have the annulment; David will claim the babe. We will keep the birth a secret—"

"No!" Allora cried. "You go too far, Uncle, too far! I have told you, I will not make this babe a bastard for you or for anyone. Now I pray that I am quite clear, and I am also quite tired. Unless you have something more to discuss, Uncle, I will leave you here, milords, and Craig will be pleased to order the servants to bring you a meal. My father's hall will always welcome you. Now, I bid you all good night."

"How could you have done this?" Robert demanded furiously.

She coolly arched a brow. "Uncle Robert, may I remind you—you were the one who assured me I could legally wed this man and still escape him unscathed. Well, you were wrong. And if you would cast accusations about, you might like to begin with God, for it seems that this is His will."

"Allora—"

"Good night, Uncle!" she repeated firmly.

She turned and left them, walking smoothly across the floor, determined that she would not lose to Robert tonight. How dared he! He hadn't really cared about sacrificing her innocence, not when it meant his escape. But now, that sacrifice was coming back to haunt him, and he was heartily sorry indeed.

Perhaps she had found her strength, and her own voice, for Robert Canadys did not try to stop her or waylay her. Nor did he seem inclined to argue any more that night.

She heard him groan and sink down in a chair. "Dear God, but all is lost! How will we ever fight to win now?"

She didn't answer him, but started up the stairs. Looking down from the curve, she could see that Duncan and David both watched her make her way to the floor above them.

David gazed at her with sorrow, and with sympathy, she was certain. But Duncan . . .

Duncan looked as if he longed to throttle her.

She longed to say more to David, to try to explain how things had changed, yet she didn't really have an explanation herself. She was exhausted. She had spent the day holding manor court, listening to all the grievances the people within the fortress and working upon the mainland had against one another. Those had seemed so complicated today! Henry the miller wanting recompense because Geoffrey, the cooper's son, had gone off with his daughter on the night of All Souls. The daughter wanted nothing more than the cooper's son, but the miller wanted two fat pigs as well, and Allora had agreed to both the marriage and the pigs. There had been other such petty problems. And one by one, she had gone through them. It had been the first court she had ever held alone, and it, too, had been painful, for she could all too easily remember sitting there with Ioin, listening to his grave judgments, always anxious when he asked her opinion first, teaching her, and delighting in her when she gave the same verdict he himself had chosen to give.

It had made for a long day.

She had really wanted to be rid of her uncle. When she passed the second flight of stairs and came to the master's chamber which occupied the whole of the third floor of the tower, she laid down upon the big bed where she had been born, and curled into a ball.

A fire burned gently in the hearth. She stared at it and closed her eyes, and felt the warmth of the flame. Sweet Jesu, but the time she had been with him had been so brief! But day and night, unforgettable. She could see his eyes in the flames, feel his heat. Remember . . .

Their time together had been brief indeed, but she was going to have a child, his child. She didn't intend to reconcile with him, for she was convinced she could not. Her people would not have it, and Bret . . .

Bret would not want it either, she was certain. He desired to see her again, of that she was also certain. Simply to take away everything she might hold dear—simply to make her pay her dues for all that she had done. She could remember his face, remember his touch . . . and she could also remember his absolute fury at what she had done.

"O God!" she prayed suddenly, vehemently, aloud. "If You have any mercy at all, please, please, let me stop thinking about him! Let me sleep, let me rest, I beg of You, O dear Lord!"

But it seemed God turned a deaf ear to her that night, for though she closed her eyes and found sleep quickly, she dreamed.

And her dreams were plagued by a man in a suit of glittering armor, a horned helmet atop his head, the whole golden length of him burning in the sun . . .

Riding. Riding a snow-white horse and bearing down upon her, closer and closer. She could feel his eyes upon her, feel him condemning her. And she longed to cry out, longed to touch him. But the steel of the sword was falling.

And she had no choice but to run, and keep running.

Elysia arrived with Eleanor and Gwyn in Normandy when the snow was piled high and the winds of winter began to set their icy fingers upon the land. Bret had been fighting in the Vexin, once again seizing back land that had been wrested from the king's control, but upon news of their arrival, he left the rebellious castle in siege and hurried to Rouen where he would find his sisters.

He was anxious to see to Elysia's welfare, but on first sight he knew, in truth, that she was fine and healthy, and unharmed. Lovely as always with her wild red hair and silver-gray eyes, serene face, alabaster skin. She hugged him fiercely, then he swept up Gwyn and held Eleanor, greeting them. He wasted no time, but stared at Elysia anxiously, demanding to know if she had been let go unharmed and untouched.

She smiled at him, pushing back a lock of black hair from his forehead. "Brother! I have already gone through this with Father, you know."

"Aye, well, milady sister, you may now go through it with me. I am responsible for what befell you. And if they dared to harm you in any way, Elysia, I will rip them to shreds, I swear it."

"I know!" she assured him. "And I told them that, and I do think it brought a definite measure of fear to their hearts."

"Not enough, apparently. What happened?"

Elysia sighed, as if it were a story she had told a dozen times already. "Mother read your message, that Allora had been ill, yet you had to leave as soon as she pulled through the worst of it." She winced. "We all felt a bit sorry for her—"

"For being saddled with me?" he demanded. "Thank you, Elysia!"

Elysia blushed. "For the circumstances, Bret! She was far from home, alone, and ill. But when I arrived in your room, I found no Allora, only Laird Ioin, and he instantly apologized profusely, then knocked me upon the head with the hilt of his sword. I did not awaken until we had come far from the city."

"And then? Who was with them? How many?"

"Laird Ioin, his brother Robert. Two border knights— David of Edinburgh and his half-brother, Duncan. Allora No more."

"And they never harmed you?"

"Bret, no. That wretched David was like a leech upon me, and I could not escape. But neither, in all his exasperation, did he ever harm me."

"And Ioin is dead. You saw it?"

She nodded. "Bret, it was horrible. For all that happened, my heart broke for your bride. She would not let him go. His blood covered her, and she held him, and could not set him down. And when she did, she was furious with them all—and demanded that they set me free. Bret, I know how angry you are. But it was Allora who forced them to free me." She shivered. "Robert Canadys and Duncan were determined that I made a good hostage. I think either of them would have slit my throat in a second if it would have advanced them in any way."

He arched a brow. "Are you suggesting I forgive Allora because she had the sense to realize we would all raze the castle or die in the attempt to free you?"

Elysia exhaled softly. She shook her head. "Perhaps not. But there is the possibility she might want to reason with you, perhaps negotiate some terms . . ."

"Well, I will be waiting," he told Elysia.

Elysia nodded, looking as if she wanted to say more. "What?"

She shrugged. "Robert Canadys would be delighted to see either the wedding annulled—or you dead. I don't think he'd care which. And I think . . ."

"Aye, Elysia! What?"

"I think you had best take care about this young man, David of Edinburgh. I tried to listen while I was in their company, pretending to sleep when I could hear whispers. Robert wants Allora very quickly freed from you, and wed to this man."

Bret leaned against a wall as he listened to her. Maybe it was good that he would have time to cool his temper. He wanted to kill her—and the Scot, David of Edinburgh. Maybe in time . . .

"But Bret, even as we arrived here today, Father received word from Damien in Rome. He has set our case before the pope, and the pope has agreed that it is a valid marriage. And as yet, no one has arrived from the Far Isle to plead a case for Allora."

"It won't matter," he said softly after a moment. "Whenever I am free, I will go there. And she will surrender the fortress, or I will raze it, every ragged outcropping of stone will fall into the sea."

"Bret—"

His eyes leveled on hers. "By then," he said wearily, "I will have lain siege to so damned many of the king's castles here, there will be no man more expert at the task!"

When March came, Bret was fighting in Brittany. He was astounded to see Father Damien riding across the battlefield toward him.

Damien reined in quickly, and greeted Bret.

"This is a miracle!" Bret murmured, clasping his hand, awaiting his words.

"It was news I thought I should bring myself."

"Tell me quickly."

"The pope has refused an annulment, but he was never asked to sanction one. No one ever arrived from the Far

Isle. I have friends in the border region and I sent them in to find out what is happening."

"And?" Bret demanded. He should have been wary of anything, but Damien, he had realized, had not come to give him bad news.

"There can be no annulment, my lord," Damien said, with a certain amount of amusement.

"Pray, go on!" Bret demanded.

"They have managed to keep the news very quiet, but now the truth is quite apparent. Within the next few weeks, my lord, you're going to be a father. And no matter what Robert seeks to do, your child will be heir to the Far Isle."

Chapter 15

~~~

*T*he winter seemed such a strange time for Allora. The winds blew fiercely throughout it. Snows whirled and fell and disappeared into the sea. News came infrequently, for travel was difficult. Within the fortress walls, men whittled before the fires. Hounds bayed strangely during the night, and each time one cried beneath the rise of a full moon, Allora would awaken, and wait, and remember.

Bret did not come. She had been certain at first that he would, but Robert had gleefully told her that the Conqueror was spending Christmas and beyond in Normandy, and that his men were constantly engaged in battle there.

And still, it was a waiting time. She waited for the harsh winter to end, because men might come to do battle then, when the spring arrived.

Christmas came and went, another quiet time, for she remained in the deepest mourning for her father. Twelfth Night came and passed as well, January grew evermore fierce, but as it ended, she felt the first stirrings of life within her. She was both elated and anxious, awed by the fact that the babe then seemed very real, and then tormented again by that fact.

There were days when she stood in the great hall, watching the incessant whirl of the snow, and longed to pick up a quill and write to Bret. But what in God's name could she say? She didn't know, but one day the urge to put something down was so strong that she did hurry up the stairs to the high tower room and sit at the table before the shafts of light with ink and quill and begin to write.

215

Bret d'Anlou, Earl of Wakefield: Forgive me the evil things I did to you, but don't, please don't come here, because my kinsmen are longing to trap and slay you; even the simple people who live and work within the fortress and the countryside loathe you and all Normans, for Robert has seen to it that you have been blamed for my father's death. Then, of course, there is the matter that I have heard you wish nothing more to do with me, that you intend to lock me away—if you do not strangle me first—then seize the isle, and seek your own divorce. God help me, I am afraid, and yet now, when I am wondering if this babe will be a boy or a girl, dark or blond, I cannot help but wish that you were here . . .

She stopped writing. It was a foolish pasttime. There had never been such hatred for the Normans in the Far Isle as there was now, because Ioin had been so fiercely loved. She slid the letter into the chest with her writing materials and stared from the tower window. It had been such a foolish thought, and it hadn't done anything to soothe the tempest in her soul. She was, admittedly, at this point, afraid of him. He thought she'd attempted to poison him, and he would never believe that she hadn't been eager for escape the second his back was turned. They'd kidnapped his sister. And she knew, if Robert did not, that Bret, with his will and determination, and even his arrogance, would come eventually. She prayed that he wouldn't be harmed, because he had somehow entered her soul, and she could not forget him, or forget the brief time between them when something had been surrendered for something else exquisite to be gained. As time passed, she prayed that she might forget him. But she could not, and it didn't help that she grew larger daily with their child.

Robert watched her constantly, and she knew that he was waiting, hoping that she would lose the babe. He asked after her health, and then seemed disappointed each time she told him that she felt wonderfully well.

"You invite disaster upon us!" he told her once.

Though Robert's manor and lands were on the mainland, as were those of David and Duncan, and all the other border lairds and their knights, they were often in the fortress, as they had always been, for the clan meetings had been held there, and matters of great importance had always been decided there. Each of the lairds was a man who had paid homage to Malcolm, and the Scottish king had taken on many of the Norman feudal systems. Beneath him each lord had several knights he trained and outfitted for the defense of their home and the realm, and for the protection of the serfs and craftspeople and freemen who lived and worked beneath the laird's wing. Thus those men who had been called housecarls in Laird Ioin's early days very frequently became knights, and they strove to earn the privileges of their overlords, hoping to be rewarded for their services with lands of their own. Most of these matters were decided within the walls of the fortress. In the olden days, the lairds of the fortress had been as kings themselves, and since those days, the other lairds had always come to the fortress; and when Malcolm sent his messages and his calls to arms, it was to the fortress he sent his own men.

But winter remained quiet, and at last turned to spring.

Allora watched the snows melt on the mainland, and then the farmers and tenants began to plant their fields. The blacksmiths began working again in the open air of the bailey; children played along the shoreline, barefoot, running in the sand.

And men began to train again. She stood at the windows then and watched them below, heaving their heavy swords upon one another, listening to Sir Christian's shouts and warnings and teachings. Robert came frequently, too, warning her that the winter had passed, roads were easily passable again.

"Wakefield may yet come. Those wretched lands given him are not so far from here that he will not eventually reach out. Now, Allora, I am well aware that you will not agree to an annulment for the sake of your child—"

"Ioin's grandchild as well," she reminded her uncle.

"But we will then have to consider the best manner for achieving a divorce. You are inviting disaster upon us."

"You tell me that Bret remains in Normandy, that William has lost all his genius and will probably die somewhere in his homeland battling someone. But *I* am inviting disaster."

"Wakefield could be killed," Robert said reflectively.

And Allora turned away from him. Yes, Bret could be killed. But she didn't believe it. He would live, she thought, if only to come after her. She dreaded the day, and yet strangely, she dreamed of it at night, seeing him as if she saw him through a wall of flame. And she was screaming his name, praying that he would come to her on his white horse, his eyes gleaming through the silver slits of his helmet.

Within her household, the spring became a pleasant season. Flowers bloomed on the hillsides facing the isle, the winds blew softly, cool and inviting. Now when she rode out, she saw newborn lambs coating the cliffs white. Does ran rampantly across the forests with their fawns. The world had become very beautiful, and she sometimes found it hard to meet or dine with the uncle she had once loved so very much. She was glad to find out that she was growing stronger in her own private realm. She met with Sir Christian daily, and together they looked to the fortress's defenses, saw the masons about the upkeep of the walls, and helped plan strategies in the event of attack. The fortress was valuable to everyone because of its near-impregnable position. When the tide was out and the sands were dry to the gates, men could pour across from the mainland on horseback with scaffolding and rams, but if the defenders just held them off until nightfall, the tides would come and sweep away the implements of war. There were freshwater wells within the walls for drinking, and when prepared, the castle could withstand a tremendous siege.

They prepared. Candles and soap were made, meat was smoked. Greens were taken from the gardens and dried, berries were brought, basket after basket. The mill kept grinding an exhaustive abundance of flour, and Allora was glad to oversee it all. She kept an even, level temper with Robert, and as the months passed, she discovered that Sir Christian would come to her first with a question, that Timothy, the tally reeve, gave her all his reports, and that even Father Jonathan came to her exclusively with problems of the more day-to-day nature. She approved marriages, solved disputes, collected revenues. She even joined in with the training sessions in war skills, not shirking from a chance to show her own skill with a sword until the babe had really grown big and she grew frightened that her own activity might injure it.

There were good times then, too. Peaceful times. In a strange way, she grew closer to David than she had ever been, for though he lived outside the castle upon the mainland, he frequently came to see her, and he would sit with her at night before the fire; sometimes they would listen to a traveling minstrel, and sometimes she would read to him, or he would read to her. He was soothing to be with after her uncle's constant harping that she must make some move soon or else she was betraying them all.

One night when June had just come upon them, and Robert had been especially strident in his condemnation of all things Norman, David stayed behind when her uncle and Duncan had returned to their own homes. He read to her endless pages of work by the Greek Sophocles while she worked on a tapestry for the north side of the wall in her chambers, determined to keep out the least chill and to make the stone fortress as warm and welcoming as Fallon's London town house had been. David had stopped reading. She looked up and found him studying her.

"What? Are you thinking that I am betraying everyone as well by not agreeing to let Robert battle for an annulment?" she demanded. "After all," she continued bluntly, "you are the one with the most to lose. Robert had intended you to be laird here."

"Allora, I have a comfortable manor and fine, rich lands. I hold them from the laird or lady of the Far Isle, but I don't fear that they should be stripped away. You do not want an annulment and, because of the babe, it is easy to understand why."

"So you do not seek to wed me?"

He smiled gently then, and she thought that she had never cared so greatly for him as she did now. "If your husband were to die, my lady, then I would be the first suitor at your door. Or if he were to disavow you, and seek another. But you see, Allora, I do love you. And I think that you are in great enough torment now not to be given more from me."

His tenderness at that moment seemed to catch upon all her wayward emotions. She burst into tears, and found herself in his arms, only the size of her abdomen a true obstruction between them. He held her, letting her cry, then he pulled away suddenly, and they both saw a shadow disappearing down the stairs.

"Someone trying to leave us alone, and encourage romance, no doubt," David murmured dryly.

She nodded, but she had an uneasy feeling. Two housecarls were always stationed just beyond the door to the tower keep. The house servants slept elsewhere, the main keep being the hall and kitchens on the first floor, guest quarters on the second, and the whole of the third being taken by the master's chambers. Her second cousin, Lilith, recently widowed, her husband lost in one of Malcolm's raids into the area known as no-man's-land, had come to stay with her until the babe was born, to help her in whatever way she could. She kept a room on the second floor here, but she had retired long ago for the night. Allora's personal maid, Mary, young and sweet and a good friend as well as a servant, also kept a room on the second floor. Allora could not imagine either of them watching her quietly and then disappearing. But there had been no alarm, and so anyone within the keep would have access there; it must have been someone slipping quietly away rather than interrupting them.

She might have worried about it more, or at least sought an answer to the question of who it was, except that at that very moment, she felt the first pain.

It was a strange thing, not so terrible. It started in her lower back, and seemed to sweep around her, like a tightening belt. She inhaled, wondering if she had imagined it, then drew away from David to sit suddenly before the fire.

"Allora? What is it?"

She smiled. "I'm not sure, I've never done this before. But I think . . . I think this is it."

"You think?"

She nodded. "Well, it's not very bad . . ."

Within an hour, she was ruing those words. The pains came frequently, and they were no longer just a tightening. It began to feel as if some awful, invisible demon was trying to slice right through her.

By then, Mary and Lilith had been called, and Meghana, the midwife from the mainland, had been sent for. She'd had to come by boat, but she did so quickly, and when she arrived, she found Allora balled up on the bed, swearing like an old berserker, and, for once, decrying Bret d'Anlou in a way which would have greatly pleased her uncle. Allora was outraged at first when toothless old Meghana made her rise and walk, but when the old woman warned her that the pains could go for hours and that walking might shorten them, Allora started a smooth pacing around the room.

The pains did last for hours. Mary tried to soothe her, and Lilith did her best as well. Allora tried not to scream, or give way to tears. Eventually, the pain became constant, and Meghana bade her be still then, and smoothed back her soaked hair, assuring her that the bairn was big and healthy, and due now any minute. Nearly insane with the agony that reached across her, Allora whispered wildly. "He did this on purpose!" she cried. "Oh, he did this on purpose! So smug, so damned arrogant, he just had to have things his way. Damn him to a thousand hells, and damn my uncle Robert for all that he has done to me!"

"Hush!" Lilith warned her, holding her hand, letting Allora squeeze her fingers with a death grip.

"Now! Push the wee bairn, push!" Meghana said.

She pushed. The pain left her. She felt the most incredible relief, felt the tiny body slip from her own, and then heard nothing for what seemed like endless time.

Then she cried out at last, terrified. "He's dead!" She gasped, sitting up, reaching out. "Oh, my God—" And then she broke off because she heard the sudden great wail, and she knew the baby lived. "Oh, thank You, God! Thank You!" she whispered, and tears slipped down her cheeks as Meghana lifted the squalling infant high before her.

"The babe lives, but it is a *she*, milady!" Meghana said with a cackle. "Now *that* will be a cross for them all to bear, eh, my lady? Your Norman husband *and* your wily uncle!"

At the moment, Allora didn't give a damn about either man. She wanted her daughter. But Mary was busy obeying Meghana's commands to clean the wailing little bundle of life, and it seemed forever before Allora could actually get her hands on her own babe. When she did, she simply stared at her with utter amazement. She was so wonderfully, absolutely perfect. She had a tiny doll's face, not crinkled as it might have been, but rosy-cheeked and wide-eyed. They were blue eyes, and the amazingly wild, thick cap of hair was darker than ebony.

Allora looked up at Meghana as the wrinkled old crone stared down at them both with smug pleasure. "She's a beauty, milady. Ah, indeed, a glory to behold is the wee bairn!"

"Will she stay like this, Meghana?" Allora asked. "Will her eyes stay blue, her hair—"

"Ah, now, lady, I don't be knowin' that! 'Tis true that most are born with blue eyes, and they change. And light hair goes dark, and dark goes light. It will not matter. It seems already she has your lovely face, Allora of the Far Isle, and will grow to haunt the future of many a poor lad!"

Allora smiled and lay back, exhausted but still determined to study her infant daughter. She wanted to watch her for hours, but Meghana reminded her after a moment that the baby was howling because she had been born hungry. So Allora rather awkwardly made her first attempts to feed her child, then thrilled anew when she felt the first hungry rooting of her daughter against her breast. Finally, the babe was fed, her tiny eyes were closed. Lilith swept her up, cooing over her. Allora smiled, and slept.

Bret rode into her dreams that night. There was a fog upon a field, and he rode out of it. She saw him coming on his great white Ajax, and she started to run. But she was carrying the baby, and the babe weighed her down. Finally she had to stop, had to turn and face him, and wait. And he dismounted from Ajax, and strode toward her in his coat of mail and shimmering horned helmet. And he reached out for the babe, seizing her from Allora with one gauntleted hand. Then he stared at her, and cried out in rage, and his sword began to swing . . .

Meant to sever Allora's head.

She woke up, screaming, shaking. Lilith, plain and plump but gentle and sweet as the warm winds of summer, came running in. "What is it, what is it, Allora?"

Allora shook her head, quickly looking to the corner of the room where her newborn infant slept in the cradle that had once been her own. "A dream!" she whispered. "But it's all right, it's over."

"I'll stay with you," Lilith offered.

Allora shook her head, forced a smile to her lips, and made Lilith leave. When her cousin was gone, Allora stretched her hands out over her bed. She felt tears slipping from her lashes, burning down her cheeks. Despite the fear her dream had generated, she missed Bret. Missed him horribly that night, and could not forget the evening she had lain in his arms, so secure, held with such gentle tenderness after such wild sweet tempest. The result of that tempest now lay sleeping so near her, so perfect a babe, and so like him in so many ways.

She knew that she cried then because she really might have fallen in love with him. Because it was impossible to fall in love with or hate a man because of his nationality; she had become entranced and seduced because of the man himself.

And she was his enemy; she *had* to be his enemy.

Or a traitor, one or the other. There was no middle ground.

She leaped out of bed and cried out, for she had forgotten how sore she was, how painful giving birth had proven to be. But it didn't matter anymore, of course. She had her daughter, and she raced across the room to sweep her up into her arms, even though her infant howled in protest.

"Sweet little lady!" she whispered softly in the moonglow and pale candlelight that filled the room. "I swear that I will protect you above all else, and as to the men in our lives, all of them—well, they are all welcome to just go hang themselves!"

She cradled the baby in her arms and walked back to the huge bed, clean and welcoming now with fresh cool sheets. She lay there with the baby, watching her again. "The Far

Isle will be yours. And I don't care what any of them say!"
Allora vowed. "I love you. I love you so very much!"

And it would have been a happy night for her, if she
hadn't realized something as she spoke those words.

Time had not cleansed her mind or soul. If only in a
secret portion of her heart, she loved her babe's father just
as well.

And feared him . . .

And longed for him.

"My lord! My lord Bret d'Anlou!"

He heard the words shouted over the din of men who
had just broken through the castle's defenses on the Maine
border, the line where the Comte de Marcus had so defied
William. Another siege, now ended in victory. Men streamed
through the castle walls, shouting victoriously. But through
that crowd, from the slope of the eastward hill that led to the
valley where the castle stood, Bret could see a rider coming
toward him. Several riders, and bearing his family colors
of blue and gold. He lifted his helmet from his head and
wiped the grime from his face. It was Damien coming with
three well-armed and mailed knights as escort, though Bret
was convinced that the strange Saxon priest who had come
to serve his Norman father so well could handle himself in
any battle of arms, whether he had taken the cloth or not.

"Father!" he cried in greeting. "Welcome to another scene
of battle!"

"Another victorious one," Damien commented, reining
in. He watched as the victors, afoot and upon horseback,
kept streaming into the bailey. Chickens came flapping out,
squawking; sheep and goats followed, bleating.

Bret shrugged. "It was a weak defense; a stupid one. The
compt was a fool to fight William."

"Most men are fools to fight him," Damien said softly,
"though it is quite possible . . ."

"What?" Bret asked sharply. He waved a hand in the air.
"Never mind. Don't answer me that. I've a tent on the field.
Come with me, out of the sun. Have some wine."

"I didn't mean to interrupt," Damien said uneasily, hearing
more cacophonous cries as more animals came streaming

out, many of them pursued by soldiers. "Perhaps your men need your guidance now?"

Bret smiled. "Father, there will be no rape, no murder, no wanton cruelty—this battle has been waged under my command, and I am seeking no revenge. The men are free to do what plundering is easy taking, but they have followed me wisely and well through many wretched months now and they will not take matters too far. Will you have some wine?"

"I would well love some good wine," Damien agreed.

They rode to the tent Bret had set up just on the outskirts of the battlefield. He had now been at this particular castle for nearly two months.

It should have held out longer, yet he was becoming amazingly proficient in the art of siege warfare. It was the one advantage that kept him from going mad here.

Damien joined him on a camp stool beneath the shade of the tent as Gillys, Bret's newly acquired Angevin squire, brought them both wine.

Bret leaned forward, his eyes showing his burning desire for whatever news Damien had brought. He had hidden his impatience well until this moment, but now it spilled over.

"Pray you, Father, and quickly. What news do you bring?"

"The Lady Allora gave birth to a live and healthy daughter one week ago today. I have just learned that she was christened Brianna Elise the following day. The infant is perfect and quite beautiful, so say all who have seen her."

Bret leaned back, startled by the trembling that seized him. A daughter. Perfect and beautiful. She was Allora's daughter; what else would she be? He wondered fleetingly if some word would come from his wife herself, but he knew that it would not. He wondered just what the gender would mean. Had Allora borne a son, Bret might well have feared that Robert Canadys might have been so foul as to arrange to smother the babe in the night. A girl was probably much safer in Robert's midst. He would not darken himself in Allora's eyes by harming a child when he could see no benefit to himself. He would surely be insisting that

Allora pursue a divorce. If she married again and bore a son, that child would take precedence over a Norman lord's daughter.

He exhaled softly, then said:

"Is there anything else?"

Damien sipped his wine slowly, as if he hesitated in answering.

"Damien, damn you—"

"Don't you damn me, my lord, I'm a priest, and well accustomed to both your parents in their wild and arrogant moods!"

"I am both of them combined, and doubly wretched!" Bret said. "For the love of God, if you've something to say—"

"Only this. You must go to the king, and get him to grant you permission and men to take with you to seize the fortress of the Far Isle, and you must do so soon."

"Why the haste?"

"Lady Allora grows closer to old friends these days. There is a young man, David of Edinburgh, surely being groomed to take the castle."

Bret rose slowly, draining his wine, fighting the tempest of rage that was unleashed within him. He'd been patient, so damned patient, serving the king—waiting. Now a daughter had been born to him, and very shortly, his wife would be ready for a lover once again. And despite the fury he had borne her, simmering over these long and tedious months, there was nothing that could still the flame of jealousy in his heart and soul at the thought of her being with another man. He wanted her back. Wanted to see her again. And even if pride and fury demanded he not desire her, he would not permit anyone to take his place.

He had served well. He had always served William well. The time had come for the king to repay him.

"Damien, if you know anything more than what you're telling me—"

"There is nothing more," the priest said with assurance. He stood, coming around to Bret and facing him squarely. "I swear to you, my good young lord, that I would warn you of anything else amiss. My only suggestion is that you hurry. I am certain that the lady has not betrayed certain of her marriage vows—not as yet."

"And how is that? Can you see into the fortress walls?" Bret demanded.

"I see into men's hearts, and I have never given you reason to doubt me."

"Nay, Father Damien, you have not," Bret admitted. He lifted his chalice to him.

Damien grinned suddenly. "It's also true that the priest there, a Father Jonathan, has served the Far Isle for nigh unto twenty years. But before that, when he was a poor young man in need of help to reach his clerical goals, I was able to help him out—and your father gave assistance as well. Gratitude sometimes has a comfortably long arm."

"Well and good!" Bret said, pleased. He at least had some contact with the inside. "Thank you for the news you have brought me. I will hasten to William."

"I will join you. And I will be at your side—now and until we have taken the Far Isle."

"Indeed, it is time. I am coming to my rightful inheritance now, as sworn by Laird Ioin before God. And I will take that fortress apart stone by stone—and my countess, limb by limb, if necessary!"

"Bret—" Damien began worriedly.

But Bret was already out of the tent and seeking his horse. He meant to ride to William then and there.

Brianna was a month old, a greater joy to her mother than ever. Allora had left her in Mary's arms by the fire when the door to the keep burst open and her uncle came striding in angrily, David and Duncan at his heels like ever-vigilant watchdogs. Sir Christian came in behind them with several of the knights of the Far Isle, her father's best men, at his back.

"You had best prepare every able-bodied man and the isle itself for siege, madam. News has reached us that Bret d'Anlou has gone to the king with a demand for men. He means to raze the castle—and slay us all. Including you, so we have been told," Robert said.

"He means to come here and murder us all?" she asked, keeping her tone cool and level, even if the length of her seemed to tremble with hot fire. "I cannot believe that—"

"Believe it, lady. You nearly murdered him yourself—"

"I!"

"You were the one put the poison in the wine."

"And drank it as well!" Allora reminded him.

"Well, we will all pay now, eh?" Robert demanded sourly.

Allora stared at him, hating him. "Some of us have been paying for a long time already, Uncle!" she said, and whirled around, staring at them all. "My father did sign a contract with this man, and if he comes against us, many lives will be lost. We can surrender the castle—"

"Allora, what of you?"

It was David who interrupted her then, his voice quiet, reasonable. He shook his head. "What of you, what of our lands beyond the fortress walls? These men will fight, because they will fight Norman rule. They will fight, because your father was slain. They will not surrender; they will demand that you fight as well."

She was silent, in anguish, as minutes ticked by. "And you are going to beat him, right, Uncle?" she demanded of him.

"Indeed, milady! I will best the Norman bastard's henchmen!"

"Pray that you do, Uncle," she said softly. She scooped Brianna up from Mary's arms and left them, starting up the stairway.

"Allora!" Robert thundered. "Will you fight, or betray us all?"

She paused, looking down at him furiously. "Oh, I will fight, Uncle. And it might well turn out to be the worst treachery I might design against my people!" She hurried on to her tower room. A moment later, she heard a light knocking, and she realized that Lilith and Mary had loyally followed her.

"Milady, is there anything—" Mary began.

"Aye!" Allora said swiftly, handing Brianna to Lilith. The baby loved Lilith with her gentle touch and wide bosom. "I'll take ale, oceans of it! Anything, just to sleep one night in peace!"

But not even the ale she drank could ease her soul now. She dreamed again.

And in her dreams, he was coming still. Riding through the mists of fog. Coming . . .

Bret received the king's permission to leave and his promise that, in addition to taking his own men, Bret might recruit what knights he could to follow him on his mission. All that Bret had to do first was ride with William on his frontal assault against the French king.

Troops from Mantes had made a foray into Normandy, and in turn, William had demanded that Philip offer him the cession of all that was called the Vexin Français. Philip adamantly refused, and so William attacked.

They crossed the Epte and swiftly attacked a French garrison which rode out to do battle. They attacked with all of William's old cunning, and did so savagely, winning the day. But though his cunning had served him well, so did his fury. William ordered the town of Mantes burned to the ground after it was brutally sacked. Bret, horrified by the king's demands, watching the wanton destruction around him, turned Ajax and started away, anxious only to meet with his father and brothers and make for home. But even as he rode down the blackened street, he saw the king before him. Suddenly, a burning timber fell from one of the buildings down upon the street, missing William by inches.

The king's horse reared and fell back. William was pitched forward, striking his head hard upon the iron peak of his saddle.

"Jesu!" Bret cried, urging Ajax quickly forward. "By God, William!"

The advance was halted. Bret and his father reached the king at the same time and Alaric took hold of the reins, leading the injured man he had served for so many years. Along with his brothers, Bret followed closely behind.

William was taken to the priory of St. Gervais. Two of the churchmen there, recommended as excellent physicians, attended the king while William's men anxiously paced the floors, awaiting their verdict.

There would be no hope for the king, the physicians told them solemnly. William was on his way to meet God.

He did not die swiftly, and on his deathbed, he finished his affairs in life. His sons, William Rufus and Henry, were both at his side, as was his brother, Robert, Count of Mortain.

Robert, William's oldest son, was in France, with King Philip.

Yet as he died, even in his great pain, he gave his forgiveness to his rebel son Robert. The great barons of Normandy all pleaded that he do so. Normandy had been promised to Robert; it was his inheritance, he must receive it. William railed that Robert was not worthy; yet, as his loyal barons demanded, the duchy would be his.

The king went on to leave gifts to the Church. Despite a lifetime of warfare, he had been a pious monarch, and on his deathbed, he remained pious as well.

Men he had imprisoned during his reign were to be released—all except for his brother, Odo, with whom he had quarreled bitterly many years before. Robert of Mortain pleaded for his brother; the other barons did as well, including Bret's own father, who had known Odo well in the distant days when they had all been fighting for a promised inheritance.

At last, William agreed to release Odo.

William seemed suddenly not certain that he had the right to give England away—he had taken it by the sword. But he wrote to Lanfranc in England that he gave to his son William Rufus his scepter, sword, and crown, and prayed that God would then give William Rufus the gift of England. He then ordered William Rufus to go—to England—and his son complied.

The king's third son, Henry, came to his father, asking what would be his. William bequeathed him five thousand pounds of silver, and suggested that he be patient, and put his trust in the Lord God above them.

William then began his smaller bequeaths. Bret stood by his father's side when William reached out a hand to Alaric and gripped his old friend's fingers with an amazingly strong grasp. "God grant you peace, Alaric. Remember how we met? Fighting, always fighting! Through a lifetime. But we swore to take what was ours and hold it well, and that we did, old friend. I confirm you as Earl of Haselford, Alaric, and pray that you hold it well in your lifetime, and that Robin will hold it equally well in his time. Bret, I gave you burned-out, destroyed land, but I gave you a title as well that I conferred upon very few! I confirm that title now, and wish your oath that you will serve my son as you have served me."

"You have my oath," Bret told him.

William winced as pain seized him, tightening his worn features. "You are free now to take what men you will to England. Take the Far Isle, as I wished, for William Rufus will have good need of all defenses he can have!"

"Aye, William, I will take it."

"God go with you then!" William said.

The Conqueror had already made his last confession, but the archbishop of Rouen hovered by the king, and waved them away that William might sleep.

Bret realized that, like William Rufus, he had been given his freedom to leave. Nevertheless, he decided to wait with his father and brothers. At this point, another day or two did not seem to matter.

The king closed his eyes, and rested. The death vigil went on. Bret slept against the wall with his father and brothers and other of the king's nobles as they awaited the end. He was just beyond the chamber where the king had slept when William of Normandy and England, Bastard and Conqueror, awoke the next morning.

It was just dawn on Thursday, the ninth of September, in the year of our Lord 1087, and the king said quietly, "I hear bells. Why are they ringing?"

"For our Lady Mother," one of the priests told him.

William folded his hands. "The bells ring to Mary!" he said. "And so, to our Lady Mary, the holy Mother of God, I commend myself that by her prayers she may reconcile me to her dear Son, our Lord Jesus Christ."

There was silence. Tremendous silence. Then the priest announced softly, "He is dead. King William is dead."

Bret, along with the others, crossed himself, and lowered himself to his knees. It seemed impossible that one so filled with vitality and determination could be dead. Bret closed his eyes and thought of the times when William had shown his brutality and excesses. But he had never been wantonly cruel, and had been brutal only when it had been a political necessity. He had been known for his sheer crushing force, but equally had he been known for his piety, and if he had somewhat dominated the Church, he had endowed it as well. He had shown mercy to many of his enemies; at times he had been not just tolerant, but kind.

He had been many things, Bret thought, and he set his hands upon his father's shoulders, for Alaric would truly mourn the king he had served for the majority of his life.

Whatever he had been, Bret thought, he now belonged to history, and history would be his final judge.

The king was dead.

And he, Bret, was free.

Chapter 16

⤜⤝

"**H**e's dead! My God, he's dead!"

David, flushed and anxious, burst into the great hall, just as Allora finished meeting with Timothy to take stock of the assets within the castle. She'd acquired a great headache through the counting of sheep, cattle, horses, and trained armed men, and then they'd gone on to wine and ale and salted fish. After the bitter winter, the summer had been rich, and the fall harvest was promising to be bountiful.

But as she heard David's words, her headache compounded into a knifing agony; her legs seemed to go weak, her breath to leave her body completely.

"Who is dead, David? *Who is dead?*"

"William. King William is dead." He strode across the room to the long table where carafes of wine and ale were kept, and he poured himself a drink of wine, not seeming to care if he drank wine or ale, as long as he could drink something.

"William!" she breathed. She had been afraid. Afraid that he had meant Bret.

David sat upon the table, drinking his wine. "He was killed assaulting a French town. No arrow struck him down—perhaps it was God Himself for they said his horse reared, the king catapulted forward, collapsed, and was then taken to a priory to die. But he is gone, Allora, William is gone."

"William the First is gone," Allora said. "There is another to follow him. William Rufus will have England, so his father said while he lived."

David nodded. "He came to London with a letter for Lanfranc even while his father still lay dying. Normandy for Robert, England for William Rufus. And Henry, the

233

third son, has a goodly sum of money and a warning—to be patient and wait." He shrugged. "Perhaps his will not be such a poor inheritance, for if certain rumors regarding William Rufus are true, it is doubtful that he will leave an heir behind, and thus his brother will have England in the end."

William was dead. She could not believe it. She thought back to the time she had sat at his side; she remembered feeling the force of his strength and power. It seemed inconceivable.

Yet all men died.

The Conqueror was like all men, dust and ash in the end. And yet he had died with his conquest complete. He had changed the world in which they lived.

"You know what it means, of course, don't you?" David asked softly.

"What?"

"Your husband will be here now, milady. And soon!"

Bret did not come immediately. As Allora nervously awaited word, more news came, but all of it regarding the dead king.

Robert brought the news of the king's funeral to her with great glee. "Can you imagine this! They were all there like a flock of vultures, the king's great noblemen, until he took his dyin' breath. Then they panicked, and all rushed off to see to their own affairs and the corpse was left alone, and there to be pillaged by the servants who served him at the last. He was left half-naked and upon the floor. Then some poor fellow did see that he was clad, and a boat was gotten, and he was brought to the outskirts of Caen. Now here, niece, is fitting irony, and surely God's own: fire all but destroyed King William's coronation, and fire sent his would-be mourners running, for a house caught flame and all were panicked again!"

Despite her own troubled relationship with William, Allora could not be glad that such a powerful man in life had suffered such indignity in death.

"And is William Rufus now in London?" she asked him.

"Oh, indeed, he was crowned at Westminster Abbey on the twenty-sixth of September."

"And what do you know of Bret, Uncle?"

"Not enough," he admitted, perplexed. "He came back to England, so I have been told, after the king's death, and came to London to swear his fealty to William Rufus. There is little else I know at the moment, but . . ."

"But what?" Allora asked him.

"London is closer than Normandy."

"Indeed," she agreed.

And again, they waited.

This time, it was not to be a long wait. On a beautiful autumn day in late October, just as the sun fell, Allora stood on the tower ramparts overlooking the mainland and saw a rider racing across the sands, just ahead of the breaking tide.

A moment later, David came galloping into the courtyard, dismounting from his horse even as the animal still moved.

"Allora!"

"Here!" she cried, and he looked up to her.

"He comes!" David warned her. "With an army of over two hundred well-trained knights! He has stopped at his lands in Wakefield, and from there, he will march on the Far Isle. He will be here within the week!"

It had seemed like forever, as if an eternity had passed, since he had first longed to come here, Bret thought on that first morning when he brought his massive army moving across the countryside to reach the hill country right before the Far Isle.

By dawn's light, he could see the majestic structure of the castle rising from the sea. It had been years and years since he had actually been here; he had been no more than a boy when he had come that long-ago time, and met Ioin Canadys when the old laird had proudly ridden out alone to confer with Alaric d'Anlou. He had been awed at the time by the rock rising so defiantly from the sea, protecting the southern rim of the isle. Ragged stone rose all over the isle, and thus helped create the fantastic barriers that kept it so safe. Many Normans were of the opinion that the Anglo-Saxons had actually been superstitious about the use of all the Roman stonework which had remained long after the Romans had departed. Not so upon the isle, for the walls had been made of stone and wood, and even the parapets that ringed it were solid and secure in their structure.

"Quite a place, isn't it?"

The soft female voice at his back caused him to stiffen his shoulders and make a firm attempt to rein in his anger.

Elysia was with him. Bret had managed to dissuade his father and brothers from joining him on his ride north since William II had just been crowned and there might well be new anarchy in the land.

This was, after all, his fight. His fight, his land.

His wife.

But Elysia, after kissing him good-bye and wishing him Godspeed in London, had procured an excellent escort in the form of nuns bound for York, and she had managed to get the good ladies to bring her to Wakefield. There, Bret had furiously denied her permission to ride with him, not wanting her anywhere near the scene of battle. He'd gone so far as to have her locked in her chamber in the poor manor at Wakefield, but she wooed the seneschal there into opening the door to give her water, and escaped from the poor man. Once she had arrived in the midst of his army, Bret had determined that she was, perhaps, better off right beneath his nose, and so she had ridden directly behind him all the way here.

He stared at Elysia, eyes narrowed. "Quite," he agreed. "All right, then. You've been in it. Tell me about the inner workings."

Elysia sighed. "There's really very little I know. The gates open to a large courtyard and bailey. There are numerous towers, and even inside the walls, the land is spacious, with many people living and working right there. The walls themselves are solid. Even the gates are thick, not easily burned or broken, I can assure you."

Bret nodded, staring again across the meadows and valley to the isle where even now, the sea began to drain away, and a white expanse of sand began to appear.

"How will you take it?" Elysia asked him.

"Carefully," he replied dryly. Then he bent down and plucked up a stick to draw in the dirt. "Men have tried before to build scaffolding and leap the walls so that they could cast open the gates. But time is needed, and the tide rushes in quickly once twilight comes; the scaffolding is lost to the sea. I intend to use a ram—"

"And the sea will still come!"

"Aye, but I have already seen to the crafting of some very special machinery. My ram is upon a bed of logs, and if my builders are correct, then we will not lose our advantage by night, but simply wait until day to begin our assault again."

Elysia's silver eyes shimmered. "Dear God, Bret, but I pray you are successful."

"My dear sister! Would that it were merely *my* welfare you were so concerned about. You're seeking vengeance."

"And you?"

He stood, staring at the gleaming walls of the Far Isle once again.

"Aye, I seek vengeance!" he declared, his voice deep and trembling. "Vengeance indeed. Father Damien!" he shouted, his voice rising over the din of the mounted men behind him. "Come, Father, lead us in a prayer for our godly endeavor!" he commanded.

Father Damien came forward. The foot soldiers fell to their knees. The knights dismounted from their horses to do the same. Father Damien prayed for a righteous victory.

When he was done, Bret shouted out his next commands. "We will set up our camp here, and have no delays. As of this very morning, we attack the gate!"

A swift cheer went up all around him and he surveyed his troops. The men were his familiars; he had fought with them so very long. Some were Saxons, many were Normans. Some were of mixed blood, as he was himself.

All sought glory—and land.

Well, he would have to gain that land for them, he thought. He paused, looking to the castle again. He closed his eyes, feeling heat race wildly throughout his body. God, how long had it been since he had last claimed his wife? Was she there, plotting her defenses even now? Arming the parapets, calling for oil, for arrows, for pikes?

Listening to the war cries of Robert Canadys?

Indeed, that bastard would be within the walls himself now, relying on the strength of the castle for his own defense.

But Robert's land was outside the walls. And Bret smiled.

The man's time had come to an end. Bret would prevail. It had seemed like forever since he had first been touched by the fury and fire to come here.

But during that forever, he had managed siege after siege. And he was ready.

The Far Isle would fall.

Allora saw Bret's colors, gold and blue, brightly waving on what seemed like endless banners of battle. She bit her lip, trembling, feeling her uncle at her one side, her cousin Lilith at the other.

"Let him come!" Robert said, and there was excitement in his voice. "Let him come then, let him do his worst!"

"Wait, wait, there now!" David said, pointing down to the sand as a lone rider suddenly came galloping across, bearing a message.

He reined in a hundred feet from the gates, staring up to the parapets.

"The Earl of Wakefield, lord of the Far Isle, demands the surrender of the fortress to his rightful rule. Pray, what message do I bring him?" the knight asked.

"Bring him the message that he must rot in hell!" Robert roared. He lifted a pike, and even as Allora screamed out a quick protest, he sent it hurtling down toward the messenger.

The pike missed, imbedding in the sand by the rider's mount. The horse reared. "Aye, so shall I convey that message!" the man shouted. Horse and man turned, and began a wild gallop back across the sand.

"Uncle, how dare you accost a messenger so?" she demanded furiously. "Jesu, we are not without our honor here!"

"Allora, this is battle now, and you've no part in it!" Robert declared angrily.

"I've every part in it. I am lady of the Isle, Uncle! Ioin's isle—"

"My brother is dead, lady."

"My father is dead, but his memory lives within my heart, and I remember his honor. You'll not betray it."

"And I'll not surrender to any Norman lord!"

"Allora, Robert, look quickly!" David warned.

Bret's men were not taking any dangerous rides straight across the sands to the castle. They had built a magnificent shield of wood, and it rose high above them as they slowly advanced, the shield covering some monstrous working they slowly dragged along beneath it.

"Archers! Be ready!" Robert bellowed.

The men with their assault machinery came closer and closer. Robert ordered the first wave of arrows be set flying. She watched them rise and fall in a smooth arc.

All were caught within the thatch and wood of the shield. "Fire!" she called out herself in a quick order. "Fire the arrows, that we may burn their shield!"

Sir Christian echoed the command about the walls, and the second arc of arrows went out blazing. They caught upon the shield, and indeed, it began to burn.

But the advance continued.

Another wave of men began toward them. Then another. Arrows kept raining down; Robert ordered that kettles of boiling oil be poured, hoping to catch the closest grouping.

Suddenly, one of the shields carried by the attackers was set back. It had harbored a group of archers. The Normans returned the fire, aiming so that their slim arrows rode high up and over the walls, and came sweeping down then upon the courtyard, bailey—and parapets.

Men screamed.

More oil was ordered poured over the wall, and from the well-armed invaders screams rose as well. Allora suddenly felt David's arm around her, dragging her from her position on the parapets. "I will not run!" she cried to him. "Not when men are going to their deaths—"

"You are the isle, Allora! You must not die. And think of Brianna. You cannot leave her."

Thoughts of her daughter swayed her at last, and Allora let him lead her from the front wall. She hurried to the keep and to her chamber there, and from the high vantage of her tower, she looked out and watched the battle.

It lasted through the day, and as the afternoon waned, she prayed that the water would come quickly, and then again, that it would not.

There were so many men out upon the sands.

Was Bret among them?

She closed her eyes. When she opened them again, she saw that he was. In his gleaming armor, upon the snow-white Ajax. She saw his sword raised high as he led his men, his face and head encased in his horned helmet.

The sun slipped further down. They were dragging something out upon the sand. Allora watched, amazed.

Bret knew that the sea came to encase the isle each night with the setting of the sun.

Then she saw that, covered by his shields, he brought out a massive ram. Behind it came rows of scaffolding, ready to carry men over the walls if the gates could not be broken.

They would sink into the sea, she thought, and she watched with fascinated horror as the weapons came closer.

But the water came, too. Men shouted, screamed. The horses began to move away. Men left the massive, shielded weapons behind and began to hurry back to the mainland while the water began to swirl around the castle walls.

She waited for the siege weapons to sink and topple.

They did not.

The invaders had been driven back for the night.

The ram and scaffolding remained. She saw, even as the sun turned golden and set upon them, that they were lifted by rafts. They had been anchored, well out of the way of the castle, but they would not sink.

And come the morning, they would be ready at the gates. Ready to break down wood, to scale stone.

"Jesu!" Allora breathed, her heart quickening.

There was a pounding on her door. Her uncle entered, and she saw in his eyes his amazement at his enemies' designs.

"We will have to leave the walls of the isle," he told her. "I'll take my men, David and Duncan theirs. We'll slip out the south beachfront tonight, make the forested shore, and wait there for weapons and horses from the countryside. We'll attack the Earl of Wakefield from the rear." He strode across the room to her and caught her shoulders hard. "You would defy me, niece, I know that you would. But hear me in this: if you must surrender the fortress, know that I'll come for you! Promise surrender, have someone stall for time, then slip from the gates and come around to the south beach as well, and I will find you there."

"Uncle—"

"Allora, heed me in this! You do not know what his revenge will be. They are bloodthirsty animals. And you are a fool if you do not think he'll despise you! What would you have, Allora? That the man should set you aside, choose another wife, and take all from us? Escape; come to me. While you live and while you are free, there is hope. Now I'm going, and quickly. Pray for us, niece, pray for *us!*"

He left her.

Even as she started to follow him to the door, the last of the sun's light fell into the ocean, and the sky darkened. By the time Allora reached the hall, her uncle, David, and Duncan were gone, their knights with them. Only her own people, her housecarls and those able-bodied workers who had learned to wield weapons, still lined the walls.

It would be a long night, with everyone looking to the sands.

Brianna was restless. Even as Allora waited in the hall with her women and Sir Christian, Father Jonathan, and Timothy, the baby cried and fretted again and again. Allora walked with her until she was exhausted, then excused herself at last to bring the baby to her tower room. Father Jonathan told her that she must get some sleep. Allora knew she would never do so.

She did get the baby to sleep, lying beside her on the broad expanse of the bed. Allora touched Brianna's tiny cheek, stroked her ebony curls, and then closed her eyes and remembered the man who had fathered her child. She trembled and tried to pray, and she wasn't sure if she prayed for her own people or for her Norman husband.

And though the words would not come, she prayed in her heart that he might somehow forgive her.

She had thought that she would never sleep, but she did.

She awakened to the awful sounds of hand-to-hand combat, and leaped out of bed, washed quickly, and threw on man's garb: chausses, shirt, and short tunic. She grabbed up her father's old sword and headed for the parapets, shouting for Lilith to come and care for the baby.

She burst from the keep and raced across the courtyard and bailey to the stairs to the parapets, raced up them, and came to the wall.

She was in time to see David lead troops from the forest, men on horseback and afoot, rushing out to attack the men bringing the ram forward once again. Yet even as David's troops attacked them from the back, more of the Norman forces appeared from behind *them*, and David's border knights were quickly trapped between the two groups of Normans. She cried out her horror, listening to the clash of steel, the scream of horses. She clamped her hands over her ears, and sank slowly down upon the wood flooring of the parpet. David was with those men. David who was gentle and kind and tender, and who had loved her too much to hurt her.

A moment later she realized that Gavin, Sir Christian's oldest son, stood beside her. He bent down, taking her hands, helping her back to her feet. "Lady, the fighting was swiftly over. The men have been taken as prisoners."

"David?" she whispered painfully.

"I believe he has been taken."

She nodded, and dared to look out over the sandy battlefield again. The ram was moving toward the gates once again. Behind it, more fighting was taking place between the desperate border knights and the Normans. Yet even as she watched, some were taken.

And some fought their way to the trees, there disappearing, and, hopefully, making good their escapes.

The ram was almost upon them. Allora sighed softly. "Gavin, follow me to the tower. I will write the terms of surrender, and you will ride out with them."

"My lady—" he began miserably.

"There's no choice. I will make arrangements for my own escape, and everything will be well in time, I assure you!"

She turned and hurried from the parapets. He followed. In the keep she strode past Father Jonathan, then paused. "You come as well, good Father. Gavin, summon your father, Mary, and Lilith. We must hurry. That ram might well crush us any minute, and I would surrender before we are forced into submission."

Gavin did as he was bade. Within minutes, Allora had her main players assembled around her, and a tearful, wary group finally agreed to her plans. She commanded that a flag of truce be flown, that Gavin might ride out, then, left the hall.

When he was gone, she stood on the ramparts, gazing at the men upon the walls and all those who had come to stand in the bailey, looking up to her. Everyone was silent and still. She saw Mary down in the bailey, her hair ruffled just slightly by the breeze. And there was Lilith, too, with Brianna in her arms.

Allora inhaled on a long note, and then began to speak. "I have just sent Gavin to surrender the fortress—" she began on a high, clear note. An outcry rose quickly and she raised a hand to still it. "I cannot let more men die, it would be a tragic waste! There are two things you must realize. First, it was not Bret d'Anlou who came in pursuit of us and slew my father. He was not even in the country when we hastened here to escape the king's hold. Second, you must understand that my father *did* sign a contract with him.

He would become laird here upon Ioin's death. My father entered into that agreement, and this Norman nobleman is one who will not quit until he has gained the fortress. I have asked that the isle be neither plundered nor ravaged, and I have asked as well that your wives and daughters be left in peace. Swear your fealty to him, and I know that he will treat you all fairly."

"Lady!" Dale, one of the blacksmiths, called out unhappily. "What of your own sweet self? For ourselves, we do not care, truly. But if this Norman fiend would in any way harm you, then we would all rather fight to the death."

A noble notion, Allora thought, yet one she was not so sure all would agree with if more of their sons and daughters were to fall prey to a battle already lost.

She smiled down at her stalwart defender. "Ah, good friend! I stand here demanding that you all be of faith and good courage, and yet I will not be with you. Thus you will not have to worry about me."

"Then where—" Dale began.

"My uncle will shortly come to take me from here by boat. Lilith has determined to await the Earl of Wakefield in my stead; hopefully, they will leave her to her prayers long enough to allow for my escape, which Mary will manage with me, along with the babe. When I can again negotiate with your new lord, I will return to you, I promise. There must be some peace made here between my uncle and my husband. I beg of you, be not afraid. The Earl of Wakefield will bear you no malice." She hesitated, then reminded them all softly, "You loved, admired, and obeyed my father. Ioin Canadys signed the agreement that Bret d'Anlou, Earl of Wakefield, would be laird here. Ioin respected the Earl of Wakefield, and you must now do the same!"

They kept watching her in stunned silence, like a group of startled lambs. She waved a hand to them, and started racing down the steps to the parapets. They would be safe with Bret.

She would not.

One particular knight among the border warriors proved to be Bret's most talented opponent of the day.

Bret himself had led the rear assault on the men who had come to attack his own forces on the beach. He had first met the knight's sword while they were both horsed, and they had thrust and parried to a great clash of steel before the border lord's horse had wavered in the sand and the animal had gone down. Bret then leaped from Ajax's back, determined to finish the affair on ground level along with his opponent. Again and again, their steel clashed. Bret was amazed by the fellow's prowess and stamina, yet in the end, the simple fact that he had been fighting for William forever stood well in his stead. With one powerful blow he managed to at last wrest the sword from the man's hand, and when his weapon lay upon the sand twenty feet away, the fellow staggered to his knees. He had been wearing a head and neck piece of the same link mail that covered his chest; now he wrested the head and shoulder sections from his body armor, and, breathing heavily, stared proudly at Bret. "If you would honor one who has fought well, my lord, then slay me quickly!"

Bret set his own sword's point down into the soil, staring at the young man with the sandy hair and green-gold eyes. "I am not accustomed to executing my enemies on the field. A fair fight is lost, but it seems you are to live. Rise; I see that we have acquired other prisoners. You may follow along with them."

Bret started off, his back to the fellow, curious. He was ready, should the man try to dive for his sword to slash him in the back, but the border lord stood and followed as he had been told. Bret whistled for Ajax, mounted him, and saw that Jarrett and Etienne had acquired a group of prisoners; all now were falling in. He waved a hand to them, indicating that he was leading the group back to their camp, where his battle tent awaited. Yet they had barely reached the camp before Bret was startled to see his sister race from his own quarters, pass him by, and approach his unusual prisoner.

"You!" Elysia raged, and threw herself against the man, pummeling his chest in a wild tumult.

The prisoner caught her by the wrists, locked his jaw hard, and looked to Bret who had reined in on Ajax and stared at them both.

"My lord, I beg of you, have her cease!" the man implored.

"Elysia—"

"This is David of Edinburgh, the wretch who held me captive through that awful journey north!"

David of Edinburgh. Bret felt a tightening within himself, but something about the man himself helped Bret to control his temper.

"Sir, I suggest you unhand my sister. Elysia, may I suggest you join us inside? I would like a word with this Scotsman myself."

David and Elysia stared at one another for a long moment, hostility flaring. David did release her, but then Bret thought that she might start up her pummeling again, and he called out softly, "Elysia!"

She spun around and entered Bret's tent. Bret stared at David. The man lowered his eyes, then proceeded into the tent, while Jarrett saw that the other prisoners passed by to be held down the hill.

Bret sat upon the camp stool behind the broad table with his battle charts and looked at his prisoner. "So you are David of Edinburgh. You should have introduced yourself."

"I had not known that you would know of me, my lord."

"Oh, indeed, I know of you. And I am damned curious to learn more about you—and my wife."

The man's eyes never flickered. "There is nothing more to know about Allora and me, my lord. Once, before she came to London with her father, it was assumed that we would wed. She married you. There is nothing more."

"That isn't what I have heard."

"Then you have been misled, my lord."

"You haven't touched her?"

"No, my lord."

"And what of my sister?"

Elysia, who had been quiet behind him, suddenly gasped.

"You may ask her yourself, my lord. Ioin never meant to take the lady, but once he did, we had no choice but to keep her. That, my lord, I did. Yet I never used her intimately in any way, and I swear, I did my very best not to abuse her as well."

There was such passion in those words that Bret could well imagine his fiery-haired sibling casting this man into all the torments of hell as they rode. Were he still not in so precarious a position himself, he might have found it an amusing situation.

"What a paragon of virtue you are, young man!" Bret muttered.

"Not so virtuous, my lord," David said evenly. "As to Allora . . ." He hesitated, squared his shoulders, and faced Bret levelly. "She has suffered enough pain without my adding to it. And your sister . . ." He paused again, staring at Elysia over Bret's shoulder. "Quite frankly, my lord, we were never alone, and always involved in the rugged adventure of the escape."

Bret lowered his head quickly. Elysia would surely long to slit his throat if she saw him smiling now.

"You may believe in your wife," David said suddenly. "When she has made up her mind, there is no swaying it. You must understand, the border lairds want no part of you, milord."

"And they did battle with me!" Bret said. He rose, approaching David. "You are a man with laudable honor, David of Edinburgh, but I am quite sure that no one in that fortress fought without my wife's command that they do so. You've seen clearly enough—"

He broke off, for there was a sudden commotion just outside. He strode from the tent, David and Elysia following behind him.

Etienne was there, walking quickly toward Bret while a mounted man from the fortress hovered a short distance away. "He's come with a letter, my lord!" Etienne told Bret.

Bret quickly took the parchment and unrolled it. It was addressed to Lord d'Anlou, Earl of Wakefield, and it promised the unconditional surrender of the Far Isle, recognized his right to the property, and begged his mercy upon those within it who were innocent of all but loyalty to those they had long served. At his leisure, he could take the fortress come morning, as long as he would swear upon his honor there would be no violence against the people therein.

It was signed by Allora, lady of the Far Isle.

He stared at the parchment for a long time, felt the breeze ripple through his hair. He strode across the field to the messenger and stared up at the young man. "Indeed, the terms are agreeable. Come the morning, I will take the fortress of the Far Isle. Tell my lady that she must be ready, for I will come with the dawn."

Gavin returned to the fortress and the gates were opened for him. He hurried across the bailey and into the great hall where he found Allora with Timothy, his own father Sir Christian, and Father Jonathan, giving them last-minute instructions from her seat at the head of the table.

She rose as Gavin entered the room.

"He has agreed to the terms as you have stated them."

"But will he adhere to them?" Sir Christian demanded worriedly.

"Aye, he will," Allora assured him softly. "Then all is ready. I will depart before the dawn tomorrow, and pray that my uncle comes, as he has promised. For now, I would be alone with my daughter in my father's room. I thank you all for your help and support, and I bid you good night."

"Allora!" Sir Christian cried. "There must be some other way—"

"There is none. God be with you all."

Chapter 17
～∞～

*H*e stood beside Ajax as the sun rose, staring out upon the castle fortress of the Far Isle. The morning light made the stone gleam white, while the white-washed sands carried a reddish glow. The sky was touched by a gentle pink, with shades of yellow and gold breaking through it. He thought again that it was a fantastic place, with the north wall composed completely of natural sheer rock, the harbor to the western sea protected in the same manner, the five different towers that stood taller than the walls like impregnable sentinels; soundly constructed, beautiful, defiant.

Maybe they would have been impregnable. Maybe not. He had not taken the battle nearly as far as he had been willing to go. Perhaps, after all, Allora's first concern was for her people, for her agreement to surrender the castle of the Far Isle to him had certainly saved many lives. She hadn't forgotten that he had come from a people who had conquered all England. Maybe she had seen from one of her high tower windows his rams and scaffolds and catapults being assembled and pulled up.

And maybe she had already fled the Far Isle.

A sharp jag of steel seemed to rip through him, and he fought anew to still the bitterness and fury that filled him with each thought of his wife. He hoped that he had sufficiently encircled the fortress so that she could not possibly escape it. But though they had captured a vast majority of the border troops, including David of Edinburgh, some of the men had slipped through their fingers. Allora just might have managed the same. No matter. If she had disappeared, he would find her. He would battle every last border clan

249

out there if he had to, until she was returned to him. Then he would seize the daughter he had never seen, and have Allora guarded day and night within one of her own tower prisons.

But first . . .

"Are you ready, milord?"

Jarrett had ridden up behind him with Etienne at his side, Jacques just slightly behind him.

Bret stared at Jarrett and the disciplined line of his troops. He nodded gravely. "Aye, onward to the castle!" But then he paused a moment. "My sister?"

Jarrett grinned. "There is a guard upon her nearly as strong as that we have set upon David of Edinburgh. She will not be arriving in the fortress until we are quite certain it is safe."

"Then it is time we ride."

He mounted Ajax swiftly, set his stag-horned helmet upon his head, and with his squire carrying his colorful banner high, they started out across the now-dry sands that flooded with the ocean at night to protect the fortress.

She had promised surrender. Still, he studied the fortress as they approached it, wary lest she had sent her missive of surrender only to trick them when they rode to the massive gates that protected the walled fortress upon the island. But though he saw a skeleton crew of men aligned along the walls with swords belted to their waists, pikes at their sides, the men made no move to attack. Indeed, their pikes were turned down, handles upward, in a sure sign of submission.

The great gates lay open.

They rode through them, Bret in the lead, his horned helmet still upon his head, his own great sword dangling down his thigh within easy reach of his ready grasp.

The courtyard was vast, he noted quickly, a place where a multitude of people lived and worked. There were numerous wooden lean-tos erected against the stone where he was certain craftsmen customarily worked upon their wares. The place was dead-quiet today, and he could see where one of their well-aimed missiles from the catapult had destroyed stonework and one of the lean-tos. The place before him was all but empty now. He heard a whinnying and noted that one of the lean-tos seemed to lead to stables that had been built right within the wall itself. He could just see that the inner wooden support beams were heavily laden with harnesses and bridles.

He began to feel a renewed rise of anger and unease, thinking at first that Allora had chosen not only to disappear herself and refuse him a formal surrender, but that she had also failed to order anyone else to take her place. But then, from the fifth tower, where the broad wooden doors were double and certainly the largest, a small group suddenly appeared, hurrying toward the mounted horsemen.

Allora was not among the group.

It was led by a priest, a short, rounded little fellow with puffy cheeks and a very worried expression. Father Damien's old friend, Bret thought, and he wondered if the man looked so nervous because he wondered if he might be betrayed himself.

Behind the priest and to his left was a very tall and lean man with a slim, intelligent face; and at the priest's side was another tall man, but this one broad-shouldered and heavyset, at least in his fiftieth year, weary and dignified.

The priest was the first to speak to him, bowing his head quickly and offering swift introductions. "Milord, you are the Earl of Wakefield?"

"And lord of the Far Isle," Bret reminded him dryly.

The chubby little man trembled slightly, but held on to his courage. "Then, milord, we have come to surrender the Far Isle to you: I, Father Jonathan, priest here for the last two decades, Timothy Tanner to my left here, castle reeve, and Sir Christian Canadys, distant relation to your lady wife and captain of the housecarls who still line our walls."

Sir Christian bowed his head, and offered his sword by the engraved handle to Bret.

"We do so surrender our arms, milord, as commanded by our lady, and pray your grace and mercy upon us."

Bret remained silent upon Ajax for a moment, eyeing the sword, but not taking it. "Sir Christian, in a moment you will attend to the needs of my men. Fifty of them will be quartered within the walls; the rest will find places in the surrounding countryside, here and upon the mainland. You will see to it."

"Aye, milord," Sir Christian agreed.

Bret looked back to the priest. "Where is Allora?" he demanded.

The priest's Adam's apple bobbed up and down as he struggled to speak. "Allora?"

"Your mistress, good Father," Bret said dryly. "Where is she?"

"Why, milord! As so many of her kinsmen have so recently died upon the field, she is in the chapel, atoning to God, praying for their souls. She really mustn't be disturbed—"

"Ah, good Father! But she will be disturbed." He dismounted from Ajax at last, and lifted his helmet from his head. "Father, you will direct me to the main keep and hall of the fortress. Timothy Tanner," he said, turning to the tally reeve, "the men behind me are my right arm, and you should know them well: Etienne, Jacques, and Jarrett. You will escort Etienne and Jacques to find the Lady Allora at her devotions, so that they may bring her to me."

The man nodded, ready to obey, yet apparently unhappy about his task.

"Father, lead onward," Bret commanded.

"Oh, aye, aye! You will be greatly pleased with the keep, milord. It is a fine place. Even when the winter gales rage, the keep is warm and dry!" He turned quickly and Bret followed him through the double doors from which he had come. It occurred to him again that there might be some treachery afoot, but it did seem that there was no more than a thin force left here within the castle, and that to seek any attack upon him now would be to invite sure disaster with so many of his men already within the walls of the fortress. His hand, nevertheless, stayed ready to reach for his sword at the slightest provocation.

But none was forthcoming. They came through the doors and he discovered that the main hall of the keep was there, right upon the ground level. The entire lower level was a massive hall, with nearly all of one side of it a huge stone hearth where a healthy blaze burned cheerily. To his left, an angled stairway led to a narrow hallway above, and even in the shadows, he could see doors to chambers there and another stairway leading to a third level.

"Come, milord, come!" the priest encouraged him. Bret strode into the room. The long table that stretched nearly from the hearth to the outer wall was beautifully and intricately carved. High-backed chairs with tapestried seats were ringed around it. Before the hearth, four similar, but larger, chairs were arranged with three-legged tables between them. Near the window where the morning's light would first enter the hall was another, smaller table, and around it, four straight-backed chairs, as if it were a place strictly for the business of the day, somewhere to study maps, charts, perhaps designs for improvements to the fortress.

Or battle strategies.

He imagined that his wife had made use of the table until quite recently, yet it was empty, clean and barren now. "Wine, milord?" the priest asked, striding to the center of the large table on his stubby little legs, reaching for the carafe that awaited there and one of the silver chalices.

"Wine?" Bret repeated softly. He smiled. "I think not. I have brought my own."

"But ours is excellent!" the priest informed him somewhat indignantly, then added quickly, "My lord!"

"Right now, Father, I think that I will just take a seat before the fire. And await my lady wife. In the meantime, perhaps you will be good enough to summon servants to see that my things are brought to the master chamber—I assume it is here, within this tower?"

"Aye, milord! 'Tis a lovely chamber, near as big and broad as the hall itself, just atop the second flight of stairs. It is all on the third floor of this, the inland tower. The views sweep around from the mainland to the sea, and it is a glorious place. You'll find it very comfortable—"

"Indeed, I will."

"My lady has resided there since her father's death, with the little angel—" He broke off, obviously realizing that in his enthusiasm he had mentioned the child Bret had yet to see. And that the lord and lady of the fortress had just done battle with one another.

"Where are prisoners customarily secured?" Bret asked him, propping his feet upon one of the three-legged tables and folding his arms casually over his chest.

"Prisoners, milord?" the priest asked unhappily.

"Prisoners. Those people one does not want escaping," Bret said wryly.

"We've seldom kept prisoners, milord. The clans do not fight in such a way. Perhaps a hostage is taken now and then, but—"

"Then where is a hostage kept?"

The priest swallowed hard, his Adam's apple bobbing up and down again. "The north tower, milord. The one facing the sea. There is a strong door that bolts from the outside, in the high tower room."

Bret nodded. "Fine. Now—"

He broke off; Etienne and Jacques had come to stride into the hallway with his heavily veiled wife between them. He rose swiftly, feeling as if the length of his body burned with his fury, and he reminded himself that he dared not touch her, he'd be too tempted to strangle her. Yet even as he stared from her to Jacques and Etienne, he realized that there was something very wrong.

"Milord," Etienne informed him quickly, "I have reason to believe that this is not your wife."

Instantly he strode to the trio, controlling his anger as he lifted the veil from the woman's face.

She was blonde. She had green eyes. She even resembled Allora to some extent. At a distance, some men might be fooled. But she was almost a dowdy little creature, and really not a bit at all like Allora.

"My lord!" she said, bobbing before him submissively.

"Where is Allora?" he demanded.

"I don't—"

"Lady, I don't know who the hell you are, and at this moment, I do not care. Where is Allora?"

The woman's lashes fell. She cowered visibly, seeking some words to say, but her courage seemed to have failed her.

Bret swore. "Never mind. All that matters is that you are not my wife, lady." He stared at her in astonishment, realizing that he had really been meant to believe that this was Allora.

Time *had* passed between them. But not that much. And he would never, never forget her face!

"Leave her!" Bret commanded suddenly to Jacques and Etienne, striding quickly for the doorway to the main keep and the courtyard beyond. His men were already involved with the task of moving in, some seeing to their horses, some with Jarrett, engaged in the task of learning the layout as they strode along the walls.

"Secure the castle!" Bret shouted to his men, his eyes darting quickly about. Before, the place had seemed near-empty; any movement might have been seen. But now, men moved about busily. The people had begun to come out, moving into the courtyard from the homes beyond the wall, shepherds herding their flocks out of the walls and over the pathway to the mainland created by the tide at sunup.

And it was now difficult to follow the movements of any one individual with all that was going on.

But then he saw a caped and hooded peddler who seemed to be hurrying around one of the lean-tos in order to reach the open gateway; his long strides brought him swiftly across the courtyard until he was running.

Freedom was close for the figure. Just a few more steps, and the gates would be in reach.

But Bret came upon the furtive, hooded individual, his hand landing firmly upon the caped shoulder.

The creature whirled, and a sword was suddenly brandished before Bret, cutting the air in a warning swirl. He leaped back, knowing that the sword had been leveled at him in desperation, with the gateway so very close! Yet he was instantly ready, drawing his own blade in one swift movement. His opponent backed away, then moved forward with a series of quick thrusts and parries that were certainly skilled enough. But he knew that strength would tell. He allowed her the fight, parrying her every strike, until he thought his temper would no longer allow him the play, even if it was to best her at her own game. He slammed his sword down upon hers, nearly splitting the blade. Her hand would have snapped had she not released the sword; its steel clattered to the ground.

He realized that they were surrounded then. The priest was behind him, as were Sir Christian and his own men. He started to lift his blade in a smooth arc, and Sir Christian cried out, "Milord, for the love of God—"

"I'll not kill her, Sir Christian. Though by God, I am tempted!"

Yet his sword still moved, drawing a huge collective gasp from around him. He'd been fighting forever, so it seemed at times, and he was very adept with a sword. He slit the loop that held the encompassing cape and hood upon her, and both fell to the ground atop the sword.

And there she stood.

She had changed so little. She was dressed in a man's tight chausses with a silk shirt and short tunic atop them, her feet booted for a long ride or journey, her hair uncovered and gloriously free and wild, longer, more golden, than he had remembered. Indeed, her eyes were greener, her face more beautiful. A pulse beat a wild and reckless pace at her throat, betraying her fear. Her breasts rose and fell from the tremendous exertion she had put forth to fight him.

She had very recently bathed—planning well ahead for this escape, he imagined—for she still bore the delicate scent of a rose soap, and that sweet allurement drifted through the air, softly, subtly encompassing him.

Somehow, she had never seemed more desirable. Or perhaps it was the passage of time and the memories that had so plagued his nights for so very long that made him think so now. It had been a long time since he had seen her. So damned long. An eternity since he had touched her.

Inwardly, he cursed her. With a tremendous effort, he willed himself to betray no emotion.

"This one, my friends," he said lightly, his voice resonant, "is, in truth, my very lovely wife!"

She stared at him, and it was only then that he noticed a second person, clad so similarly to her, trying to smoothly sail past the men in the rear now. The person carried a well-bundled something within his or her arms . . .

He raised his sword, calling out to another of his men, Gaston de Ville. "Secure the gates! Now!"

The caped creature froze, then turned. The hood fell back and he saw the fresh, freckled face of a young servant girl, looking now to Allora with apology in her eyes. The gates were closed. Bret strode away from his wife with long hard steps to quickly close the distance between himself and the girl. He reached out his arms for the bundle.

"I will take my daughter, lass," he told her firmly.

She hesitated barely a second, then handed over the well-swaddled babe before dropping to her knees before him. "My lord, I beg you for mercy—"

"Mary, rise!" Allora cried, hurrying forward and lifting the girl, keeping her arm around her shoulder, her eyes defiantly upon her husband. "She has done nothing!" Allora quickly told Bret. "She is innocent—"

"Indeed, your Mary is innocent," he agreed. "She has but served her mistress." He turned his back on Allora, feeling the life within his arms, amazed at the strength of the emotions that surged within him as he held the tiny, squirming bundle. He was desperately anxious to be alone for a moment, to see his child, to study her, to count her fingers and toes.

Even Allora could wait for a moment or two.

He started back for the keep, calling his orders out over his shoulder. "Etienne, you will have the Lady Allora delivered to the master's chambers when I have settled there. For now, I will not be disturbed!"

He strode long and hard, reaching the doorway to the main keep with everyone still and silent behind him. Yet he was not to be left entirely in peace.

"Milord!" As he entered into the keep, the priest tried to stop him. "Milord, you must understand! None of us thought to deceive you—"

"Not a whit, Father," he replied, his attention on his child.

"Your lady wife was charged to leave this place by her family. You must realize, her uncle is loath to see it go to any Norman lord. She was convinced she must join those men beyond our gates who had escaped the battle, and she has watched for those who would come for her from the tower window throughout the morning; but Robert did not come when he should have to help in her escape. You must realize that all this was not her fault—"

"My good Father," he charged the man, "I must be left alone for a moment! And by God, I demand that you see to it!"

Leaving the priest behind, he climbed the first flight of stairs, staring down at the tiny face beneath his. He climbed the second flight until he came to a huge oak door and, pressing it open with his shoulder, entered the master's chambers.

The room was all that the priest had promised: huge and warmed by a hearth nearly the size of that below. A massive bed covered with linen sheets and warm furs took up half the far wall. There was a writing desk before the window, a high-backed chair before it. There was a dressing screen, a handsomely carved washstand, and a huge tapestried chair before the fire. He strode to the chair, then sat, unwrapping the woolen blanket from his daughter and studying her anew. Again he felt a tremendous flood of warmth and emotion, looking at the so-serious little creature. She was dressed in a white linen gown that seemed to encompass her, but her tiny fists waved outside of it, and now, with the blanket unwrapped, her tiny feet began to move, too. She stared at him with eyes as deep a blue as any that had graced anyone in his family.

And her hair was ebony. A curling cap of ebony.

Yet something of her delicate face seemed to belong to her mother as well. At four months, this little lady was already a beauty. His daughter was perfect. As perfect as he had ever judged his wife to be.

She hadn't cried as yet, but now, as they stared at one another, her tiny rosebud lips began to quiver. "There, there!" he said soothingly, and he rocked her upon his knees, allowing her to curl her little fingers tightly around his own. "I may look like a stranger, little one, but I am not. I am your father, and you will know me well now, I swear it!"

There was a light knocking on the door. "Come in!" he called out, and waited as Etienne led in his errant wife. He nodded briefly to Etienne, and the man left them alone, closing the door carefully as he departed.

Allora stood where Etienne had left her, trying to keep her eyes level with his, but they kept falling upon the babe in his lap, and he was quite certain that she longed to rush over, scoop up the babe again, and run wildly from his sight. But she held herself very still, very dignified, her beautiful face pale, her stance firm. She was afraid, he thought. Tall, slim, proud, beautiful—and very much afraid.

As she damned well should be!

"My daughter is quite exceptional," he told her at last, studying the child, then offering her a dry smile. "Customarily, I should have owed you quite an exceptional gift at her birth. Ah, but then, I wasn't informed at the time."

Allora's eyes lowered swiftly. He noted the way she curled her fingers into her palms, fighting to stay calm. He longed to rise, to shake her, to strike her.

Yet more than anything, he realized, he longed—no, *burned*, to have her.

Nay! He would not forgive her—by God, he would not!

Her voice was husky and pained when she spoke. "We have surrendered the fortress, my lord. You have won. All is yours. What more do you want?"

He stared down at the babe again. She had liked his rocking motion. Either that, or she had been ready for a nap. Her sweet little eyes were closed, black lashes curled like winged shadows upon her cheeks. A bitter smile curved his lip and he looked from the babe to his wife. "Ah, the fortress surrendered, milady. Aye, you sent out your white flag, and you offered up your terms of peace. And they were all lies, lady, for when I arrived you were trying to escape the fortress, no doubt to join your uncle and recruit more border troops to try and wrest the place back from me!"

The flush upon her cheeks assured him that he had hit upon the truth.

He rose suddenly, striding to the bed. Allora cried out with alarm, starting to hurry toward him, stopping, pale as he swung around on her.

"What—what are you doing with her?" Allora demanded breathlessly.

He arched a brow. "The babe sleeps. I am lying her down upon the bed. I would not waken her again when I deal with you."

She stiffened, swallowed hard, her chin up, her eyes flashing. So much time had passed! Yet it still seemed that he could feel the softness of her hair without touching the golden tresses, that he could recall the fluid beauty of her smile and movement, could remember holding her . . .

Jesu, he would not be swept into such unforgettable obsession again.

Allora remained where she was, in the center of the room now, waiting. She would have liked to have run, he thought.

But she would not do so. Not with their daughter in the room.

He laid the baby down carefully. She wiggled and stretched, but did not waken. He turned back to Allora, then sent his arm out in a sweeping gesture to encompass the room. "You may see that some of your things are packed quickly, milady, that they may be taken from this room. The north tower will be your new domain, and I do assure you, the door will be bolted and guarded at all times."

She gasped and stood stock-still, silent, for a long moment.

"You mean to imprison me here—" she began.

"Aye, lady; you meant to escape me! By God above us, madam, you *did* escape me and rob me of my child and property. Ah, lady! There are moments when I'd find great pleasure in flaying you until you were but half alive, so pray, don't find your imprisonment such a brutal decision!"

She lowered her eyes quickly. "You judge me too harshly, milord. I had no choice, for my uncle's life was at stake! You have always known that!"

"I did not see your uncle's life threatened today when you tried to escape me again!" he reminded her.

She lifted her hands. "I was giving you this place!" she whispered, her voice strangled. "I was certain that you would take no vengeance upon the people themselves, and so I thought—"

"To steal my daughter and depart, to seek my death or a divorce, and enjoy your life with your young Scottish lover."

Again, she went very pale, and he swore inwardly, feeling the fire of jealousy rake through him.

Had David been telling him the truth?

"You—you're mistaken," she said softly. "I was not seeking a divorce and I could not allow Robert to seek an annulment once I knew about Brianna. And I . . ."

"You what?" he demanded, arms crossed over his chest as he stared at her.

Once more, her eyes fell. "You have obviously heard a great many things. Some of them are true, some of them are not." She lifted her eyes to his, in staunch control again. "David of Edinburgh is not my lover," she told him.

Damn the pain that could rake through him when she spoke! He arched a brow again, determined that he would not falter. "Indeed, my lady, he is not your lover *now!*"

"What do you mean by that?"

He walked away from her, leaning upon the stone hearth, staring at the flames. He was tired. There was a great deal he was going to have to attend to himself, securing the Far Isle.

He turned back to her. "If there are things from this room you wish to take with you, milady, you must make haste to get them now, for I shall summon one of the men to escort you to the north tower."

She lifted her chin higher, her eyes narrowing. He wondered if there wasn't just the slightest trace of tears within them. "Most of my belongings are in the trunk at the foot of the bed. They will suffice, if you will be so good as to allow the servant to bring the trunk. Also, the smaller trunk there contains the baby's clothing and blankets. It does not matter when you send them. I will take Brianna now. She is all I really need."

"Ah, lady, and she is all you will not take!" he informed her angrily.

"But—"

"She will remain with me. I see her cradle now on the other side of the bed. It will remain there."

She stared at him in astonishment. "You can't keep the baby, Bret! She is but six months old!"

"Aye, and you have kept her from me for those six months, lady. She stays."

"Bret, you cannot separate me from her, I beg of you. She is still so little. She needs me—"

"Madam, women to nurse babes are quite plentiful. There is nothing she needs that must come from you."

"*I* need her, then! For the love of God, Bret, I cannot be without her!"

"Perhaps you should have thought of that before you fought me. And then again, my lady, perhaps you should have thought of it before you tried your own escape—with *my* child."

She turned away from him, shaking, obviously very agitated. She walked across the room as if she would come to the bed, but he blocked her way, and she stopped by the window that faced the sea. She stood very still there, staring out at the sunlight, at the freedom of the rolling sea.

"Please, Bret!" she begged softly, her back to him. "Aye, perhaps I have wronged you, and perhaps I sought to escape you still. But sweet Jesu, do not do this to me!"

Her voice drew upon every fiber of compassion within him, but he fought it. He stared at her straight back, at the golden hair flowing down the length of it. Heat seemed to whisper and wave on the air, and it was the greatest agony not to touch her.

It was hard to forget all that she had done, and he dared not, could not do so. "I have no choice, milady."

She turned back to him, the tears in her eyes naked now, her lips trembling. She walked forward suddenly, falling gracefully upon her knees before him. "I beg of you!" she repeated. "I will do anything, anything . . . !"

He caught her arms suddenly, fiercely, dragging her to her feet. God, but the scent of her was sweet, the liquid shimmer of her eyes compelling. The softness of her flesh . . .

"Just what will you do?" he demanded of her harshly.

Her head cast back, she moistened her lips. "I will beg your forgiveness before everyone, swear an oath of fealty, turn the entire isle over to you."

"That's fine," he said, keeping his voice hard. "And what else?"

"Anything!"

"Anything I desire?"

She met his eyes, then could not do so. She nodded.

"Tell me just what you'll do."

"Sleep beside you—"

"Ajax has slept beside me. I require much more."

"Lie with you—"

"Please, be more specific!"

She gritted her teeth, her eyes flashing once again. "I will make love to you, my lord. I will use everything I learned at your not-inexperienced hands to entertain you through the darkness. I will do whatever you wish!"

Dear God, but it was tempting. Tempting unto death. The length of him burned with a desire he had never known. He would burst into sheer flame, explode, implode. It was nearly unbearable. Holding close the woman who obsessed him, listening to the promises that she made. He ached to hold her even closer to him, but his very desire for her infuriated him further.

"Whatever I wish!" he exclaimed softly.

"Aye!"

He shook his head very slowly. "Once, it would have been enough." He released her arms suddenly, turning away from her to stride back to the bed and look at his sleeping child. He looked to Allora. "Not now. You ran from me in London. You closed the gates of this place against me. I don't think that you ever meant me to know that we had parented a child, and even this morning, you did your best to escape me once again."

"You don't understand!" she cried out. "I *had* to do what I did—"

"Aye, lady, you had to marry me. But you did not have to follow your fool uncle and get your father killed—"

A sudden sob escaped her and the back of her hand flew to her lips to still it. She stiffened regally, forgetting her plea for the moment. "You killed my father, and if not you, your Norman king, your all-conquering Norman lords! If a man does not bow to you, slay him and be done with it!"

"Lady, I admired your father, and I did not kill him. I was across the English Channel when he perished. And he perished because of your uncle's reckless desire to compromise with no man and serve only himself. And you know that what I'm saying is true. With all of my heart, I am sorry about your father, lady. You do not know how sorry."

"You have no heart!" she cried heatedly, emerald eyes so very liquid, bathed in her tears.

He arched a brow. "You stood beside me and before God and spoke vows you never meant to keep for a single moment. I am quite certain I conveyed to you, before you did so, that should we wed, it would be a marriage in all truth. I never abused you or harmed you. *I* did not do my best to escape you or hide a child. You, my lady, I will point out once again, did all these things."

"You refuse to understand—"

"Aye, you were forced to wed me for your uncle's life. We all have our reasons for what we do. And I do pity you there, Allora, for you bought Robert's life with the sacrifice of your father's. Again, I am very sorry for that. But it changes nothing now, for you chose your way after his death, and your choice was to battle me."

"You cannot, you cannot do this!" she cried, racing toward him suddenly, dignity lost, her hands wound into tight fists, amazingly strong and powerful against him in her desperation and fury. She caught his chin with a good strike, and it was damned painful. He swore, sweeping her up, catching her ankle with his foot and causing her to fall to the foot of the bed where he pinned her down, his weight atop her, wrists captured by his hands.

"You can't do this!" she cried again, and he saw the dampness of the tears on her cheeks. He was nearly swayed. His heart did ache for her. And he longed to forget the battles between them and all that she had done, to bury his face in the sweet-smelling softness of her hair, touch the silk of her flesh, let his anger burn and cool to ash in the fires of passion and desire. It would be so easy now. So damned easy.

Perhaps if she had just been there when they had surrendered the castle. If she hadn't chosen to escape him yet again, to take the babe he hadn't even seen.

But she had made her choices.

And he had to stand by his.

The baby suddenly shifted on the center of the bed, drawing their attention, causing them both to go still and silent for a moment.

Then her eyes touched his again. "You can't!" she whispered.

He stood, pulling her up with him.

"Ah, but I can. Watch me, my love," he told her wearily, and as she struggled anew, he carried her out of the room himself.

Chapter 18

$\sim\!\!\infty\!\!\sim$

Nothing that she could do now would mean anything to Bret, Allora realized, and the thought terrified her. She had expected his anger, she had even imagined that he might want nothing to do with her.

She had never thought that he would deprive her of their child.

Yet she wasn't quite sure at that moment which hurt the most—his utter rejection of her, or the threatened loss of her child. In her heart, she couldn't believe that he would deny her Brianna forever.

Yet he was cold as ice with her, unrelenting, unforgiving. Not even the fever and fury she felt in his arms as he touched her seemed to warm the ice within his eyes, or soften his tone as he spoke. His hold upon her awakened wild, sweet sensations within her that had lain dormant since his last touch.

Yet he did not seem to feel those same sensations, for despite all the fire it aroused within her, his hold was simply one of steel, and if any emotions raged within him, they were composed of that cold fury and hatred he bore toward her. He had picked her up merely to expel her from her chambers. *His* chambers now, the master's chambers.

Her weight seemed as nothing to him. He carried her as easily as a sack of grain, shifting her carelessly to open the door. She was forced to cling to him. Fighting tears, mired in her indignity, she charged him softly, "Sir, you have received today the surrender of a proud people; this will hardly endear you to their already ravaged hearts and souls!"

"My lady, this will assure them that I will brook no more disobedience from anyone."

"Wait, then!" she pleaded. "Sweet Jesu, wait, and I will walk! I don't want any of them rushing forward in my defense to meet nothing but your wrath. Set me down, and I will walk!"

She found herself instantly upon her feet, breathless, breasts heaving, meeting the icy blue of his eyes, the hard set of his jaw, a cool stare that still denounced her. She had not heard anyone come up behind her, but Bret suddenly nodded his head slightly, and spoke. "Etienne, will you please be so good as to escort the countess to the north tower? See that she has all that she requires, since she will not be leaving the tower."

"Aye, milord. Milady?" Etienne said, and his bow to her was polite, and somewhat pained, she was certain. She bit her lower lip, determined that she wasn't going to cry.

If it would have done her any good she would have sobbed out her heart at that moment. But Bret's own heart was closed against her, and nothing would serve to change his mind. She needed time to think, she told herself. He was sending her to the tower, not away from the fortress.

"Etienne!" she said softly, and lifting her chin, she accepted the arm he offered.

She felt Bret's eyes boring into her back as she walked down the stairway, past the second floor, and down to the first. As they passed through the bailey where people paused to watch them, Etienne said to her, "That is the north tower there, I assume? With five of them . . ."

"That is the north tower," she assured him.

They walked the distance to it. The ground floor here contained a massive fireplace and a table and chairs, comfortable enough, yet arranged merely for a guard of several men. It was a place for those on duty to come to warm themselves when the winter was harsh, to eat, to whittle, to rest.

And to keep tabs upon hostages above, if and when there were such hostages in the tower.

Allora had never imagined that she could be a hostage in her own house. Years ago, she had been told, the wife of a Viking jarl, having displeased her wild Nordic lord, had cast herself from the tower into the sea. Allora had never liked the tower because of that story, and she had seldom come here.

She hesitated on the ground floor; Etienne waited politely. She started up the stairs. The second floor held sleeping quarters for the guards, and she walked on higher until she came to the main chamber, similar to her own, yet colder, duller, untouched by warmth or comfort. There was a sizable bed—since border lords did grow to be big men!—and there were tables and chairs before the fire. There was a washstand and a dressing screen. She wouldn't suffer here; the quarters were not tight or confined, but even as Etienne began to leave her, she felt as if the walls were closing in.

She was far from Bret. He couldn't see her, or hear her. He could so easily forget her.

"Milady, if there is anything you need—" Etienne said.

"There is nothing, Etienne. Thank you."

He hesitated a moment, but she said nothing more to him. He turned and the door closed behind him; she heard the bolt slide home.

She walked to the bed and sat upon it, shaking. What would happen when Brianna awoke? When she cried and cried, because she was hungry. Women to nurse a babe were easy to find, he had told her, and she felt a stinging in her breasts and a fresh rise of tears to her eyes as despair began to overwhelm her.

She rose and paced the room.

He would come; he would have to come for her.

But the hours passed, and he didn't come, and she spent the time reliving the past, remembering certain things so acutely, then damning her uncle silently for all that he had done to her.

She had known not to fight. She had known the mistake before she had made it, and yet she had let Robert and the others talk her into taking a stand against Bret's men. And what had it gained them in the end? Robert had always been a wily fighter, disappearing into the forest as soon as his forces were overwhelmed. It was a good manner of fighting; they had survived many years by following just such tactics.

But once again, she was the one left behind. This time a prisoner in a tower.

She paced anew, unable to forget that one afternoon she had spent with Bret in the sweet security of the cottage in the woods beyond London. She trembled, remembering the tenderness he had shown her, the pleasure he had discovered in her. She had longed so to touch him today when she had seen him. But the fight had begun . . .

And he had finished it.

Suddenly, it all seemed too much for her. Her breasts were really beginning to pain her. She longed for the baby. And she longed for a chance to start over.

She threw herself on the bed and sobbed, certain that no one could see or hear her now. But even as she gave free rein to her torrent of grief, she was startled by a knocking upon the door. "Allora!" a soft voice called to her.

Someone slid the bolt. "Allora, may I come in?"

She dried her tears with her hands and leaped warily from the bed, still not replying. She stood uneasily at the foot of the bed as the door opened and she heard Etienne say quietly, "A few minutes, Lady Elysia, no more. Your brother has not said that she may have visitors.".

"I'll not get you caught!" Elysia promised him.

And Allora found herself staring then at the wild, red-haired beauty she had last seen on the night of her father's death.

"Elysia!" she said, startled. "Ah!" she murmured softly then. "Ah, yes. Well, you were right. Your great and magnificent brother has come down upon us, and your revenge will surely be complete. I imagine you have come to gloat, or perhaps you wish to offer me a few slings and arrows of your own."

Elysia lifted a delicate brow. "After such a greeting, I should just walk away."

Allora lowered her lashes for a moment, praying that Elysia hadn't seen just how wretched she was. "Then why have you come?" she asked.

"Actually, I am in a bit of sympathy with you—"

"I don't want your pity."

"Don't be such a prickly creature!" Elysia charged her. "If you'll just listen for a moment, I'll tell you why I've come."

"Why?" Allora asked her.

"To help you."

"How? If you mean to help me escape—"

"Oh, Allora! Never! I am no fool! I know when to test my brother's temper, and when not to do so, I do assure you!"

"Then what is it you have planned? And—and why would you help me?"

"In all fairness, Allora, I am well aware that neither you nor your father had a wish to abduct me, and perhaps I do have my own vengeful streak; but you are the one who insisted I be freed. I cannot forget that night—when your father died."

"Oh," Allora murmured, her lashes sweeping over her eyes once again. "Well then, I am glad that you have come, and I am grateful for your concern. But I don't believe there's anything you can do for me, since you don't intend to help me in an escape."

"Think about it, Allora. Are you really so eager to escape?"

Allora stared at her. "Elysia, there is nothing else that is open to me."

"Ah, but there is. I have watched my brother for a long time now."

"Your brother will not forgive me."

"You haven't asked his forgiveness."

"But I have—"

"Allora, he came, you tried to escape. Coming here has been like a fever raging in him! And surely not just to lay claim to a pile of stone. If you really wish for peace, reach out for it. Have Etienne bring him the message that you must speak with him again."

"He won't see me; he has already cast me out. Elysia, he did so bodily!"

Elysia smiled. "Are you so willing to accept defeat?"

Allora fell silent.

"I must go," Elysia said quickly. "He is already furious with me for being here at all. Heed my words, Allora!" she urged, then she turned and slipped from the room.

"Elysia!" Allora cried, ready to hurry after her. But the door closed, and the bolt was slid fast. She listened as Elysia's footsteps fell upon the stairway, fading away at last.

Then she began to pace the room again, and at last stood stock-still. She had done so many things because she had believed she must. She had married to free her uncle, and that she had done willingly and with her eyes open.

But once Robert had failed to rescue her on that first night, things had changed. She had nearly poisoned herself to death, again for her uncle, and her father had at long last come to rescue her when she no longer desired to be rescued. But she had ridden north, because she didn't dare take the time to argue with her father, and she had been a party to Elysia's kidnapping because she could not let any of her kinsmen be caught.

She had failed to inform Bret about the baby because she hadn't wanted to pitch her people into war, nor had she wanted him to come when nothing but warfare with her uncle awaited him.

But she had never wanted to fight him. She had let Robert's rash determinations sway her when she knew that she would have been right to accept Bret here—her father was dead. By her father's own agreement, Bret was rightfully laird of the Far Isle.

Her fingers clenched. "No more!" she said aloud. No, no more. She would not be influenced by those around her, and she'd be damned if she'd let Robert rule her any longer. They were beaten.

She hurried to the door and slammed her fists thunderously against it. "Etienne! Etienne!"

The bolt slid quickly; the wiry Norman burst quickly in, his eyes wide with alarm. "What, what? What is wrong, my lady?"

She inhaled deeply, trying to gain composure. "Nothing, Etienne, I'm sorry. Nothing is wrong. But I wish you to summon someone else to guard me; I wish you to bring a message to Bret that I beg to speak with him again. Will you do that for me?"

Etienne nodded swiftly. "Aye, my lady. I will go to him myself."

"Beg him, Etienne."

"Aye, milady! I swear, I will do what I can!"

He left her. It seemed like an endless time that he was gone. Without the babe to nurse, her breasts grew heavy and more painful. Dismay filled her heart. The day began to disappear; sunset shadows played upon the room; then the longer stretches of darkness began to invade it. Exhausted from her constant pacing and turmoil, she lay upon the bed, despairing, and waited still.

Then she suddenly heard footsteps, and her door burst open. She rose up on her elbows. "Etienne?" she whispered in the shadowy darkness.

"Nay, madam. It is I. You asked to see me?"

Bret. He had come himself. Perhaps he had determined not to let her out of her tower, even to speak with him.

Rivulets of cold fear seemed to run through her. It had been so easy to come to the determination that she had been wrong!

And it was so hard now to find words. It was dark, yet she could see the height and breadth of him, the strong contours of his face. She could see the blue glitter of his eyes so hard upon her.

"You wanted to see me," he repeated. "What is it?"

She was at such a disadvantage, stretched out on the bed as he towered above her. She gained a sitting position and inched back, wishing that they were in the light, and that his expression was now covered by the shadows of the coming night.

"I pray—I pray that you listen to me!" she began quickly then, digging her nails into her palms, willing herself not to stutter and fail. "I have been wrong in many things, and I know that you do not believe me easily; but half that you would condemn me for was not by my choosing. Aye, I meant to escape you the night of our wedding. But after that night, I—my father came, and I was so afraid that the king would have them all slain if I did not quickly come with them and get them out of the city! And dear God, I swear upon Brianna's life that I knew nothing of the poison in the vial. I couldn't think or reason when—when you touched me. I wanted you to sleep, nothing more."

She fell silent because he was standing so utterly still. The silence stretched out.

"Go on!" he ordered sharply.

"I fought you because I thought that I *had* to fight you!" she whispered. "I did not wish to. And I tried to escape you because I knew how deeply you despised me, and I was so very afraid!"

Again he was silent. It seemed that an eternity passed, and she cried out again. "Bret, I will swear my fealty to you. I am so cold and weary! My battles are over, I swear to it. I will bow to a Norman king—and a Norman lord."

She watched in the shadows as he turned and started to the door once again. A sob threatened to tear from her then and she pressed her hands against her lips, desperate to silence it. "Bret!"

He stopped at the doorway, and again, all she saw was his silhouette there.

"Etienne will bring you to the babe in the keep's tower," he said dispassionately. "When I have secured my men and the fortress for the night, I will return."

He left her. She inhaled sharply, then squinted, for Etienne entered seconds after his master left, carrying a candle that seemed to burn very brightly.

"My lady, are you ready?"

"Aye!" she cried. "Aye!"

She had eaten very little since the morning, yet her stomach was in absolute turmoil. It didn't matter. She leaped up, ready to follow him. He led her across the bailey and back to the main tower, and when they entered, she could hear the sounds of Norman French now filling the main hall.

She knew a few of the men there. Jacques, Jarrett, and her own Sir Christian. Some of the others she had seen before. Some she didn't know at all.

They stood as she entered. In silence, they bowed gravely. She nodded in return, and hurried on up the stairs, still afraid that someone would try to stop her.

She reached her room. Nothing had changed—but more trunks had been added.

Bret's mail and accoutrements of war were carefully piled upon one of the new trunks. The room was empty.

She spun around, staring at Etienne. But even as she did so, she heard Brianna wailing, and in a second, Lilith was hurrying in with the babe. "Oh, Allora, Allora!" her cousin exclaimed, tears dripping down her plump cheeks. "Lady Elysia assured me that all would be well! When our poor wee lass here awoke, she cried and cried! The earl sent for a woman from his camp, but the babe continued to cry, and would have nothing to do with her. Mary and I tried a linen teat and goat's milk, and the poor babe managed to keep some down. Oh, she needs you! She has cried and cried for you! The only time she would stop was when he was with her himself, can you imagine? That great muscled wall of a man, and his touch made her quiet! But he couldn't stay, and when he left her in my arms, she wailed again, and he told me that if I did not care to serve him and the child, I was free to join my kinsmen in the woods. Allora, of course I would never leave Brianna, nor would Mary. But, oh, lady, it was a mistake! I knew it was a mistake, that I could not fool him, even from a distance!"

Allora didn't care about mistakes. She was reaching for Brianna, tears of joy now dampening her cheeks as she held the babe close to her. She hurried to the chair before the fire and nursed the babe, grateful to ease the swelling in her breasts, even more grateful to be touching her precious daughter again.

"Thank you, Lilith!" she said softly. But then she realized that her cousin was gone. The door to the chamber was closed, and she was alone within it once again.

She was shrewd enough to realize that she had exchanged one tower prison for another, but that didn't matter at the moment. She had Brianna.

The baby drank and drank, and then fell heavily asleep. Allora had just set her into her cradle when there was a soft tapping on the door. Mary was there, with a tray that carried food and wine. She hugged Allora fiercely and then, without a word, quickly disappeared.

Allora started to call after her, but fell silent. Bret had come right behind Mary, and now walked in, closing the door behind him. He stared at Allora, and she felt a swift trembling seize hold of her.

He crossed the room to where the food and wine had been set down and poured out two goblets, offering one to her. She stood still and he lifted it anew with an impatient gesture. "There's nothing tainted about this fruit of the vine, my love. I brought it myself."

She stepped forward. "I didn't—"

"You may eat and drink anything safely, you know. Were I to seek vengeance for any deed, it would not be done in so devious a manner."

She took the chalice from him, determined to control her temper. She lowered her lashes quickly. "I did not assume that it was poisoned."

"The babe sleeps?"

Allora nodded, keeping her eyes downcast.

He drank his wine, striding across to the fire. He turned to stare at her again, studying her from head to toe, still so aloof and arrogant. She felt his eyes, like a touch of fire, and she swallowed more wine quickly, wondering what in God's name might be passing through his mind.

He lifted his chalice to her. "Why so silent now? Your speech such a short time ago was so very eloquent. I hurried business as best I might to come and hear more of your lofty resolutions. Have I understood you right? You wish to make amends, to find peace in this household? You are willing to do anything to achieve this peace?"

His tone was making her increasingly nervous. Earlier she had offered him everything—he had flatly rejected her.

"What is it that you want?" she asked him painfully.

"You offered me everything. And that is what I want," he said, his voice low and yet deathly vehement. "Everything."

"But what—"

"Those—for a start!" he told her, pointing at her legs.

She looked down in confusion.

"Nay, perhaps the tunic and shirt first, for they offend me as well. They remind me that you were so willing to escape in masculine costume."

She was willing to do anything to stay with her child. Anything. But she hadn't expected him to do this to her, to taunt her so.

"Well?" he demanded.

She gritted her teeth hard and wrenched the tunic over her head. She threw it down upon the floor before him. His eyes didn't fall from hers.

"Keep going, my lady."

She drew off the shirt as well, shivering from his stare as much as from the sudden cool touch of the air against her naked flesh.

"The boots, and the chausses. They offend me mightily."

She kicked off her boots, and, burning, skimmed the skintight chausses from her hips and thighs.

"Ah, yes, grit your teeth—but get your clothes all over here!" he ordered softly.

Naked, only her golden hair curling around her, she stared at him with an outrage she could little conceal.

"My lady, bring me that distasteful pile of clothing!" he commanded her.

"You are a bas—" she started to charge him.

"Careful, careful. You are seeking my trust and forgiveness, remember."

She fell silent, her eyes glittering green daggers as she plucked up the clothing and forced herself to walk to him with it, looking up into his eyes when she reached him at at last.

"Thank you." He took first the tunic from the top of the pile and cast it into the flames. An involuntary cry escaped her as the sparks flew and the fabric burned. He didn't say a word, but continued to set her clothing to the fire. As each piece left her arms, she felt more and more naked. She inched away from him as the blaze burned brightly, then swept a blanket from the bed, clasping it quickly around her shoulders.

He left the fire, striding toward her. "Give it over," he said softly.

Her eyes glittered; she fought tears. "Truly, if you have done this to humiliate me, you have well succeeded. There is no more need—"

"I have done this because I will not have you dressing as a lad to escape me again. And I will have that blanket from you because I am damned anxious to see just how eager you are to appease me. Come, my love. You have said that you will do anything. Give over the blanket."

"Dear God, Bret—"

There was suddenly no patience left within him, for he reached for her, wrenching the blanket from her grasp.

"I'm sorry!" she gasped out quickly. "I can't . . . I . . ."

She was suddenly swept into his arms and borne down to the wide expanse of the bed. His eyes with their searing blue fire raked into hers, and she was startled at the rise of a fierce trembling within him, to feel the rampant pounding of his heart against her own.

"I taunt you no more, milady. And neither will I wait a moment longer . . ."

His lips came down upon hers. For the briefest flicker of time, she resisted his touch, frightened by the very heat and intensity of it. But then the longings of what had seemed like a lifetime since she had seen him took flight deep within her. Her lips parted swiftly to his savage kiss, yet his own did not remain long upon them. His mouth sheered across her cheek, the tip of his tongue stroked over her throat. His hand cupped the heavy weight of her breast, and his tongue flickered over it, his mouth closed upon it. Deep within her throat she groaned, feeling the swift rising sensation of something liquid and hot and sweet racing through her. Her fingers threaded into the ebony darkness of his hair; and she arched to his touch, nearly crying out again. His hands, his mouth, the sweet, savage caress of his lips and tongue were all over her as if he could not taste and have her swiftly enough. She felt the stroke of his fingers down the length of her inner thigh as his mouth continued to arouse her breast, teasing . . . stroking. His palm brushed over the soft golden triangle at the juncture of her thighs, then swept lower again, catching her thigh, drawing it apart from the other. The sweet tingling thigh became fire, and fire the sweetest hunger. She was dazed when she felt the fullness of his weight as he knelt there, between the length of her limbs. He was silent as he stared down at her, wrenching shirt and tunic from over his shoulders. His chest naked, he leaned against her, catching her lips again, stroking her body with the weight and heat and muscled fever of his own, his lips leaving her again to travel downward, tending her right breast, her left. Farther downward. She dug her fingers into the bed as his tongue laved her navel and belly. Then his hands were suddenly roughly upon her thighs, parting them still farther, and she cried out at the searing liquid caress that stroked her next. She was certain that she would die as a blinding sensation swept through her like fallen rays of the sun. It had been too long since she had known this fleeting fire of ecstasy. A taste so long denied, and now scorching through her like the blue fire of his eyes.

She felt the stroke of his fingers upon her, within her. The ravaging fire of his tongue. Whispers escaped her, cries, soft, desperate pleas . . .

And she didn't even know just exactly what it was that she begged. Then he loomed above her, all rigid brown muscle, eyes cobalt with the hunger of his passion. His lips touched hers again as she felt him sink against her, wrenching at the tie to his chausses, freeing himself. She felt the hardened length of his sex fall against her flesh in startling, pulsing dimensions, and then he shifted, and seemed to sink swiftly yet eternally within her . . .

He moved like jagged lightning, a startling force of hunger and demand, a ruthless, relentless storm that was not to be stopped. So swiftly the winds rose, so wildly, so violently. She feared she would shatter, break. But rather it seemed that she melded more fully to him, gloved him ever more deeply, encompassed him until she was filled to the womb, the heart, the soul. It seemed to last forever; it was all so swift. She had sailed so high, reached so desperately, and then the wonder and awe and sweet ecstasy burst over her again, even as it seemed he burst into her, a floodgate, filling her with himself, with all the time and hunger that had passed with such rich anguish between them . . .

When it was over, she lay beside him silently. Moments later she felt his fingers moving in her hair. "And I had thought that memory must have deceived me!" he said softly. "But it did not, and I don't really seek to taunt you now, my lady, by saying that your gallant apology was hardly necessary. You'd not have remained in that tower long."

She met the blue fire in his eyes, and was stunned by the tenderness within them. She had dreamed of him looking at her so once again.

But she had never thought that it could really come to pass.

She closed her eyes, trembling as she curled against him, feeling his chin upon the top of her head, warm within his embrace, her nose tickled by the coarse ebony hair that grew on his chest.

"I didn't want to escape you!" she whispered painfully. "But after the wine . . . I didn't think it possible we could ever share . . . this . . . again."

"*This* is easily enough shared, milady," he said rather dryly. "No matter what else may reign in the world! Yet creatures of such exquisite beauty are quite hard to come by. Ioin knew that I would come for you."

"Had he lived—"

"But he died."

"Had he lived," Allora continued determinedly, "he meant to write to you, to . . . negotiate."

"No annulment," Bret said, his tone acid now.

She swallowed hard, ready to turn from him. But his arms around her were tight, and tonight, there truly was no escape.

"No one has demanded that you be anything but what you are, Bret. Norman-English. A subject of a Norman king— William the First, or William the Second. You have asked me to turn my back on my people. You owe me some measure of understanding!" she told him boldly.

She felt his fingers go tense within her hair and she winced as the golden strands pulled tight. Then his hold eased. "Aye, maybe I do!" he said at last. "But a problem remains, my love."

"And that is?" she whispered.

"How do I trust you now?"

She rose and knelt at his side, finding his eyes hard upon her, their blue depths dark and wary. "I told you," she said in a husky whisper, "that I would swear fealty to you."

He nodded. "Oh, aye! And your father signed a contract with me, remember?"

She bit into her lower lip. "My father's word really was good, Bret. He was frightened when you wouldn't let him see me, and once we had come here . . . he died," she said hollowly.

Her lashes had fallen over her eyes; her eyes had fallen low over his body. His chausses were untied, and though they still covered his buttocks and legs, the deep V created where he had unlaced them left his sex exposed in a nest of ebony hair. She quickly drew her eyes away, startled at how the sight of it had seemed to create the simmering of a fire within her once again. She could want him so very quickly! It seemed indecent. Maybe it *was* indecent . . .

Her eyes slipped again. And the sight was even more erotic, more arousing, for that which had been nestled quietly was now growing again to startling dimensions right beneath her eyes.

"My—my word!" she whispered.

She heard his husky laughter, and he rolled suddenly, sitting up at the edge of the bed to peel the chausses from his body. He stood and turned to come back to her but Allora found herself already upon her knees, and reaching out to him. She buried her face against the wall of his chest, felt the hair tease her face again. She stroked his sides with her fingers, curved her arms around his body and caressed his buttocks with the cups of her hands.

"Sweet Jesu!" he breathed, his arms around her, pressing her closer against him.

She kissed his abdomen, teased a rib with the tip of her tongue. She slid her body down lower against his, then instinctively caught his fullness within her hands. She felt the massive shudder that shook his body. Hesitantly, she closed her mouth over him. Touched him, stroked the length of his sex with the tip of her tongue . . .

A deep, ragged cry exploded from him and she found herself swept up again, thrown down . . . and quickly, quickly filled. Once again it seemed that the winds of tempest rose to fever pitch in mere seconds. And then the stars exploded in shimmering, liquid pleasure, and she was left breathless, her heart thundering, her body, slick, her hair damp . . .

And soul somehow so sweetly filled. He held her securely, even when the storm had passed. His light stroke upon her remained achingly tender.

He didn't speak for the longest time. He held her, he touched her, his fingertips moving gently over her arm. She was bone-weary. She had spent the night consumed with worry about what the morning would bring. She had spent the day pacing, and the afternoon wretchedly anxious and sobbing. His sweetly gentle touch was putting her to sleep. Tomorrow would come, and she knew it. Happiness was fleeting; she had learned that well. And she was happy now. Content. She had no wish for words, even had she the strength to find them.

She was more than half asleep when he spoke at last.

"Ah, my lady," he whispered, "how do I trust you? There's the quandary still!"

"I gave you my word—" she tried to murmur.

"And I hold it sacred," he warned her softly.

She curved against him, so very tired. "I'll not fight you again," she murmured sleepily to him.

"How can I be so sure?"

She didn't stop to think; she couldn't. The truth simply escaped her.

"Because I know that I love you," she mouthed against his flesh, unaware of her words as the comforting darkness of sleep claimed her, even as she moved her lips.

Sleep . . . ah, she slept! Bret thought.

When, dear God, after that, he would surely never do so!

But then again, what was sleep?

He held the Far Isle.

And . . .

He held his wife.

Chapter 19

∽

She awoke in the morning alone.

For several minutes, she was simply aware of the coolness of the sheets beneath her cheek, and the warmth of the blankets that covered her. She became aware of the sun, streaming into the room through the window slits, and of the dust motes that danced upon the air. Within her room, nothing had changed at all, except for his things being added. If it hadn't been for yesterday . . .

But yesterday had come. And everything had changed. Bret was not in the room because he was downstairs somewhere surveying his new empire. She closed her eyes, drawing the blankets more tightly around her nakedness, and she remembered the night. She should have been ruing her loss of freedom; mourning the battle waged and lost by her kinsmen. Yet she felt oddly at peace; memories of his long-remembered touch caused her to tremble even now, and she was glad that Bret had come, glad that the contract she—and her father—had agreed to between them had come to completion.

She wasn't certain anymore it mattered whether the laird of the Far Isle gave homage to Malcolm or William Rufus. For the laird was often all-powerful in such a place as this, by the old customs or the new ones, and a fair and noble laird was far more important to the people than the man the laird himself gave his homage to. Bret, she had learned, could be ruthless and relentless. He could also be tolerant, and, in her case, he had proven himself fair.

When she—and her kin—had all proven themselves devious time and time again.

She rolled in the bed, a sudden fear suddenly rising within her breast. But when she looked across the room, Brianna was there, sleeping sweetly in her cradle. Her fear subsided.

Allora rose, shivering. She washed hurriedly and dressed, and by that time, Brianna had awakened, hungry and crying. She quickly fed the baby, and just as she finished, she heard a faint tapping at the door. She rose swiftly, Brianna on her shoulder, and hurried to open the door.

Mary stood there, her pretty young face furrowed with concern. "Milady, is all well?" she asked anxiously, then rushed on before Allora could answer. "I did my best to disappear once the Norman took the child from me. I failed you, I'm so sorry—"

"Mary, you didn't fail me. If you'd have left with Brianna, she wouldn't be with me now. Everything is well. It will simply be—new. No one—attempted any harm to you last night, did they?"

Mary shook her head. "Nay, lady, the place was subdued, and nothing more. The Norman laird spoke with the housecarls and the knights, and assured them he did not fault them for defending what was theirs, and that any who vowed an oath of allegiance to him as rightful laird would suffer no reprisals for anything that had happened. Sir Christian said it was only right, since Laird Ioin had signed the contracts, wedding the two of you, and naming Bret d'Anlou laird upon his own death. To a man, lady, the men within the castle vowed fealty to your Norman laird. And when they were done, the servants and the others were called, and one by one, lady, we also swore our oaths to him. It has been amazing, I do assure you! Even as the sun rose, men were all back to their tasks; the masons worked upon the walls, the housecarls here were given over to Norman knights to command them at their new stations."

"Then—it seems that all *is* well," Allora breathed. Then she asked anxiously, "What of my cousin Lilith?"

"She is down now in the great hall, sampling a fine breakfast of kidneys and fish. She begged your husband's pardon for her part in the deceit, milady, and he quickly forgave her, warning her only that she would be out of house and home were she ever to think to betray him again. There is a strange way about this Norman laird of yours, milady. He has beaten and subdued us, but in his victory he is merciful. His voice is firm and rings out clearly when he speaks, and his words are all believed. He gains men's trust so easily!"

"And women's too?" Allora asked.

Mary flushed. "Aye, milady, for he looked me square in the eye, and when I vowed to serve him, I meant the words that I said."

"I'm glad," Allora said softly. "I am tired of living in fear. He has come, and he has been more tolerant of us than I had imagined possible. My uncle will have to accept what has happened."

"Your uncle will never accept what has happened, milady," Mary said.

"Then he will have to avoid the Far Isle in the future," Allora said simply.

Brianna, who Allora had absently held over her shoulder as she patted her back, suddenly let out a staggering burp for so tiny a child. Both women laughed, and Allora gave Brianna over to Mary. "Watch her for me, Mary. I will see how the wind blows this morning."

"You'll be surprised at just how sweetly!" Mary told her.

Allora nodded and hurried out of the bedroom. She quickly ran down the flights of stairs to the great hall, then slowed her speed. There was a difference within the fortress, for her hall was filled with Norman knights now. Etienne stood by the fire, warming his hands, Jarrett was at the table, speaking earnestly with Elysia, and Gaston was engaged in a game of chess—with Sir Christian. Lilith was at the end of the table, happily munching upon a thick slice of fresh-baked and fragrant bread.

"Milady!" Jarrett stood quickly when he saw her entering the hall. Elysia, beside him, smiled warmly and mischievously, and Allora averted her eyes from her sister-in-law's.

"Please, sir, sit," she said to Jarrett, and nodded to Etienne as she discovered the need to warm her hands before the fire.

She could still feel everyone staring at her. She turned to them, maintaining the coolest facade she could muster. "Where is Bret?"

"Surveying the fortress from top to bottom, milady," Etienne volunteered.

"Oh," Allora murmured. "Then perhaps I will look for him, and see if I can be of assistance," she said. She waited for someone to stop her; to tell her that they had been ordered to see that she made no attempts to leave the main keep tower.

No one said a word. She still felt their eyes as she hurried to the doors, and then beyond them into the courtyard and bailey.

Once again, she was amazed. Life had not missed a beat. She could hear the ring of the blacksmith's hammer against steel. The cooper was at work on a barrel, seated on a stool beside his lean-to, just as he had worked as long as Allora could remember.

The parapets were heavily lined with men.

Even more heavily than they had been when the fortress had prepared to go to war against Bret. Yet perhaps that was to be expected. Bret had brought many men with him, and he would not be expecting to live peaceably here, not with Robert still roaming the forest.

And no matter what Mary had said, no matter how many men had given him vows of fealty, he would still be waiting for treachery from within, and so his own showing of guards would be strong.

She hurried to the stables, certain that Bret would be on horseback. When she entered the shadowed chamber within the walls, she was startled to see Briar tethered to the wall. She had left the horse behind in London so long ago now, it seemed.

She hurried to the mare, and crooned softly to her. "Ah, but it is good to see you, my pet! I've missed you. I am delighted to have my good horse back."

"*My* horse," she heard, and she turned quickly, only to discover that Bret was not mounted and about, but standing just twenty feet from her, feet planted firmly on the ground, arms crossed over his chest. He walked to her and stroked

Briar's silky neck. "My horse now, milady. You did leave her behind, you know."

Allora let her lashes sweep her cheeks as she wondered if he was serious, or merely mocking her. "I left you behind in London as well," she said softly, "yet you still claim to be my husband. Therefore one might think that the horse might still be mine as well."

"Hmmm . . ." he mused, and her eyes met his. In the shadows, his seemed as dark as ink. "Perhaps she should still be yours, but only upon good behavior."

"Mine—or the horse's?" Allora asked.

"I meant yours, milady."

"But I thought that my behavior was excellent last night!" Allora said, and then felt her face burning. He laughed softly, a husky, warm sound that seemed to touch her all along the spine.

"It was—excellent," he assured her. "And therefore, for the time being, the horse must once again be yours, just as the husband is. Come, we'll have her saddled, and we'll ride together."

He called to a groom quickly. The boy bobbed his head to them both, looking at Allora apologetically, as if he were sorry to be obeying Bret. But she smiled, and he beamed, and moved quickly to his task as if remembering that she had been the one to advise them all to bow down before a new laird.

In a few moments she was mounted, and Bret led Ajax outside and mounted his great horse to join her. "Come then, milady. Show me the fortress," he told her.

She stared at him, then shrugged. "Follow me!" She kneed Briar and started off, racing swiftly ahead of Bret, knowing her way around the lean-tos and craftsmen. He followed close behind her, and one by one, she pointed out the towers, and the direction they faced, and fine frame of defense each managed. She came at last to the north tower and reined in suddenly.

"The north tower—which you already know, of course. It's where we keep our prisoners."

He nodded, looking upward.

"It has most oft been vacant," she assured him with a definite arrogance.

He scowled at her suddenly, and she was startled by the look of dark anger that tightened his features. "Well, it is not empty now, milady," he told her.

"But I just vacated it last night—"

"And I have filled it anew, milady."

"Who—"

"It is not your concern, and I demand that you keep your distance, do you understand?"

His voice had seldom seemed so icy, or so flat—other than when he had come yesterday. But she had thought that the night had warmed that terrible chill; she knew now that it had not done so completely, and that she must still tread carefully around him.

She also felt a burning curiosity about the prisoner in the tower.

"If you are holding my uncle—" she began.

"I am not holding your wretched uncle," he said irritably, his voice still icy. She felt as if the very coldness entered into her limbs. "And I am warning you, Allora, stay away from the tower!" He spurred Ajax, turning from her to race swiftly across the bailey once again. At his call, the gates were let open. He raced out onto the stretch of land connecting fortress and mainland. Allora rode hard to the gates, hesitated, and rode on through them.

She came upon the mainland and a bleating herd of sheep. The sheepherder's daughter waved to her across the expanse of undulating white. She didn't see Bret anywhere, and so started riding to the south, into the tangle and mire of trees that rose atop the cliffs, and followed the sharp incline to the small stretch of smooth white beach below. She rode among the trees, then let Briar make her way down the steep incline to the sand. She dismounted there, and walked along the white sands, looking to the sea, and then behind her, nervously. She wasn't afraid for herself. She was afraid for Bret. Robert knew these woods like the back of his hand. So did his swift and wily men. Her people, so many of them distant kin . . .

But even as she walked, she was suddenly swept off her feet, and borne down to the sand. She shrieked, starting to fight, and then she heard rich masculine laughter.

She looked up to find that Bret was straddled over her in the sand.

"Did I startle you, my love? I'm so sorry!" he taunted.

"Aye! You startled me, Norman."

"I had to let you know that, in the future, you would still have no chance to escape me."

"And what makes you so certain I was not trying to escape you now?"

"Because Brianna remains back in the fortress. You are free to roam about it, but my men will know where my daughter is at all times."

Allora clenched her teeth together hard. "You are still too assured, milord. These woods—"

"Besides," he said swiftly, waving away her warning. "I seem to recall some fascinating words I believed I heard just before I slept last night. I think you murmured something about the fact that you had discovered that . . . you loved me? Could that be true, milady?"

How easily those words had escaped in the darkness, in the sweet aftermath of passion! How fragile they seemed today, how frightening, with him staring down at her, eyes cobalt fire, lips curled in a curious, taunting smile.

"I believe I was willing to say anything last night—"

"Ah! The words were tortured out of you!"

"There are many different means of torture, milord," she assured him coolly, and he laughed again, a husky sound from his throat that brought hot streaks sweeping along her limbs.

"You shouldn't be so amused!" she charged him, and there was a note of seriousness in her words. "You are beyond the walls of the Far Isle here, alone, without your men. My uncle knows those woods and the forests—"

"This is wonderful, fascinating," he said, stretching out on the sand at her side, perching upon an elbow to study her face. "Would you really seek to warn me about your uncle?"

She leaped to her feet. "Fine, let him take you. And let me warn you, they've their own laws here. They won't see you brought north to imprisonment with Malcolm! The clans judge men and carry out sentences, and upon extreme provocation, they've been known to condemn men to death at the stake! I'm quite sure that my uncle considers you to be a man who has given them extreme provocation!"

She stared down at him, angrily waiting for him to rise as well. But he plucked a piece of the wild grass that grew at the edge of the beach and chewed upon it, studying her, unconcerned.

"Why are you staring at me?" she demanded. "I won't warn you about danger in the future if all that you choose to do is laugh at me!"

He rose at last, tossing the blade of grass aside and reaching for her hands. His voice was grave, and only the slightest smile curved his lips. "I am grateful for the warning, my love. I am just curious that you should have so despised William and his Norman reign. For William went to battle, yes, and conquered, and there were a few occasions when he was furious and even cruel. But in all his reign, Allora, he actually executed just one man, Waltheof, and that after the man had rebelled time and time again, and left him little choice."

"My uncle does not carelessly execute men!" she cried defensively. "And neither has he ever laid waste half a countryside!"

"He was quite willing to poison me."

Her lashes fell swiftly. "I'm sure he couldn't have known just what potion—"

"The one thing the man is not is stupid, Allora. Never mind; I do not care to argue the point," he assured her. She was startled when he turned away from her, walking over to mount Ajax, leaving her on the beach to follow or not as she chose.

He infuriated her so with his arrogance that she longed to stay right where she was. But he was right about one thing: she would not leave Brianna.

And there was more, of course. The words she had refused to repeat were true. She had dreamed of him the long months she had not seen him. She had waited for him, knowing he was coming. She had seen the strength she had expected, and a careful mercy she had not. He fascinated her. She was never so comfortable as when he held her during the night, never so alive as when he touched her. She did love him. She wanted him to stay. She wanted to find peace with him, and she even believed an even footing could eventually be found.

She turned from the water, and looked to the woods. This was insanity on Bret's part! Robert could too easily bear down upon them here, on this beach.

But Bret was mounted, waiting for her, watching her as she strode to Briar and mounted the mare. Then he turned back over the mainland rise, and together they raced over the already dampening sands back to the gates of the fortress and within.

Bret swiftly dismounted from Ajax before the keep door, throwing the reins to a groom, calling, "Give him a good rubdown, boy!" and striding on into the main hall.

She dismounted from Briar, but stood her ground in the courtyard for a moment, determined that she wasn't going to follow him any farther since he was so damned confident that she would. She found herself looking to the north tower, curiosity burning hotly within her once again.

He wasn't holding Robert; he would have told her the truth about her uncle, she was certain. He might well have sent Robert back to London, to imprisonment with William Rufus or perhaps even death or banishment to the continent. But he wasn't holding Robert, so it had to be another man high in the leadership of the clan Canadys.

It came to her swiftly then, and with a shattering anguish.

He had to be holding David.

The breath nearly left her; a terrible weakness so pervaded her limbs that she almost fell. Then she gasped in air, finding new strength. She swung around and marched into the hall, practicing the words in her head with which she would demand a private audience. But when she strode into the great hall, there was no one to be found. Everyone, including Bret, had gone about their business elsewhere. A fire burned brightly in the great hearth; pitchers of wine and ale sat upon the long table, waiting to quench the thirst of those who resided here. But despite the warmth of the hall, it was empty.

She started for the stairs, quickly reaching the second level and then her own. She thrust open the heavy door to the vast bedchamber at the top of the tower and found Bret there. He stood leaning idly against the wall, staring down at Brianna who napped in her carved wood cradle.

"You have to let him go!" she cried out, then winced inwardly, for that was not at all the tactful beginning she had planned on.

And it was not taken as such. An ebony brow arched high with cool rebuke at the brash audacity of her words.

"There's very little that I *have* to do, my lady," he informed her, arms crossed over his chest as he surveyed her. "But just who is it you believe I must let go?"

She braced herself, shoulders squared, head high, eyes straight upon his. "David. You're holding David of Edinburgh."

He didn't blink; he gave nothing away. "Any prisoner that I'm holding, milady, I took in battle. And there is no reason as of yet to release anyone who so willingly fought against me."

She shook her head, very afraid for David then. "You don't understand. I'm telling you this for the good of everyone! David is loved, he is admired."

"Is he?" Bret queried coldly.

"His is one of the few voices of reason now that Father is gone!" Allora persisted, wishing that she could start over. "If you free him, the other men might well be swayed to give up the battle, to recognize you as the rightful laird here."

"They will all recognize me as rightful laird here, my lady, or perish in their attempts to prove otherwise," he assured her, something savage in his tone, though he kept his distance and was very still, staring at her.

"You have to let him go—"

"Don't tell me what I have to do, Allora."

"Oh, you wretched *Norman!*" she cried, fighting for control, losing the battle. She moved across the room, sweeping around the cradle, slamming her fists against his chest in a violent fury. She managed to act but once; then her wrists were caught and she felt the icily furious touch of his eyes upon hers. "Let him go! Let *me* go! If you don't—"

"If I don't, you'll vow to escape me? Try to slay me? What tired threat will you have against me now, lady?"

Tears stung her eyes. "No threat!" she cried. "A vow, indeed! I'll not come near you, I'll not sleep with you, I'll not . . . touch you while he remains a prisoner here. You can lock me in another tower, do what you will, but—"

"My lady, maybe I don't give a damn about your tender touch, and maybe you should know this: I have tolerated all that I am going to tolerate from you. You had your way long enough. *I'm* here now. You'll sleep where I tell you to sleep, and if I want you, wife, I will have you, and your interest in the procedure need not sway me at this point!"

She jerked hard at his hold upon her wrists. "Damn you! Do what you will with me, but David does not deserve—"

"Right! David is loved. Well, perhaps I keep him in a tower to torture him so that I may discover once and for all just how deeply he was loved by you!"

She gasped, suddenly still. "You don't believe—"

"I believe that I will not be commanded by you after all that has happened between us!" he shouted, his fingers still vises around her wrists.

"But—"

She broke off as Brianna suddenly let out a wail that rivaled both her parents' shouts.

"See to your child, Allora!" he ordered angrily, releasing her with a push away from himself. "And haunt me no more about this matter!"

He strode to the door, his steps long, his boots clipping on the floor.

"But I will haunt you!" Allora cried desperately after him. "I will haunt you, I will fight you, I will reject you— as long as you cause harm to him."

"Then you pay the price of your own rebellions as well," he told her curtly.

"Not if I am not here to pay them!" she cried defiantly.

"There is but one gate to the fortress, milady. Be assured that my Norman knights will be watching it. Fight me, reject me, do what you will. But I will keep you beneath my power—if only to make you as wretchedly miserable as you are forever striving to make me!"

The door flung open at his angry yank. "You wanted to be with your daughter! See to her now!" He spun around. The door slammed in his wake.

"You woke her up! You should see to her!" Allora whispered heatedly to the closed door. She should have shouted the words, and she might have, except that she was too afraid they might make him think that she didn't want to be with her daughter. Her own stay in the tower was too recent for her to take chances with Brianna.

She plucked up the baby and held her, crooning to her, soothing her as she walked around the room, thinking desperately. Bret was lying, she told herself. He would never torture David. He couldn't really believe that anything had gone on between her and David; if he had thought that . . . well, one of them might well have been bereft of a head by now.

But how could she be sure? She had to *speak* with David, at the very least. She couldn't, by any means that would be decent or right, accept Bret here and her marriage if David was being tortured or ill-kept in the tower.

Brianna continued to wail, hungry, and Allora sat down to feed the babe, her mind working furiously.

Elysia sat idly at the table in the great hall, sipping wine and wondering why she had been so determined to defy everyone and come here.

Vengeance, plain and simple.

But she'd had her revenge. Once Allora had been freed from the north tower, David had been taken to it, and he was there now, her brother's prisoner.

Maybe that was it. Maybe she hadn't had enough vengeance. She didn't think that she'd wanted Bret to do anything completely evil to him . . .

But then, Bret hadn't really done anything to him at all. In fact, Bret seemed to like his rival.

So David was the prisoner; but she was the one tied in knots. As she sat there, Bret suddenly came hurrying down the stairs, tossing his mantle over his shoulder as he swiftly

strode down the length of them. She started to speak, then
saw the darkness of the scowl upon his face, and fell silent.
He hadn't seen her; he seemed in a rare fury indeed. He went
straight out the door to the keep, allowing it to slam wildly
in his wake.

Elysia looked up the stairs, biting her lower lip. Well, it
was apparent that her brother was not residing in marital
bliss, even if he had allowed his wife out of the tower.
Strangely, she liked Allora, maybe because she had known
that Allora had been so forcefully opposed to Elysia's
own abduction, and maybe simply because she did feel
an empathy for the beautiful girl who'd been forced into
so much and torn in so many directions.

And maybe it was because Elysia was convinced that
above it all, Allora really did care for Bret. After all, she,
Elysia, had lived with him and knew that dark scowl just
about as well as anyone. He was arrogant and confident,
savage when he was determined enough—and noble to a
fault, of course. She would definitely long to scratch out
the eyes of anyone who would seek to harm him.

Like David. And perhaps that explained her moody
restlessness now. The wretched Scotsman just hadn't paid
enough!

Elysia stood suddenly, noticing an old servant woman—one who had long been with their family and had
come with Bret's retinue—emerging into the great hall
from the huge kitchen beyond. She carried a tray covered
with a linen cloth, and Elysia hurried to her on intuition. "Jeannette, where are you going with this? Is there
a hungry guard somewhere? Mmmm, this food smells just
wonderful."

"It's for the Scot prisoner, Lady Elysia," the old woman
told her. "And if you'll give me leave, I'll take it quickly,
for the tray is heavy for my old bones and the cold is fearful
and wicked as I pass from tower to tower."

"Indeed, these northern winds are horrid!" Elysia agreed,
though she privately had to admit that she loved the wind.
She loved the Far Isle, and she loved the rough, rugged
border country. "My bones are not so old. You give me
the tray, and I will take it."

"My lady! Lord Bret would surely have my bones cracked to dust for giving my work to you!"

"Jeannette, when have you ever seen my brother violent with any trusted servant? Besides, we'll never tell him. I shall swear a vow of silence, and so will you."

"You'll be seen—"

"Give me your cloak and hood, and no one will be any the wiser. Come now!"

"Aye, milady. I thank you. I could have sent a younger girl, of course, but I don't think your brother does trust the servants here as yet. They are a group to keep an eye upon, and there's the truth!"

"Indeed!"

Elysia quickly grabbed the encompassing hooded cloak and swept it around her, then took the tray swiftly from Jeannette's hand before the old woman could argue with her again. "Not a word to Bret!" Elysia.

"Aye, lady, not a word. I vow it!" Jeannette agreed.

Elysia turned and hurried from the great hall to the courtyard, lifting her head just slightly. Life had returned to normal here. The cooper again labored industriously. Masons were at work on the wall. Sheep were bleating, hounds were barking. She could hear the high squeals of children at play.

She lowered her head and hurried across the courtyard, pausing before the entrance to the north tower, at one of the watering troughs. She lifted the linen cloth and found a steaming haunch of venison along with a sweet-smelling hunk of fresh bread. There was also a goblet of wine.

Poor David! Such a wretched imprisonment, she thought sarcastically.

She quickly dumped the wine out of the goblet and refilled it with water, then she whistled softly. One of the huge hunting hounds that roamed the fortress hurried to her, its massive tail wagging. She tossed it the venison, and placed the hunk of bread in the center of the remaining juices. "We'll give him just a taste of it, eh, boy? I do hope he's *starving!*"

The hound whined and sat, staring at her, hoping for more. Elysia drew the hood more closely about her and stepped into the tower.

Etienne and Gaston were on guard. They sat at a rough-hewn table in the center of the hall, playing a dicing game.

"Food for the prisoner," she said, holding the cloth of her hood against her mouth.

"Come then, he's up the stairs," Etienne said pleasantly, not recognizing the servant as Bret's own sister. He stood. "I'll be back immediately—no cheating!" he told Gaston, who offered him a grin in return. Then Etienne led the way up the two flights of stairs to the high tower room and pulled the heavy bolt. Elysia kept her eyes lowered, her hood shielding her face, and mumbled swiftly, "I'll wait for the tray."

"I suppose that will be well enough; he seems honorable, but if you've trouble, woman, scream hard, and we'll be here quickly!"

Elysia nodded, her heart thundering wildly. What would Bret do to her were he to catch her here? She didn't want to imagine what his punishment might be. Worse, he might send her to their father, and Alaric would be both astounded and furious with her behavior. Even with her mother's intervention, she might find herself wed to some iron-fisted baron who would scarce let her breathe!

She couldn't worry about it now. She had come this far. She slipped into the room. Etienne closed the door behind her.

She could see David standing by the narrow archer's window, looking out on what he could see of the dying day. The twilight breeze flowed through the window, ruffling the thatch of wheat-colored hair on his forehead. He was dressed handsomely in light-brown chausses, bleached white shirt, and short green tunic, and he didn't seem to feel the chill of the breeze that touched his face. But then, this wild country was his. He had known the chill breezes all his life.

He knew she was there. "Set it on the trunk," he said, and did not turn around.

He didn't seem to be starving. Her brother fed his prisoners all too well.

She walked further into the room and set the tray down on the trunk as he had directed. "I'll wait," she said.

"Nay, woman, don't."

"But—"

He turned then, perhaps recognizing her voice. She lowered her head quickly but he strode across the room and lifted her chin. Her eyes, blazing, met his.

"You!"

"I brought you bread and water!" she said, startled to discover it was difficult to breathe. He let go of her chin and walked away, stopping at the tray to lift the linen cloth. He picked up the goblet and sniffed it. "I assume some tail-wagging hound has enjoyed my meat?" he queried. "What of my wine?"

"Soaked into the ground."

"A pity. Your brother carries excellent wines."

"The very best from Normandy!" she agreed.

"So you tossed my meal!" he said, moving toward her once again. Slowly. Somehow, there was menace in the movement.

Elysia backed away quickly. "Come near me and I shall scream for my brother's guards!"

"*You're* going to scream! I should be the one shouting out for deliverance from the torture I'm quite certain you've come to inflict!"

"How dare you—" Elysia began, but she had backed against the wall, and there was nowhere else to go, and he was suddenly in front of her, tall and broad, emitting waves of warmth, and yet there was a compelling cool touch of laughter in his light eyes.

"I shall shout for help, I swear it!" she warned him.

"Do so quickly, for I need help badly," he assured her.

She wasn't sure who made the first move. And if she had come to torture him, she was creating equal torment in her own soul. Her lips touched his, and the world exploded. All the sweet, forbidden flashfires of hell seemed to explode within her and she was on her toes, pressed against him, craving more and more of his touch. His arms swept around her; the cloak fell to the floor. Trembling, he lifted her, and they came to the bed; her heart thundered wildly as he laid her down, and came to lie beside her. He touched her cheek.

"Surely, I will die for this!" he whispered.

"Oh!" she gasped, struggling suddenly against him.

"Ah, but life itself is well worth the price!" he told her.

"Nay, nay! I would not have your life on my hands!" she cried to him.

"I will die a happy man," he whispered, his lips finding hers again.

She wanted to protest. His touch swept away thought. They were in incredible danger. Etienne was just down the stairs. Someone could come in upon them . . .

No, someone could not surprise them, for David paused, and rising, thrust the trunk before the door, then returned to her. He ripped his shirt and tunic over his head, and she discovered that she trembled with anticipation, that she longed to touch him, to feel the heat of his flesh, the contours of his well-muscled chest. This was horrible, absolutely horrible. Her mother would be shocked, her father would be shocked, her brother would probably rip her hair out.

And she just didn't care . . .

She watched as he came to her again, stretching out beside her, taking her tenderly into his arms.

"Sweet Jesu, but you could be made to pay for this!" she whispered to him, the warning desperate, hard-torn from her lips.

"Only one thing could stop me now!" he assured her.

"And that is . . . ?"

"You," he whispered, nuzzling her forehead. "Would you stop me, Elysia?"

Suddenly, she could find no words at all, and so she slipped her arms around him, and kissed him.

Chapter 20

When Brianna slept again, Allora was ready. She dug into her trunks to find a plain, dull-gray woolen tunic. She slipped it over her head, drew a heavy veil over it, and nervously slipped down the stairs.

The great hall was again empty. She hurried to the kitchen doorway and slipped just inside, looking for one of the long-handled brooms used to change the rushes that were strewn about to soften the scents within the living quarters.

Servants argued in the kitchen. One of Bret's Norman cooks quarreled with her own woman, Jane, over the proper way to prepare a shoulder of wild boar. Allora slipped back out before either of them could see her. Head lowered, she then hurried across the courtyard and bailey, seeking the north tower.

He had warned her his men would be at the gates. If she had tried to leave, she was certain that her encompassing disguise would have meant nothing. But perhaps she would be fine trying to reach the north tower.

And if she wasn't . . .

Well, she had already thought of ways to deal with more of Bret's anger.

But no one stopped her as she neared the tower. Etienne and Gaston, well-wrapped in their own capes, were just outside, drawing water from the trough, their heads close together, their conversation intense.

She slipped by them, unseen, dropped her broom on the lowest level, and went tearing up the stairs.

She reached the landing before the high tower room and was ready to break in when she paused, going stock-still.

She heard moaning. Deep-throated moaning.

She gasped, drawing her hand back against her mouth, fighting the wave of tears that stung her eyes. Ah, it was easy for Gaston and Etienne to be so lax! Someone was in with David, and indeed, he was being tortured! "Oh, sweet Jesu, David, I am so, so sorry!" she whispered. She heard a slamming sound below and bent over the stairway, looking downward. Etienne had come back into the low chamber.

She turned again swiftly, ready to fly into the room to stop whatever awful procedure was going on. But when she pitted her weight against the door, it would not budge.

The moaning stopped.

"Shall we see to the lad?" Etienne called to someone below, and Allora could hear him drawing closer.

She couldn't reach David, she thought, and she was nearly blinded by a sudden flurry of tears. She would still see that he was rescued from his horrible plight.

She slipped swiftly down the stairs, hovering in the shadows as she waited for Etienne to pass her by, going up the stairs.

She burst out into the night, then paused, gasping for breath in the bailey. Her plan was madness!

It was the only way. And not really madness. She had done what she meant to do once before. She had been about ten at the time, and indeed, she had done it with David, and they had both been switched for the daring act.

But they had survived. They had survived, and so it hadn't been such terrible madness!

But first things first. She hurried back as fast as she could to the main tower keep and prayed that she would not now run into her husband in the hall.

She did not. As she came silently in, she could hear Lilith speaking softly with Sir Christian at the table, but no one else seemed to be about, not even the servants. Ah! Father Jonathan sat in a corner, his head down as he apparently contemplated life.

Allora didn't want to see any of them. She hurried to the second floor and then to her own bedchamber, and found Mary there, folding Brianna's tiny, newly washed garments and setting them into her trunk. The baby still slept sweetly.

"My lady!" Mary said, on sight of her. Allora thought that she must truly look wild indeed to have startled her servant so.

"Mary, I need you to help me once again," Allora said quickly, and Mary instantly wore a look of weariness, and actually backed away from her. "Mary, I'm not asking anything except that you care for Brianna if—if anything happens to me."

"Happens to you!"

"Mary, I have to go to my uncle—"

"Nay, lady, you cannot do so! *Why* would you do so?" Mary demanded, baffled.

Allora inhaled and exhaled, tears nearly splashing from her eyes. "I have to, Mary, because Bret is holding David hostage. And if I go, Uncle Robert can trade me back for David. I know that Robert will do so easily enough, and I know that Bret will do so—" She broke off. Bret would do so because he had sworn he would keep her, if only to make her miserable. And he might well do so.

But still. It was true. David was in agony. She had to do something, and she had already begged for his freedom. This was her only chance.

"How will you reach your uncle?" Mary asked.

"I'm diving from the parapet by the southern tower. It is the only place where—"

"The rocks, milady! Are you forgetting the rocks? You will be dashed to your death, you will leave this poor babe orphaned—"

"Mary, I know where to dive! Don't you remember, when we were young, when we had heard the tales that the Vikings used to dare one another to dive from the rocks? And David and I started to make the same dare to one another. It was the only time I ever saw my father absolutely furious and I thought he would whip the skin from our backs when we came up! But I can do it again, Mary, and I must. Now, you cannot ever allow anyone to know that you knew what I was about—but when I've gone, you must find Bret, and tell him what I've done; that way, he'll have to make sure that David is not harmed any more, that he can be a decent hostage in return."

"Milady, you'll freeze—"

"I'll find my uncle easily enough. Give me time to reach the tower and gather my courage. Then go!"

She gave the unhappy Mary a quick kiss on the cheek, and then paused, looking down at Brianna. Now the tears slipped down her cheeks. "I must have him freed!" she whispered. "Else, you could not love me as I would have you do!"

The babe continued to sleep. Allora cast aside her wool cape and dug into her trunks for her lightest shift. She didn't want any added weight to drag her down into the depths of the sea.

And once she touched the frigid northern water, it wouldn't matter if she was clad in wool or linen.

The slam against the door had come just as they lay in one another's arms, replete, in new awe with the wonder and beauty of the world.

Yet that sound alarmed Elysia and she leaped to her feet, not nearly as worried for herself as she was for David.

"Dress! For the love of God, David, dress quickly!" she commanded him.

"Elysia—"

"You fool—"

"I'll not cower before your brother."

"Then you *are* a fool! Get up and get dressed, and don't you dare say a word to him."

"I will say what I must—"

"Nay, don't! I will renounce you for being the wretched barbaric Scot that you are!" She was dressed now herself, fumbling with her cloak, ready to burst into tears. What had she been thinking? This had been sheer madness. She had to make him see it.

"I hate you! I never meant—this!" she cried, swinging an arm out to encompass the bed. "I will deny it until I die!" she spat out.

Then she whirled and rushed to the door, finding herself incredibly frustrated when she reached the heavy trunk that blocked it. She strained and grunted but could not move it.

He had donned his shirt and chausses and came over, bending to move the trunk. His eyes met hers. "You're a liar, Elysia. And one day, I believe, I will have to abduct you again to prove it!"

The trunk was out of the way. She opened the door and looked nervously out, wondering who had knocked so heavily against it, for no one was there.

That frightened her all the worse.

"Abduct me!" she exclaimed to him. "Indeed! Laird of the tower prison, David, that's what you are. Dirt beneath my feet, and that you'll remain!"

She hurried outside, closing the door behind her, determined not to let it slam. She leaned against it for a moment, then realized that someone was coming up the stairs.

She lowered her head and ran down them swiftly, mumbling a swift good evening as she passed by Etienne.

As she reached the bottom of the stairs, she could hear Etienne plainly as he spoke to David.

"My lord wishes you to come to him, David of Edinburgh," Etienne said. "If you would be so kind as to follow me?"

"A moment," David said.

Panic filled Elysia's heart. Did Bret know? Oh, what a fool she was! What could Bret possibly know?

She ran on outside the tower and waited, wondering where they would take David. Had Bret had him summoned to the main keep?

But he had not. Elysia followed carefully behind as Etienne led David far across the courtyard and bailey to the chapel. They entered, and Elysia followed, keeping her distance. The men disappeared within. She came around to stand in the stone entry, shivering, her back against the stone. She could just see inside. Bret was standing before the altar, his dark head lowered, his hands clasped behind his back. Etienne brought David forward, then left him by Bret, and went to stand silently at the rear of the chapel.

Bret turned to David. "I am loath to keep you here, David. I am often at odds with my wife, but she mentioned one thing to me which I find to be true—you are perhaps the only voice of reason here, now that Ioin is dead."

"I have never been inclined to warfare for its sake alone, milord," David said, inclining his head.

Elysia bit her lower lip, glad that he neither defied her brother nor bowed too low before him.

"You did abduct my sister!" Bret reminded him.

"Nay, milord. Ioin abducted her—I was given the task of keeping her."

"A wearying task, no doubt."

Elysia straightened indignantly, about to run to Bret with her fist raised.

Prudence ruled her. She stayed where she was.

"I swear to you, I would allow no harm to befall her!" David said passionately.

Elysia saw her brother nod gravely. "I believe you. And I believe as well that you are perhaps the one man who can bring peace to these other border lairds and myself without too much more bloodshed and destruction. That's why I've had you brought here, to the chapel. Swear an oath that you will no longer take up arms against me, that you will accept me as Ioin's choice as overlord, and you are free."

David hesitated for a long moment. Elysia didn't realize until her lungs nearly exploded that she had ceased to breathe while he remained silent.

Then David suddenly went down on one knee before Bret. "I swear, Bret d'Anlou, Earl of Wakefield, that I, David of Edinburgh, will honor you as overlord, and never again take up arms against you." He rose and added wearily, "But I cannot make promises for other men, and there is no guarantee that the violence will stop. You—you do not know Robert Canadys very well if you think he will pay me any heed. I think that he has coveted the Far Isle all his life, and is determined to have it in the end."

"I am grateful for your honesty," Bret said. "And you are still free to go."

David, disbelieving, turned, and walked down the stone aisle, and out of the chapel. Elysia was ready to take swift flight, but David paused suddenly, turning back. "In this chapel I swear to you as well that everything between Allora and me was always—innocent."

"I believe you."

"It wasn't that I didn't love her. I did; I do. We have known one another for all our lives, and we have shared a great deal. But, my lord, there is nothing that you need fear from me, ever."

"I wasn't afraid," Bret told him quietly. "But I am curious. Why such a passionate denial?"

David hesitated. "Well, milord, if truth be told, I am in love with your sister. With that so stated, then, I will take my leave, as you have given it."

He turned again, and Elysia was frozen, not at all ready to run quickly away.

Yet it didn't matter. She didn't have a chance to run. Mary, Allora's servant, suddenly came tearing by her, bursting through the stone entry, not even seeing Elysia.

"Milord! She has gone, my lady has gone!"

They were all frozen in place then. Bret, his back to the altar. David, nearly out of the chapel. Etienne at the wall, and Elysia in the entryway.

"Gone where?" Bret bellowed. "I have my best men on the gate!"

"She didn't go by the gate, milord. She dived! Oh, I begged her not to try it, but she is convinced that David of Edinburgh suffers greatly here and that you will trade him for her with my lady's uncle."

"*Dived?*" Bret gasped. Elysia watched her brother's fingers wind into his palms, the whole of his hands knit into tight fists at his sides. "The little fool!"

"From near the south tower!" David said quickly.

Bret stared at him hard.

David shrugged. "I did it with her once. We were both whipped severely."

"She will die; she'll be dashed to death—"

"Nay, my lord. She'll come up freezing on that patch of beach before the southern forest," David assured him.

Bret paused just a moment longer. "You, sir, are free!"

he told David, then he strode swiftly by him. "Surely, my lady wife would be delighted to know that I am somehow the one who wears the shackles!"

Elysia turned away, racing across the courtyard before her brother could come stamping furiously out of the chapel.

"Bret!" she called, racing quickly behind him. "Bret!"

He stopped short and spun around. "Get back to the keep, Elysia, now! Etienne, knock her over the head and drag her there if she will not go!"

"Bret—!"

"Jesu, isn't one wretched female enough for one man to deal with?" he demanded angrily. "Go, Elysia!" For one moment, his hands grasped her shoulders. He pulled her close and absently kissed her forehead, but his words were heated. "I am worried to death, Elysia! For the love of God, obey me!"

Elysia felt Etienne's firm clasp upon her shoulder. She was drawn to a halt as Bret and then David strode by her. She bit her lip, watching them go. What had Allora done? Fear gripped her heart, and she suddenly gasped out loud. Dear God, it must have been Allora at the door . . .

Allora, convinced that David . . .

Elysia's cheeks turned red, and she turned on her own, hurrying back toward the keep. Jesu, the cold, and the rocks! Who would think to dive from these forbidding, windswept towers? Elysia prayed desperately that her sister-in-law had survived her desperate dive.

For Elysia was certain it was her fault that Allora had taken that dive.

The night seemed so dark, though it was scattered with stars. The sky was beautiful, an ebony sweep with just those touches of glimmering light within it.

The breeze was cold, whipping now and then. Brutal.

She was insane.

Nay, she was not! She had stood just here all those years ago with David while they called one another cowards! She had been the first to jump. And the dive was fast, so fast, that once begun, there was no time to be afraid. She had done this before!

Ah, yes. And last time, there had been guards staked out along the ramparts as well, and she and David had been left alone, just as her own men and Bret's Norman knights left her alone now.

They would never assume that she meant to plunge into the icy depths below her . . .

She let go of the warm cloak she had worn this far, set her hands upon the stone wall, and leaped up upon it, looking swiftly around her. One of the Norman men had seen her; he was hurrying down the wooden walkway to reach her now, shouting out to warn the others.

This was it!

She stood. She stared into the Stygian darkness far below.

She was a fool!

Nay, she could do this; and if nothing else, David would be free.

The guards were closing in on her now. She had just seconds.

The wind whipped her linen tunic around her. She felt its sharp bite, and she dreaded the deep water below. She raised her arms above her head, caught her breath, and dived.

Jesu, what a strange sensation, plummeting so swiftly downward in blackness. Then the water. She hit it hard, and nearly had all reason knocked from her as she was shocked by the coldness of it. For long seconds, she couldn't move. She could only feel the terrible cold biting cruelly into her. Then she realized that she was going deeper and deeper, that she had to force herself to move or perish. She began to kick her legs, and to paddle strenuously upward with her arms. Her chest began to burn. She could see no light! She kicked harder and harder . . .

She broke the surface, gasping. Dear God, it was cold! Her lips were surely blue, she could scarcely move. She tried to swim and became entangled in her sodden tunic. It added nothing for warmth, and, afraid that it would drag her down again into the midnight depths, she managed to shed it. She breathed in a great gasp of air, and started swimming hard then, determined to reach the beach and the shelter of the forest. She envisioned some of the poor cottages there, deep within the woods. Hunting cottages, but places of warmth where she could find blankets against this bitter cold!

The beach! The beach was just ahead of her. She had only a little farther to go.

She kicked her feet hard, decrying the numbness within them. She paddled harder and harder, not daring to look ahead. She kicked rock and sand, and then felt it beneath her feet. She staggered up, her hair a sodden cloak that melded over her breasts and buttocks, nearly reaching her legs. She hugged her arms to her chest, trying to walk through the crashing surf.

And then she went stock-still, feeling the coldness of the night as she'd had yet to feel it, stunned, dismayed.

For he was there. Seated atop Ajax, towering in the night. Alone on the beach, he waited for her, his expression one of the darkest anger she had ever seen.

How in God's name could he be there? The sun had set; the tide had rushed over the sand bridge from the Far Isle to the mainland.

How, in God's name, indeed? But he was there, Ajax seeming so much bigger than life, the man atop him a raging giant.

Such a panic seized her at his cobalt stare that she turned, ready to fling herself wildly back into the ocean. But Ajax was suddenly bearing down into the surf upon her, and before she could go far, she cried out in alarm as she was plucked out of the ocean by her husband's strong grasp, thrown over Ajax's saddle and haunches.

His fingers threaded cruelly into her hair. "Dear God, but I prayed you would live! Just so that I could skin you alive myself, milady!"

She was jerked hard against the horse as Ajax struggled to clear the sand and water. They reached the beach; Bret dismounted from Ajax and pulled her down before him, his eyes furiously raking over her nakedness, then meeting hers again. "Running naked to my enemies?"

"I was afraid of drowning—"

"You should have been afraid of breaking your fool neck! I would willingly drown you myself this moment, if it weren't for our daughter! The one you were willing to sacrifice everything to be with not so very long ago!"

She felt as if she were drained of blood, freezing. "I knew that you would trade David for me. I knew you tortured him—"

"Tortured him! I did nothing to your precious David! He was free before I ever heard of your wretched attempt to dive your way to freedom. You risked your fool life—"

"I risked nothing!" she defended herself staunchly. "I knew that I could do it!" Her teeth chattered. She had never been so cold in all her life. "And you wouldn't listen to me, you wouldn't pay any heed to me at all! You're like your wretched William, you think that you can just conquer things and people and make demands and—destroy lives!"

He ripped the mantle from his own shoulders and swept it around hers.

"We'll return to the fortress. I'll deal with you there."

His hand fell roughly upon her upper arm and he started walking, pushing and dragging her along. She saw then how he had come, for a large raft was drawn up on the beach, with Jarrett awaiting them, his hands hard upon a long oar that anchored him to the beach while he awaited Bret, Ajax, and her.

"Milady," Jarrett said courteously, not blinking an eye as Bret led her, dripping and naked other than her husband's cloak, aboard the raft. She nodded miserably in return.

Bret released her and she sank down to her knees, wrapping the cloak around her as the breeze grew stronger when Jarrett shoved them back out into the sea. There was another oar, and Bret picked it up, and he and Jarrett called back and forth to one another as they made their painstaking way back to the fortress over the surf. They came to the sand before the entry, and even as they arrived, Allora was startled to hear a loud cheer. She looked up. Men lined the walls, her own men, Bret's men.

She stared at Bret in confusion. Surely they cheered because he had brought her back.

"There's a lot of Viking left in all of us," he informed her coldly. "They are cheering your bravery."

She winced and lowered her eyes. But as the raft dragged along the sand, Bret slapped Ajax and sent him walking his way through the damp sand to the dry. Two men rushed out to help the ever-loyal Jarrett pull the raft ashore, and then Bret had a firm hand on her arm again, dragging her through the gates and the cheering crowd, and straight through the courtyard to the keep.

Her face burned. She felt all eyes on her.

"Sorry?" he asked.

"Sorry that I did no good," she replied, head high, teeth still chattering. "Not sorry I made the attempt, for I felt that I had to."

They had reached the door and Bret threw it open. "Get upstairs!" he hissed into her ear, and she was only too ready to oblige, to escape his furious hold if only for a moment. He strode into the room, assuring those who waited there—Sir Christian, Father Jonathan, Timothy, Lilith, and a few more of his own men—that all was well.

Allora continued up the stairs, freezing in earnest, shivering fiercely. She burst into her room to find Elysia awaiting her, and bringing a hand to her lips instantly. "Oh, dear God! You are all right!"

Allora was astounded when her sister-in-law wildly swept her arms around her, hugging her. "I was so afraid!" Elysia whispered.

"I—I knew what I was doing," Allora told her, still puzzled. She and Elysia had hit it off well enough together, but . . .

"Elysia," she asked quickly, "where is the baby?"

"Gurgling away below in Mary's room—she is fine."

"And David—Bret said that he had freed him, before I dove from the parapets. Is that true as well?"

Elysia nodded. "He was on the raft that sailed across to retrieve you."

"Oh, Jesu!" Allora pressed her cold hands to her freezing cheeks. "I was so certain he was being tortured! I heard these awful moans—"

"They were not awful moans!" Elysia protested, her own cheeks flaming.

Confused—and then stunned—Allora stared at her. "Oh,

my God!" Her knees had gone very weak. She would have fallen if Elysia hadn't grasped her arm and led her to one of the chairs before the fire.

"Allora, I pray you! You mustn't say anything!"

Allora continued to stare blankly at her for a moment. Then she felt like laughing hysterically. She had risked her life because David and Elysia had been . . .

Oh, dear God. It was rich!

"Please!" Elysia implored her softly. Her lashes lowered. "David would never deny it, I know, but I'm so afraid. He swore peace to Bret tonight, and I'm so afraid of what my brother would think or do. He would feel responsible, and then there's my father . . ." Elysia's voice trailed away, laced with anxiety.

"It's all right," Allora said. "I won't say anything."

"Then how will you explain—"

"Oh, he will not expect much of an explanation from me!" she said softly.

"Oh, Allora!" Elysia said miserably, hugging her fiercely once again. "He won't really hurt you! At least—I don't think so!"

The last words were less than encouraging.

"You'd better go!" Allora whispered. "He'll be here soon enough, I imagine."

"Oh, Allora—"

"Elysia, go quickly, please!" Allora begged her.

Allora felt the brush of a swift kiss on the top of her wet head, and then Elysia left the room. Allora stood, anxious to get closer to the fire, but even as she approached it, the door Elysia had just closed so quietly banged open with a violent thunder. She jumped and then turned, her back to the fire. Bret had come. He closed the door with another slam and leaned against it.

Allora swallowed hard.

"I would have never done it!" she said softly. Then she gasped out, "Bret, please, what did you expect? You led me to believe that while I—while I made peace with the conquerors, you had cruelly imprisoned a good man who had defended me and mine for years! Bret, you had locked me in a tower—"

"Madam, a bit of meek humility might serve you well now, rather than these grasping attempts at reproach!" he retorted quickly.

Her eyes fell, then rose to meet his again defiantly. "Sweet God, Bret! I could not be any meeker or more mild than I had been as I begged your pardon the other night!"

He was silent, watching her. She continued, fighting a chattering in her teeth. "I didn't do what I did with any desire to escape you or the Far Isle. You must realize that! You expect me to acknowledge the near-brutal carelessness of my uncle's actions, and I'm afraid that I do realize that he will often do anything for his own gains. But equally, I've seen the actions of the men around him, and David is a good man, one to whom I am in debt—"

She broke off at the sudden sound of his irritated oath and realized that she was getting herself into worse trouble. "I'm telling you, he understood when no one else did that I could not go for an annulment! And you deserved what I did! You let me believe that you would torture him—"

"You were so determined to think that it might be so!" he reminded her harshly.

She flushed furiously, lowering her lashes. It occurred to her then to tell him he should be looking to his own sister, not her; but she had promised Elysia, and even if she had not, she could not betray either David or her sister-in-law.

"I only did it because I thought I had to!" she whispered fiercely.

"And that's what scares me the most," he told her, his tone unnervingly soft. "When else will someone, something, arise from your past again? You are loyal to me—unless you must be loyal to someone else."

"It was just David—"

"Perhaps you shouldn't keep reminding me just how important you find the man," Bret suggested coolly.

"There was never really anything between us—"

"Other than the fact that he comforted you, eh? You're a fool if you don't think I know what went on here, Allora."

Just what information had he had? she wondered. But

she could answer him easily enough. "If you know what went on, then I have nothing to fear; aye, he comforted me, and no more."

"Comfort comes in many guises."

She fell silent, stubbornly refusing to argue the point. She realized that he did believe her—or else he had believed David—and was baiting her, no more. She would not take the bait.

Yet she felt herself shivering again despite her determinations and best resolves. She gritted her teeth hard, lifted her chin, and spoke with all the quiet dignity she could summon. "Well then. If it was a tower before, what will it be this time? What do you intend to do with me now?"

He was silent for a long time, his eyes moving over her. Then he shrugged.

"A bath."

"What?"

"Water is coming," he said flatly. "You're a wretched, freezing, salty mess. I believe that streak of green in your hair is seaweed, and you are dripping all over the floor. And I wouldn't want you ill; I think you should be in the very best of health, so that I can take my anger out on you very slowly. A bath is definitely in order!"

Her heart slammed against her chest, with fear, with anticipation.

"And then?" she whispered.

"*And then* remains to be seen!" he promised softly, and turned.

He left the room, and the door closed firmly behind him.

Chapter 21

Little in life had ever felt as good as the steaming hot water in which she immersed herself to bathe. She had scrubbed her face, her hair, her body, and still she had been loath to leave it. Even when the water had begun to grow cool, she had not wanted to leave the bath. Absurd. As if the small tub of wood and metal could somehow protect her from his wrath.

It could not. She longed for him to come back; she dreaded that he would do so too soon. Wrapped in a massive towel before the fire, she brushed her hair while it dried, soft from the washing and the gentle warmth of the fire. She gazed into the flames, and was startled by the rush of memory that swept over her. That long-ago time when they had first wed, when he had held her tenderly and they had so lazily watched the flames together seemed like something she could almost reach out and touch.

Of course, it was really his fault. If he had just told her that he hadn't harmed David, that he was planning on freeing the man . . .

And then again, if David had just managed not to be quite so vocal when he was actually in ecstasy rather than pain, she would not be in this predicament now, with the night drifting past her as she waited and waited . . .

She had almost lulled herself into a sense of security when the door suddenly opened again with a wicked slam against the wall. She set her lips in a thin line, refusing to move, her towel wrapped warmly around her while she continued to run her brush through already-brushed hair.

The door slammed again. Closed, this time.

She didn't turn, but bit her lower lip and waited. She heard his movements around the room, heard him cast aside his own clothing. And still he hadn't said a word to her.

She turned just slightly to see him from the corner of her eye. He stood by the bed, naked and bronzed in the firelight, pinching out the candle flame there on the trunk with his thumb and forefingers. The room darkened to shadow. He crawled beneath the sheets, turning his back on her, and Allora was startled by the immense sense of loss and loneliness that seemed to settle over her. It was one thing to fight a man on a point of honor.

It was quite another not to be wanted.

And if he didn't want her . . .

She could well spend a lifetime in the north tower.

Her fingers numbed, she continued to brush her hair. Time seemed to stop, then to rush along. The fire did not burn so brightly.

Then, suddenly, he spoke so quickly and harshly that she jumped and the brush went flying out of her hands. "Be done with it! Get in bed!"

She thought later that she was certainly startled because she obeyed with incredible speed, slipping into her own side of the bed, still wrapped in her towel, and drawing the linen sheets and warm furs straight to her chin. She shivered, feeling then the expanse of bed that stretched between them.

Once again, time stood still, then careened on by her. She wondered if seconds, minutes, or hours had passed. She stared at the ceiling, wondering if he slept.

Then she nearly screamed again, for he touched her with force and impatience, drawing her into the center of the bed, half-sitting up to wrench the sheets away from her and touch the fabric that encompassed her.

"What is this?" he demanded harshly.

She swallowed hard, miserable, and yet unable to keep herself from making a sarcastic reply. "A towel, my lord. The same here as one finds in London town!"

"Well, what is it doing in bed?" he inquired sharply, blue eyes searing.

"I—was cold."

"I see. You were quite willing to leap naked from a tower to the sea—"

"I wasn't naked when I leaped."

"You were certainly so when I discovered you upon the beach."

She flushed furiously, her lashes falling. "I wasn't quite as good a swimmer as I remembered myself to be," she whispered. "I was afraid that I might drown."

"And commendably, you cast modesty aside for the sake of life. And there you were, as glorious as some little sea nymph for all men to see—"

"You are the only man who saw me!" she reminded him.

"But you meant to find your uncle and his men. What a wondrous reunion that might have been!"

"There are hunting cottages in those woods, crude, but they do have blankets and furs within them—"

"The point is, my lady, get the damned towel off and out of our bed!"

She stared at him blankly. She didn't obey quickly enough. He gripped the towel, she was suddenly rolling out of it, and the offending linen was thrown to the floor with a sniff. She lay upon her stomach, startled by the sudden violence of his action, just catching a gasp when she next felt his touch, for it was anything but violent.

His fingers smoothed her hair from her back. Then drew a line, slow, subtle, soft, down the length of her spine. Her breath caught. His lips touched her nape; his tongue drew a slow trail where his fingers had so recently traveled, his lips touching here and there, the slow, sensual movement beginning again. His palm moved over her buttock, cupping it, still in a slow and sensual movement. Then she found herself rolling once again, and his lips were against her abdomen, a gentle kiss here, the slow lazy stroke of his tongue there. His hand came upward, fingers closing around her breast, his palm massaging over it until she thought that she would shriek with the fierce burning that suddenly seemed to explode between her legs. She wanted him so desperately.

He seemed to know what she longed for, and where. He did not come to her, though she whispered that he should. He touched her anew, his stroke upon her upper thighs, his kiss suddenly searingly intimate until she did cry out loudly in the night. And still he stroked her, his kiss found her flesh, worked its way upward along her body until the bulk of his weight was between her thighs, and the hard pulse of his sex teased her as it never had before. She reached for him, meeting the cobalt of his eyes, then closing her own. She felt his lips upon her breast, then upon her own. And at long last, she felt his staggering thrust into her, slow as well, with him holding above her as he seemed to press harder and harder and endlessly deep within her . . .

She buried her face into his neck and shoulder, feeling the slickness there. Now there was nothing gentle, subtle, or slow in his movement, but rather it was ruled by a reckless passion and near-blinding speed. She clung to him, and felt the mercurial wildfire of his passion soar and spread, the incredible sweetness that seemed to pervade her limbs, even with the harsh demand of his lovemaking. Sheets and furs fell swiftly from them. She had been so cold, and now she knew incredible warmth. Tightening within her, driving her. She felt her fingers digging into the knotted muscles of his shoulders and back, vaguely heard the soft, gasping cries tearing from her lips. She was achingly aware of the length of him, hard and rigid, vital, bringing wonder, bringing magic. She arched against him, savored the slickness of his flesh, reached and soared . . .

Wave after wave of shattering ecstasy filled her and she pressed her face hard against him again, bracing herself as the shudders swept her body. She felt the steel hardness of him against her with a sudden fierceness, then sweet warmth filled her all over again, and she gasped, still clinging to him. Moments later, he eased himself to her side. She waited for his arms to sweep around her, waited to be held.

He didn't touch her, and she realized that he lay beside her on an elbow, studying her. She bit her lower lip, and turned to meet that gaze.

"No sweet words tonight, my love?" he queried, and there was a taunt to the words.

Her lashes swept her cheeks. He had made her forget that they had not been on the best of terms.

"What could I say that you would believe?" she asked.

He shrugged, and she found herself looking at him once again, and trembling inwardly because she liked all that she saw. He was lean, muscled, bronzed; his features were both fine and masculine, his clean-shaven Norman chin firm, his jaw set. His eyes were blazing into hers.

"It's not that I don't believe you, Allora—it's that you tell me quite honestly, again and again in different ways, that you will accept me—until you don't care for the way I do things. You have this wondrous knack, my love, for absolutely humiliating me. Imagine! My wife would rather pitch herself into the sea—an incredibly cold sea!—than remain with me."

"It was over David, you know that—"

"Over another man. That does improve things a hundred-fold!" he told her acidly.

"I didn't know—" she began.

"But you should have. You know me. By now, you know me. And I can't begin to imagine how you could have believed in your heart that I would have tortured your fair-haired friend!"

But she couldn't tell him what she did know about David . . . and Elysia.

"You locked me in a tower!" she reminded him.

"I felt I had to do something. Perhaps I acted too quickly, behaved foolishly—"

"You never gave me a chance to prove myself to you."

Bret groaned. "There's the rub, my love. When will I be able to trust you to come to me—"

"I came to you! I told you—"

"You started shouting orders!" he interrupted curtly.

"And you do not do so?"

"Only under extreme provocation. And lady, you do provoke me to extremes."

"And I tell you again," she said softly, "no one has ever asked you to be what you are not! You have not come here as one of Malcolm's barons. You are William's man, the Conqueror's first, and William Rufus's now. I have spent

my entire life considering myself Malcolm's subject; my
father vowed his fealty to him. My uncle has done so as
well. If I had burst in upon your father's house denouncing
Normans—"

"My mother would have delightedly grabbed you a chair,
no doubt, and made you warm and comfortable before
the fire."

"Don't mock me!"

"There is no mockery in my words." He sighed. "And
you may have all sworn fealty to Malcolm, but even by
the records of Edward the Confessor's reign, the Far Isle
lies within England's borders."

"So there we are!" she said softly.

"Indeed." She felt the chill of his eyes, as if it were
stinging her naked flesh. "So I must keep a wary eye
upon all my enemies at all times—including my enemy,
my wife."

She inhaled painfully, her lashes falling. "I'm—I'm not
your enemy!" she told him. She gazed at him again, pleading for something this time, and she didn't know exactly
what. "You have come here and taken the fortress. The people within it have all bowed down to you. You locked me in
a tower upon your whim; you released me upon your whim.
Don't you understand, you can force me to do whatever you
wish. I had to try to find a way to force *you* to free David."

"David. Well, David is free now. But what of the future,
Allora?"

She rolled from the bed, finding her huge linen sheet on
the floor, wrapping it quickly around her shoulders as she
walked to the fire, prodding it to make it flame and sizzle
and bring greater warmth to the room, for she grew cold
once again.

In a moment he was up, and crouched down naked
beside her, adding a log, causing the flame to spit and
rise, red, gold, and blue. His eyes met hers. "No words
of love, milady? No protestations that you will never defy
me again, because you are so enamored of me?"

"This evening, milord, it seems that you are enamored
enough of yourself for the both of us."

A smile curved his lip.

"What of you?" Allora whispered.

He reached out, touched a lock of her hair. "You already know that I find you fascinating. That I have desired you above all reason."

"As preferable to a hedgehog?"

"Far."

"But nothing more? You ask me to lay my heart at your feet so that you can tread upon it, but the best words you can summon for me are that I am far preferable to a hedgehog?"

He laughed softly. "Oh, milady! If I were to trust you with tender words, anything less than a total guarding of heart and soul, I would have to brace myself for your casting the gates wide open to invite in all my enemies! It might well be like setting my own head upon a block!"

She started to rise, to turn around. But he was up with her, catching her shoulders, spinning her back to meet him. Her towel fell. He lifted her into his arms, and her fingers instinctively laced at the nape of his neck as he walked with her back to the bed.

"Hold me before the fire!" she said to him suddenly, her voice husky. "Please? Can we draw the furs from the bed, and sit there, and watch the fire burn?"

"Aye. That we can do."

He eased her to her feet, then plucked furs from the bed and brought them directly before the fire. He found another, and wrapped it around her. Then he lifted her again, and sat leaning against the wood of the tub, with her curled on his lap close before the warmth of the flames. She watched them rise, blue and gold and orange. She leaned back against his chest, and felt his fingers moving gently through the length of her hair.

"What are you going to do to me?" she whispered.

"Do?"

She should have kept her mouth shut, she decided ruefully. She had never thought it would happen again, this feeling of being held, of being secure, of being cherished. Even if it was illusion, she wanted to cling to it.

But she had spoken. "Do to me or with me!" she whispered softly.

He was quiet for a very long moment. "Nothing."

"Nothing?"

"Aye, milady. Nothing. We'll go on. Learn to live together."

"You'll forgive me, forget—"

"Nay," he warned, and she felt the tension in the fingers that stopped moving, then threaded through her hair once again. "Nay, I'll not forget a thing. Defy me in any way again, and I will easily consider whipping you myself— before consigning you to the north tower to remain this time. Until I can find a tower in Normandy, perhaps. Then you can join custom, rather than custom joining you."

She was silent, finding her throat constricted. "I don't want to hurt you," she whispered. "I never did. Well, except, of course, when I first met you. And you were an insufferable bastard."

"You were a spoiled brat."

"And you were in love with Lady Lucinda."

"I was not in love," he said quietly after a moment. "Merely prepared for another life."

"Ah. And you are not in love with me."

He was quiet again. Then she felt him lift her hair, and press his lips to her neck, just below her earlobe. "Wildly, passionately, extremely infatuated, milady. Is that enough?"

Nay, it was not!

But he turned her within his arms, and his lips found hers. In seconds she found herself stretched out on the fur, and with the fire casting its golden glow over them both, he made love to her again, slowly building to a shattering climax that seemed to burn with the fire before them. And when it was over and she began to doze, he lifted her and brought her back to the bed, and his arms curled possessively around her. She closed her eyes, sweetly weary. *I do love you*, she thought.

And she wondered if he knew, for she heard his whisper again at her ear. "Passionately, desperately, hungrily infatuated, my lady. I wonder if you realize just how hungrily!"

She felt her own lips curl into a small smile, and she discovered that though he didn't trust her, she was beginning to trust him completely. If only he could begin to trust her, then . . .

She could lay down her heart and soul before him.

If only . . .

For the next few weeks life seemed so normal, it was hard to realize that things had changed at all, that Bret had come, that Robert and his men had gone. That a new reign had taken over.

Allora had decided that for the time she would take things slowly, and keep out of her husband's way. But one month after he had come, he called a manor court to settle disputes among the people, and he did so while she sat in the great hall, working on a tapestry, Brianna set in the cradle beside her.

She rose to leave. It would be best if she were not here; she had become too accustomed to dealing out justice herself, and she would be too tempted to tell Bret what to do.

But even as she rose, he arched a brow. "Stay, my lady."

"Perhaps I should not—"

"But I have commanded that you do, and I cannot imagine that you will be without an opinion here today!"

Uneasily, she sat again, vowing that she would keep her peace.

Unless he were being unfair, of course.

The complaints were the customary ones—they did not change before the Norman lord, the only difference being that Father Jonathan came forward with some of the people, those who spoke the border-country Gaelic only, and he translated their words carefully for Bret, who listened intently.

Allora felt that she could far more easily have translated for Bret, but she knew they were walking a fine line, and she didn't want to make the suggestion herself. They were actually establishing something of a relationship that went deeper than the simple hungers that had driven them together despite mistrust and anger. He'd warned her that he wouldn't love her, and she took a wary care in all that she said and did, but by night he often came in to rub his hands before the fire, and then ask her some question about the fortress itself, one of the craftsmen within it, or the land just beyond. She tried to explain the differences in their laws, and he quickly understood them, for he was well aware of the differences that had come with the Norman invasion, and that Saxon women had lost almost all of their legal rights as a consequence.

She liked the nights. She enjoyed his questions, even when he baited her purposely, only to sweep her into his arms when she would grow irate, laughing, ready to make love to her. And then hold her through the night.

Indeed, he had warned her that he would not love her, and he did not imply that he did. But she knew that he did care for her, and she was certain there was no other woman in his life, no one else for him within the walls of the keep, and that alone pleased her.

He left her entirely alone to deal with matters within the household, yet there was never any doubt that he had come as lord here, and lord he would be.

Two men argued the price of a lamb; one accused the other of having hit it with his cart on purpose. Bret asked for details, and was told that the man who had owned the lamb had upset the other's cauldron in the painstaking making of soap, and that he had perhaps done so on purpose.

Bret stroked his chin. Allora sat on the edge of her chair, ready to reprimand them both.

"You shall help your neighbor in the making of a new batch of soap," he told the complainant, "and you will pay the price of a new lamb. And if you continue to argue, I will take the soap and the lamb, and you will both start anew. These are truly petty matters with which to burden a court—next—!"

Bret watched his wife as the next disputing men came forward. The argument here was over a patch of land to be worked, the one man claiming he could not make his payment of grain to the lord of the fortress on the lands he had been allotted, as they were too frequently filled with brackish seawater. He'd asked for only a small section of his neighbor's land, while his neighbor could not see why he should pay the price for the other man's misfortune.

Charts were brought. Bret studied them, as did Allora. She was bursting to speak, he thought. She watched the proceedings with interest, but each time he would glance her way, her head would be bent over her needle again.

She could do beautiful work. He had seen it, admiring this piece or that piece within the keep time and time again, only to learn that the Lady Allora had fashioned it herself, soon after returning from London.

Yet the sewing of a tapestry, he was certain, held little interest for her. She was accustomed to governing. She had ruled here—if somewhat beneath Robert's thumb—before he had come, and he was sure she had to feel some resentment that he had swept power from her grasp, even if he had tried to take care in the doing of it.

He hadn't wanted to sweep it away. He recognized that he was a product of William's invasion, and that although his views about women had certainly been tempered by having a strong-willed mother, he was still strong-willed himself, determined to be master of what was his; he was not so certain that he would have been fond of the Saxon laws giving too much legal power to the fairer sex.

They could be dangerous. He knew that well.

Yet this morning he had very purposefully kept Allora here in the hall, while he made the judgments on the minor arguments himself.

There was a more difficult trial coming before them. Father Jonathan had drawn his attention to it earlier in the week.

The good father stepped forward now, unrolling a parchment, reading from it. "My lord, the charge here is one of rape."

As he had expected, Allora stiffened, her fingers going still, her eyes on the group gathered before them. The girl standing with her head bowed, wild dark hair all but hiding her youthful features, was one of the shepherd's daughters.

The man himself, tall and thin with a mane of white hair, came forward. He knew no Norman French, but his knowledge of the Saxon language was good, and he quickly spoke for himself.

"Milord, Sarah is a good child, an innocent child! I beg for justice, for she carries a bairn now, we're all but certain, and she'll not now marry a good lad on her own. She'll suffer mightily in the days to come; my wife and I have eight of our own, and will not be able to feed them all through the winters if we must care for this child as well. I beg of you, let us at least have justice against our offender!"

The old man was eloquent, Bret thought. He watched Allora. In the olden days, the punishment for any proven act of rape was castration.

"And the accused?" Bret said, though he knew well enough. It was one of his own men, a young man of Breton descent who had only recently been knighted. A handsome lad, not much older than the girl.

The boy stepped forward. Bret heard his wife gasp softly, and saw her jaw set with indignation.

The old sheepherder continued his complaint with dignity. "I have been told I am a madman to accuse one of your men so, milord. But they told me you are just, and I have come for your justice."

"Raoul, what have you to say?" Bret demanded.

Raoul spoke as well as did the old sheepherder. "Sire, I have served you long, first in the stables, tending your horses, finally riding with you, in Normandy earning my knighthood. You have known me these many years . . ."

"And you have known that I have never condoned rape or pillage, and though we have taken treasures at times when our enemies were bested, I have never allowed the maiming, rape or execution of surrendered peoples. This is far graver even than most circumstances, for this is my land, and I am lord here. Is the child yours?"

"Aye, milord. But I swear before God, it was not rape."

"Milord, the lass knew nothing of carnal pleasures!" the sheepherder insisted. "What will you do?"

Bret relaxed into his high-backed chair, his fingers curving over the arms. "What shall I do?" he repeated. Then he stared at Allora. "It may well be a matter of the heart, my love," he told her. "Why don't you judge this offense, my lady?"

He spoke as lightly as he could manage, his body filling with tension, and he wondered if he wasn't a madman himself. If she did judge that Raoul should be castrated, what would he do then? Wrench the authority from her?

Her eyes, on his, widened incredulously. "You jest!" she said very softly to him, so that others would not hear.

He shook his head. He leaned forward. "I think that I have judged the people here—including you, my love—with temperance and mercy. Milady, I am deeply interested in your insight into such matters. What do we do here?"

He kept telling her that he didn't love her. He tried to tell himself the same thing. But as her brilliantly green eyes, so wide and so beautiful, rested on his, he felt a tremor in his heart. He forced his expression to remain emotionless as he watched her rise, golden hair sweeping around her beneath the pale-mauve gauze of the veil that chastely covered her head, held in place by a gold filigree circlet. She walked forward, slowly, gracefully, and paused at last before the girl who stood with her eyes downcast.

"Sarah, did he hurt you?"

"Milady!" the girl's father said indignantly. "She would not seduce a man!"

"Sarah," Allora repeated, "did he hurt you? Was it rape?"

The girl's head fell even further forward.

"Was it rape, Sarah?"

The girl shook her head, tears suddenly appearing on her cheeks. But Allora didn't comfort her. She came to stand before young Raoul like a beautiful, but definitely vengeful, angel.

"The girl was young and innocent. And if you did not rape her, sir, you did seduce her."

"Milady," he said miserably, "I truly meant no ill—"

"Yet ill has occurred."

"I beg you—" Raoul began, his voice rasping. He was well aware of the possible punishments for rape.

"Don't beg me!" Allora told him. "The girl is but a shepherd's daughter, I grant you that, and you are knighted now. But if you would beg someone's pardon, let it be hers. And if she will have you, and if her father agrees, I would consider that a marriage be in order here."

Both Raoul and Sarah gasped. Bret leaned back, grinning, deeply pleased.

"Sir, perhaps you might wish to fall upon a knee, take the girl's hand, and pose the question," Allora said.

"Aye, milady, aye!" young Raoul quickly agreed. And he was most eloquent indeed as he went upon a knee before Sarah, softly requesting her hand in marriage. Sarah looked to her astounded father, who looked to Allora. "The boy's come with the Normans!" he said.

"The boy is a knighted warrior," Allora informed him.

The shepherd nodded slowly. "Aye, then. Aye. Every babe needs a father, no matter what his homeland."

"Sir," Raoul said, "this is my homeland now."

There was silence. Then Elysia, who had been sitting in the rear of the room with Bret's Saxon priest, Father Damien, suddenly stood with a little cry, and went tearing from the room.

Bret started to rise, confused and puzzled, ready to follow his sister.

But Allora stopped him. "I'll go," she said. "You must finish with the manor court, and approve this marriage of vassals upon your land."

She hurried after Elysia, who seemed to be heading for the room she had chosen upon the second floor, beside Lilith's.

Allora found Elysia there, atop her bed and sobbing. Allora quickly stretched out beside her, patting her back. "Elysia, what in God's name is it?"

Elysia jerked up, staring wildly at Allora. "I'm so afraid!" she whispered. "So very afraid!"

"Of what?" Allora demanded.

"You can't tell him! You can't tell *him!*" Elysia cried.

Him. Allora realized suddenly that Elysia was talking about Bret.

What an irony! The time had come now when Elysia was begging her not to speak with her own brother!

"Elysia, I'm trying to help you—"

"Then you must swear that you won't say a word to Bret!"

Allora sighed. "But Elysia, if he can help you in any way—"

"Nay, nay! Swear to me, Allora. Swear!"

Allora sighed. She already sensed that she was sinking into danger. "I swear, Elysia, I will say nothing to Bret. Now what is it?"

"I'm so afraid—"

"Of what?" Allora demanded with exasperation.

"I think I'm having his child."

"Whose child—oh! David's child!" Allora whispered.

She was apparently right. Elysia burst into another spate of tears.

"Hush, hush! He'll hear you and come up here, demanding an explanation!" Allora warned her quickly. "Elysia, David is a very fine man, I know that he will want to marry you—"

"Bret would kill him, my father would kill him. He was one of the border lords who abducted me, Allora. You can't tell Bret!"

"But you must tell David. Perhaps you can both go before your brother then—"

"As you know, David has been gone since he was given his freedom. He lurks beyond the walls with your wretched uncle and his barbaric army—"

"Elysia, please!"

"Oh, Allora, I'm sorry! But he has made no attempt to return. He has not tried to reach me. He has not asked for me, he has vanished. Back to the border lords!"

"I can find him," Allora heard herself say.

"Can you?" Elysia gasped, staring at her with tear-filled but suddenly hopeful eyes.

"Aye, I'm sure that I can. The border lords do not spend all their lives seeking battle. It is winter now. Most are surely at their manors, striving to see that their harvests last the cold."

"My God, but how will you do it? If Bret finds out what I did, he will kill me. Nay, he will let my father kill me. Maybe they will both kill me—"

"They will not kill you, Elysia."

"Dear God, but they will be furious, and so disappointed, and if I do not reach him first . . ."

"What?"

"They might well kill David!" Elysia said, and started sobbing softly again.

How much longer would the manor court go on? How much longer until Bret came up the stairs to find out that his sister had been dishonored by the young man he had chosen to set free?

Allora shivered fiercely. "Elysia, hush now! I'll go, and I'll find David. Christmas is nearly upon us; then comes St. Stephan's Day, and there will be a great deal of confusion here, for it is the servants' day, and they celebrate wildly. There will be coming and going and I shall be able to slip away."

"Oh, Allora, would you really?" Elysia asked her, still crying.

"Stop weeping! He might well be here any minute. I will find David for you now, I swear it!" Allora assured her.

And she felt a trembling begin deep inside of her. Sweet Jesu, what had she promised?

And worse . . .

What if she was caught?

Chapter 22

Christmastide came swiftly upon them, and once again, Allora marveled that the people of the Far Isle had come to terms so quickly with their new lord. Despite the winter winds and the snows that fell upon the mainland and whirled so whitely upon the dark sea, they all seemed of exceptional good cheer. Matters went on as they had before.

Except in matters of the soul, so it seemed.

She came to the chapel early on the morning of Christmas Eve in search of Father Jonathan, for she'd had a cloak of the warmest wool made for him as a Christmas gift, and she'd wanted to bring it alone. When she reached the chapel and saw a priest upon his knees before the altar, she came forward quietly, ready to wait until he had finished with his prayers.

The man had heard her, and moved instantly, rising and turning to her. It was not Father Jonathan, but rather the Saxon priest who had come here with her husband.

Father Damien. The same man who had wed her and Bret, who had saved her life when she might have died from the poison intended for Bret. She had been grateful then; she had surely thanked him. Yet it hadn't made it easy for her to welcome him here, and indeed, it seemed that she had scarce seen him since he had come with Bret's troops. He had kept his distance from all the tempest that had erupted between her and Bret then.

Perhaps it had been she who had kept her distance from him, for he unnerved her. He always seemed to watch her with the strangest, far-too-knowing eyes. He was a tall man, broad-shouldered, and appeared more suited to be among her husband's knights than among his churchmen. He was well-liked here, she knew. Her people came to him frequently, not just to confess, but for advice, and they all seemed to think that he heard whispers of the future from God Himself, or that he had magical powers. The people here were very swift to believe in such things, and this strange Father Damien had captured their imaginations well.

"Milady," he said quietly to her, "what may I do for you?"

"I was looking for Father Jonathan," she said, lifting the cloak. "He gets cold so very easily . . ."

"A kind gift," Father Damien said, "and one I'm sure he will deeply appreciate." He raised a silvery brow. "And yet I had thought you'd come to confess!"

She knew now why she had avoided him so strenuously, even after the fact that he had saved her life. It was the way he looked at her, taunted her—and seemed to know when she kept any secret in her heart.

"You're implying I need to confess, Father?"

"All God's children within His Church need to confess their sins, and remove the burdens from their hearts," he told her, and it seemed that his eyes twinkled.

"Perhaps our opinion of the definition of *sin* differs, Father," she murmured coolly.

"I remember, milady, I was officiating when you swore before God to love, honor, and obey your husband."

She gritted her teeth, wishing she had turned back when she saw him there, yet determined she would not let him have the upper hand. An uneasy feeling like a little rivulet of ice water seemed to dance along her spine. She intended only one more act of disobedience against her husband's wishes, and one not even an act of open defiance. If things went well, Bret would never know what she had done for the sake of his sister. Yet Father Damien seemed to know already, before she had even done anything!

"Where exactly is it, in my vows, Father, that I now fail before your eyes?"

"Well, milady, you must admit . . ." he began. "First there was the poison—"

"I never knew I carried poison!" she protested with a cry. "I had thought you believed—"

"I did believe you. But from poison, you went on to escape, and from escape, you came to battle; from battle, milady, it cannot be forgotten that you pitched yourself into the sea."

Allora set her jaw hard, staring at him. "These are matters for Bret and myself!" she choked out. "Perhaps you would look to him about *his* vows!" she suggested, then bit her lip, her lashes falling quickly. What a foolish defense. Bret had never sought anything but honesty in the marriage, and he had treated her more than fairly. She had to admit that she was happy now, happier than she had been in all of her life, and that if only they didn't live in a world so filled with hatred, she might well be completely content. Yet even so, despite the things they shared, despite, even, the tempest of heat and passion that could so easily arise between them, he kept a distance himself. He had warned her that he would not love her. He had never come near, even in his wildest, most intense moments, to whispering such words to her.

"Where has he failed, milady? Are you not honored and cherished?"

"These are matters between Bret and myself!" she cried again.

Father Damien nodded, staring at her. "Indeed, my lady. I do not mean to distress you—I wish you all God's blessings for His Christmas season. It is only that I warn you as well: remember your vows, lady. Remember them well. For to break a vow is a sin, and punishment must follow, be it your lord husband's, or that of the Almighty Lord above us all."

She'd had enough. If he had such wondrous sight, why wasn't he going to Elysia? She would not be in this predicament if her sister-in-law hadn't . . .

Fallen in love. And if David had just managed to keep his clothing on . . .

"Father Damien, the servants have planned a great repast for us following our devotions in the chapel tomorrow. We pray that you will join us," she told him, and she turned quickly to flee, leaving Father Jonathan's rich wool cloak upon one of the rough-hewn pews.

Allora didn't see much of Bret during the day, but she knew that he was out on the hard-packed sand in the morning and the afternoon, working with his own men and Sir Christian, training the fortress men in Norman means of warfare, and training them all to work together, molding his men—Norman, Saxon, and Scot—into one working army. When it came to battle once again, Allora wondered, who among her people would honor their vows of fealty to Bret, and who would turn swiftly to fight on her uncle's side once again? She was sure that Bret must wonder the same question. But then, he had never been foolish in his assumption of command. Though many of his men had taken up residence within the many towers of the fortress, others even now built a fortress upon the mainland across the sands. Already, and despite the cold, a wooden palisade was rising high. She shouldn't have been surprised. These were Normans, the same men who had come and conquered all England, and dotted the landscape with their castles and fortresses with every movement they had made.

The fortress, though not completed, already stood as a defense for the Far Isle across the sands. No one could approach from land now without being seen.

But the woods that surrounded the plain, and the hills and the valleys so near it, were still enemy ground—surely, Bret must realize that. Her uncle's only lands were just over the next rise, along with his well-guarded manor. David's fine home was beyond it, and his brother, Duncan, had claimed lands to the north of that. There were others of them known as lairds to the people, all ruling in what was still known as their "hundreds," yet all of them linked to the family Canadys. Once, they had all answered to her father, and her father to Malcolm.

They had even answered to her, she knew. But she didn't know if they would ever accept a Norman as their overlord here.

Bret returned to the hall with the coming of darkness, when all the men were in from the blustering weather, when the sea rose to darken the white sands.

Allora realized how glad she was when he entered the room, his stag-horned helmet in his hands, his coat of mail glimmering upon the breadth of his chest. She watched him, feeling a strange trembling within herself, and she wondered a bit dully why words should matter so very much to her. He had always been honest with her. He had been anticipating marriage with Lucinda—maybe even *eagerly* anticipating marriage with Lucinda—but once Lucinda herself had asked him to cease his quest and his mind had been made up, he had strongly pursued his commitment to Allora, and when he had come here after all that she had done, he had brought no mistresses or whores in his company to taunt her. No man could be more passionate, and few could offer such tenderness, and fewer still, she was certain, would find such fascination such as he took in his determination to bring her to the wildest pleasures. She was very much in love with him, and for good reason, for the longer she knew him, the greater respect she had for his wisdom, intelligence, and determination, the greater she understood his capacity for mercy and tolerance. No one could ask for a finer figure of a man, a knight, molded more tightly with muscle, more fleet of foot, more graceful upon a horse. He was a fair ruler here.

If only those last barriers did not lie between them.

If only he loved her.

His helmet and mail given to a servant, he strode across the hall to the fire, stripping his gauntlets from his hands, dropping them upon a low table, and stretching his fingers to the flame. His gold shirtsleeves glowed in the light of the fire and his royal-blue tunic, rimmed in ermine fur against the bitter cold, took on a richness that looked well on him. He looked across the room, obviously searching her out, and she found herself rising and coming to him, smiling. He reached out to her then, and she placed her hands in his; he drew her into his arms, pressing a gentle kiss to her lips, his eyes blazing blue as they touched hers. "Sweet Jesu, lady, but the cold does burn fiercer than a fire in these northern parts!" he told her.

"But the fortress is here to welcome you in from the wind with warmth," she assured him softly.

"And you, lady, do you welcome me in with warmth?" he asked softly.

A blush tinged her cheeks. "I have welcomed you so warmly at times, milord, I am amazed that you might doubt such a thing—especially with your inestimable confidence."

He laughed softly, and whispered, "Perhaps we should move to the table. Our household is watching us, and I assume they wish to sit to a Christmas Eve dinner before watching the lord of the manor sweep the lady away!"

She turned quickly. It was true. All the members of their household were standing expectantly behind their chairs at the table. Lord and lady customarily sat together at the far end. Along one side were Sir Christian, Timothy, Father Jonathan, and Lilith. Down the other side were Jarrett, Etienne, Jacques, and Elysia.

Father Damien had not appeared tonight. Perhaps he would come tomorrow.

Bret took her hand and led her to the table. They sat, and the others followed suit. Wine and ale flowed, platters of meat were served. Allora was startled that they seemed to have so much.

"Boar and deer," she murmured.

"We've been hunting a great deal lately," Jarrett said, pleased.

"Out across the sands?" she asked.

"We are careful, milady, if you are expressing concern for our safety," Jarrett told her.

She looked to Bret and discovered him staring at her intently. "Is there something that you know, Allora, that lurks beyond the sands?"

"Everyone knows that danger lurks beyond the sands! Call this England if you will, but your neighbors are still Scots."

"But it's winter. My neighbors should be busy upon their estates, surviving this weather."

"And that's where they are certainly."

"But they hunt by winter as well," Father Jonathan commented, "and the woods are filled with their cottages, though I am sorry to say . . ." He broke off.

"You're sorry to say what, Father Jonathan?" Bret demanded.

Father Jonathan's puffy little cheeks filled and flattened as he inhaled and then sighed. "The people come and go here, my lord, as you well know. For example, the miller's daughter is wed to young Swen, groom on an outside estate; this daughter sends butter to her mother, and her mother sends fine wool to her. I've heard that the winter is proving harsh for the people, that the fields were too long neglected as they prepared for battle with—with you, and that now . . . now the men do not hunt enough, the cottages stand idle and empty, and the little children are often very hungry."

Bret was silent for a long time. Allora awaited some explosion, but none came. "They are my vassals," Bret finally said. "I am overlord here whether Robert Canadys or Duncan of Edinburgh will admit such as yet. If the children are hungry, let the cooks know that they can be fed here. Even with all of my men and the men of the Far Isle, including those who camp outside the walls and build a new fortress beyond them, we have an abundance. When winter is over, they will all learn that I am the overlord here. Until then, the children must be fed." He stared at his wife again. "It's good to know that there are many cottages in those woods; I'm sure my men will be grateful for their usage."

"We've an exceptionally talented harpist with us this eve, milord," Father Jonathan said quickly.

Elysia was not so subtle. "And it is Christmas Eve," she announced from her end of the table. "In the gentle spirit of the Lord Christ, my dear brother, you really should cease to taunt your wife!"

Once again, Allora awaited an explosion. But Elysia had said the words with a charm that brought laughter to the table.

There was no explosion. "Aye, for Christmas Eve, then, sister, I will cease to be an ogre."

Platters were passed again, more wine was served. Allora felt Bret watching her now and again, but he didn't say anything more. A lute player came to entertain them, and the harpist joined the man; their music was beautiful and soft and lulling. In time, they finished with the meal and the entertainment ended, and Bret rose, reaching for Allora's hand.

"It will be a long, illuminating day tomorrow, Father, and so I think we will bid you all good-night." He drew Allora around the table, pausing to kiss his sister on the top of the head. Elysia clasped his hand, which lay gently on her shoulder as he kissed her, and Allora was newly touched by the tempest that was surely raging inside Elysia. She did love her brother; she had spent a lifetime honoring father, mother, and family. And now . . .

Things could still be set right, she was certain. If only David would return and ask for Elysia. Though maybe it wouldn't be all that simple. Maybe her father had other plans for her; perhaps he would never agree to her marriage with a border laird, even if that man had sworn his own peace with and paid homage to her brother.

The moment they reached the high tower room and the heavy door had been closed behind them, she forgot about Elysia, startled by Bret's swift and enflamed touch. She found herself swept off her feet, carried to the welcoming breadth of their bed, and laid down with him atop her. His eyes pinned hers as his hand slid along her leg, over the length of her hose, to the bareness of flesh above it. She was startled by the very bold touch of his hand upon her, one finger sliding within her and then another. She closed her eyes, her breath leaving her body, her lips parting. She felt his kiss upon them, felt as if he breathed fire within her. Her tunic was thrust high around her hips and he barely adjusted the chausses about his own before she felt the long hard shaft of him within her, driving with a staggering force, impaling her again and again, filling her. The tingling between her thighs grew to a burning need and she felt a cry building in her along with the hunger and rise of desire. Her eyes opened and she met his; she was trembling and burning anew with the piercing fire she found within them. "Sweet Jesu, cry out!" he commanded her. "Cry out, whisper to me . . ."

She did cry out. The world around her exploded with the sweetness of her climax and she was barely aware of the thrust then that brought him to his own. She drifted in sweet sensation, yet still disturbed by the light in his eyes. Moments later, he rose, shed his clothing, and pulled her to her feet, helping her to discard her own. He was careless of where the garments fell, sweeping her back into his arms the moment their clothing was discarded. The bed coverings were swept aside as he laid her down once again, coming beside her to draw that warmth back around them both, his arms around her. She felt his knuckles then, up and down her spine. She moved, curling against him, returning the touch, running her own knuckles over his thickly furred chest, her head slightly bent to the task. She continued at it for some moments, then let her hand stray lower, fingers delicately teasing upon the flesh there, then curling around the length of him that hardened and found life with an amazing speed. She caught his eyes again, saw the passion within them, and threw back the covers that had warmed them. She held him, stroked him, and pressed her lips to his shoulders, his chest. She lowered herself very slowly against him, teasing, stroking, touching, holding. Covering him with warm, liquid caresses. He seemed a willing-enough participant to her leisurely play.

"Cry out!" she commanded him, rising above him, seeking his eyes. "Whisper to me . . ."

"Indeed!"

She was suddenly lifted cleanly from him, and found herself upon her knees, her fingers wound tight around the wooden headboard of the bed. And he was behind her, his hands around her breasts, caressing, the fullness of him wildly and deeply inside her again, thrusting in a sweet rhythm that drove all reason from her head . . .

She didn't know if he cried out or not; she was certain she heard no whisper, for once again, it seemed, he had taken her where he would choose to go, and he would not be coerced into words by any torment of lust. She told herself it didn't matter, yet felt unwarranted tears stinging her eyes. She lay beside him, and was then startled to realize that he studied her still.

And rolling toward her he said softly, "One would think that you were totally resigned."

"To what?" she inquired.

"To me."

The tears stung again. She rolled from him, but found her arm caught, her body brought back against his. She felt his muscled length, the pounding of his heart. For a moment the hair on his chest tickled her nose, then he lifted her chin and met her eyes once again. "As you keep telling me, no one has asked me to change what I am. Here I am, a Norman, sleeping in great Ioin's bed; still, at times, I believe in my heart that you are content. Yet what of the honorable Laird David? It's certainly true that in your mind he was meant to be laird here—a Scottish laird, Malcolm's chosen, I would well imagine, and your own."

"Aye, once I would have wed David!" she told him. "And you would have wed Lucinda. Do I need still fear that you long for her, and for distant places? Warmer places?"

He threaded his fingers through her hair, easing himself down once again. "Lucinda went her way, and I went mine—"

"And I did hear her say that marriage would not cause her to end a relationship she cherished—"

"And you heard me tell her even then that she was to wed a friend I would not dishonor."

"Hmmm. You did not mention dishonoring your worse-than-a-hedgehog bride."

His lips curled into a smile. "I have told you quite frequently that you are far preferable to a hedgehog."

"Such compliments, my lord! My head will shortly be spinning with them."

"You are, I think, well aware of your assets. I fear to mention them too oft—"

"I assure you, you do not."

"For I would not let you think I had become too daft a fool over beauty and bounty."

"Oh, I am aware of my assets! Well aware," she said softly, "that too many men are willing to fight and die not for me, but for the Far Isle."

He kissed her lips suddenly. "You are part and parcel of that prize!" he told her, then leaped from the bed again, crossed the room, and bent down before one of his trunks. He came back to her, sat beside her, and offered his hand to her, long calloused fingers opening from the palm. Upon it was a brooch made of golden filigree, finely crafted and extremely beautiful, at the center of it a large and beautiful emerald. Still the beauty of the piece was in its workman-ship; the filigree was so very fine, and it was evidently very old.

"It's lovely," she murmured, puzzled. "But what . . . ?"

"It's your Christmastide gift, my lady. I thought long and hard on the matter, and wondered what to give a woman known as a princess, who might have had all that she desired all of her life—other than complete freedom. I cannot give you that freedom, but this I thought you might enjoy. It came to me from Mother, and came to her through Harold Godwinson; it's of old Anglo-Saxon craftsmanship, and is a rare and precious piece. The emerald reminded me of your eyes. And I thought that you would like the fact that the gift has no taint of anything Norman about it— other than that it has passed through my hands—and is, perhaps, a part of our history."

She bit her lip, feeling the sting of tears at her eyes again, but aware that she was absurdly happy. He had given her gift great thought, and she had wondered if he might think she even warranted one at all.

"It's—it's beautiful."

"Take it."

Her fingers were trembling, but she took the brooch from him, her fingers curling around it. She came to her knees and quickly kissed his lips. "It's wonderful and I am grateful, and there is truly nothing more I could imagine being so beautiful and courteous a gift." She leaped up, blushing just a little to realize it seemed natural to move about naked before him, and strode to one of her own trunks. She carefully set the brooch into a compartment within it, tenderly placing it there, and picked up the bundle of cloth that lay topmost within the trunk. She brought it to him almost hesitantly, then shook out the fabric to show him a cloak made of the finest wool and dyed cobalt-blue, with fine embroidery upon the back in gold, the design his coat of arms.

He arched a brow.

"You made this?"

"One of the sheepherder's wives—Sarah's mother—fashioned the cape. She spins the softest, warmest wool. The embroidery I did, along with Lilith and Mary—and even your sister. The trim is golden fox. I thought of ermine, but the color of the fox blended so well with the coat of arms—"

She broke off, startled to find his arms around her; he bore her down upon the beautiful new mantle and kissed her. "It is an incredible gift. I am delighted that you made it for me."

"I told you, I did not—"

"But you did," he said, and kissed her again.

She smiled. "I've another gift," she told him. "But I cannot give it to you tonight. I think it will be a wonderful gift—nay, I am sure it will. But it is not quite . . . ready yet, and so I am convinced that I must wait to give it to you."

"Tell me," he insisted.

She shook her head.

"Allora—"

"Nay, milord!" she said primly. "You may come and conquer and dominate us all, but you'll not get another word from my lips!"

He arched a brow high. "Then, perhaps, I will coax a whisper from them, another cry . . ."

He swept her off the cloak. He kissed her again, and in moments, her arms wound around him.

They slept very late in the morning, barely arising in time to dress for the lengthy services that took place in church. As was the custom, Allora brought many of her poorest vassals there that day, bathed their feet within the chapel, and saw that they were well fed within the hall. She had not said anything to Bret about the ancient Christian ritual carried out here, but it seemed he knew it well, and was more than willing to take his part, as lord, in the cleansing.

Perhaps he was a little less than totally pious in a few of the teasing remarks he made to the people, but they smiled; watching him, she was certain that he gained more loyalty daily, and she wondered if her uncle was aware that he did.

She felt some guilt about her uncle. She was happy, and he most certainly was not.

And he was surely bitter, living upon the fringe of all that he had considered to be his.

She said a prayer for Robert, certain that it would not alleviate her guilt. But her mind quickly strayed from Robert, and she began to wonder if she did indeed have another Christmas present for Bret, not one that could be handed to him now, but something—someone—he could hold in the future. She hadn't really let enough time pass to be sure, but she suspected that she might now be carrying another child, and she wondered if it might be a boy, and if that would matter greatly to Bret. A son would be important here, for though she had managed to keep the Far Isle, she had been wed in a political gesture, as part of a battle between kings, and she could not help but fear the same fate for her daughter, while a son . . .

A son gave Bret roots here. It was a natural thing in their world for fathers to long for sons, and it was a natural thing as well for a people to recognize a male child as his parents' legal heir, an heir that none could argue. But she might have another girl, she mused, and thought of how she adored Brianna, and spun webs of dreams for her, and she thought that she would be equally happy no matter what the sex of the child she bore, if the babe were just healthy, and born well. But it wasn't really something she could seriously ponder as yet. She was but days late, and she'd been so erratic since Brianna's birth as it was.

The day was a busy one. From the chapel they moved on into the great hall, where the doors remained open despite the cold, and the ale flowed and the plenty within the fortress was shared with all who resided there. Tithe and homage were paid to the lord and lady of the Far Isle. The feasting went on through the day, and Bret formally rewarded some of his men, and some of those who had resided in the castle before he had come, with land and gifts of stock. Though pleasant, the day was long and exhausting, and Allora looked forward to the day that followed.

And still, tired as she was, her night was sweet. She came up alone, for Bret had disappeared, and as she closed the door she saw that a hip bath awaited her with steam rising from the water. She gave a glad cry, hurrying toward the tub, stripping as she went. She crawled in and shut her eyes, luxuriating in the warmth seeping into her. When she opened her eyes, she discovered her husband by the fire in an open crimson robe, and nothing more. He came to her, knelt by the tub, and teased that the bath was a Christmas gift as fine as any other, and when he began to soap and massage her shoulders, she quickly understood how rich a gift it could be. His soothing touch slowly worked its way into a sensual one, his hands, his fingers deliciously erotic beneath the steaming water. Even as he lifted her from the tub, and she discovered that furs awaited them on the floor, she began to shiver, and not from the cold.

She was afraid. Afraid that she would lose what she held—that this happiness could not last.

He stilled her shivering. His lovemaking was achingly slow, drawing her sweetly along at first, then suddenly casting her into a frenzy.

Later he held her close against his chest, within his legs, and they watched the fire. He kissed her throat, told her that her hair was gold, that her eyes were precious, haunting gems of emerald-green. He said nothing of love, and though she craved the words from his lips, it didn't matter. She had never longed so deeply to hold on to a night as she did that one. Yet even as she prayed that it could last forever, her eyes began to close before the fire, and he lifted her and brought her to bed, holding her.

She was half-asleep when she heard him speaking to her.

"If you could have something for Christmas, what would it be?" he asked her softly.

She smiled, her eyes closed, and curved against him. "To have this night forever!" she whispered. "To . . . to feel so safe, so secure and cherished—" She broke off.

"Go on," he commanded.

"To be cherished forever by a knight so strong; one who listens, who gives support, stands his ground, and yet does not dominate."

His arms curled around her.

"What would it be that you would have?" she asked him.

"Honesty!" he told her, and suddenly, no matter how warm and secure his arms, she felt shivering within her once again, and she prayed fervently that just once—just once!—her determination to do something good for others did not in turn do ill to her.

She didn't sleep until it was very late.

For once she lay awake longer than Bret, for she could hear his even breathing even as she lay and cursed both David and Elysia for being such passionate fools.

Fools for whom she cared too deeply . . .

The day after Christmas the entire castle seemed to awaken early. It wasn't exactly like May Day, but it was a similar occasion, when the nobility and the mighty were to tend to themselves, or to join in the festivities of the servants and the villeins. Very early on, there was a huge bonfire set out on the sand, between the fortresses of the Far Isle and that one rising upon the mainland far across the shifting sea and sands. The music was wild, with a pagan beat. When Bret and Allora arrived upon the scene, the fire already burned huge and fierce, with flames shooting up to the sky. The day was extremely fair, without harsh winds to seize the flame or a chill to freeze the bones. Skewered deer, lamb, and boar roasted upon the flames, and there was merriment everywhere, the people dancing, drinking, laughing in their celebration that honored distant gods as well as the birth of the Christ child.

"There was nothing quite like this in London," Bret murmured.

"Or in Haselford?" she asked.

He shrugged, his lip curling. "Perhaps, upon occasion. Yet I thought May Day the wild celebration."

"This is not so wild," Allora assured him. Another chill swept through her but she smiled up at him. "You are expected to dance with every lass here, young and old," she informed him. "And you needn't worry about my feeling a whit of jealousy, for I shall be on the arm of every creaking old knight and every squire and stable boy. Ah, and you needn't tarry long in one place, for there will be many lasses!" she warned.

Even as she spoke, she was swept up by Sir Christian's tipsy son, Gavin, who was yet sober enough, thank God, to quickly see Bret and to humbly murmur that it was the custom today for all good men to dance with the princess of the Far Isle.

"I see a milkmaid yonder!" Allora whispered.

Bret scowled at her, but as she was swiftly jounced away by Gavin, he was accosted by two buxom lasses at once, and chose the slimmer of the two with whom to begin his duty.

Allora took grave care at first, making sure that she saw him at longer and longer intervals. Then she came upon Gavin again, and whispered quickly, "You must find David for me, Gavin. Beg him meet me at the southernmost cottage, as soon as he can come."

"Milady," Gavin said miserably, "if you're now asking me to betray the new laird—"

"Gavin!" She took his slender cheeks between her hands and forced him to meet her eyes. "This is no betrayal. I need to see him upon a matter that does not concern myself, only his own good and that of another. No matter what comes of it, Gavin, you'll not have betrayed anyone, and I will never breathe your name, I swear it."

"I'm not afraid of serving you, milady. Not for myself. But for your own sweet person."

"I am afraid enough on that for both of us! Go for me, I beg of you. I will wait until I'm certain you're well gone, and then I'll make my way to the cottage. David will trust you, Gavin, as I do."

Gavin nodded, still very unhappy. But Allora knew that her message would be delivered.

And she had no doubt that David would come.

Gavin left her. For a moment, she stood on one side of the massive bonfire, which burned brightly upon the noonday sand. The flames, gold and red and blue, flickered high into the sky. Through them, she caught Bret's eye as he paused, engaged in conversation with Father Damien. They both watched her. She waved to them through the mist of the smoke and flame. Someone whirled by her. She allowed herself to drift backward across the sand.

She reached the far rim of the crowd, which had spilled onto the mainland beach and nearly into the woods. It was a simple-enough matter to drift back enough to slip between the trees. And from that point, she gave no thought to subterfuge. She had known the woods all her life. She followed the trails as swiftly as a doe, and in thirty minutes' time, somewhat breathless, she had come to the cottage.

She lifted the iron hinge and slipped into the cottage, anxiously looking around. But David hadn't come as yet, and it seemed far colder inside the cottage than it did beneath the sun outside. She began to pace the small confines, nervously waiting.

The place was very cold. No fires had warmed the crude hearth for a long time. A dusty wool blanket lay on the straw bed, and a long-stagnant and frosted bowl of water was perched on a small table near the one window. The cottage smelled musty and stale, and gave her an uncomfortable feeling.

"Please, David, come quickly!" she whispered, seeing the frost from her breath on the air as she spoke.

Then she heard swift hoofbeats followed by footsteps. She started for the door, stopping stock-still as it suddenly swung open. For a moment the sun was in her eyes. She saw a tall, tawny-haired man there, yet she could not see his face.

"David?"

"Nay, lady."

Not David. Then who . . .

"Duncan!" she gasped, stepping back quickly, away from the man. Though he and David were only half-brothers, they looked very much alike, with their sandy hair—though Duncan's was darker—and their glittering hazel eyes, though Duncan's glittered more fiercely. He was a tall man, strong enough, attractive enough. And yet, despite all that, and his resemblance to David, there had always been something about him, an edge, a leaning toward cruelty, that had always unnerved her. She felt that full-force now as he walked into the cottage, closing the door firmly behind him.

"Milady," he said softly. That was all. And yet . . .

She felt trapped. She *was* trapped, for his body blocked the door, and the window was narrow. She had simply never taken this man seriously enough to think that he would dare presume to trap her.

"Where's David? I sent for David."

"David is not coming."

"Why not?"

Duncan had scarcely moved. He leaned his muscled bulk against the door, watching her. "My brother is not coming because I did not bring Gavin's message to him. I managed to waylay your messenger."

"Waylay!" she exclaimed. "If you've harmed Gavin—"

He waved a hand impatiently in the air. "We do not harm our own, lady. Only when they become traitors unto us. Yet my fool brother has sworn some oath, and so is no longer one of us. Therefore, I have come in his stead. Milady, I will now make good your escape!"

She shook her head. "But I am not escaping—"

"This message from you today was extremely opportune, my lady, for Robert Canadys has planned an attack upon the sands just before dusk tonight which will lay flat your wretched Norman! None there are ready to fight; 'tis Christmastide, and surely our own people will be quickly ready to lay down to us what arms they might grab, then take them up again to fight the trodding foot of the Norman!"

She shook her head again, growing more frightened. "You don't understand, Duncan. I would never wish to hurt my uncle or anyone else, but I was not attempting to escape to him. There was something I needed to discuss with David that had nothing to do with the Far Isle at all! I cannot believe that you would be so presumptuous—"

"I remain a border laird, lady, not the strumpet of a Norman bastard's son!"

She slapped him as hard as she could, a tumult of emotions sweeping through her. Her uncle had planned an attack for this evening—she had to get to Bret and warn him!

Yet if she were to escape Duncan, what then? She couldn't warn Bret—he would ride out in full force and possibly slay her uncle.

She stared blankly at Duncan, trying desperately to find some means of escape. In the cold his cheek turned a mottled red with her fingerprints clearly outlined. He didn't respond for a moment, then told her, "I will take that but once, my lady, and give you fair warning—I'll see that vengeance comes your way for any more ill you do to me, or our people."

She inhaled and exhaled, furious. "You remain an inflated pig's ass, *Laird* Duncan, and you'll never frighten me. Now if you'll get out of my way—"

She strode toward the door furiously, hating herself for being so confident that this would work! But David would have come, she'd no doubt of it, if his brother hadn't ruined things with his own ambitious machinations.

She reached the door. He didn't move. Instead his hands fell firmly upon her shoulders. "I think not, milady. I think you'll be coming with me. You'll not go back and betray us!"

"I don't intend to betray anyone, Duncan!" she said heatedly. "Let me go!"

"Listen to me!" Duncan cried to her fiercely. "My brother is worthless now; he's sworn some oath, and will neither take up arms against the Norman, nor us, his kin. Robert is raging, and is deeply bitter that you have so easily accepted the dominance of an enemy laird! These men killed your father! Where is your pride, your decency? Bedded with that arrogant henchman of conquest! You will come with me now and I'll take you deep into Malcolm's country, far from this place. I'll keep you safe while they battle this out; then we can return, and you will be lady of the Far Isle in truth again, and I shall guide you in a peaceful ruling."

She stiffened in his hold, trying to remain calm, not realizing until she saw the gold sparkle in his eyes and the wild tension in his features just how determined he seemed on his course. A hand eased from her shoulder and his fingers slid down the length of her cheek. "For some time my brother stood in my way, so it seemed. But he is practically gone traitor himself now, and I swear to you, lady, I will be all that you need in life, in the rule of the Far Isle, in your bed at night. You'll ride with me now—"

"No! No!" she cried, jerking free from his hold as she stared at him. "Duncan, I will ride with you nowhere! You're mad! Your brother never stood in our way—no one ever stood in our way. I despise you. And if I did not, I am wed, I have had a child, I—" She broke off. She had almost told him that she was about to have another child, when she hadn't even shared the information with its father. "Duncan! You and Robert are driving everyone here into battle and into death, and surely, this winter, into something akin to famine. You are so eager to oust him from land that was never yours that you don't care what you do to the people, you don't care if the children live or die, if they eat or starve. They don't know Malcolm, and they don't know William Rufus; all they know is bloodshed now and starvation!"

"Ah, but you've come high and mighty, Allora! But I do not mind a noble shrew!"

She was growing truly frightened, but she could not allow herself to take Duncan seriously as her enemy. This was all madness.

"Let me go!" she commanded him again.

"Aye, we'll go—" he began, and she knew that he did mean to drag her off somewhere, and she knew not where. Into the highlands, somewhere far and distant. He really believed that her uncle could win his war, and that he could ride back to the Far Isle with her, triumphant.

Well, perhaps she had spent a great deal of her life pampered and sheltered. She had also learned how to wield a sword, and, more importantly, she had learned to look for an enemy's weakness. Neither of them was armed, but Duncan had the strength. She must strike first.

She did, suddenly kneeing him as hard as she could in the groin. Instantly he bellowed in pain, bending over. She slammed her folded fists down over his back and he fell forward. She sprang for the door, throwing it open.

"Allora!" she heard her name shrieked with fury, and knew that he was up and would be upon her in an instant. She started to run across the cold expanse of near-frozen earth before her. She turned back to see if she was being followed, and paused, startled to see that Duncan had disappeared.

She turned to run again, and gasped, crashing hard into the huge white haunches of a horse. A white horse. She looked up slowly in horror, realizing that Bret had come for her.

She looked up very slowly and met the chilling blue gaze of her husband.

"Find him!" he commanded, his voice a rich thunder that carried, and she suddenly realized that there was a host of horsemen with him, and they were all rushing by her, crashing into the clearing and among the trees.

But Bret's eyes did not leave hers. His coming, she thought fleetingly, might well have saved her from Duncan. And yet . . .

"Well, milady," he said very softly, bitterness edging his words like a razor, "you have been warned, time and again."

She moistened her lips, parted them to speak. What words could she say? Tell him that she had only been trying to reach David, because the man she had one time thought to wed had gotten his sister with child?

Would his fury abate even then?

Nay, and his eyes were terrible to behold. Ice-fire, like the blue blaze against the sky. There was nothing she could say. No excuse that would serve her, even if she did seek to betray friends to ease her own lot.

"You're wrong," she said quietly. "I did not seek to betray you."

"Nay, lady! It seems there is never any wrong that you do! But then, aye, you are a Scott, milady, and it was my grave mistake ever to forget it. Fate has set you beneath my rule. I am your enemy, and thus you are mine. And you have gone against me one time too many, my love. And therefore, Allora, as I have promised you, you will now pay the price!"

She would have run if she could. After everything that had been between them, the intimacies they had shared, she suddenly felt that she did not know him anymore. Didn't know the utterly ruthless tone of his voice, the searing cold of it, the fury, the absolute finality. Indeed, she would have run . . .

But he leaned down too swiftly, and set his hands upon her far too strongly. She was up and set before him upon Ajax before she ever thought to move her feet.

And the winter's icy wind that blew upon them as he rode hard back to the fortress seemed as nothing against the glacial frost that seemed to congeal around her heart and soul.

Chapter 23

They rode hard past the festivities that continued on the sands, heading through the open gates. Allora looked up at the sun in the sky and thought that it was just past noon—it would be some time before the twilight began to fall.

But Robert was well acquainted with the tides and the sand. He would know just when to come to inflict the greatest damage upon them, and if he did not gain the fortress gates, he would surely weaken the forces within tremendously.

She could tell Bret, and perhaps save herself from some of the deadly fury about to fall her way.

But if she told him, she would condemn numerous Scotsmen, loyal to her uncle as they had been to her father and her, to a sure death.

She couldn't do that, she couldn't be responsible for so many lives, for their children, for their families. Somehow, she had to manage to warn someone about what was to happen so that the people were all in before the sun began its first descent.

How, when she would probably find herself swiftly within a tower prison once again . . . ?

When they came through the gates and he at last drew Ajax to a halt, his touch was still as cold and strong as steel as he let her down before dismounting himself. She had only a split second's freedom from his touch, but she saw quickly that Sir Christian had ridden in behind him, and she was certain she had found her chance to avoid disaster, and the risk of anyone's life.

For the time.

Yet that was all that she could do, she realized; try day by day to keep what peace she could.

She moved like lightning, rushing to Sir Christian's horse, clutching the old man's leg, and speaking as swiftly and sincerely as she could in her native Gaelic. "My uncle is planning an attack for tonight, right on the sands. You mustn't tell Bret, for his knights might well then slay too many good and noble men, but you must see to it that no one is left upon the sands to be slaughtered. Sir Christian, do you understand?"

"Aye, lady, I ken!" he answered her quickly in Gaelic, looking over her head, and she knew, long before Bret's hand fell upon her shoulder, that he had come upon her.

"Tell me, Sir Christian, how did the Laird Ioin deal with those who constantly sought to escape and betray him?" Bret demanded. His tone remained quiet, controlled, almost pleasant.

"My good Laird Bret—" Sir Christian began miserably.

"I've heard tell that the Scots are quick to fight fiercely, nobly, and ably. And that they are equally bent on revenge, and that they do not tolerate treachery among their own. Ah, but Sir Christian! I will not trouble your conscience and loyalty with such a question. Await me in the hall, good sir, and I will be with you as soon as I may."

The force of his hand upon Allora's shoulder turned her quickly. Her unwilling footsteps led her to the door of the keep, and she didn't know whether to be relieved or not that so far, she was not being taken to the north tower. And at the moment, at least, she wasn't sure if it mattered. At least she had gotten her warning out to Sir Christian, and no one would die.

"Up the stairs, Allora," he told her, his voice still deceptively pleasant. A sliver of resentment stole into her heart. Perhaps she hadn't given him much cause to trust her, but he never even paused to question her motive. He had discovered her running away from Duncan, but he hadn't seemed to give that the least bit of thought.

"Up!"

She started moving because she didn't really want to do battle with him there on the stairs. The servants were out, dancing, feasting, celebrating, but she was certain one of his men would be quickly following behind to report on whether or not Duncan had been seized. With her back very stiff, she started up the first flight of stairs, and then the second. She reached their room and hurried in, walking quickly to the fire, warming her hands. He came in. The door closed. She awaited his words, trembling despite herself, trying to close her mind to the fears of just what might happen now that she had tested his tolerance this far.

He would speak to her, she was certain. Speak to her from his distance, with his ice-cold voice. And she would reply in kind, she told herself, but she would also defend herself to the very best of her abilities.

But he didn't speak from any distance. His hand upon her shoulder, he wrenched her around. His hand raised as if he would strike her to the ground, and despite her intention to stand against him, a cry of fear left her lips. His hand fell. She could hear the ragged grating of his teeth, and she was suddenly lifted and thrown atop the bed with a force that left her breathless.

Then he did not come near her. Hands folded behind his back, he walked to the window, looking out at the startlingly blue sky.

"There is no help for it!" he said, the words quiet. "Maybe you have been right all along. No one has asked me to change what I am—and nothing *can* change what you are."

Trembling, she wondered if she should simply keep her silence, then she knew that she could not. "You don't understand!" she whispered. "You don't want to understand. And you should! I was running *away* from him when you found me—"

"Running away?" He looked at her, arching an ebony brow. "Running away? Ah, how foolish of me! And I thought that you were running from your secret assignation with Duncan and back to the festivities upon the sands."

"I never meant to meet Duncan, I was trying to reach David—"

"Ah, and that is supposed to set my mind at ease? Yet it seems that David knows something more about vows and honor than you, my lady, for it seems he did not choose to meet you."

"David never knew I was trying to reach him."

"But that didn't matter. Duncan came."

"You don't understand."

"Indeed, I do not. Pray, give me an explanation."

She lowered her head, biting her lower lip. "I simply needed to speak with David. It was on a personal matter—"

"Sweet Jesu, but you do know how to ease my temper!"

"It did not concern you or me—"

"Never mind!" he thundered suddenly. "I do not want any more of your lies or protestations."

Tears stung her eyes. He stood far away from her, shoulders squared, eyes like blue ice, features harder than the sheer stone walls of the fortress. She felt again that he was a stranger, a cold, ruthless stranger, and one that she had somehow created herself.

"You don't want to hear anything from me—"

"By God, Allora, I can hear no more! I have listened again and again—I have forgiven again and again, like a fool. My grave mistake, my cruelty to us both! Had I but left you in the north tower a while, you might not have presumed that to defy me again and again could bring about no ill."

He still kept his distance from her. She stood, keeping her back to the bed, her eyes on his. She tried to straighten her spine and her shoulders, lift her chin.

"Come then, my great Lord Bret, you wish no trial, so go ahead, give your judgment!"

He stared at her a long moment. "It seems there is a large post in the courtyard for just such an occasion, my love. I am having you whipped—merely forty lashes, since we are still in the Christmas season. It seems fitting, does it not? Then . . . well, milady, I will be leaving in the morning, so you will remain here. Until I return. Then I will make my decision on whether you should remain within the fortress, or bide some time at my father's estates in Normandy."

He spoke quietly, and, oddly, without venom, and she realized he meant his every word, for it seemed they each pained him to say.

She wanted to be strong. She didn't want to care. He was wrong in this, and she wanted to have complete courage and dignity and suffer his unjust punishments with a composure that he would find haunted him daily.

But her knees were shaking. She didn't think that she could stand, she was so afraid. Forty lashes. She had seen strong men swoon at twenty. And then . . .

Banishment.

"Tell me," she said softly, "do you intend to wield the lash yourself?"

"Nay," he returned. "For I would either find my fury so great I could not stop at forty—else I would not manage to raise it at all. Nay, lady, I intend to be gone when the sentence is carried out."

The chill determination of his words made liquid of her limbs. She sat quickly upon the bed before she could fall. She was startled when he suddenly decided to dissolve the distance between them, striding swiftly to stand before her, lifting her chin and causing her to rise once again.

"What? Do you not intend to beg for mercy, my love? Tell me again that you are resigned to my being here— nay, lady, tell me you have discovered this magnificent love for me, in all things—" he demanded harshly, his eyes cutting into her like a blade, his voice every bit as razor-honed.

His fingers suddenly threaded into her hair, hard, fierce. His lips descended upon hers, hard, bruising. And despite his anger, nay, his *hatred*, the touch was arousing still. Yet she could not breathe, and her fists came up against his chest, and his lips rose from hers.

"No words, no whispers?" he taunted harshly. "You'll not tell me again that you love me?"

She felt a burning sizzle at the back of her eyes and refused to cry. "Only a fool would love you, my lord! A Norman fool."

He smiled. "Ah, honesty! So you do not love me, my lady. Yet I had thought it truth that you had come to need me! Come, lady! Use those wiles you wield with such gile and talent! Tell me that at least!"

"Aye, my lord!" she cried furiously. "I have come to— want you!"

"In this, then, you are obliged!"

His mouth crushed hers once more. She felt the force of his teeth and tongue. She thought she tasted blood. His lips left hers once again. The blue fury of his eyes remained to impale her.

His touch did not leave her. His fingers set upon the bodice of her gown and ripped forcefully. She fell back, and he was swiftly atop her, and she cried out with alarm at his tremendous force, yet he was heedless of the sound. His fury seemed as much directed at himself as at her, for the words that broke from his lips then were harsh and bitter. "Ah, but I am cursed, lady, wanting you, seeking to have you, when no matter how tightly I hold, you escape my grasp! Yet I would hold you again and again, have you till I should be drunk with you, done with you!"

She heard a startling anguish in those words, but his anger seemed to override all else. With no sweet play, with no tenderness, he was suddenly within her, driving like the wild pelting of a winter's storm, hard, fast, his eyes never leaving hers, no softening look coming to the rugged contours of his face, even as he arched, grated out a cry, and filled her with the richness of his heat. Even then, his eyes remained upon her. He did not fall by her, did not hold her, offered no word of tenderness.

He rose, adjusting his clothing within that fluid movement, and Allora found herself curling away from him upon the bed, trying to draw the remnants of her own about her. He walked away and stood by the fire, his back to her.

She closed her eyes tightly, then refused to be so used and beaten. She leaped up, ripping the torn gown from her body and hurling it across the room. She wrenched the covers from the bed, sweeping them around her, staring at him.

"You cannot have me whipped," she told him, her voice quiet and level and determined.

He turned around at last, a taunting smile curving his lip, somehow giving him the appearance of a handsome demon.

"Ah, my lady! You are mistaken. I am quite taken by your charms, as we both are well aware! But alas, they are not enough to change my judgment!"

She longed to strike him. To run across the room and strike him as hard and swiftly as she could manage.

She stood her ground. "You cannot have me whipped, my lord, because—" She broke off. She had meant to state the words with such dispassion! But she failed in the effort, going silent.

"Because—?" he demanded, mockingly.

She no longer stood her ground. She did go tearing across the floor, slamming herself and her fists against him.

She lost her covers with the effort, and was naked when he caught her wrists, stilling her wild impetus of motion. Her breasts rose and fell, her heart thundered against her chest.

"Because why, Allora?"

She threw her head back. "Because I think that we're going to have another child. And because I don't believe you want your *Norman* offspring's life endangered."

He continued to hold her wrists, stock-still, his eyes blue fire on hers.

Then he slowly released her. He turned swiftly and left the room, slamming the door behind him. She ran after him, casting the door open again.

But Bret was halfway down the stairs. A wide-eyed Etienne was left standing there, staring at her.

She reddened from head to toe and slammed the door. And ran back into the room, pitching herself upon the bed. And she cried, slow tears trickling down her cheeks as she despaired at the life they had been cast to lead . . .

An hour or so later she managed to dress and returned to the door, hoping that Etienne would be gone.

He was.

But there was another Norman knight there, one she had seen, but whose name she scarcely knew. He wore his battle helmet and mail and held his sword before him, the point biting into the wood of the floor, his hands upon the hilt. He spoke before she could.

"Milady, I'm afraid I have orders that you're not to leave the room," he told her unhappily. He was an older man, at least fifty, she thought.

One who had been loyal to Bret and his family for years and years, no doubt.

"I need to know, sir, if the people have come in yet from the feasting and bonfire."

"You needn't worry about anything, milady. All is well," he assured her.

Frustrated, she returned to her room. She looked out the window. The sun was just beginning to fall. The day was tinged with brilliant colors—golds, yellows, reds.

Now . . . Now was when Robert would have come to wage his battle!

She closed her eyes, then suddenly heard a shout, a cry . . . and a thunderous clashing of steel.

No . . .

She ran to the corridor, throwing the door open again. The Norman knight remained. "What is happening?" she demanded. "I had thought the people would be in—"

"The people *are* in, my lady. Robert Canadys attacks only armed men, who were pretending to be the villeins, drunk and disorderly about the bonfire!"

"Oh!" she gasped, closing her eyes. Oh, God! The slaughter she had meant to prevent was happening despite her efforts . . .

Sir Christian. Sir Christian had betrayed her; he had gone to Bret.

"Dear God!" she whispered.

She had to see what was happening. She flew past her Norman guard so quickly that he hadn't a prayer of stopping her. He followed as she raced down the stairs and out to the courtyard, tearing across it to reach the ramparts of the wall so that she could see the sands beyond. But even as she started upon the first step, she felt a hand on her arm. A very strong one. She turned, wrenching hard, desperate to free herself, only to meet the knowing eyes of Father Damien.

"Father, let me go! I have to see—"

"Nay, you do not have to see!" he told her softly.

"But—"

"There is nothing you need see, my lady." He drew her from the steps. She winced, hearing a cry rise high on the air. She heard the clash of steel again, and longed to drop to her knees and cover her ears. But then another shouted order came: "Open the gates!" It was Bret's voice; she knew the command in it very well.

And the gates opened, and Bret and his army came pouring in. Father Damien drew Allora back from the huge war-horses that tore their way in.

The men reined in. A massive cheer went up among them. Allora stared at the mounted and armed knights, then realized that they had obviously taken the victory.

She saw Sir Christian, riding in behind Bret, and broke free from Father Damien to go rushing over to him. "Dear God, sir! You betrayed me, you betrayed them! I warned you to save lives, not to spill them!"

Tears fell upon her cheeks again and she dashed them quickly away with the back of her hand. Sir Christian dismounted swiftly from his horse, answering her sorrowfully. "My lady, I swear, I never had a chance to tell the earl anything at all. He knew of your uncle's planned attack, and gave orders to be ready for it."

She had to believe him. Looking into the old eyes that had stared with such honesty at her so many times before, she knew that he was telling the truth.

Then . . .

"My lady!" It was Bret, his fingers biting into her shoulder. "How amazing that I should find you down here when I had thought you so anxious to rest—and care for yourself and all that is mine."

She spun quickly, eluding his painful touch. She met his eyes with her own hate-filled glance and refused to answer him, heading back for the keep instead. She entered swiftly, ignoring Elysia, who called to her from her great hall. She raced up the first flight of stairs and the second; she went into her room and closed the door firmly behind her, leaning against it. Oh, dear God! The sounds had been horrible. How many men had died, how many had died . . . ?

The door moved at her back. She braced herself against it.

"Allora, move!"

She didn't. Bret's next thrust was powerful enough to press the door inward, even with her weight upon it.

He came in, slamming the heavy wood closed with angry force. She hurried to the window, dully staring out of it, not looking his way.

"If you're mourning for your uncle, don't bother. He was not taken. Nor was Duncan. And your dear David was not part of the fight."

"I am mourning the blood of good men, spilled upon the sand!" she cried. "I am mourning the wretch within this fortress who would betray his or her own people—"

"No one betrayed them, Allora. Except you yourself."

She spun around, staring at him at last. "I don't know what you're talking about. You won't believe that I would never betray you, but before God, I would not see those poor men butchered by your Norman knights!"

"Many of them are Saxons," he reminded her politely. He was still clad in his mail and helmet. The helmet he removed carefully, setting it upon his trunk. He started to remove one of the leather straps that held his mail to his shoulder, then sat down wearily. "Come here. Come help me with this."

"I will not!"

He rose and strode to her, grabbed her arm, and dragged her along with him to the bed where he sat down again, his fingers a vise around her wrist as he held her there.

"Undo the strap."

"I'll not! I don't know what—"

He pulled her closer, bringing her down to her knees between his. He leaned close and smiled and whispered softly, "Here you are before me, my love. So obedient and sweet! *Céad mile buiochas!*"

A hundred thousand thank-yous, in the Gaelic she had spoken to Sir Christian earlier. Bret had never spoken it here before. She hadn't had the least suspicion that he knew a single word of the language.

"Oh, you bastard!" she whispered. "How dare you, how could you—"

"How could I not, milady? Sweet Jesu, madam! I have no wish to kill men endlessly! But as long as your uncle keeps planning on waging battle against me, I have no choice!"

"Let me go!" she cried, choking. "Oh, my God! I hate you! I hate you—"

"You hate me for speaking your language? Or for making you feel like a fool? You have done it to me oft enough."

"Let me go—"

"In time!" he snapped, suddenly impatient. "I want to know, were you telling me the truth? Or is it some game to escape your just rewards once again? Are you expecting a babe?"

She tried to pull free. How strange. She had imagined telling him on Christmas Eve, when their world had seemed so warm and secure. Something sweet and beautiful to be shared. But she had waited then to be sure, yet this afternoon, she'd had to tell him, or else risk the babe.

And now . . .

"Allora!"

She tossed her hair back, eyes emerald afire. "Aye, my lord, it is no game. I wanted to tell you before, but I thought I should wait longer, be certain. Yet the first months are the most precarious for the bairn, and so I had to speak today."

He released her and stood, striding by her where she was left upon her knees. She felt desolate, and sank down wearily upon her ankles. She no longer cared. There was no way out of the tempest of her life. She had killed men today, just as if she had ridden with her husband's men. She had never meant to kill them. But she was certain that many lay dead . . .

He could manage his mail very well himself. He stood by the fire, found the leather straps, and released them, then eased the heavy cloak of linked steel over his head, draping it over a trunk. Allora remained where he had left her, and he came back, sitting upon the bed, staring down at her again.

"Aye, lady, men died beyond those walls. Would you rather that their death had fallen upon me?" he asked her.

"I would rather that no one died!" she said dully.

"I asked you—"

"No!" she snapped, looking up at him at last. "If you understood what I said to Sir Christian today, you must know that!"

"Aye!" he said softly after a moment. "And though you are so heartily dismayed that I understood you, my love, it has somewhat redeemed you in my eyes."

She glared at him. "I do not need to be redeemed, my lord!"

"You are redeemed *somewhat*. Not completely, my love."

She grated her teeth, looking downward, feeling the hot burn of tears again behind her lids.

There was a tapping at the door. Allora did not look up. Bret rose and walked to it, opening it, then stepping outside. Allora still did not move. She vaguely heard him speaking with someone, saying that he would leave in the morn. Then she heard someone coming into the room, and she looked up. Mary, carrying a tray with goblets and covered trenchers, came in and quickly set the tray upon the trunk at the foot of the bed. Allora met her eyes, silently entreating her to tell her whatever news she might have, but Mary looked away, and wouldn't risk Bret's wrath, not at this time. She quickly left, and Bret returned to the room, closing the door behind him once again.

"I am weary, and have had our meal brought here," he told her.

"I am not hungry."

"I am ravenous."

"I imagine killing men does create quite an appetite."

He strode to her, reached down for her, and pulled her firmly to her feet. "Your uncle has been trying to kill me since he met me. He was the one willing to stoop to poison, and nearly killed you. When will you see that the man is ruthless and ambitious beyond all reason?"

"My uncle is alive, so you have told me. Other men are dead."

"Your uncle stands in the background, directing others to their deaths."

"He is a brave man, a hardened warrior!"

"And a smart one, not willing to risk his life until he is sure he can triumph."

"You hate him—"

"With good reason!"

He suddenly swept her up and before she could struggle, she found herself seated before the fire. And he set one of the trenchers upon her lap; despite herself, she found the scent of the meat tantalizing.

"You need to eat," he told her curtly.

"How strange," she murmured. "All in one day. I should suffer Christ's forty lashes, but I must eat in the meantime!"

"You've one babe and perhaps another," he said bluntly.

She speared a piece of meat with the small table knife beside the trencher, yet despite the pleasant scent, she knew she couldn't eat it. She set the trencher aside and rose, walking to the window. "You don't understand," she said. "Half of those people are relatives, distant cousins, but cousins nonetheless. Dying."

He spoke curtly once again. "Robert Canadys is killing them, milady—neither you nor I. The moment he seeks peace, he shall have it."

"On your terms."

"Malcolm himself is not disputing that this land is English," he told her quietly.

There was a very soft tap at the door. "Aye?" Bret called, and Jarrett entered with two of the Norman squires behind him. "Milord, we've come for your things, assuming you wish them ready for the morning."

"Aye, come. The trunk there—" He pointed to a large leather trunk against the wall "—goes. My mail and helmet are there."

The men took Bret's belongings. Jarrett offered Allora a smile she thought was an encouraging one. He liked her, she realized. She smiled back wanly. She liked him, too. And she liked Etienne.

She wasn't sure she wanted to see them for a while, though.

She frowned suddenly, watching as the men left with her husband's belongings and accoutrements of war. When the door closed, she asked him, "Where are you going?"

"I told you I was leaving with the dawn."

"But where are you going?"

"To York. There has been a summoning of the king's barons there, and I believe William Rufus fears a possible revolt again. I had thought to bring you with me, but I must split forces, since I will have to leave men here to guard the fortress along with your carls."

"So that my Scots and I do not turn the place over to Robert?" she queried.

"You won't be doing anything, my love. Jarrett will take command of the Far Isle."

"In which tower do I reside?"

"I haven't decided that as yet!" he said softly.

Allora started to speak again, but broke off before she began hearing a lusty wail from the hallway that easily passed through the barrier of the door. Bret, at the mantel by the hearth, pushed away from the wall, going to the door. A moment later he returned to her with Brianna, placing the babe in her arms.

She was red-faced and indignant, very hungry and very angry at having to wait. Her eyes were incredibly blue and filled with tears. Allora laughed softly, forgetting the horrors of the day for the moment, and sat near the fire, away from Bret, crooning to the baby and untying the laces of her tunic and undershift to feed her.

Bret didn't speak; neither did she. When Brianna slept, Allora rose carefully, setting her to sleep in her tiny cradle. She rocked it gently for a moment, then strode to the bed and laid down upon it, closing her eyes.

She opened them again slightly when she heard him move. He stood at the cradle, rocking it slightly himself, smiling as he watched his daughter sleep. Allora bit her lip, and closed her eyes wearily again. Her heart had never seemed so terribly heavy. Bret was leaving her. She wondered if he might not decide just to ride on forever . . .

"Allora, you cannot sleep so. Get up and undress."

Her eyes flew open. Indignation brought a sizzle to them. "If my clothes disturb you, it does seem you know how to rid me of them."

His mouth was grim. She found him pulling her up, spinning her around, unhooking the delicate gold filigree girdle she wore low on her hips. He turned her once again, loosening the ties on her tunic and shirt. "I can manage myself!" she murmured, backing away.

"As you wish. I thought you had implied you needed my help."

"I implied you had the manners of a boar."

He turned away from her, walking around the bed to sit and shed his boots and chausses, tunic and shirt. She set her back to him, stripped, and crawled in on her own side.

It seemed there was a vast, vast distance between them, but Bret made no effort to lessen it.

Allora felt as if she were choking, as if she could not breathe. She wondered just how many men had died . . .

And she wanted to curl against the man who had gone to battle against her people, and she wanted to be comforted by him. It would not happen.

She began to doze, watching the fire. She remembered how warm and sweet it had been to watch the flames, when she had felt his arms around her. Yet, perhaps as part of a dream, the sight of the flames suddenly frightened her. She could see them rising, reaching out to her, trying to touch her. She must have cried out.

"Allora, wake up. You are dreaming, nothing more."

Her eyes opened upon his. He was on an elbow, lifted above her, stroking damp strands of hair from her face, blue eyes tender now, she thought, as he stared down at her. "Hush, my love, it was but a dream."

She closed her eyes, soothed by his voice. "I love to watch a fire burn," she whispered. She bit off the words *with you*. "I've always liked the flames. But they suddenly seemed evil, malignant . . ."

"It's just a fire in a hearth, burning low!" he told her. He lay beside her, drawing her back into his arms. "It brings warmth and comfort, and is nothing to fear." His words were soft and gentle. Her fingers curled over his where they lay upon her hip. She caught his hand and held it close to her.

A few moments later, she felt his gentle, seductive kiss upon her nape and shoulder. She closed her eyes and savored the sensation. Her pride told her to protest. Her heart refused to do so.

He made love to her tenderly, slowly, erotically. She felt she exploded in his arms, and drifted back to a sweet world where she felt secure again. "I hope it's a boy," she whispered after a moment.

"Why?" he asked. "I have always adored my sisters."

"You don't care about a son?"

"We're both young, my love. You could have a dozen children. It is immaterial to me if this babe is male or female, as I assume you'll eventually bear a son. And if it is not God's will that you do so . . . then we will be content with daughters."

She felt warm again. She wanted to hold him tight and tell him not to leave, but she could not do so. She shivered and told him, "You really don't understand. A son—a son will weaken Robert's hold upon the nobles. A son is a true heir no man can argue."

"Robert will bow down to me, one way or the other," he assured her after a moment. And his voice seemed cold again. She wished she hadn't spoken.

"But so many die—"

Perhaps he heard the thin veil of tears in her words. "Go to sleep, Allora," he told her. "Rest."

His fingers stroked her hair. She was so very weary. Held in his arms, feeling the sweet comfort she had not thought to know again, she slept.

When she awoke in the morning, she was shivering. She couldn't quite understand her discomfort.

Then she realized that she was cold, very cold . . .

Because Bret was gone, and held her no more.

Chapter 24

*B*ret had seen to it that he and his men began their ride as early as the dawn broke, and he had been glad, for the ride was a long one. Hours had passed in which he had ridden ahead, Etienne and Jacques holding pace about ten feet behind him, and the fifty men riding with them, staggered out behind. The day was crisp and cold, but the sky was clear, brilliantly blue, beautiful. For once, the harsh winds that so often tore at the northern counties were still, and the snow that stretched before them was settled and as pure a white as could be imagined.

He had come to realize, though, that he did not mind the gale winds that normally blew. He liked to stand on the parapets, smell the sea, feel the mist touch his face, and welcome the wild wind that ruffled his hair and, sometimes, soothed his soul. He loved the Far Isle.

And he loved his wife, he admitted to himself, if never to her. It had seemed to rip something inside of him apart to leave her with the dawn just breaking into the room. She had been deep within the covers, sleeping so serenely, a picture of beauty and innocence, her golden hair spread out upon sheets and blankets of fur, her lips slightly parted in a small smile, honey lashes sweeping the alabaster of her cheeks. He had paused to touch her, to kiss her lips, and her smile had seemed to deepen as he straightened, but she didn't awaken. And Etienne had stood quietly in the hall, waiting to tell him that fifty men-at-arms were in the courtyard, ready to ride.

And so he hadn't touched her again. He had left, aching to do so.

The slim fiery creature he had once deemed such an annoying child had slowly chinked away the barriers of both his anger and resolve. He had realized the night of his wedding that her beauty was unmatched, and he never really wanted to look back. But she had been something to possess then, to fight and fight for. He had been in wretched anguish when she had poisoned herself rather than him, and yet he had believed the denial in her emerald eyes. Nay, Allora might plunge into reckless battle with a sword, and she had admittedly put the poison in his chalice. But Robert had been the one with the deadly intentions.

And still . . .

He had wanted to forgive her then—but she had fled with her kinsmen. And she had said that she would not allow an annulment—once she had learned about Brianna. He had wanted so badly to throttle her, to thrust her away, to leave her in a tower and forget her forever!

But once again, he had believed her, in the emerald beauty of her eyes, in the softness of her words . . .

In the arms that held him in the night, the limbs that wrapped around him, the sweet, sensual body that melded so swiftly with his own. She had said that she loved him. Words she would not repeat, but they had slipped out once.

Aye, she had loved him! She had nearly plunged to an icy death, she loved him so damned much. But that had been for David, and he should have understood that she was willing to die for another man.

And still he had forgiven her.

Then had come yesterday, and the bonfire, and the wild crowds feasting and drinking . . .

And Allora, disappearing into the woods. He had barely gathered his men and horses quickly enough to follow her trail. And once again, she'd had a tale to tell him. Once again, she'd been trying to reach that young figure of absolute nobility—David! So she had said. But she had learned about Robert's planned attack . . .

And she had warned Sir Christian to see that her people were not slaughtered outside the gates.

She hadn't told Bret himself a thing, and he wouldn't have known if she hadn't made a major mistake in assuming that a child of Fallon and Alaric would not have been taught any language spoken by the peoples surrounding their own country. Thank God. He had dealt Robert and his barbarians a severe blow. Dozens of men were prisoners in the new fortress on the mainland, many of them hurt, but being as carefully tended by Father Damien as any Saxon or Norman might be, and Damien had left strict instructions with the villeins working in the new fortress on how they were to be cared for in his absence. Robert was weakened, but then, Robert was also careless with human life, and Bret had no doubt that he would call in any untrained man or boy to take weapons out on the field if it would further his own cause.

He wished he'd managed to seize Robert Canadys yesterday. There would have lain the victory. For as long Robert kept up his fight . . .

Bret would never be able to trust Allora. Love her, yes, but not trust her. He should have kept her in the north tower from that first night he had come here. He should have admired her elegance, grace, and beauty from a safe distance.

Maybe even visited her upon occasion, he mocked himself. But it didn't matter. He could have never left her there, for the very fact that she had wound her way into his heart. She was an obsession with him; he needed her, craved her. He thought of touching her again, even as he rode now . . .

He gritted his teeth, nearly groaning aloud. She had run out to meet that sly Duncan, and she should have been whipped, and instead . . .

He couldn't have had her lashed at a whipping post. He wondered if he would have ever really carried through with the threat. It didn't matter; he would never know just what he really would have done. She was expecting another child. Or so she had said. She wouldn't have lied, he thought. But, oh, by all hell, there lay the torment, for he looked at her, he touched her, and he forgot anger and resolve and the desire for truth, and knew only that he desired her. It was good that he was summoned now to York to meet with other landed barons on king's business.

He needed the distance. Aye, she should have been whipped and imprisoned within her tower once again, and instead . . .

She would pay no price. He had left, telling Jarrett and Sir Christian only to see to her welfare. They would do so, he knew. And as long as they stayed within the walls of the fortress, they would all do well enough, he was certain. Robert would know now that he couldn't attempt an assault on the isle. He hadn't the strength for it. He would be holed up somewhere in the hills, on his own estate, planning some new and devious warfare for spring. But that wouldn't matter, for Bret had no intention of being away any longer than necessary on this business.

He winced, thinking ahead. He had brought a furious complaint to William the Conqueror about Jan de Fries presuming to ride north and slay Ioin Canadys. William had promised him justice, but then had died. Bret had taken the same complaint to William Rufus, and he had learned, when his father's messenger had reached him at the Far Isle, that William Rufus had done no more than fine de Fries for the murder, that fine to be paid to him in gold. Jan de Fries went free, and many of his fellows could not understand Bret's argument with the man; Ioin had been a rebel when he died, running with a Norman lord's bride, and from a contract he had duly signed.

Yet many understood, as the now-deceased William had understood, that Ioin had been the only sanity there. Bret wished suddenly and severely that Jan de Fries had been there—to battle Robert himself, and thus see from whence Bret's anger sprang.

Well, Jan de Fries was not with them at the Far Isle, but according to Alaric's message, he would be in York.

His thoughts returned to Allora, and he knew that another reason he had determined not to take her with him had been the fear that they might see Jan de Fries, and that she wouldn't be able to keep her distance, but would try a headlong rush with a carving knife against the man who had slain Ioin. She was loyal to Robert, but it was her father she had adored.

Well, she wasn't with him. She was safely at home. And when he returned, he would be better prepared to deal with her. Perhaps he could bring her south, to Haselford, to spend time with his family there, far away from her warlike kin. Maybe then the barriers of mistrust could be broken.

He shook his head, even though it was with himself he argued.

No, that would not do. The Far Isle was their home—his now as well as hers. He had never imagined that he might want it, but he did. And by right, he was laird there, and Allora was the born heiress. Brianna had been born there— without his presence, a bitter note—but now, there might be a new child, and it seemed as if roots were spreading out beneath him. He couldn't define all the reasons, but the Far Isle was his; it was home.

Just as Allora was his. And just as he loved her, no matter how much anguish that love brought him.

He was startled to hear a rider coming up close beside him. It had been his obvious preference to ride alone that morning.

He reined in, slowing Ajax and turning slightly, to see that it was Father Damien. Bret lifted a brow. He'd known the strange priest all his life, had been baptized and married by him; his mother had been the one to insist Damien accompany him here. He hadn't argued the point. He was not sure if Damien had a special ear through which God whispered, but the good father did know things, and even on those occasions when he exasperated Bret, Bret was grateful for his wisdom, expertise, and advice.

"What is it?" Bret asked, frowning, because Damien's silvery brows were furrowed, his striking features, as yet unlined, were drawn.

"We need to halt," Damien said.

It was going to be one of those occasions when Damien exasperated him, Bret could see.

"My good father, we are trying to reach Wakefield tonight, York tomorrow. If we don't ride until dusk—"

"My good *Lord* Bret, if we don't hold up, I fear something far greater than a delayed arrival."

Bret's frown deepened. "What? What is it that bothers you? Are we being followed?"

Damien shook his head. "I don't know. I've been uneasy since we left the Far Isle this morning. Bret, it is near enough to dusk now. At least stop and make camp for the night here. Post a guard. I am seldom wrong in these matters."

And Bret knew he seldom was.

Bret reined in hard on Ajax, turning to raise a hand high to the mounted men who followed.

"We'll find shelter in the trees, make camp here. Etienne, call a halt and post a guard."

Bret dismounted from Ajax, entering into the midst of the forest itself, for there the high bowed branches of some of the evergreens had left a clean hard sweep of dry ground. It would do for a camp.

Leaving Ajax to Etienne, Bret walked out from the canopy of trees and stared homeward, then looked to the sky. It was cloudless. There was a light breeze, and nothing more stirring. Yet he was deeply disturbed. Damien's uneasiness had now crept into Bret's own soul . . .

Allora sat in the great hall with Brianna, working on a tapestry even as she longed to run outside, if only into the courtyard. She could see that the day was beautiful. The weather had been so rough as of late, but a strange and peaceful lull seemed to have settled over the Far Isle. She could feel the air as she passed the windows, and it was cool; snow blanketed the ground, but the sun was shining, playing now through the slit windows, striking upon the dust that stirred in the air to create dancing motes. She envied Bret his ride through the countryside, though she was certain that his men-at-arms had grumbled at the prospect of the trip. She paused in her stitching, staring at the flames that burned in the hearth, feeling her heart pound. How strange, she'd had such an awful dream about a blue blaze last night!

Aye, and yet what a strangely good and erotic dream that nightmare had become! she reminded herself, and she felt warmed, her face coloring, and she quickly looked down to her needlework again. Jarrett and Sir Christian were in the hall with her, gaming at the table. She didn't want the two of them to suddenly realize that she was staring at a fire and blushing. But she couldn't keep her mind on her task. She looked at the flames again, and it seemed that her heart constricted. She missed him. He was barely gone, and parts of yesterday had surely been akin to a shadow ride into the nether regions of hell, and yet . . .

She felt incredibly alone with him gone. The hall had lost its life. In the warmth of the sun, it could still be so cold. He mistrusted her, and he probably always would. He didn't love her, had sworn that he would not.

And yet . . .

She did love him. And she suddenly ached to tell him so again, to curl into his arms and let him mock her if he would, but to whisper to him the simple fact that she needed him in her life, craved and desired him . . .

Loved him.

The baby stirred suddenly. Allora reached down to Brianna where she had been playing with a toy lamb Sir Christian had whittled for her, and swept the babe up into her arms. Mary came into the hall and smiled, looking at the baby upon Allora's shoulder. "She's getting so big, so quickly!" Mary said. "Shall I take her to bed, milady?"

"Aye, she needs her nap," Allora agreed, and smiling, gave the baby over to Mary. Alone again, she sat staring at the flames, wishing that she dared leap to her feet and run out of the hall. But she was moving very warily today. She was supposed to have been tied to a whipping post right about now, and when finished there, she might well have been put in the north tower.

No one had said a word to her as yet today about any of the events of yesterday. She was not about to bring them up. When she had come down this morning, Jarrett had been unfailingly courteous, and had offered her his encouraging smile. Sir Christian had been somewhat grave, but courteous as well. Neither of them had denied her the right to leave her tower and sit in the hall.

But she hadn't yet taken a chance on stepping into the courtyard . . .

Even as she looked to the doors into the hall, they suddenly opened. Elysia came in, glancing swiftly, almost furtively, to Allora, then smiling sweetly to Jarrett and Sir Christian.

She walked to the table, sitting, leaning her elbows upon it, and commented idly, "It's a beautiful day. Stunning, really. Cool, crisp, and the sky is *so* blue!"

"Indeed, milady, it's a glorious day," Jarrett assented politely.

Elysia smiled again and pushed away from the table. "Allora, you must come out. Just to take a quick ride out onto the sands."

"Elysia—" Jarrett warned.

"Jarrett, come now! Sir Christian, it's my understanding that you all gave a crushing blow to the Scotsmen beneath Laird Robert Canadys!"

"Aye, lady, that's true!" Sir Christian agreed unhappily, his mist-colored eyes meeting Allora's.

"We needn't ride out then," Elysia said with a shrug. "Come with me, Allora, we'll simply ride within the fortress walls themselves, feel the sweet touch of the sun and the gentle hand of the breeze."

No one said or did anything to stop them. Allora waited, her heart beating hard. Jarrett did not deny her the right to leave the hall, and so she forced herself to slowly come to her feet and to smile at Elysia. "Aye, let's see this wondrous day," she murmured softly.

Elysia started for the door with another shrug. "Even a walk would be lovely. There is no snow within the walls; even while the mainland is blanketed, so little falls upon the isle. We can run up to the parapets, and see the work still going on at the mainland fortress." She set a hand upon Elysia's back, urging her forward more swiftly.

A moment later they were stepping out into the courtyard.

"Hurry!" Elysia said, catching her hand and starting to run for the stables.

"Why?" Allora gasped, pulling Elysia back. She looked around quickly. The customary guard lined the walls. The gates, however, were ajar—ready to be closed swiftly at either the first sight of danger or dusk, one or the other— but they stood open now as they did in times of peace.

Robert could not attack the fortress anytime soon. Everyone knew that. He hadn't the strength to attempt a siege, and he hadn't Bret's expertise in breaching a fortress's defenses.

"Allora—" Elysia pleaded.

"Elysia, tell me what is going on!"

Elysia stepped closer to her, whispering swiftly, "One of the miller's daughters asked Mary if she could get a message to you. Mary couldn't speak to you in the hall, not with Jarrett and Sir Christian there, and so she came to me.

"David has sent his apologies for what happened with Duncan. He had no idea you were trying to reach him, and he has sworn to come today to find out what he can do for you. He will see you just within the first copse of trees in the southern forest."

Allora bit her lip, hanging back.

"Oh, please, Allora!" Elysia begged. "You won't be alone, I'm coming with you. And Bret is well over half the way to Wakefield by now! I have to reach David. Oh, Allora, I said terrible things to him! And if he does care for me, he must come to Bret as soon as my brother returns, or else my condition will too quickly become apparent for all to see."

Allora crossed her arms over her chest. "And just how are we to manage this feat?"

"You're asking me?" Elysia demanded with a trace of humor. "The woman who dove from the parapets into an icy sea?"

"Aye, and was dragged right back out of it!" Allora reminded her.

Elysia smiled, shaking her head. "We will simply mount our horses and ride right out of the gate. Allora, I know Bret was in a fury yesterday—"

"You truly cannot imagine!" Allora said dryly.

"But he is gone. And when we ride back in, neither Sir Christian nor Jarrett will wish to present himself as the fool who let you slip out."

Allora smiled slowly. Elysia had a point.

"And," Elysia said with wry amusement, "if David and I do manage to wed, Bret will cease to hound you about him."

Elysia had another good point, Allora thought.

"All right, then!" she said softly. "Let's go."

"Hurry!"

Elysia caught her hand again. They went running for the stables but then Allora pulled back and began to walk, forcing Elysia to a casual dignity when they told one of the stable boys they wanted their horses. They discussed the brightness of the sun, the blueness of the sky, and the lightness of the breeze as they waited. When the boy brought Briar forward, Allora thanked him as she always did and mounted with no apparent need to rush. Elysia's roan gelding was brought forward next, and Allora commented that they would ride around the entire circumference of the walls, and Elysia would realize then just what an accomplishment nature and some ancient builder had managed.

They did ride along the walls, and then Allora felt her heart begin to thud as they came to the gates. She looked up at the guard there and saw he was one of the very old carls who had served her grandfather as well as Ioin. She was in luck. She waved gaily to him.

He waved back, and called down a warning.

"Darkness and tide come quick, now, milady. Take care!"

"Aye, that we'll do!" she called back.

Elysia was right behind her, the roan crowding Briar.

Allora kneed Briar. They went flying out across the sands, and she felt the refreshing freedom of the wind against her face, tearing at her hair. It was a wonderful ride. Far ahead, she could see the new fortress rising. She veered quickly away as they came to the mainland, heading straight for the southern forest, Elysia still right with her.

They came to the trees and dismounted; laughing giddily, they hugged one another. "How very, very easy!" Elysia said, her silver eyes twinkling. *"Très facile!"*

Allora had to smile, leaning back against one of the trees. They had covered quite a distance very quickly—and they had not been stopped or even delayed. Allora felt alive and warmed with the pleasure of that fact. Bret had left his men no dire warnings regarding her—if he had, Elysia wouldn't have even been able to get her out into the courtyard.

"Easy indeed," Allora agreed, then added mournfully, "But it seems the beginnings of these excursions are always very easy. It is the endings that seem so hard as of late!"

"Nothing ill can happen. Bret is not here!" Elysia insisted, leaning against a tree as well, breathing hard from their wild race through the crisp air. She hesitated a moment, then added, "Thank you. With all my heart, thank you for all that you have endured on my behalf."

Allora nodded after a moment. "It has not all been on your behalf. I seem to find discord on my own as well!" she whispered. She looked out across the blanket of snow that shimmered in the sunlight. She couldn't see the new fortress any longer, for it sat too far back. She could just see the towers of the Far Isle, where the land sloped and rolled. The trees were behind them now, anyway, making the ride back somewhat of a maze.

"If it means anything," Elysia said very quietly, "I believe in you with all my heart. And I believe that you love my brother. I believe the stubborn ox even knows it himself sometimes, but Allora, you did fight him."

Allora started to nod, then paused, stepping forward. She could see a rider coming toward them. It seemed that he came alone, but she couldn't tell. The sun was shifting slightly in the sky, and she was glad the rider had now come; the sands would not stay dry much longer, and when the sun began to fall in earnest, it would do so quickly.

"It's David!" Elysia cried happily. She had been standing behind Elysia, and she started to walk around her, ready to wave her arm in greeting.

"Wait," Allora warned.

"But I can see him!"

"Go back, Elysia, that isn't David!"

"It must be David—"

"It is not, I'm telling you, it's Duncan. I don't think he's seen you as yet, you have to go back!"

"We'll *both* go back—"

"No! First you. He can't catch us both."

"Allora, come with me—"

"Someone may be riding with him, and if we both run,

we might both be caught. Then there would be no hope for escape."

"I forced you here; you go back!" Elysia insisted. "I won't be in any danger—"

"You don't know Duncan," Allora said. "And I do know these woods. For the love of God, Elysia, don't argue with me now. I'll buy some time—we can't run together. We could very easily both be taken then, with no prayer for help to come. Elysia, go back! Bret would *never* forgive me if anything happened to you."

"Allora, please—"

"Elysia! I am going to run as well, I promise you. But you've got to get a head start, one of us must make it back. The faster you go, the greater my own chances. I beg of you, go now!"

"I'm going!" Elysia cried, but she hadn't moved. Allora gave her a push that sent her stumbling into the snow, toward the trees where their horses waited. She gave her sister-in-law a chance to escape, staying in front of the trees on the white snow and waving as if it were David riding toward her. When the horseman came so obviously near that she could pretend to be fooled no longer, she turned swiftly and made a mad dash for her horse. She leaped atop Briar's back, rode out into the drifts of snow, and saw clearly that she had been right—it was Duncan, not David, riding hard now to accost her. She swung Briar about and slammed her knees against her mare's ribs, whispering heatedly to her, "Run! Run as you have never run before, I beg you!"

Briar was a fine mare, but was no match for Duncan's horse, and even as Allora started into a swift gallop, she heard the war stallion riding up hard on her. She leaned against Briar's back, very low, and veered into the trees, thinking to take a reckless loop.

"The trees!" Duncan shouted, and she realized that she had guessed right; he hadn't come alone.

It didn't matter. She plunged more deeply among the trees, racing hard. Briar came around a curved path, and suddenly reared up high, then fell to all four hooves again. One of her uncle's most trusted companions, white-whiskered Bruce of Willoughby, firmly blocked her path.

She spun Briar around to run again, but Duncan had come up behind her.

She reined in, staring from one of them to the other.

"Milady," Duncan said, "today you will come with me."

"Where is your brother this time?" she asked him bitterly.

"Tending his fields and flocks, like some poor, cuckolded villein!" Duncan said contemptuously. "And if he gives us trouble where you are concerned, then he, too, will pay the price of traitors."

"How dare you—"

"Thirty good men were killed or captured, lady. Thirty. Their blood rests on your hands."

"Nay, their blood is on your hands!"

"Ah, well, those who survived the battle will be your judges, lady!"

"My uncle will—"

"I am bringing you to your uncle, lady," Duncan told her with a self-satisfied sneer. "You thought to ridicule and debase me, did you, princess of the Far Isle? Well, 'twas your mistake, and you will now pay the price for all your sins."

"If I don't return immediately, there will be a horde of men out to look for me."

"That there will not, for your husband's men are divided, are they not, lady? And indeed, those who remain do not know the hills and valleys and craigs here! There is no out for you now, milady. Your wretched Norman is gone. And you will at last be made to answer for your treachery!"

He rode close to her. She tried to strike him or his horse with her reins. He reached for her, and though she struggled wildly, it was a losing effort.

"Easy there, Duncan!" old Bruce commanded. "She's still Ioin's daughter, lady of the Far Isle, and ye'll not be hurting her till we've made our judgments."

But Duncan had at last managed to wrench her from Briar onto his own horse, and as she fought against him, he gritted his teeth.

"Ioin's wildcat!" he exclaimed heatedly, and somehow

managed to tie her hands with the cord from his own tunic. "Get her horse, Bruce! Don't let that mare go running back over the sands. We need what time we can buy."

"Aye, I'll manage the horse!" Bruce replied.

Allora cried out as she was suddenly slammed against Duncan's chest. She gasped in fear, aware that Duncan was a reckless rider and was now crashing wildly among the trees—with her hands tied, there was no way for her to save herself should she fall. As the snow flew up beneath his horse's hooves, she lost her fear of Duncan for the moment, overwhelmed by her fear of falling as she teetered precariously, swaying, as they raced. She leaned back into the safety of Duncan's arms, as hateful as that was, and closed her eyes, ruing this new stupidity of hers, and wishing fervently that, her affection for her sister-in-law notwithstanding, she had told her to go jump in the ocean.

She should have run. She should have never let Elysia go alone.

But she had been so sure that she would be safer with Duncan than with Elysia. Elysia was Bret's sister, and Duncan wouldn't hesitate to hurt her. He had frightened Allora, but she had also assumed that her uncle would have the final word over Duncan's actions.

Her uncle did, so it seemed. And she was being brought to him now.

They rode deep into the hills, away from the ocean. Duncan kept up his speed until his horse was exhausted, snorting, spitting flecks of foam. He slowed his gait, and they continued.

She knew the road they followed. They were coming to the town of Stone. It was an ancient place, with great stones set in a strange cross-shaped pattern and a massive circle right in the center of the cross. The stones had fallen as if seats had been arranged for a council, and for as long as Allora could remember, the border lairds and the lairds of the Far Isle had come here to discuss matters of importance.

When they arrived, Duncan dismounted quickly and lifted her from his mount. She saw the flicker in his eyes, and wondered how long he had hated her as deeply as he did. She looked at him, then raised her chin and looked beyond him.

Her uncle sat upon the center stone, his beard grizzled, his eyes bright and hard upon her. Arrayed around him were a number of the border lairds.

Some polished armor.

Some sharpened knives and swords.

And all of them stared at her.

She walked forward, head high, standing in the center of the stones before Robert Canadys.

"What is this indignity, Uncle? Since when have you taken to sending your hounds to make a captive of your own kin?"

"Since when, Niece?" Robert echoed, standing and coming to walk around her. She followed his movement. "Since you have turned traitor, murdering your kin!" he told her savagely.

Allora shook her head. "Nay, Uncle—"

"Duncan has told me that you knew of our plan. Your husband might have been taken or killed, the isle returned to you—to us. Yet you warned the Norman bastard, and it was our good people who were slaughtered!"

"I tried to stop the killing—"

"Stop it? Tell that to Bryan Miller there, whose only son lies bleeding now, a hostage behind a Norman wall! Speak those words to old Jamie Peterson, dead and buried just an hour ago!"

She felt herself trembling. She had blamed herself for the deaths; why wouldn't these men do so?

"Uncle, nay—all of you!" she cried, turning to meet the doleful, grim, sorrowful faces that stared her way. "Remember this: I fought as long as I could!" She stared at her uncle again. "I fought, and yet was left behind, while you all disappeared into the woods. I was left with no choice but surrender. I—"

"Allora Canadys, lady of the Far Isle!" Robert thundered out in interruption. "You are accused of willfully betraying your family and people, of causing the slaughter of countless men, leaving widows and orphans and cripples! You are brought here to to be judged and punished."

"Judged and punished—" Allora began.

This time, Duncan jumped in upon her words. "She was given every chance! She could have come with me yesterday, she was warned! She could have joined with us, and she could have chosen to ride with her kin. But she raced back to him, nearly costing me my life as I fled into the forest to save my throat! She was given every chance. She chose to ride to the fortress, and to bring the savage Normans down upon us! Willfully did she kill our friends, spill the blood of kin!"

"Do you deny, girl, that you refused to come with Duncan to us yesterday?"

"I would refuse a walk of five feet with Duncan!" she lashed out.

Then she winced. She should have kept her peace regarding the man. The other lairds would not see the evil in him.

"And swear, niece, swear before God, and on your sainted father's grave, that you did not let the Norman lord know of our planned attack."

"Perhaps he learned it because of me—"

"There! She admits her treachery!" Duncan cried.

Robert leaped up to stand upon his rock. "We've laws, ancient laws! We know the sentence for traitors!"

"Aye, then, she is sentenced!" Duncan yelled.

"Let her pay the full price!" shouted one of the injured men, lying upon a litter, blood seeping from the bandage that was wrapped about his arm. It was old Andrew Canadys, a distant cousin. His face was mottled with fury and with the passion Duncan and Robert were quickly managing to whip up among the men.

"She would kill us all! Make slaves of us all to a Norman master!" Duncan continued.

Allora stared at the men surrounding her, from old Andrew on his litter to bitter Duncan, who all looked so very pleased to see her being so harshly judged.

"You are wrong," she said very quietly, and with dignity. "I deplore death and bloodshed, as did my father. The men within the fortress have followed my husband, you have seen, and they have done so because he is no Norman monster, and seeks not to slay or enslave men."

"Niece," Robert said quickly, and she realized that he had no intention of letting her speak, to sway any of those who listened, "you've been accused of the worst kind of treason: that practiced against your own people, your family. And it is your family who judges you now. The lairds have agreed on their penalty."

She looked around the ancient arena of stones once again. She was sure there had been a great deal of pressure put on these men. Duncan and Robert had spoken so passionately and persuasively against her.

One by one, grim nods were given as the men stared at her. None of them appeared happy with the judgment demanded.

And yet . . .

"Allora, as head of the family Canadys and the border lairds, I condemn you, as have these clansmen. You'll be executed upon the slope beyond the sands, there burnt upon the stake until dead, a death as so befits a traitoress!"

She gasped, unable to believe his words. "How dare you," she began softly, then her voice rose. "How dare you! You—of all men. I married this great Norman you so despise to save your life! My father died because of it—indeed, countless men have died because of it, and dishonorably! You tried to poison him and nearly killed me! *You* keep the fight going—"

"Aye! I keep the fight going!" Robert agreed, his face florid with anger as he came before her. "And I'll do so—until I've taken your Norman knight! Only one thing could save you now, Allora Canadys—his life for yours. Else you will burn at the stake!"

She wanted to strike him. With all of her heart, she wanted to strike and beat against him. After all that he had done, he still had the audacity to judge her.

But she couldn't strike. Her hands were still bound before her. She took a deep breath.

"God will judge you, Uncle!" she said very softly.

"Aye, well, you will speak with Him soon!" Robert said.

Allora smiled. Then she spat in his face, and stood tall, waiting for him to strike her in return.

He did not. He wiped his face. Even as he did so, someone suddenly cried out.

"Rider coming!"

"Just one?" Robert demanded.

"Aye—'tis David!" old Andrew told him.

And indeed, David, tall and handsome in the saddle, rode hard right into the center of the gathering. "What in God's name is going on here?"

"You've no part of this, David!" Robert said furiously.

"Indeed I have! Duncan, Andrew—Bruce! What in God's name is going on?"

Duncan stepped forward quickly, catching the reins of his brother's horse. "She's condemned, David. Allora saw fit to betray us, you must know. Now she is condemned. To death."

"Death!" David cried, astonished. He looked from Allora to Duncan and Robert, and to the men who surrounded them all, and realized that they were in earnest.

"By what right do you condemn her? She is lady of the Far Isle, she is Ioin's heiress! I will not let you—"

"The judgment is made, lad," Robert said wearily. "And you will not stop us."

"Indeed not," Duncan agreed.

"By God, but I *will* stop you—" David began.

"Take him; do so gently," Robert urged.

And Allora winced as she saw the men move in on him. In seconds he was dragged from his horse. He put up a valiant fight, but his hands were then tied behind his back as well, and he was left to stand helplessly beside Allora.

"You still cannot do this, are you daft?" he demanded.

"You watch your tongue, or you'll perish as well!" Robert warned him.

"What will you do, Robert, kill everyone?" David demanded.

"David!" Allora cried at last. "Hush, I beg of you! They will condemn you as well, don't you see? They are like lambs—and my uncle is the wolf leading them to slaughter."

"No more!" Robert cried out. And he strode to stand before her once again. "You have heard the judgment!" he announced clearly. "You made your choices; you turned upon kin, upon us, and spilled the blood of your own! Come the dawn tomorrow, you will pay the traitor's price."

"The Norman will come for her!" David said assuredly.

"The Norman rides south. But, aye!" Robert said, his eyes glowing. "The Norman may well ride for her, and thus, perhaps, burn as well. Perhaps my lady niece will even cease her treachery and send for him, that he may taste the flames for her."

"Nay, I will not!" Allora assured him.

"Then," Robert announced firmly, "come the dawn, she will burn! We'll bide the night in my manor; she can taste the sweetness of wine and bread one last time, and confess her sins, if she wishes."

He took her arm, leading her from the circle within the stones, while others began to follow behind and others to disappear into the surrounding woods and the night. Allora walked forward with her uncle, bound hard, and surrounded by those who had condemned her. They came at last to the edge of the stones, and Robert set her upon his own horse, mounting behind her. They traveled deep through the woods with a number of men following, until they came to his manor.

Men quickly dismounted from their horses and went to stand at their guard posts. Robert brought her down, and she looked back to search for David, but it seemed they had taken him elsewhere.

"Into the house, Allora."

It was not so grand a place as the keep on the Far Isle, but Robert's manor was still exceptionally fine, with beautiful carvings throughout the great hall, a handsome stairway winding to the second floor, and an abundance of good hardwood furniture strewn comfortably about. A half dozen hounds had been dozing by the fire. They rose, barking, and wagged their tails.

"Up the stairs, niece. You may be a guest this night, but you are also a prisoner, condemned."

"I have no wish to be your guest, Robert," she told him cooly. She felt numb. She still couldn't believe that the uncle she had once fought so hard to save had now condemned her to death—by flames!

"You are possessed by the bastard, and are, in truth, his strumpet! Move, girl!"

She walked up the stairs and felt his hand at her back, hurrying her along. She felt him thrust her suddenly into the darkness. He turned around then and left, slamming the door behind her. She paused, blinking against the complete darkness. "Where is my priest for confession, where the bread and wine of which you spoke?" she called out in the darkness. "Would you really so dishonor Ioin's daughter? Aren't you in the least afraid that the men you have so twisted might turn against you after all? And what of the servants and craftsmen, the simple people you surely must arm to fill your ranks of warriors, with so many lost?"

"In time, girl, in time!"

She heard a bolt sliding heavily across the door, slamming into place.

She was left in the darkness, afraid to move lest she fall. Finally she took small steps, and found that she was in a bedroom. She came at last to a pallet that lay upon the floor, and she eased herself to it and leaned against the wall. She still could not believe what was happening. Even staring into the darkness, she could not believe this. That Duncan might have abducted and raped her, aye, that he might even have slain her in his fury and hatred.

But that her own uncle would condemn her . . .

She fought a sudden rise of tears. It couldn't happen. Someone would stop him.

But there was no one. Bret was gone. If Sir Christian and Jarrett were to come, they'd leave the Far Isle undefended. Even if they came, Robert's men knew the terrain, battered and bleeding as they were. Bret's men wouldn't have the numbers to save her on open ground.

The door opened. She winced against the shaft of light that came in on her.

It was Robert himself. He brought in a tray with fresh bread and wine, and a candle burning upon it. He set the tray at her feet, and leaned forward to untie her wrists.

She stared at him, then gasped suddenly, for she had remembered something. "You cannot execute me," she told him.

"Aye, but I can. It has been judged."

"I am expecting a child. You cannot slay an innocent."

"You are as slim as a reed. It is a lie."

"It is not."

Robert reached down for her, gripped her upper arms, and drew her to her feet, close before him. "If you do carry a child, Allora, it is but a spawn of hell, and must perish along with its mother. You've one salvation, lady, and that is to give us your husband's life for your own."

She didn't try to fight his hold. "Bret has gone to York, a fact of which it seems that you are aware. Even if I wanted to give him over to you, I could not."

"There is surely some manner—"

"More treachery, Uncle?" she asked him. "Nay, milord Robert, no more! For everything that I—nay, that *we*—inflicted upon him, he has been merciful in return. You are right, Uncle. I have made my choices."

"Your father would be in tears! Surely he twists and writhes within his death shroud!"

"Indeed! To see what bitterness has done to you!"

"If you would but see reason—"

"I'll not betray Bret in any way."

"You will play the traitor only against your own people, so it seems!" Robert hissed. "Then be damned with you. With the first cock's crow in the morning, we'll hie to the appointed place and set our stake and faggots, and there, niece, to my eternal sorrow, I will watch you burn until death itself is your salvation."

He turned and left her, slamming and bolting the door once again. She sat upon the bed, cold and numbed, then picked up the chalice of wine and drank deeply; it did not help.

She stared at the candle. She watched the flame, burning and rising, yellow, gold, white. She remembered suddenly and with anguish how she had first discovered that she loved to watch the flames when she was with Bret, held by him, kept safe by him. She thought, too, of the dream that had plagued her about the fire reaching for her . . .

She brought a single finger near to the flame, and felt the searing heat when it came too close.

She drew her finger away.

She closed her eyes tightly and leaned back against the wall. The flame was so beautiful, and it promised such agony.

Aye, her uncle was right. Death would be her only salvation.

Chapter 25

❧❦❧

*E*lysia reached the keep with staggering speed, shouting for Jarrett even as she rushed through the fortress gates. She rode hard and breathless into the center of the courtyard, then dismounted from her horse, casting the reins aside, and rushed to the doorway of the keep as fast as she could manage without stumbling.

"Jarrett!" she shrieked.

He had surely heard her cry, as had half of the fortress, so it seemed, for several men were hurrying down from the parapets and towers to surround her, even as Jarrett and Sir Christian rushed together from the keep.

"What—" Jarrett began.

"We were tricked again! Duncan came and took Allora. I should have waited, but she made me come! She said that someone must be able to come for help, and it is true, we must do something—"

"Duncan took her from where?" Jarrett demanded, puzzled. Then he stiffened, his face taut with fear, fury, and denial. "Lady Elysia, you went beyond the gates—"

"Aye! I was fooled by that wretched Duncan! I thought David had sent for her, and as he has sworn a peace with us, there should have been no danger. But it was not David, and Allora saw that quickly. And if she has not come as yet, then she has not escaped."

"Dusk is falling," Sir Christian said.

Elysia looked to the sky. It was true. The night was coming on them already.

And the ocean would be racing over the sands.

"A rider!" one of the guards suddenly shouted from the

parapets. "He has paused on the mainland, and waves a banner of truce."

Jarrett went running across the courtyard to the closest steps to the parapets, leaping up them two at a time.

The ocean was already crawling over the sand. The rider had paused. He shouted with a booming voice, "Let it be known that the Lady Allora faces trial for the death of her kin. Let it be known that, if she is found guilty by those who bear the bloodstains of her sin, she will die upon the dawn tomorrow!"

"Wait!" Jarrett shouted.

But the rider turned as swift as lightning, and went tearing toward the woods again. Jarrett swore profoundly and turned, only to discover that Elysia was all but on top of him, her face whiter than the snow that littered the mainland ground.

"My lady—"

"We've got to find her."

"You'll not get near her," Sir Christian, who had joined them on the parapets, warned. "It would take us till dawn to move any kind of a strong force across the water, and there is only a skeleton guard left on the mainland—if we weaken their numbers, those left will be slain by the men they hold prisoner. We could withstand a tremendous siege here, but if we were to try to fight beyond the walls here . . ."

"What are you saying? That there is nothing to be done? That we are going to let Allora's wretched uncle execute her for yesterday's battle?" Elysia was incredulous.

"No, we are not saying that, my lady!" Jarrett snapped. "It's just that we must think—"

Elysia pushed past them both, going to the steps that led back to the courtyard. "I know what I am doing. I am riding for my brother."

"Lady, he is surely the distance to Wakefield by now—" Jarrett started to warn her.

"I don't care if he has ridden all the way to hell! I am going for him!" she shouted. Tears were stinging her eyes. She had caused this. She had been tricked, she had been such a fool! Yet the message had come from Mary, and she was certain that Mary had been fooled as well.

"Lady Elysia, wait!" Sir Christian begged. "I've men who can still walk into one of Robert's strongholds. I'll send them—"

"Fine! You send them, Sir Christian. And they'll come back just before the execution to tell us that the Lady Allora is dead!"

"Elysia!" Jarrett protested. "You were the one to lead her out there—"

"And I am going for my brother, and you'll have to put an arrow through my heart to stop me, Jarrett, do you understand?"

He stared at her, then accepted defeat. "Aye, fine. Then listen, and you, Sir Christian, as well, I beg you. Elysia, you and I will ride after Bret, with just a few men. We'll take the barge across the water just twice; we dare waste no more time. Sir Christian, you will send out your men to find out all that they can, and come the morning, you will meet Elysia and me behind the trees at the crest of the hill. With God's grace, we will have escaped Robert's men tonight and secured help."

"Aye!" Elysia cried.

"Sir Christian?" Jarrett asked when the older knight remained silent.

"I don't think that you will have any trouble escaping tonight. I think that Robert intends you to bring Bret back with you. His troops will be exhausted from riding through the day, and from night until morn again. He will expect Bret's forces to be divided. He will think it his one chance to conquer—"

"So you do not believe that he will harm his niece?" Jarrett said hopefully.

Sir Christian shook his head slowly. "Nay, I think that he *will* seek her death. And he will strive to kill Bret as well. I would even say a prayer tonight for the sweet babe who sleeps in the tower keep, for Robert wishes the Far Isle to be his, and though many of the border lairds are noble, I do so swear it, Robert holds deep sway, and is in league with men as ruthless as he is himself."

"Jarrett," Elysia cried, "come now! For the love of God, come *now!*"

*   *   *

Bret's men made a makeshift camp for the night, settling themselves and their mounts beneath the trees, seeking open copses where they could build their fires and thaw the cold from their hands.

Bret strode through the snow, trying to decide what to do. After a moment he determined that, though he could scarce afford to spare even one man, he would send a messenger to his manor house at Wakefield, for it was likely that his father would have come there to confer with him before they were to meet with others. His brothers would be with Alaric as well, he was certain, for given the magnitude of this meeting, all who were able to come would be in attendance.

He called to young Gavin, Sir Christian's son, to select a second man to go with him and make the ride throughout the night, warning him to take care that he not fall prey to bandits in the woods. Robert's men were no threat to them here, for by now they had traveled into land that Bret could call his own: land within the realm of the earldom William had granted him, even if it remained scarcely inhabited and offered little more than wood for sustenance.

"You know the north country as well as any of my own men, I am certain," Bret told Gavin.

"Aye, milord, I know the country well. And my horse is a fleet creature, accustomed to the rocky terrain. I will carry your message as quickly as I can."

"Tell my father that Damien warned me to stop, and that will be enough for him. Tell him that there is no more that I can say now, and he will still understand. See that he knows where we are, and let him know that if he wishes, I will be heartily glad of his company."

"Aye, milord!" Gavin agreed, turning quickly to do as bidden.

"Gavin!"

"Aye?" The young man paused.

"Bring Conan, the Breton, with you. He is stronger than ten oxen, and you will need him should you be set upon in the forest. I would not have you endangered, after the service you and your father have given me."

"Milord," Gavin said quietly, "you have dealt with us fairly, as was promised. It is no hardship to serve you."

Bret nodded gravely. "Thank you."

"Milord, just why are we stopping?" he asked.

Bret arched a brow. Gavin did not know Father Damien that well as yet. "I don't know exactly myself," Bret admitted. He forced something of a rueful smile to his lips. "Bring the message as I gave it to you. As I have said, my father will understand. Go now."

Gavin nodded, and was gone. Bret walked to one of the campfires that had been lit, stretching out his hands to warm them. He watched the blaze burn. He felt the uneasiness settle over him again, and he cursed aloud, suddenly wishing he had never ridden out.

But he was a nobleman who held his land from a king, and when the king summoned, a nobleman was bound to give his strength to that king. Perhaps Robert Canadys still refused to see that Bret's land came from the king of England—it didn't matter. One day Robert would have to admit defeat, Bret thought wearily. And yet he wondered if the man would ever do so.

And if he did not . . .

One day they would come to combat between them, and by God, he would rue the day, but he would slay Robert Canadys, and pray that Ioin, surely in heaven, would forgive him the deed, for surely God Himself would.

But then there was Allora . . .

He cursed again, slamming his fist against the trunk of a tree. She refused to see the evil in her uncle. What would come if and when the man lay dead at last? Would she turn away from Bret again?

He reminded himself that it was not her uncle Allora had defied him with for so many times—it was David of Edinburgh. Yet he was convinced that nothing lingered between the two, for they both denied that it was so.

And David had told Bret, before he had left the fortress to return to his own people, that he was in love with Elysia. Still, there was that closeness between his wife and the Scot that he could not touch . . .

Sweet Jesu, where will it end? he asked himself, and he

stared into the flames once again, wishing again that he had never ridden out.

He suddenly wanted Allora with him. He should have brought her, even if it had been necessary to gag her and lock her away from de Fries. He should have had her with him now, and he should have been holding her against the cold. He should have felt her touch, her warmth . . .

And instead, he had only the night.

And the occasional cry of a wolf.

At best, the barge could carry three people and three horses, and even at that small number, they had to pray that the horses didn't panic and go plunging into the sea.

Elysia didn't think she had been so frightened in all her life. She had been born the child of a noble Saxon lady, and had learned at a young age of the atrocities that had befallen England, but she was also her father's child, and she had looked back on all that happened before her birth with sadness. She couldn't blame her grandfather Harold for claiming England as his own; after all, the witan, the wise men of England, had proclaimed him king by their own choice.

And yet William had believed that the kingdom had been promised to him and was thus his to conquer by right.

It had happened before she had been born, and due to her father's place in William's court, she had lived a fair and sheltered life. The only exception being when she had been abducted in her own home by the Scots.

And David.

And with him holding her, she had never really felt herself in danger. She had been far more furious and indignant than frightened.

And now she was terrified.

Allora would have never allowed Elysia to be harmed on that long-ago ride.

And now Elysia felt with certainty that Robert would as easily slay Allora as he would any poor creature standing in his way. And if he hurt Allora now . . .

Elysia didn't think that she'd ever manage to live with the guilt of it. Yet she wasn't of a temperament to bemoan things when she still had the power to act. And she was ready to ride, as soon as the second barge, with Jarrett and two more armed and mounted knights, arrived upon the shore.

She could just see the barge coming now. She looked out into the night around them, listening intently.

No one was coming, no one was riding out to impede their progress. Perhaps Sir Christian was right; Robert Canadys wanted somebody to go for Bret.

He surely wanted to slay the lord and lady of the Far Isle in one foul deed . . .

"Jarrett, hurry!" she cried.

And without assistance from those two men who would have died to serve her, Elysia leaped up on her horse's back. "Hurry, we must hurry!" she cried.

Even as the barge beached,. Elysia kneed her horse, racing through the snow. They had a great distance to travel.

"Horsemen coming, fast and hard across the snow, milord!"

It was Etienne who gave the warning. Bret had sat down at the trunk of an old oak, his saddle blanket beneath him to keep the cold from his limbs. He had tried to sleep, but sleep had eluded him, and he had known he was waiting, yet not knowing what he waited for. He had closed his eyes, dreamed again, seen her in his dreams . . .

And longed for home.

But at Etienne's call, he was instantly upon his feet, hurrying from the hardened ground beneath the trees to the snow-covered earth beyond them. The ten men on guard this hour stood within the shadows of the trees: five archers with their bows and arrows ready, five swordsmen ready to combat any man to come upon them.

Bret lifted a hand, warning them to be steady, to wait. He looked across the white snow, the night illuminated by the glow of a half moon and dozens of stars. He narrowed his eyes. There were not many . . . Six of them, and coming fast, with no effort at any subterfuge.

He recognized the first rider, and he swore softly. "Elysia!

Will that sister of mine forever haunt me!" he swore out softly.

"She rides with Jarrett, and our own men," Etienne said beside him.

Bret strode out into the snow, ready with a quick tongue-lashing for his sister—and for Jarrett, who had apparently been willing to follow her here on this madness.

Yet if Elysia and Jarrett were here . . .

"Sweet God!" he gasped, stepping forward as Elysia reached him at last, well-cloaked against the cold in a furred, hooded cape.

She leaped down from her horse and raced to him, gripping his arms. "Thank God, you're here! Thank God, I never thought that we'd reach you, that we'd have a prayer of making it back!"

She was exhausted, shivering, collapsing in his arms. He looked over her shoulder to Jarrett, who had now dismounted as well. The anger he had been feeling for the two had swiftly been overridden by the fear that now filled his heart. He should have started back. The second Damien had spoken of unease, he should have been riding straight back . . .

But Damien hadn't known the cause of his unease. He had said to wait.

"What has happened?" Bret thundered.

"Duncan took Allora. A messenger rode to the shore when we were trapped by the tide. Allora is going to be judged for the deaths of the Scotsmen yesterday. If she is found guilty, she is to be executed tomorrow at dawn."

His fingers tightened convulsively around his sister's arms. He wanted to bellow out his rage, and yet knew that it would stand him little good.

"How in God's name did Duncan get his hands on her?" he demanded heatedly. His words were so angry; his stance so taut. And inside, it seemed that he melted like the snows beneath the sunlight. If Robert dared harm her . . . if he dared touch her, Bret would slay him. Slowly, slicing him to ribbons, ripping the skin from his frame . . .

And if he managed such an act, he would still feel the

agony inside, the hollowness. The rest of his life would be filled with the emptiness, the void, the anguish. She would be gone. Vivid life, emerald eyes, pastel beauty. Her smile, her laugh, her whisper, the way she entreated him to believe her, the valor with which she was determined always to make him understand . . .

"How did Duncan get her?" he repeated.

"It was my fault," Elysia told him. "She thought that David sent for her—"

"That wretched bastard. Would that I had slain him when I'd had the chance!"

"No, Bret, you don't understand. She had tried to reach David—"

"Pray, tell me no more!"

"For me!" Elysia insisted.

Bret paused, and stared at his sister. They'd gathered quite an audience around them—the men who had ridden with Jarrett and Etienne, and the men who had ridden with him: those who had been on guard, and those who had quickly awakened and gathered their arms at the possible approach of danger.

"Perhaps I should hear more," Bret said, furiously. Then he shook his head. "Nay, we dare not waste the time; we must mount and ride hard, prepared for battle."

Elysia stood away from Bret, turning quickly to reach her horse again. Bret helped his sister up on her mount. When she took the reins, she found his eyes on her, and they were like ice. "It's a long ride, Elysia. I want the truth from you as we make it, and if any ill befalls my wife . . ." His voice trailed away and he swallowed down his bitterness and anger once again. They had to hurry. Time was everything. He had to find out exactly what Robert Canadys planned before the dawn could break.

He turned, assuming that one of his men had resaddled Ajax and brought the horse forward.

Ajax was indeed ready to ride. But it was Father Damien who brought the mount forward.

"Time is of the essence, my lord," Damien said.

Bret nodded, took the reins from Father Damien, and leaped atop Ajax. He started out at the head of the party, then turned to look back at the ten feet between him and his sister.

"Ride with me, Elysia!" he commanded.

She bit her lip and hurried forward. She didn't think that she could face his wrath. Yet . . .

Allora might well meet some awful death. While Elysia remained afraid of her brother's anger.

And feared for David's life! she reminded herself.

But when she brought her gelding up alongside her brother's war stallion, she was ready to speak. She met his eyes evenly. "I was very wrong," she told him, her chin high. "I was the one who had to reach David. And so I used your wife to do it for me."

"And why was it so necessary that you reach the Scotsman?" Bret demanded.

She had tried valiantly to keep her eyes locked with her brother's. They fell.

"I am expecting his child," she said very softly.

"You're what?" Bret thundered.

Elysia was certain that every man riding behind them must have heard them. "I'm expecting a child—his!" she repeated quietly.

"By all the saints! I had the man imprisoned! He was locked in my tower, and you . . ."

"Aye!" Elysia said quickly. Heat coursed through her. "It wasn't his fault—"

"Surely not! You held a knife to his throat!"

"I was in love with him. Love. It's an emotion I wonder if you comprehend at times!" she cried out.

Bret's jaw set firmly, and he stared straight ahead.

"Please . . ." she whispered. "Don't tell Father."

"Elysia, you were in my care."

"Please, I beg of you."

"At this moment," he said grimly, "I cannot be assured that I will survive to tell our father anything. Though I do swear to you, by God, I will take Robert Canadys to the grave with me!"

Elysia shivered miserably. She watched her brother. She didn't believe that she had ever seen him so darkly dangerous, and she bit her lip. She had been wrong to accuse him of not knowing what love was. He loved Allora. She had become his life, and he turned from her only when he was forced to see that her loyalties remained divided. He was bitter at times, furious at times . . .

But he loved her.

And Elysia was suddenly certain herself that he would not want to survive if Allora did not.

"Bret—?" she said softly.

"What is it, Elysia?" he responded, glancing her way, and then tears burned her eyes for she realized too late that he would not have condemned her for the child she carried; he might have helped her, with far better results. But he didn't say these things; she just knew them. Still, the words he did say were both reassuring—and chilling.

"I'll not let that bastard harm a hair on her head!" he swore. "By God, I will have my wife back, and come what may, I will have that bastard's throat!"

They rode in silence then.

They had a long distance to go.

And very little time in which to ride that distance.

Darkness still reigned when they came through the forest trail and approached the craggy hills.

Dawn itself was not far off.

For the last miles, Bret had ridden harder and harder, giving no heed to animals or men. He watched the moon ride across the sky and fall low within it, and he forced them onward, racing the dawn.

Bret reined in on Ajax as he heard the screech of an owl that was not really the cry of a bird. He dismounted, his men still and silent behind him.

Then they saw a single man coming their way, and Bret saw that it was Timothy, the reeve, running through the snow on foot, keeping cover within the trees. He was breathless when he came to Bret.

"Dear God, hurry, milord, hurry! They condemned her to death last night—by burning. She is already staked upon the hill just beyond the mainland fortress. Sir Christian is in the woods with the entire garrison from the fortress, yet he is desperate, for though he would willingly risk his own life and that of every man, Norman and Scot, in his command, he fears that his appearance will only cause them to light the fire, and that he will not be able to reach Allora before—before she is consumed by the flame. And my lord, I must tell you that Sir Christian's spies discovered—"

"Timothy, for the love of God, we have no time, tell me what you know!"

"She told her uncle that she was expecting a child. He either refused to believe her—or did not care. Other men would wait until the innocent bairn were come into the world first, but I don't think that Robert Canadys wants another child born, another of his brother's heirs to claim the Far Isle."

"Get to the rear, Timothy. Take my sister with you, well behind the armed men." He turned in his saddle, so desperate he was ready to leap from Ajax and run the distance to his wife—yet he dared not chance her life any more than Sir Christian did.

He couldn't even take the time to rage before God and damn Robert Canadys for the murder of his unborn babe.

He called out sharply, his voice echoing in the chill morning air. "Keep within the forest until we are all abreast to hold a battle line!" he commanded. "Let no one be seen until I am ready. We will join with the men from the fortress, and I pray you all, let God and justice be our right!"

He raised his sword high.

Down the line, swords rose to the sky in a silent salute.

He turned again then, and rode hard across the valley and up the hill, and into the woods there. A soft cry welcomed his coming, and he saw Sir Christian within a copse of hemlocks, waiting for him. "Thank God in His infinite wisdom and mercy!" Sir Christian breathed.

"Have they seen you?" Bret demanded.

"Not as yet." Even as he spoke, he looked around him. "The light is coming," he said quickly.

Indeed, day was dawning. Beautiful colors stretched across the snow-covered hill. The white blanketing was now touched with shades of pink and crimson and gold . . .

Bret lifted his sword, then reached to his saddle pommel for his battle helmet and set it firmly upon his head. He lifted his sword again, his motion a command for his men to fan out within the trees, to form their line.

He stroked his sword in a whish across the sky.

They urged their mounts forward, stepping from the trees.

And then he saw her. Allora. Bound to a stake . . .

Beneath the touch of dawn's first sunrays, her hair shimmered with golden light. Her chin was high, he thought, and he damned her even as he thought he would die if he could not reach her. She would have defied Robert again and again, she wouldn't have pleaded for mercy from him, and . . .

Too late, she had discovered her uncle's absolute ruthlessness.

Rage and fear built and spilled within him. She was so young, so innocent, so beautiful there, dressed in white, like the snow, that golden hair tossed by the breeze, swept around her beautiful face. And Robert Canadys meant to burn her, his own blood, slay her in a horrid and gruesome fashion, destroying all that beauty, snuffing out life . . .

And taking, as well, the innocent life of the child she now carried . . .

She was looking at him. They were so far away, and he couldn't see her eyes, but she looked his way, and he knew that she saw him, and he thought that she smiled. Perhaps she didn't believe that she could be rescued, that no one could beat the flames . . .

Yet she knew that he had come. And a smile touched her beautiful features . . .

"*He's come!*" someone shouted, and he saw that the men aligned around the stake were pointing at his well-armed line, that they had realized he had come.

Had they been awaiting him?

Were they ready for a pitched battle?

"Light the fire!" came a harsh command.

Bret knew the voice; knew the hated voice. It was Robert Canadys. Robert Canadys, glad that he was there, glad that he would see the carnage.

And even as they faced one another across the snow-covered slope, Robert Canadys rode forward, toward the stake, and snatched up one of the burning torches.

And set it to the kindling at Allora's fair feet.

Part II

...and the End

Chapter 26

Sweet God! But she had not imagined him, Allora realized, nor had it been any play of memory upon her.

Bret had come.

He could not be there . . .

But was.

Yet now, even as she saw him, Ajax throwing great bursts of mist from his nostrils as he breathed against the cold morning air, Bret in his stag-horned helmet, glittering beneath the sun, so powerful and proud a force . . .

Even as she saw him, she smelled the deep, acrid scent of fire . . .

She twisted her head. Robert! Robert Canadys had come forward on his horse to set the flame!

Yet even as the kindling caught and began to burn, Allora saw movement. Bret. Alone upon Ajax. The sun still glimmering down upon him . . .

Smoke was rising quickly all around her. Even against the chill of the morning air, she felt the heat, reaching out, touching her. She looked down, and saw the flames growing. Gold, red, orange . . .

Her eyes watered. Yet she stared through the mist, and it seemed he covered the distance in an elegant slow motion. She could barely breathe. She was losing consciousness. She would waken, she knew, when the flame touched her flesh . . .

"He's coming!" someone shouted.

Aye, it was through a mist, but she could see him. He had broken from the line, and rode with his sword sweeping the air in a flash of silver defiance. Closer and closer. Ajax leaped through the stretches of snow, the mist still streaming from his nostrils, as if he were some great winged dragon out of a fairy tale, coming, riding against the wind, coming ever nearer and nearer . . .

He could not make it. He could not. Not before the flame came to touch her . . .

"Stop him!"

She heard the words as if from a distance, yet they were spoken by her uncle, not far behind her. One mounted man ventured out.

And met his death upon that swirling sword, barely halting Bret's swift ride across the snow.

"Stop him!" Robert Canadys bellowed again.

Yet no one moved. Bret let out his shattering battle cry. It seemed as if they had all become as bound to the earth as Allora was to her stake, or perhaps they simply did not believe that one man would cry out with such a rage and attempt to ride through scores of armed warriors and directly into the flame.

She could almost see him now. Almost see the color of his eyes beneath his helmet. She could see the magenta of his mantle, flying behind him. The silver mesh of his mail, shining beneath the sun. She could see flecks of foam, spitting from Ajax's mouth. She could almost feel the mist of his breath as he rode down upon her.

The giant war-horse came crashing straight up the dais, heedless of the burning kindling, of the flames that even now began to shoot upward, and which would, in seconds, catch hold of the stake itself, and consume all within its fury. She saw the fierce blue eyes beneath the helm, and saw his sword rise and fall, slicing with razor-sharp ease through the ropes that bound her. She had so little strength. She could barely move her limbs.

"Up!" he roared to her.

She found strength and reached for the hand he offered her. He pulled her atop Ajax, and the great horse crashed back down the now-flaming dais once again and began a wild gallop back across the drifts of snow.

"Archers!" she heard her uncle roar as huge drifts of snow were plowed up by Ajax's hooves and sent flying behind them in blinding flurries. She rode in front of Bret, his mail-clad chest protecting her. She looked back, gasping as she saw the rain of arrows that was now cascading down upon them.

Miraculously, the first volley missed them and the horse. And when Robert shouted again, they had come to the protection of the trees, and the arrows fell short of them.

Ajax whirled around.

Allora saw the stake where she had been bound just seconds ago.

It was fiercely ablaze. Flames, blue, gold, crimson, wrapped around it, stretching high to the pink-streaked blue of the morning sky. Her breath caught; she shivered fiercely. In such an inferno, she would be dead already, spared swiftly from the agony that would have consumed her. If he hadn't come, if he hadn't come . . .

But he had come. Somehow he had arrived, and now, as they came within the line of his men, a great cheering went up among them. She wanted to turn and bury herself in the broad mail-clad chest at her back. She was close to tears; she wanted to thank him, to tell him that she loved him, that he had saved her life, that she would make up to him the tempest and travesty of all that had been . . .

But she had no chance. Even as the men shouted, Bret's voice rang above the cacophony. "Take care, for we may well be attacked!"

Allora had no opportunity to say anything at all. Bret's hands were strong upon her as he lifted her again, and she was thrust down quickly from his saddle. Then she heard the wild shouts as Robert's men suddenly surged forward. Bret still wore his helmet and she could see nothing of his features as he harshly commanded her, "Get back, lady! Jarrett, take her!"

"Aye, my lord!"

She was swept up again by strong arms, and found herself seated now on Jarrett's bay steed, being taken briskly among the trees.

She looked back as best she could.

The Normans let out a fierce sound with their own battle cries. Bret, at the fore, went tearing up the snow-covered hill to meet her uncle's wild forces, rushing to meet them. She cried out, and Jarrett grimly moved deeper into the trees, keeping her from harm's way. In the shadowed depths of the forest, Allora could see that other riders waited; one of them was a woman. Elysia. She would have pressed from Jarrett and made her way to her sister-in-law, except that she heard another roar as men met in hand-to-hand battle, and she told Jarrett, "Please! I have to see what is happening."

Men collided in bloody combat, Scotsmen unseating Norman knights, wickedly wielded Norman swords slashing down all that stood in their way. She saw Bret, still atop Ajax, deep in the center of the melee. She gasped as he took a blow to his back, but his mail held its purpose well, and he spun around, sword raised upon his attacker.

"Oh, Jesu!" she whispered, looking away. Then she suddenly heard a new rush and roar of cries coming from the trail to the east, leading from the southern forest.

"By God!" Jarrett gasped. "By God!"

"What, what?" Allora shrieked, twisting in his protective hold, finding that no matter what her fear and pain, she could not hide from the bloodshed. She looked back to where new battle cries and the clink and clash of steel filled the air. There were more men. Normans, she thought fleetingly. Dressed in well-tended mail, armed with glittering swords, riding huge, majestic war-horses. "Who . . . ?" she whispered.

"Why 'tis Alaric, Count d'Anlou, Earl of Haselford!" Jarrett said with great pleasure, and she quickly saw why. Bret's sword rose high on the air in a swinging motion, and his forces regathered and rode to meet his father's in a triangular pattern, one she was certain they had practiced before; it set a squeezing stranglehold upon her uncle's men. Scotsmen broke and ran, horses and men wildly reeling over the hill and into the woods beyond.

There the Normans stopped their pursuit, reining in. She saw her husband ride forward, clasping hands with a tall, helmeted man who sat in chain armor similar to Bret's own atop a pitch-black stallion.

They spoke a moment, then started riding back.

But as they did so, there came a cry from the trees through which Robert's men had so recently escaped. Allora shielded her eyes against the bright rays of the sun now raining down. A man without armor was racing back onto the field. No armor, and a tawny head of hair that glistened in the burnished sun. A man heavily collapsed over his horse's neck.

David.

He toppled still lower as his horse reached the mounted men, and then he fell to the ground. The tunic he wore beneath a forest-green mantle was white, and even at her distance, Allora could see that blood seeped rapidly upon the white of his tunic, and spilled upon the snow.

"No!" Allora gasped in anguish and astonishment. Was he dead? Dear God, no; was he injured? How could he be, how could he have fought when his hands had been tied behind his back when the melee had broken out?

Then Robert appeared from among the trees, pausing there upon his horse, his own sword high in the air.

"Murderer!" he roared to Bret. "You've murdered Ioin, and now David! No man will rest until you are dead, Norman bastard!"

As Allora watched, Bret slammed his heels against Ajax's body, ready to give chase.

"No!" Allora shrieked, twisting wildly in the saddle to plead with the knight ordered to keep her from the danger. "Jarrett, let me go! Quickly!"

Jarrett was not prepared for her shove. She wasn't sure if he would have listened to her or not, but her sudden thrust upon his chest sent him spilling from the horse, and she didn't have the time to apologize. She slammed her heels against the horse's ribs, flicking her reins sharply over its neck, and began to thunder across the hill.

She had been ready to ride like the wind to David's side, yet now she dared not pause to see if her good friend lived.

Her husband might be racing toward his own death . . .

She passed the still-burning stake where she had so nearly perished, and plunged past the men who now grouped around David's body upon the ground.

She caught up with Bret just as he had moved into the shadows of the trees, where he had reined in to try to ascertain in which direction Robert would have ridden after he had shouted out his accusations.

"Robert! Robert Canadys!" Bret roared. "If you'd fight me, man, then do it!"

"Bret!" Allora shrieked. "Leave it! Don't—"

"Allora!" he cried angrily, and she winced. He had saved her life; she had wanted so badly just to throw her arms around him and forget the fear, to drown in the warmth and security of his touch. Now he was angry.

Now he was untouchable, appearing so indomitable and distant, the ultimate warrior.

He rode back to her swiftly, chastising her. "Little idiot! Would you risk yourself and the child once again by riding into these woods where your uncle's men reign? I gave you to Jarrett for safety—"

She didn't mean to lose her temper, and she certainly didn't mean to provoke him, but she had been far more frightened for him then than she had been for herself. "You're the fool, my lord!" she told him quickly. "Robert wants you to follow him, alone, and they can all set upon you. He will not meet you in any fair fight. Don't you see?"

There was a rustling in the trees as a pitch-black stallion left its spot within their shadows to step forward. She saw the man Jarrett had pointed out to her as Alaric d'Anlou seated tall upon it, his helmet now stripped from his head, his handsome, dignified features bared now to her inspection as she stared at him.

"He'd not be alone, my lady," Alaric assured her with a curve of his lip which reminded her very much of the way her husband smiled. In fact, it seemed Bret was very similar to his father in many ways. Alaric was older, of course; silver lightened the darkness of his hair and his eyes were a silver-gray like Elysia's. Yet Bret resembled his father greatly in the ruggedly handsome contours of his face. They moved alike and their voices sounded much alike.

"Allora, these are rather tempestuous circumstances, but I would give you my father, Alaric. Father, my wife, Allora."

"And you are still getting on just marvelously well, so it appears," Alaric said, and seemed amused. "My lady daughter, it is a great pleasure to meet you at last. I knew your father, and rue his passing."

"My lord Alaric!" Allora murmured swiftly. She inclined her head to Alaric d'Anlou, and felt the strangest trembling sweep down her spine. Once upon a time she had hated all things—and people—Norman with such a passionate determination. This was the man who had sailed with William the Conqueror, and had subdued a nation in his service. And yet she realized that she was concerned she had met him under such horrible circumstances, and she found herself oddly warmed to realize that he had ridden here on her behalf. For his son, of course. But for her as well. And the support of his troops might have saved them many lives that day.

What did it matter? She was alive, Bret was alive—

"David!" she cried suddenly. She stared at Bret, stricken. There was still so much to be said. She hadn't meant to argue . . .

She had longed to apologize, to thank him, to speak the truth no matter what the cost. But she could not. Not now. She loved her husband, she would risk anything for him; but David had been the one friend to stay by her side throughout everything, and she would not forget him now.

"Bret, David!" she whispered again.

She slammed her heels against the poor exhausted horse once again and went plunging back out to where there was now a tight circle around the fallen man. Allora forgot both Bret and his father as she leaped down from her mount, making her way through to David. She fell to her knees, grateful to see that Father Damien was already there, and that David's tunic had been ripped away. Father Damien was pressing hard upon the wound to stop the bleeding.

"He's not dead?" she cried.

Father Damien shook his head. "Not yet. His would-be murderer was hasty!" He looked at her, seeing the white linen of her gown. "Lady, I need strips, quickly," he told her. She understood him instantly and ripped the fur from her hem, then began to make ragged bandages from the linen beneath the fur.

"We've got to move him as gently as possible," Father Damien called. "We'll need a litter for him, and fast, for the snow is cold and he must be warmed soon!"

Bret's men were swift; a litter was hastily constructed from two mantles and two spear shafts. Even as Damien ordered him carefully lifted upon it, a new cry broke loud and high on the air.

"My God, no, my God!"

Elysia. Apparently, she had just ventured from the depths of the forest where she had been commanded to wait, only now to realize what had happened. She leaped down from her horse as Allora had done, pitched down upon her knees before the silent, bleeding man.

"Oh, my God!" she said again, reaching for his hand. "You mustn't die, you mustn't—"

"Elysia!"

The word was gentle; there was a sudden clamp on her shoulder. Allora looked across the litter to see that Alaric stood behind his daughter. "It seems you wish him well. Give Father Damien a chance then to let him live."

Elysia rose slowly, her beautiful face still stricken. Her eyes met Allora's, then she turned into her father's arms, sobbing. Allora bit her lower lip, looking past them both to see that Bret remained seated upon Ajax now, and was staring at her as well.

"Bring him back carefully!" he commanded. Several men started to bear the litter. Jarrett, huffing and puffing from his run across the field in his mail, came wheezing to a halt before Bret. "My lord, I'm sorry, I—"

"Jarrett, trust me, I am aware that she is wily. Allora, return the man's horse. Come to me."

Jarrett's mount remained standing where she had left it. Allora went for the horse, returning it in silence. Trembling, she lowered her head and quickly walked to Ajax, and Bret reached down to sweep her up before him.

As quickly as they dared with the injured man, they covered the distance from the battlefield and across the mainland where the new fortress rose and across the sands to reach the Far Isle.

Allora stared up at the high walls as they entered. She had thought she might never see her home again. Yet she lived; Bret had managed the most incredible rescue, and yet . . .

David might well lay dying now.

When they entered the courtyard, she eased herself from Bret's hold, rushing forward to offer Father Damien whatever help she could. Elysia was at her elbow, and together they followed as he was brought into the keep hall, and no farther, for Father Damien warned softly that they had to treat David right where he lay first, and stop the flow of blood. Oddly enough, he ordered snow, and the household serfs—now gathered around them—quickly and silently dispersed to do as they were bidden.

"The cold will congeal the blood, while the man himself needs to be warmed," Father Damien explained, then he told Allora, "The wound must be sewn." She leaped up herself to supply him with needle and thread, and then Damien looked at her again. "Have you green moss, from inland rivers?" he asked, and she nodded quickly, for the remedy was one they had used often enough themselves, and she supplied him with all that he needed from the earthern jars kept in the kitchen.

Elysia, pale and subdued, sat at Father Damien's side, applying pressure where he told her, following his every command in silence.

Allora saw that Father Damien had stopped the bleeding with both pressure and his usage of the cold snow; when he was done, he sewed gaping flesh together and packed it well with the green moss she had brought him, carefully wrapping the whole of it. Then he sat back.

"Now?" Allora whispered.

"Now, we wait. But he is young and strong. He stands a good chance, I think. The bleeding has stopped. Is there a room where he can be taken?"

"Mine, just up the first flight," Elysia said. She moistened her lips, looking across the hall to where her father and brother stood by the fire. "I can move in with Lilith," she said quickly.

Then David's eyes suddenly opened. He blinked, then focused upon Elysia. His lips even seemed to curl in a smile. "Elysia," he said clearly, though his voice was weak. "Elysia!" he repeated her name, and that was all.

Kneeling beside him now, Elysia cried out and clasped his hand. It seemed the pale young man smiled again; then his eyes closed.

"My God—" Elysia gasped.

"He is unconscious again; he lives still," Father Damien assured her.

Bret, who had remained by the mantel, trusting in Father Damien's abilities, came striding across the room then. He stooped down, gently taking his sister's hand. "Elysia," he said firmly, "you must now leave him be. Let him rest. Pray, and wait."

Alaric d'Anlou, who had waited by the fire with his son, quietly conversing with him, came to Elysia next, setting his hand upon her shoulder once again, looking down at the white and silent David. "Ah, daughter! How I remember your anger against this man! Yet it seems in my absence that things have changed. Once you wanted me to come self-righteously to the border and slay this young man. Which is it now, daughter? I assume that I am not to finish him off. Do we pray that he lives, so that I might summon your mother for a wedding?"

"Oh, Father!" she whispered, and leaped up and turned into his arms, crying softly.

Father Damien was already ordering men to take David as gently as they might and with the gravest care to the room up the steps. Elysia then turned from her father, saying something softly to her brother. Bret lowered his head close to his sister's.

Allora suddenly felt as if she were the stranger in the house. The three heads were so close: father, daughter, and son, bound in so many ways, their closeness within the family, the caring, so very visible. It was something she hadn't known in a long time. Her father had loved her—but now Robert had made a mockery of her family to her, and Allora was surprised by the sudden pain that seemed to tear into her heart.

Then she heard a lusty wail from up the steps and fierce tears stung her eyes even as her breasts seemed to swell at the cry of her daughter.

Brianna. Allora had all that she could really ask from life; she did have a family, she did have love.

She raced up the stairs two at a time, and found her daughter waking from a nap in a temper, fists flying, face red. Allora scooped her up, holding the babe close, inhaling the sweet clean scent of her and shaking anew.

Brianna fell silent at her mother's crooning words, then began to press her little fists against Allora's chest, seeking nourishment.

The door burst open suddenly. Allora spun around, but found it was only Mary.

"Oh, Allora!" Mary cried, rushing forward. "I was tricked, we were all tricked. No evil was intended by anyone other than Duncan and—and your uncle. Oh, dear lady, we were so frightened . . ." Great tears welled in Mary's eyes.

"It's all right," Allora said softly. "It's all right. I'm well." She carried Brianna with her and gave Mary a one-handed but strong hug. "It's all right!" she whispered again.

"We tended Brianna with the greatest fear!" Mary told her. "She ate bread and cheese and mashed apple, she drank goat's milk; she did so very well, and yet she knows when you are gone! She cries, and none of us can soothe her."

"I'm here now, back with her!" Allora said smiling. She walked back to the fire, sat in a chair before the hearth, and fed her daughter. She sat in silence, suddenly overwhelmed by the fact that she was alive and able to hold Brianna again. She was so absorbed with holding her babe that she forgot for a moment she wasn't alone.

Brianna finished with her meal, smiled lazily, and burped with no thought of finesse. Allora turned, her mouth opening to speak with Mary again. But they were not alone. Bret had come into the room. He stood in silence, just inside the doorway at Mary's side, watching Allora. Mary came forward then, instinctively murmuring, "Let me take her for you, milady." She quickly swept Brianna from her mother's arms and quietly slipped from the room.

Neither of them was really aware of Mary's departure. They did not take their eyes from one another.

"So, milady, I must remember from now on that, should I leave, for your own protection you must be locked in a tower. You did leave the fortress willingly, so I understand from Jarrett. In fact, the poor fellow is suffering mightily. You and Elysia wound him quite easily around your little fingers, and to add insult to injury, you then stole his horse!"

"I—I meant him no ill. I . . ." Her words trailed away.

"I know. My sister decided a little belatedly to confess."

"Then you know—"

He nodded. "That Elysia will bear David's child? Aye. And I am equally aware that she loves him very much. Before he left from his stay here, he had convinced me rather passionately that he loved her. It seems that my father has no objection to the marriage, even though he is unaware as yet as to why a great deal of haste will be in order—as long as the young Scot survives."

"He must survive!" Allora whispered. "You must understand why. He is like my father. He . . ." She paused, and felt the fire of his eyes upon her again. He'd risked so much for her, and everything had seemed such a tempest since, and she hadn't said so much as a simple thank-you for the fact that he had ridden into the threat of an inferno for her.

Allora couldn't read the emotion in Bret's eyes. He stood as tall and stern as ever, his helmet shed but his glittering mail still upon the breadth of his chest. She didn't know what his feelings were for her at that moment, but suddenly, she didn't care. He had saved her. Perhaps he had saved her for honor, and perhaps he had even saved her because of the babe she carried. She didn't know, and it didn't matter. She let out a strangled cry and raced across the room, throwing herself into his arms.

He clasped her up, crushing her against his chest. Through the chain mail she could feel the pounding of his heart. She whispered, "Dear God, Bret! Thank you, thank you for my life. I'm so sorry that I am so slow to speak these words, and I—" She broke off painfully, looking up, slipping from the tightness of his hold to stand upon her own feet, but still within his arms. "I had to care for David, though I am so glad you know your sister loves him now; but Bret, he risked his own life for me as well. He stood against Robert and Duncan, and he has never asked anything from me in return."

"I know," he said.

"I didn't mean to be ungrateful—"

"I know," he said again.

"Bret—"

"I have to speak too," he told her, smoothing back a wild gold lock of her hair. "I want you to know that I didn't try to kill David; I was not the one who wounded him. I don't know if Robert stabbed David himself, or if he simply took advantage of someone else's deed. Your uncle rode through the trees to cry out that I was his murderer. I never touched David, I know that I did not. Things are wild and hectic in the midst of battle; yet I have fought your fine young Scotsman before, and I swear it, I did no harm to him today. I would not have slain the father of my sister's babe no matter what my differences were with him; and I *had* no differences with the man, for he had sworn an oath of fealty to me."

She stared up at him. "But—but I know that you did not harm him. Robert did accuse you of the deed, certain that everyone would turn against you if they thought you had slain David. Bret, David tried very hard to fight for me. They made a prisoner of him, too. They might well have condemned him on their own, at another of their trials. Robert really meant to hurt you, Bret. I think it has become an obsession with him. He wants you dead. Surely, you know that—"

"I know it!" he said very softly, the blue of his eyes burning into hers. "I did not know if you believed enough in me to know it yourself."

She moistened her lips. "Aye, my lord! You rode through flames, and faced a hundred men alone to sweep me from the promise of hell's own inferno. I never thought that you could come. Then I wondered if—after everything—I would be worth saving to you. I swear that I did not mean to go against you again, and still I had. Yet I could not help but pray . . . I am your wife. You are very proud, and very possessive. Perhaps, if it were possible, you would come for those reasons. Perhaps you would come because of the child I am carrying now. I prayed, but could not believe, and then suddenly . . ." She broke off, trembling so that she could not speak. "Suddenly . . . you were there!" she whispered, and she felt tears trickling down her cheeks.

"Aye, lady, aye!" he cried, and swept her up into his arms, carrying her to sit upon the bed, and there to hold her close and tenderly within his arms, rocking slightly. "Aye, milady, I came because I am proud, because you are my wife. And I came because of our child, and because I am possessive, and because I will not be bested by Robert in any way. But most of all, milady, I came because I could not imagine life without you, sleeping without the anticipation of having your golden hair tangled all around me. Without your smile, without the entreaty in your eyes when you plead a case with me. I could not imagine life without holding you through the night, making love, lying together, living together. Indeed, my lady, I came because I love you, and I could not bear life without you."

Allora gasped softly, wound her arms around his neck, and pressed her lips to his, finding all the passion and fever and sweet wildfire of his words within his lips. She held fast to him, and when his lips parted in return she whispered to him again and again.

"Oh, Bret! Oh, Bret. Oh, my lord, I do love you. Time leaped while I was bound to that stake, and yet it seemed that my life passed before me. And I thought of us . . . and everything, and I thought of how I loved Brianna, and the new babe I carry. I thought of the sun, the fields in spring, the wildness of the wind, the hills covered with summer flowers, and still I knew, that what I loved most, what I would miss above all, what I suffered to leave—was you."

"Allora . . ." he breathed very softly. "I swore that I would not love you! For you are like Robert Canadys in a way—"

"Nay!"

"You have his reckless passion, yet in you, Allora, it is a refusal to ever concede or back down when you feel that you are battling in a righteous fight. I feared your passion, even as I admired it. You were always so damned stubborn—and defiant."

"I did not mean to be!" she declared, then admitted, "Well, perhaps at the very first, but not after a while."

He smiled, then eased her back onto the bed. He kissed her lips, then rose, shedding first his mantle and mail, then the tunic and shirt beneath them. He sat upon the bed again, slipping from his boots, then leaned over to catch her lips once again.

"I am half burnt and half frozen, my lord," she warned him as his mouth left hers. "Quite disheveled."

"Ah, but I have been burnt and frozen as well, and am more than quite disheveled. And I care not. All that I do care about is this wretched desire to hold you again, to touch you, taste you, drink of you, love you . . ."

She needed to hear no more. She had no protest, nor did she desire one. He crawled upon the bed, palm capturing her cheek, one leg cast lightly over her hips. "I died a thousand deaths, seeing you upon that stake."

She smiled. "And I felt life again, the moment I saw you come forward upon Ajax."

He kissed her, lips just touching hers, something almost like reverence in their tenderness. But the passion of the kiss deepened, his tongue stroked deeply within her, and the sweet pervading heat of desire began to burn inside her. Still he kissed her, and her fingers twined within the hair at his nape, stroked his shoulders, moved down his back. She stopped, lifting her lips from his, rising to look over his shoulder. A black-and-blue bruise had formed in the center of his spine, and she cried out, thinking that the bruise must be where the arrow might have pierced him today had it not been for his armor.

"You're injured—"

"I'm not."

"It must hurt—"

"Soothe it then, my love, with a kiss," he commanded, grinning. She bit her lip, then pushed him from her to let him fall flat upon his stomach. Kneeling over him, she ran her fingers tenderly over the hard-muscled structure of his back, and then pressed a kiss that was nothing more than a breath against the bruise. But she let her lips wander upward, softly caressing spine and shoulders with her kiss, then following the length of it downward once again, her fingers easing the waistband of his chausses to tease the flesh there.

"Is it better?" she whispered.

A groan was her reply. And then he turned with sudden fierceness and she found herself embraced within the heady capture of his arms, her lips and tongue passionately entwined with all the heat and fever of his. His fingers were upon her gown, tearing at the laces, ripping fabric in their haste.

She stared into his eyes as he gave up and with a groan continued to rip the soft white tunic from her body.

"I would have *obediently* removed it for you," she teased.

He shrugged, his lips curving into a slow smile. "But it was ripped already," he whispered, and with a sharp tear, he managed at last to split the fabric of her clothing to her ankles, and when he did, the length of him crushed against hers, as did his mouth, no longer teasing . . .

Yet even as his hands raked over the length of her, kneading, touching, arousing with a fervor, his whisper found her ear, and his words were sweet. "Dear God, but I would brave a thousand fires to have you so . . ."

His kiss touched her throat, her flesh. Her arms wrapped around him. In seconds he had dislodged his chausses, and sank deeply into her until she thought she could take no more, until she could know no sweeter contact of fulfillment, and then he began to move. He had made love so tenderly at first. Now the winds rose, so it seemed, and his lovemaking was pure fire and passion, both possessive and giving. Her ankles wrapped around his buttocks, arms around his shoulders, and she felt the power of those winds, lifting her, bringing her ever closer to the sweet explosion of ecstasy. And even as she went flying ever higher, she suddenly discovered the richest pleasure of all. For just as the honey-sweet moment of climax burst within her, she heard the gentle whisper of his words against her ear once more.

"Dear God, Allora, but I love you, I love you, I love you, I love you . . ."

And all of the world exploded into a shimmering rain of silver-and-gold splendor.

They had everything, she realized. Everything between them. Hunger, longing, love . . . and at long last, peace.

Yet even as the thought seized her and she trembled in the aftermath of their tumultuous union, she curled closer to him, suddenly needing more than ever to be held.

For she was uneasy. Indeed, they had everything. Love, and life. And peace between them.

But the world they lived in was not at peace at all. And she was suddenly very, very afraid.

"What is it, my love?"

"Nothing," she lied. "Just hold me. Please, hold me. Don't leave me."

"I'll not," he told her.

And so they lay together, entwined, his arms tightly around her. Allora sighed deeply, and, after a while, fell asleep.

They had neither of them had any sleep, Bret thought. And his wife had now closed her eyes—and dozed upon his shoulder. For a long time he lay still, holding her so, thanking God that he was able to do so.

Then he heard a light tapping at the door, and he sighed. Allora needed to rest. She had surely not slept at all the night before, awaiting her own execution. And she was expecting a child. She must be exhausted, and he didn't want her disturbed.

But David was lying within the house, fighting for his life. Alaric had come with his men, riding hard to be at his son's side when he hadn't even known the danger to be faced. And someone was trying to summon him, even now.

He eased her from his shoulder and rose, dressing quickly and silently.

Then he strode noiselessly to the door.

Before he opened it, he turned back and stared at his sleeping wife, feeling a surge of protectiveness and warmth—and love—as he watched her, blonde hair tumbling across the bed in a wild tangle, lips curled in the slightest smile as she slept.

He shivered suddenly, thinking of how close he had come to losing her.

He turned away, ready to leave the room. A deep sense of unease seemed to trickle down his spine. He shook it off, and opened the door.

And did not know that another trial would await them, threatening the slender threads of peace they had at last grasped . . .

Indeed, threatening their very lives once again.

Chapter 27

*I*t was Jarrett who stood outside his door, tense and weary-looking.

Weren't they all? he thought. For those on the Far Isle had kept a vigil of fear through the night, while he had driven those with him on his desperate race against time.

But they had won.

Or so it seemed.

"What is it?" he asked Jarrett, then groaned, surprised by the depths of anguish within himself. "David—sweet Lady Mary, has he—"

"Nay, nay, the Scotsman sleeps. Come down to the hall, milord, for your father is there with the message that has recently arrived."

Bret looked at Jarrett, then hurried down the stairs. The hall, which had seemed so full just an hour or so ago, was now empty—except for his father. Alaric had shed the weight of his chain mail and sat atop the long table, a scroll unrolled before him, which he studied carefully.

"What is it?" Bret asked his father. Jarrett followed him into the hall and stood with his hands folded at his back.

"This is a wild and reckless land!" Alaric commented dryly. "Why, even William paused in his conquering of the isle—upon occasion. This Laird Robert Canadys is a persistent foe!"

"What—"

"He wants you, alone, to meet him upon the sands an hour before the sunset. He thinks that your trials should now be decided by single, hand-to-hand combat. He writes that God will be on his side—as you are nothing but the issue of a bloody bastard Norman. You're also a heinous murderer, despoiler of the land—" Alaric paused, shrugging, his silver eyes hard on his son.

Bret swore violently, taking the scroll from his father, staring at Robert's eloquent denunciation of him. With an oath of pure fury he hurled the scroll into the fire that burned in the hearth, then heaved his shoulders against the mantel, weary beyond words. "I would gladly rip his throat from his body!" he savagely told his father.

"That is the invitation," Alaric reminded him. "At least, the invitation gives you the offer to try."

"Aye. And how do I win?" Bret asked miserably. "If I kill Robert Canadys, I have murdered my wife's closest kin. If not, I let him murder me! As it would not be in my nature to accept death too easily, I would slay Allora's uncle. And then, no matter what her words, I will be damned in her eyes."

"I think you're wrong."

All three of them in the room started, turning to the stairway to see that David, his palm flat against the bandaged wound at his abdomen, his other hand holding fiercely to the carved-wood stair rail, now stood at the foot of the stairs.

"Are you daft, man?" Bret charged him. "You're half-dead! You're not supposed to be out of bed—"

"I heard the messengers coming and going," David said. He grimaced. "And everyone had left me to rest in peace, so it seemed that I had to come down."

He stared past Bret then, a puzzled frown knitting his brow as he looked at Alaric.

Alaric arched a silver brow.

"David," Bret said, "my father, Earl of Haselford, Count d'Anlou." He smiled a little wickedly. "Elysia's father, as well."

Perhaps he shouldn't have spoken. David had been pale enough.

"My lord," he said, and bowed deeply. He started to fall. Jarrett was there quickly to help him.

"Don't lose consciousness on us now, David!" Bret warned him lightly. "Now that you've met my father, and you're still standing, make this official—and take this wretched affair off my hands. Ask my father for Elysia's hand in marriage."

David then turned every shade of red imaginable. Bret was glad. He was certain it meant that the man might truly survive.

"My lord—"

"Done," Alaric said flatly. "If you can live. Jarrett, get the fool boy up the stairs so that he can live long enough to wed my wild child!"

"Aye, milord!" Jarrett agreed quickly.

Bret found himself smiling. But David protested then. "Wait! Bret, you mustn't let Robert deceive you. He is assured in his own prowess, and he is a formidable warrior. But his hatred for you is quite intense—and he is convinced that he can again rule the Far Isle if you are but dead. He has no sons of his own—he will not mind telling every lie imaginable to your child and raising her beneath his command. I believe, milord, that many of the lairds, even those who were swayed to condemn Allora, are ready for peace. They are weary of battle, and wish to start living again. Robert will not let them rest."

Bret nodded slowly to him. "I thank you for the warning."

"Don't fight him!" David warned.

"Jarrett, return the noble fool to his bed. Find my sister—surely, she will keep him there, and he will know he's had a tenacious keeper set upon him!"

"Aye, milord," Jarrett said.

"Wait!" David said quickly. "You must be aware—my brother did this to me. Duncan is as tormented and—and *mad!*—as Robert himself."

"Again, my gratitude for the warnings," Bret said firmly. "Jarrett—"

"Aye, my lord, get him to bed!" Jarrett said, and he lifted David, staggering a little beneath the grown warrior's weight, and returned him up the stairs.

"You heard the man," Alaric said to his son softly.

"Yet I must meet him!" Bret said. "I cannot cower within the castle walls—it is another of his tricks to make me appear the wicked, murdering conqueror, as he did today."

"But David is not dead."

"The border lairds will not take my word for that, Father. And I cannot send a half-dead man out to prove it!"

"Not today, but perhaps tomorrow. Or the next day, or the next."

Bret shook his head slowly. "The longer this goes on and the more men who die, the harder it will be to ever find peace. He says he will meet me on the sands. Alone. An hour before sunset. Thus, the ocean will sweep away the carcass of whichever of us is defeated."

"Or perhaps the ocean will come to cut off aid when he has his bands of men come sweeping in for the kill!"

"Aye, Father, that may well be true." Bret leaned against the mantel, wearily rubbing his temples. He straightened, and stared at his father. "There is only one thing that I can do then."

"What is that?"

"Kill him—before the water rises high enough for me to be cut off from the fortress."

Allora woke and was startled to find herself alone. She ran her fingers over the sheets, frowned, and then leaped up, a feeling of foreboding quickly taking root within her. She dug into her trunk for a clean linen shift and warm woolen tunic, dragged on hose and shoes, and hurriedly ran out of the bedroom, heedless of the fact that her hair was wild, streaming in tangled waves down her back. She reached the hall to discover that it was empty, save for Father Jonathan, who sat at the table there, talking to himself.

"Father Jonathan!" Allora said quickly, hurrying over to him. "Where is everyone? Where is Bret?"

He looked up at her with bleary, red-rimmed eyes, and she realized that he had been helping himself to the wine on the table for quite some time.

"I never meant any ill, you know, lady. Never. It was I who always let them know what was going on here."

Allora sat beside him, feeling a growing sense of alarm. "Father Jonathan, I don't know what you're talking about. I just need to know—"

She broke off as his fingers wound around her wrist and his words became more frantic. "I never meant to hurt you, but I brought word beyond the gates once you'd come back from London, lady. Understand, if you can; I was orphaned, with nothing, a castoff, starving, begging for scraps. In good King Harold's day, it was. Father Damien picked me straight up from the dirt and gave me my training. He taught me to read and to write, and he had King Harold himself support me through the priesthood. I was sent here when Ioin became laird of the Far Isle. I held you when you were but a babe. But when Father Damien needed to know what was happening here, I let word go through. Do you understand? I was the link to the Norman."

He seemed so plagued and worried. He was sometimes a lax priest, but always a good and kind one, caring deeply for the people here.

Once, it would have troubled her greatly to discover that he had been betraying her all along.

Robert might well have . . . had him burned at the stake. But now . . .

"Father Jonathan," she said, shaking her head, "it doesn't matter. I love my husband; I am glad that he is here."

"Ah, lady, but he is not!"

She jumped up, truly alarmed. "What do you mean, he is not here? Where is he?"

Father Jonathan didn't answer the question. Someone else did from the stairway.

"He's gone out on the sand to meet Robert!"

Allora spun around. David was there, supported heavily on Elysia's arm.

"David!" she cried. "You shouldn't be up! Elysia—"

"He insisted, he said he'd crawl!" Elysia whispered miserably. "He says he must get out there himself, because Robert will have other men staked out to join the battle if he were to begin to lose. He wants the lairds to see him, that he lives, and to tell them that Duncan is a treacherous fiend."

Allora stared at the two of them. "I don't understand—"

"Robert sent Bret a challenge. To meet him alone on the sand. An hour before sunset. They must be there now," Elysia said.

"Sweet Jesu!" Allora gasped. Elysia and David must be left to fend for themselves. She knew that Robert could not be trusted. She tore out of the hall, and saw that the walls were lined with those who stared down to the sands from the parapets. She came racing across the courtyard to the closest steps to the parapets and ran up them, pressing between two guards who protested, then saw who had come and swiftly begged her pardon and gave her room.

Bret and Robert were indeed upon the sands. Both men were mounted.

Circling one another.

Allora looked up to the sky, weighing the downward drop of the sun. How many minutes were left before the tide began to wash in . . . ?

Robert rushed Bret. Allora cried out, biting her lip. She couldn't bear to watch.

She had to watch.

Bret parried Robert's first thrust. Her uncle came in hard, slashing again and again, and Bret just as swiftly met each slash. When Robert hesitated to seek an advantage, Bret found his, striking upon Robert's sword with a stroke that sent it flying across the sand, and Robert catapulting from his mount.

Her uncle rolled quickly across the sand, retrieving his sword. Bret, clad in his mail again, yet without his helmet, dismounted from Ajax and walked across the sand. Robert leaped back to his feet. He rushed again. He was a strong man.

Bret was stronger. He slammed a blow against Robert's sword that brought her uncle staggering to his knees. Robert held his weapon hard, fighting the strength that weighed him down.

Then she heard her uncle shouting out an order. "Now!" he roared. "Now, now!"

From the northern woods, a group of Scotsman came running out swiftly on foot, racing down the beach tearing for the sands. They were armed with swords and dirks and maces, answering Robert's call. Allora quickly saw her uncle's strategy—the sands next to the beach would remain above the water longer than those that dipped toward the isle. Even now, her uncle's men came plummeting toward her husband, while Bret—

"No!" she shrieked, yet the sound was drowned out by another voice, one of ringing command. "Archers, now!" She looked across the parapets. Alaric d'Anlou was standing tall and rigid, watching the crowd advance upon his son, calling his order with deadly precision.

Arrows went flying into the air, arched—and then began to fall. Screams rose; some men continued onward, some fell back. "Again!" Alaric d'Anlou shouted. "Take aim . . . Fire!"

The deadly rain fell once again. There were shouts and screams. Men fell, some rose . . .

Some staggered on, and some retreated.

But the surge had come forward and Allora cried out as she saw at least five men streaking toward the sands. She looked to the sky. The sun was dropping ever further. At any moment, the treacherously cold waters would begin to rise.

She watched as the first of the men reached the sands. Two of them rushing Bret, Robert rising again to join in the fray. "No!" Allora cried again. "Dear God, no . . . !"

"The shore again, archers! Keep his numbers down!" her father-in-law commanded.

Allora bit her lower lip. Her husband and his father had waged war together year after year, she tried to remind herself. William had given Bret his earldom when he had ridden with his father when he had been very young. They knew what they were doing. Oh, dear God, they had to . . .

Indeed, she could see the strategy. They had known that Robert would wage a fair fight only so long as he was winning. They had planted the archers, but so many men were rushing Bret upon the sands . . .

One fell. Bret swung his sword in a clean circle, the single stroke of the blade taking down two men. Robert surged forward again with his sword, delivering a blow that knocked Bret to his knees.

Bret staggered up again.

It had to stop.

She turned and ran down the steps. In the courtyard, she found David and Elysia.

"David, will you ride with me, can you get on a horse?"

"He'll rip his wound—" Elysia began.

"Your brother might well die," Allora said flatly.

"Allora, I will manage," David said.

She tore into the stables. No one was there—even the stable boys had rushed to the parapets, or else demanded news of the fight from below. Allora slipped bridles over the first two horses she came upon and hurried back out to the courtyard. Elysia helped David to stand upon a trough, and then to slide himself atop the horse. Allora leaped up on her horse beside him.

"The gates are closed," David said to Allora.

"I know," Allora told him, and he followed her right to them, where she called out the ringing command, "Open the gates!"

The gates didn't open. A moment later, her father-in-law was staring down at her.

"Allora, you are supposed to be sleeping in the tower."

"Milord, you are supposed to be in York."

"I must keep you safe—"

"And I cannot live if your son does not. I swear, milord, we know what we are doing."

"We? You've that half-dead Scot with you?"

"Aye, milord, I am here!" David called wearily.

"Please!" Allora said urgently. "I shall keep a safe distance. David has mounted—the people must see him. Please?"

"Keep back!" Alaric warned her sternly. "Don't interfere with our missiles, else all of you may be lost."

"Bret is fighting so many men—"

"Aye, lady, and holding his own."

"But can he do so forever—or until the tide rises?"

"Open the gates!" Alaric called, and Allora watched as the heavy wooden gates creaked open.

"Come then, milady," David said. Gritting his teeth, holding tight to his abdomen, he trotted past her. Allora kneed her horse quickly to follow. The sands were already wet beneath their feet, she thought . . .

She rode with David until they neared the fighting men upon the shore. Then she shouted out, and in fury:

"Uncle!"

The clang of steel ceased. Bret, panting, gasping, paused, his sword downward.

The sands were littered around him now with the men who had surged across to kill him—and who had failed in the attempt. Robert stood stock-still before him, as did the border lairds at his side.

"Uncle, you called me a traitor. You condemned me to death. As you have condemned all these men! You accused my husband of the murder of David of Edinburgh, yet here is David alive beside me, because my Norman husband's men cared to give him back life."

"Aye, Robert!" David bellowed out, and Allora ached to think of the effort it was costing him. "Aye, Robert, you accused the Norman, and it was a lie! You accuse others of treachery, and it is all lies. The one who stabbed me and left me for dead was my own brother. It was done by your bidding, Robert Canadys! By your bidding. Duncan stabbed me *as I sat with my wrists bound* upon my horse. He slashed the ties as I collapsed, and sent me out to die upon the hill."

There was silence. An awful silence.

"You're the liar, lad!" Robert roared. "You're the liar, you're with them—"

"Aye! Rather with them, than with you. You're a shame to the family, Robert! Your greed has made you a madman!"

"My greed! It's you who've lost your mind!" Robert cried out. "The Norman must—nay, he *will* die!" With those words, he spun around again, calling out his command. "Take him, kill the Norman!"

Yet this time, his men did not spring to his defense. They stared at David, alive and well upon his horse. And as Robert Canadys surged forward this time, Bret swung his sword in self-defense.

It ripped across Robert from his groin to his throat. A thin ribbon of blood appeared across the distance of the strike, and Robert grasped his neck, falling to his knees.

Allora was startled to see Bret step forward, trying to catch him. Robert grasped hard to her husband's wrists, clinging to them as Bret slowly eased him down to the sand.

"By the saints, Norman, you have won!" Robert gasped out. Then his eyes closed. His body fell slack, the fingers eased from Bret's wrists.

There was a sudden roar behind Bret. He turned, just in time to see Duncan racing toward him with a dirk wielded high. He raced forward at an uncanny speed, and Bret ducked and rolled to elude him, having dropped his sword to catch Robert before he fell.

"Help him!" Allora cried to the Scots lairds. "Help him!"

Yet they stood there, perhaps stunned by the events so quickly unfolding before them.

She could no longer heed her father-in-law's warning. She raced forward, weaponless herself except for the horse she rode. When Duncan made his next lunge, she thundered between him and Bret on her horse.

The water was rising. Bret just managed to sweep his sword from it as the bitter-cold water began to rise to the ankles of his boots.

Duncan came staggering back from his slam against Allora's horse. But Bret was prepared. He came forward, his sword swinging in both hands, his eyes furiously narrowed upon his adversary. Duncan backed up, hurling water and sand into Bret's eyes.

Bret blinked, barely skipping a beat, coming toward him again. Duncan continued to back away.

He backed into David's horse.

"Brother!" David said hoarsely.

Duncan turned with a jerk. His knife raised.

But David carried his own, and he plunged it into his brother's neck.

Duncan slipped downward. The tide had risen high. Black, swirling, it encircled his body.

Allora watched him for a moment in horror. Then she looked up, and met Bret's eyes, blazing blue upon her. The water was up to his thigh, and rising high against the horse's limbs. Cold, so bitterly cold. Still, she could bear it herself, she knew it well. She could swim . . .

But David could not. Yet . . .

"We can't make the Far Isle!" Allora cried desperately to Bret.

"We will ride to the fortress on the mainland."

"My uncle's men still cover the beach—"

"I don't believe that they will stop us," Bret said. He leaped atop Ajax again, and stared at David who leaned ever more heavily upon his horse's neck.

"Fool, Scot! Will you make it?"

"Aye, my fine Norman overlord. I am going to live just to annoy you!" David vowed.

"Allora, we ride at his side!" Bret told her. "And we had best move fast."

The men who had battled Bret had already staggered back through the rising surf, one of them screaming as he was suddenly swept away by the swirling waters. Bret, Allora, and David continued to ignore them until they had made their way through the treacherous waters and come to the mainland beach.

When they were there, Allora was certain that Bret would take the lead and spur them toward the walls of the mainland fortress, where surely archers had been warned to watch for them as well.

But he didn't run. He reined in and allowed Ajax to spin upon the sands in the sinking twilight, his shout encompassing anyone hiding in any of the woods around them.

"Hear me! I never sought the life of Ioin Canadys, and I never wanted that of his brother, Robert. I am heartily sorry for the bloodshed, and sick to death of it! I have offered my hand in peace to David of Edinburgh, and he knows that the peace I offer is a valid one. You claim this land for Malcolm, yet Malcolm himself has granted it to England. I will promise you this—that the matter will be taken before the kings again, and if they claim that it is England, you will swear your oaths to me, and I will swear mine to William Rufus. If they claim that the land is Scotland, then you will still swear your oath to me—and I will swear mine to Malcolm!"

There was silence for a moment. Then a loud cheer went up.

Allora was stunned when the first of the Scots warriors came from the trees. It was old Andrew. He looked her in the eye. "Forgive me, lady. Forgive us all. We never thought that Robert would really try to carry out such a sentence." He turned to Bret then, and offered him his sword, hilt forward.

"Keep it, my friend," Bret said softly.

Andrew kissed his sword. His old voice rang out. "For peace! I swear my oath of fealty to the new laird of the Far Isle, Bret d'Anlou!"

One by one, the men started coming forward. The sun fell ever further, the sky turned crimson.

David began to fall forward. "We must get him to bed!" Allora cried out.

She started riding the distance to the mainland fortress, calling out. There were archers upon the thinly manned walls, awaiting a command. And as they saw her, riding, David's horse following, they opened the gates.

She leaped from her horse, and fell back as David's heavy frame fell upon hers. "Help me!" she cried out softly, and men were quickly there to do her bidding. "He needs a soft bed, cooling cloths perhaps . . . Oh, that Father Damien were on this side of the water!"

David opened his eyes, wincing as men set him upon a litter. "Don't fret so, Allora. I am going to live. I swore an oath to your husband, and I must be an honest knight!"

"You must sleep!"

He nodded. The men lifted the litter, taking him to a room to rest. Allora walked across the barren bailey of the new fortress.

Then she saw her husband's horse coming through the gate. Ajax, snow-white against the crimson-colored twilight; Bret, silhouetted in black against the dying sun.

She cried out and ran to him, and he dismounted from his horse.

And long before she could reach him, he had come to her, sweeping her up, spinning with her in his arms. She touched his face, pressing it between her hands, eager to kiss his lips. He held her there, crushed to him.

"Dear God, my lady, dear God! We have come through."

"Aye!"

Yet he held her face then, staring into her eyes. "I killed your uncle."

"Aye."

"Tell me that it does not hurt."

"Aye, it hurts! It hurt that he would use me the way that he did, that he set the fire to the faggots today, that he wanted me dead, for loving you."

He drew her close again and nuzzled her head with his chin, his fingers wound through her hair and held firmly at the small of her back, as if he would never let her go.

"Allora—"

"You are laird of the Far Isle, overlord here. But you cannot be the head of clan Canadys, nor can I. Yet it will be David, Bret. We will live in peace."

"What peace we may," he said softly.

She pulled away from him. "Bret! Did you mean what you said? That you would . . . bow to Malcolm?"

"Aye. I keep the promises I make, Allora. I will bring the matter before William Rufus, and he and Malcolm may again bicker and argue, yet I will demand they come to some decision together. And I will honor that decision."

"So you would change!" she whispered softly.

"Aye. For the Far Isle."

"For the Isle?"

He smiled slowly and leaned down his head, and tenderly kissed her lips.

"Nay, lady. For love. For you."

Five days later, Fallon arrived. She came with Robin and Philip, whom she had met with at Wakefield, and with Eleanor and Gwyn, quickly filling the tower of the keep with Bret's family. Even Bret seemed amazed that his mother had managed to arrive so swiftly, but Fallon, happily upon her husband's arm in the great hall, waved a hand dismissively in the air.

"My son forgets, Allora, that I was with my father at Stamford Bridge to fight the Vikings and rode with him on his mad ride south to meet his death at William's hands. I can move very quickly when need be."

"And let that be a warning," Alaric teased.

Fallon had been there but a day, yet they were gathered tonight for Elysia's wedding.

David had healed with a remarkable speed, and though he was still pale and too thin, he had begged Alaric's blessing to wed Elysia as speedily as possible, and so the ceremony was now to take place.

Allora had been with Fallon, Eleanor, and Elysia as her sister-in-law had dressed for the occasion, and it had been merry, with them all laughing and talking. And then Elysia had made some comment about the duties of a wife and Fallon had sniffed, "Aye, daughter! If I'm not mistaken, we had best be absolutely delighted that this poor boy didn't die, since it seems you were practicing a few duties before the wedding."

"Mother!" Elysia gasped.

"When is the child due?"

"Too soon!" Elysia whispered.

But Fallon laughed and hugged her daughter tightly, winking to Allora over her shoulder. "I cannot believe this! I am far too young to have two grandchildren."

"Three," Allora said softly.

"Oh!" Fallon laughed, then hugged her, too. "How very, very wonderful!"

Later, Father Damien led the ceremony, for Elysia had known him all her life, and he had, with his care and careful remedies, saved David from death. Yet Allora had insisted Father Jonathan be in attendance as well.

They had all made their confessions, and she did not think his was so terrible. She wanted him happy again, for he was a part of the Far Isle, a good part, and she wanted him confident, happy—and a bit lazy!—once again.

The ceremony was beautiful, Allora thought. There was so much tenderness and love shared throughout the bride's family. She remembered her own wedding, and wished that she had known how much she was going to love her husband then. But perhaps that didn't matter.

What mattered was now.

They feasted in the hall; they had wonderful entertainment. Yet when the hour grew late, Allora looked at her husband to discover him giving her a fierce stare.

"You really didn't need to give them *our* bed and chamber, my love."

She smiled. "I didn't. I gave our tower to your parents, and the north tower to Elysia and David. They both have a fondness for it."

Bret sniffed.

"I've really a wonderful night planned for us!" she told him sweetly as she rose, catching his hand.

"All right, my love, where are we going?" he asked her.

"Well, for a bit of an adventure."

He arched a brow.

"We have not had enough?"

"This adventure you will like."

He remained skeptical as Jarrett politely took them on a barge ride with Briar and Ajax across the surf that covered the sands. He seemed more intrigued as they started into the forest.

She brought him to one of the hunting cottages, one she had carefully tended during the day. A fire glowed within. Wine and cheese and sweet-smelling fresh bread awaited them, along with a bed covered in the softest of furs.

He looked around the room, a smile slowly curving his lips. "Aye, lady, I like this adventure well enough!" he declared, and swept her up in his arms.

"I watched you tonight," he said huskily. "And I saw that you wished we might have had such a wedding."

She shook her head. "Ah, my lord, perhaps the wedding was lacking. But the wedding night . . . well, it made up for all that might have been lost, other than the fact, of course, that you were wishing you had wed a hedgehog."

He laughed softly. "I am well delighted with the prickly hedgehog I have wed!" he told her.

"Alas!" she cried. "What—"

His lips touched hers . . .

"Aye, lady? What were you saying?"

She thread her fingers into his hair, smiling. "Fine, my lord. Hold your prickly hedgehog then. Make love to her, hold her close through the night, and watch the fire and the flames until the dawn . . ."

"Aye, lady, that I will."

And the gentle warmth of the flames surrounded them, and grew within them, and the night was given over to the sweetness of passion . . .

And love.

Unforgettable Romance from

Shannon Drake

"She knows how to tell a story
that captures the imagination"
Romantic Times

KNIGHT OF FIRE
77169-1/$5.99 US/$6.99 Can

With gentle words and sensuous kisses, the steel-eyed
Norman invader, Bret D'Anlou, vanquishes beautiful,
defiant Princess Allora.

BRIDE OF THE WIND
76353-2/$4.99 US/$5.99 Can

Innocent Rose Woodbine curses cruel fate for leading
her to an unwanted marriage with Lord Pierce DeForte,
a man she dares never love.

DAMSEL IN DISTRESS
76352-4/$4.99 US/$5.99 Can

For her own protection, beautiful, headstrong heiress
Katherine de Montrain is forced to marry, but vows
never to submit to, the handsome, virile Lord Damian
Montjoy.